Our Little Secret

Jenna Ellis is a freelance photographer who has lived and worked all over the world. She is currently based in Harrogate, England, where she teaches life drawing. *Our Little Secret* is her first novel.

4.5.17
14.95
4\17

Our
Little
Secret

JENNA ELLIS

PAN BOOKS

First published 2015 by Pan Books
an imprint of Pan Macmillan, a division of Macmillan Publishers Limited
Pan Macmillan, 20 New Wharf Road, London N1 9RR
Basingstoke and Oxford
Associated companies throughout the world
www.panmacmillan.com

ISBN 978-1-4472-6678-5

1 3 5 7 9 8 6 4 2

A CIP catalogue record for this book is available from the British Library.

Typeset in Goudy Oldstyle Std by Palimpsest Book Production Ltd, Falkirk, Stirlingshire

Visit **www.panmacmillan.com** to read more about all our books
and to buy them. You will also find features, author interviews and
news of any author events, and you can sign up for e-newsletters
so that you're always first to hear about our new releases.

For Em

Our
Little
Secret

1

The DJ's doing this retro-beat set and Scott, who loves his techno, is entranced. The guy's a pro, Scott shouts above the music. Fucking awesome. He nods appreciatively and sips his beer. In another life, Scott would be a DJ himself, instead of a computer sales rep. His foot is tapping, his neck turkeying, but this is as close as he's ever going to get to dancing. He's standing by the pillar, away from the sweating, dancing throng, looking like he always does – cool. He has this air about him, that he's just a bit aloof and superior. It drives girls crazy, but I know it's just because he's shy.

I listen too, my pulse throbbing, staring out across the club, lit in violet laser-light. My torso is slick with sweat. Tonight has been better than any workout at the gym. I dig into the pocket of my jeans shorts and grab a hairband, hoisting my long hair up into a high ponytail. The air on my neck is delicious. I want Scott to notice, to kiss me, but he doesn't; but then, he's not one for public displays of affection. I lean up and force a kiss on him and he stiffens, not letting me snog him. I laugh and stick my tongue out at him and he squeezes my bum, blushing that I'm teasing him. Even so, I'm not going to hang around being a wallflower when the music is this good. When I hear someone shout my name, I turn. Lisa is waving me towards her from the dance-floor, and in a moment I'm swallowed back into our gang.

There's a definite tango beat to the next track and, maybe because I'm pissed and hot and horny, when I see the Spanish-looking guy across the club on the metal stairway and our eyes meet, I find myself strutting through the slightly parted crowd towards him in time to the music, my intention blazing in my eyes.

I'm showing off and hamming it up, I know. Lisa, Tiff and everyone else we're here with tonight are watching. This is our favourite club night in Manchester, and a blow-out we've been planning for months. And now, right now, this is part game-play – a laugh, to prove I can create a 'happening' this late on. But the other part of me is deadly serious, being carried along by the momentum of my own daring and the beat of the music that finds a home in my limbs, making them move as if of their own accord. I haven't danced properly for years. I certainly haven't performed a tango with a stranger. But somehow, this seems like the right moment.

He sees me in the crowd and, when he stops still, I know straight away that he knows what I'm thinking. He stiffens, his torso puffing out, blanking his friends, who stare curiously in my direction, but I don't see them. My eyes are locked with his. He's wearing smart jeans and a loose shirt. He's not good-looking in the traditional sense. Not like my Scott. He has a wolfish quality to him. Thin fingers, dead-straight hair, but as he gets closer to me there's a sexual proudness to him that sends a hot flush through me.

Wordlessly, he holds his arm out, barely looking at me, expecting the contact that he knows will come.

I'm in sneakers and short shorts with a cropped vest top, my glitter make-up smeared, no doubt, but I feel like I'm in a swirling black dress and heels, as my slow steps scrape towards him. I hear Tiff squeal with laughter behind me – this is, after all, hilarious – but I keep a straight face, tuning them all out as I get closer and closer.

And then he's got me. My dance partner. He grabs me, forcefully, pulling me around into his embrace. It's sensual, loose, but firm, and I feel the pressure of his hand on my back. Man, this guy knows how to move. He's all hips and grip and perfect arms, but I know straight away that he's danced properly – professionally even – and all my earlier chutzpah melts. This is serious.

In seconds, we're instinctively mirroring each other, which is why I'm ready when he flings me backwards over his arm, so that my long ponytail flips over and touches the sticky floor. The lights temporarily blind me.

Almost immediately I'm back up against him, pressed thigh-to-thigh and we're off together in perfect unison – slow, slow, quick, quick, slow – the thumping base-beat booming in my chest. I notice the sheen on his forehead, the black marble-like glint in his eye, even though he's not looking at me, his head rigid, his eyes front. I don't know him at all. I've never set eyes on him, and yet I feel like he's seeing me in a way my friends don't. In this very public space everything has suddenly become personal and I feel a pulsing, hot connection to this stranger that pins me in his arms like a magnet.

For a split second I consider breaking away. I should back out now. It's not normal to dance a tango in a club like this, but I don't have a chance, because we're doing it. We're getting the tango *on*.

I feel his hand in the back of my hair, pulling it – violently almost, as he twirls me around and around, like I weigh nothing. Then, unexpectedly, it's a hoist and he's got my waist, lifting me, his knee suddenly between my legs. I can see the pulse in his pale neck, but he doesn't utter a word.

I'm vaguely aware that the crowd has parted and we have a space of our own on the dance-floor, but my eyes don't leave his black stare. Soon I have my knee up in a passionate embrace, my hand running down the side of his face. His skin is smooth, hardly stubbly at all. He has a mole by his left ear. I feel a kind of Latino passion throbbing through me, as he stretches me out and runs his hand up my leg.

'Hey!' Scott shouts above the music. 'Hey. Enough.'

Suddenly I'm aware of the club. Scott sounds so cross that he breaks the spell immediately. I turn to look at him, sliding down my partner's torso until my feet finally touch the ground.

Then I disengage, my knees shaking. I spring away towards Scott and grin manically, brushing away a strand of my hair from across my lips. I'm out of breath from dancing, but I breezily grab Scott's hand as if it's really no big deal. I don't turn back, I don't look back. If I do, there'll be a fight. I know it. Instead, too scared of the feeling I can't put my finger on, I quickly pull Scott away.

'Do you know that guy?' Scott asks. 'What the fuck—?'

He's stopped, ready to wade in. Blood up, hands clenched.

Still I don't turn round. I tug at my crop top. My pulse is racing. It takes everything I've got not to turn back and give the guy I've danced with some token of acknowledgment. I feel his energy burning into the back of my head.

'Course not. I just fancied a dance, and he was just there. I was having a laugh, that's all. It wasn't serious.'

I tug Scott away into the safety of the crowd, which has already filled our private dance-floor, like our performance never happened. A wave washing over a heart in the sand.

'You can dance with me,' Scott says in a petulant tone.

'Then you'd better learn to dance properly,' I say, half-teasing, but also sort of rubbing it in. I'm bluffing my way out of this, by turning this on him. He's refused ever to even try dancing. Even at his sister's wedding at the barn dance, he refused to lose his cool and do the doh-si-doh.

'Fuckin' hell, Soph, that was awesome,' Lisa says, breaking the tension between me and Scott, jumping towards me, like the Labrador puppy she is. 'I thought you were going to fucking devour that guy. Everyone was watching. Didn't you see?'

I laugh, but I glance at Scott and his look is dark. He's furious. Despite everything, I feel a deep stab of satisfaction that I've made him so jealous. He announces that we're all going to the bar for a final round of shots.

The moment passes, the dance forgotten, but when I get a chance I turn back to look for my dancing partner in the crowd. I can't see him anywhere. I feel strangely bereft that I didn't say something. I wish I'd thanked him. Although maybe it was better that it ended like it did, before I got completely carried away. Because I can still feel him. The way he held me. The beat of his heart close to mine. His leg against my crotch and, despite Scott's arm being around me, I feel dangerously aroused.

2

I don't have to open my eyes to know that it's early. Too early. Still dark. My head is fuzzy against the warm, vaguely armpit-scented pillow. It can't be that many hours since we left the club. Rain patters softly on the window. There's no heavy traffic outside yet, but a siren wails towards the town centre in the distance.

Scott's familiar body is partially spooned against me, his head up at an angle on the other pillow, a wedge of coolness between my back and his chest. I don't move, yet, making him wait, knowing he's not fully awake either.

But his cock is. Its fat length twitches against my buttocks. Like he's knocking on a door. *Let me in.*

My breathing doesn't change, but I wriggle backwards a millimetre, just the faintest motion to let him know I've responded. For a second, I remember my dance partner from last night, but quickly push him out of my mind. I'm not going to think about him, or how I felt dancing with him. That was then, and this is now. And I'm with Scott. Good-looking, gorgeous Scott, and this is a make-up shag. He claimed he was too exhausted and pissed to go for it (despite my best efforts to entice him) when we got back from the club a few hours ago, but now he's apparently changed his mind. I sigh with relief. He's not going to sulk for days, after all.

I move now a little more, his length sliding stiffly down the crease between my buttocks, and I tilt my pelvis further until I feel his moist tip graze against the soft folds that are guarding me.

I'm not wet yet. Not like we're both used to, and as he pushes more insistently, my body resists. I'm still sleepy. Wanting to be teased out.

There's a faint whoosh of air as Scott moves to close the gap between us, his smooth, waxed chest against my shoulder, his hand snaking up around my waist to find my breasts.

From above, he runs the side of his hand down between the intimate sweaty crevasse where my boobs have been pressed together in the night, then underneath my right breast to cup the ample handful of flesh, squeezing ever so gently, pushing my breast up into an impressive mound, like I have an eighteenth-century décolletage. Oh, if only Scott's hands could be my permanent bra.

His thumb and finger lazily reach up to find my nipple and we both know he's got me. He knows this is the ignition key to my sexual motor and, already anticipating that he'll gently pinch – and later (hopefully) maybe tug them with his teeth – my nipples stiffen. He rolls the right nub in between his thumb and fingertip. Below, his cock pulls away then twitches back, slapping me harder now. *See you want it, really. Come on. It's time now.*

I rock my pelvis back, arching my back, uncomfortably contorted now, then reach between my legs to open myself. Scott is already there. I can feel the moisture on his tip as I guide the fat end between my lips. I'm ready now too, my body one step ahead of me, as usual.

He takes a gasp of air in, as he eases inside me a little way.

'Morning,' I say, an amused accusation in my voice, but he's silent. I don't have to look over my shoulder to know that his eyes are shut. This is no time for conversation.

Instead, I clench my internal muscles around his tip, wanting him now to ease in further, letting him know that I'm surrendering myself to the inevitable. That I'm up for it.

Like I ever refuse.

His hand slides onto my hip and presses down as he slides a little deeper inside me. My nipples ache for him to return, but I already know he won't. That this will be quick, the way he likes it in the morning. Urgent. No face-to-face. No morning breath. Just carnal. Focused.

For a minute, he slides in only so far, then withdraws and I know what's coming, even before he's moved and I'm turning, moving onto my knees. I can feel his cock quivering behind me, waiting for me to be in position. I know the drill.

On all fours now, he pushes easily – deliciously – into me and I can't deny that it's satisfying, both intimate and yet reassuringly familiar. This is, after all, what Scott and I do best.

We move together in a synchronized rhythm and, after a while, I pivot my elbows to slide my hands beneath me to seek out my nipples, which bump against the pillow.

I'm secretly fascinated by the graceful movement of my swaying orbs and, for a second, I imagine that they belong to someone else, that I'm beneath them, that it's someone else's hot, ripe nipples dangling above me. To whom they belong,

I don't know. They're not attached to a body, a face, a person even, just a feeling. I stroke my soft skin and let the silver fish of disembodied fantasy slither through my mind as I raise myself to Scott.

He grips my hips, but I wish he would grip my buttocks, to splay them open and gaze at my bum. Touch it. Explore it. Something we've never done – never will do. I'm shocked by how filthy the thought is for this hour of the morning, and almost chuckle to myself at how unlikely it would be for me ever to tell Scott what I'm thinking. For all the frequency of sex we have, it's still pretty conventional. Not that I'm complaining.

Through the curtain of my long brown hair, I glance sideways and catch sight of us in the mirror that is propped up against the wall. I can just make out Scott's lithe and agile body in a sliver of street light through the gap in the curtain. His bum is firm and pert from playing football, the muscles on his thighs standing out where he's kneeling on the crumpled sheet.

It's hard to make out in the dark, but I know that all around us is the detritus of his bedsit – or 'studio' as he likes to call it. His crumpled jeans, boots and pants upright on the floor where he stepped out of them, next to two mugs, some sideways beer cans and an empty Pot Noodle. I close my eyes, too. Shut it out. This is why we have sex so much, perhaps. To pretend we live in a different kind of reality.

I do, anyway. Because, with my eyes closed, I can begin to believe we're in a sun-drenched villa, like in a movie. Or on a plush four-poster bed in a five-star hotel. Not here, in a rain-soaked, recession-ravaged suburb of Manchester, where life is all mapped out.

I can feel Scott deep inside me now. Really deep. I've stretched to fit him, as I always do, but it still astonishes me how far he can push into me. There's something triumphant in his thrust. Like he's claimed me. I make a sound to let him know as much.

But it's not true. He can't claim me. Not all of me.

And before I can help it, the door has opened to the secret place. Just like that door opened on the last day of school five years ago on that hot, overwhelming summer's day.

In my mind's eye I see myself step inside into the library area and, just like then, my pulse is racing. I know he is waiting for me like we've planned. I sense his aura, like the huge presence he is, even before I see him. He's standing, pretending to read by the corner shelf. He's next to the window, which has its blind drawn down, casting him in a glow of sinner's orange.

In the muffled silence of the romance section, I hear his breath as I walk towards him. He says my name. 'Sophie.' Like it's a surprise. A delight. Like he feels like a child, too. But he's not.

His hand reaches mine. We're both shaking. We both know it's too illicit. Too naughty. It could ruin us both. He's older, married. My A-level teacher. But this is a roller-coaster thrill like never before, and I know when I look into his deep-blue eyes that we've tipped over the edge and neither of us can stop.

He pulls me to him suddenly, like time has just run out, like it's the last moment on Earth. He kisses me, gasping with desire, like he's never known desire before. His lips, his smell engulfs me, and the power. It's a whole new kind of aphrodisiac. It hits my veins like a drug. *I made this happen*, I think, my senses screaming. It's single-handedly the most exciting moment of my life.

Behind me, Scott speeds up and cries out as he comes.

3

Leticia lolls against the counter in the reception area, one long, elaborately decorated claw of a fingernail scratching against the corner of her TV magazine.

'If there was a hell, do you think this would be it?' I ask her.

Her dull brown eyes flick up at me and then lazily over to where the fifty or so under-fives are screaming around the shabby play area in the FunPlex Dome where we both work. Why doesn't the noise bother her? How can she shut it out?

It's Monday morning, but the place is still crammed with buggies and exhausted-looking mothers, who have brought their hyper toddlers to bounce in static joy down the bumpy slide. The sound is deafening, not least because the FunPlex radio-station playlist that Dean, the manager, insists upon us playing all day is thumping out Pink at full volume. I sniff the FunPlex uniform Aertex shirt I've had to borrow this morning, having come straight from Scott's. It stinks.

'Yeah, but's it a job. Better than McDonald's.'

Sometimes Leticia's lack of aspiration floors me. But then her bovine attitude to life appears to mean that she suffers far less angst than someone like me, who feels like I'm suffocating most of the time; like I'm caught in an hourglass, the sand slipping away beneath me.

'I thought you liked kids, anyway,' she says, accusingly, flipping over the page to study the Photoshopped 'fat' pictures of some poor soap star.

She's right. I do like kids, but this wasn't what I imagined when I got the job here. I thought that working with children would be fun. That's why I qualified as a nanny, after all. But nobody around here can afford a nanny, it seems. Even the footballers' wives have been slow on the uptake to employ me, opting for Polish live-ins, who will empty the dishwasher, clean, iron and cook *as well as* doing the night-feed.

I haven't told Scott, but I've sent my details off to an agency in London, but it's a pipe dream, of course. Could I really cut it as a nanny for a posh family in Chelsea? Would I fit in with those cashmere Fionas, with their tight jeans and designer handbags? Would I be able to drive the family Range Rover around the streets of London, to drop the little darlings at the overpriced nursery school?

Yes, I would, part of me thought as I sent off my application, kissing the envelope for good luck. I've imagined it, these past few days, spinning across the countryside to London, in a shimmering, sparkling, magical glow. But I've heard nothing back, and the truth has dawned. There are a million better-qualified nannies, with more experience and better references than me. Let's face it, real-life Fionas want to be nannies themselves these days.

So I'm stuck here in FunPlex until something happens. And please, God, let *something* happen.

Leticia sighs and heaves her considerable bulk off the counter, as the door opens and there's a blast of icy air and the next gaggle of women and kids pile through the door.

One of the women in the front is new. I haven't seen her before. I notice her because she has nicely highlighted hair and her kid in the buggy is wearing a tanktop and cords. Posh, then.

She has tastefully done make-up and normal eyebrows, which is rare for our clientele. She has what looks suspiciously like a proper designer leather handbag on her arm, and she's holding a large Starbucks coffee cup in her manicured hand. I watch her kid, a sweet little boy with curly blond hair, wriggle free from his buggy and make a beeline for the ball-pit.

'Jasper, NO,' the woman cries. 'Wait.' She lunges forward, accidentally chucking the contents of her coffee cup at me in the process.

I gasp as the hot liquid lands mostly on the desk and splashes all up the front of my shirt. It's scorching.

'Oh,' the woman exclaims, flushing. 'Oh, I'm so sorry.'

'It's OK,' I say, fanning the shirt away from my stomach with my fingertips. Leticia, unimpressed, moves her magazine away from the brown spillage and then the computer keyboard. She stares at me, like it's my fault.

The woman dumps her toffee-coloured leather bag in a dry patch on the counter and quickly unpacks.

'Here, take this,' she says, handing me a bulky rolled-up magazine, then rummaging inside to find a packet of tissues, which she hands me, apologizing again. I mop up the coffee as she hurriedly pays and runs after the little boy.

'What about your magazine?' I call after her, but she flaps her hand. She clearly doesn't want it. I unfurl it, to see that it's *The Lady*. I've heard of it, but never read it.

I go into the staff loos whilst Leticia goes to get another shirt for me from the locker. Whilst I'm waiting, I flick through the magazine. At the back I see an advertising section for nanny jobs and greedily read through them. Why haven't I looked here before? One in particular catches my eye:

Articulate, presentable, well-mannered English girl required for an exclusive domestic position immediately in Upstate New York. Preferably aged 20–25. References and photograph essential. All travel and expenses paid. Salary details at interview. Basic qualifications required.

Exclusive. I wonder what that means? But it's in America. Wow! Upstate New York. I bet it is super-posh.

I stare in the chipped mirror at my shabby coffee-drenched reflection, the words whirring in my head.

'Sophie, I've got a new shirt for you,' Leticia calls from the other side of the door. 'You decent?'

I'm twenty-two. I have good skin. Scott says I'm pretty. And I can pass as articulate.

Upstate New York. Dare I?

'Yes, I'm decent,' I call back. Then I rip out the advert and fold it carefully, stuffing it deep into the back pocket of my jeans.

4

Tiff is sitting cross-legged on my single bed sucking a lollipop. Behind her is a pin-board with a montage of ancient photos – mostly selfies – of the pair of us, on the Big Dipper in Blackpool and in various pubs, and of me and Scott kissing at New Year.

'What about this one?' I say, looking over my shoulder at the back-view of the little black dress in the slim ward-robe mirror. This is the one I've selected for the interview in London tomorrow. I stand on tiptoes, as if I'm wearing heels. The dress is short, but it shows off my legs, which I know are one of my best assets. Dancer's legs, like Mum's were. I grab my hair and put it up, as if it's already in the smart updo I'm planning.

I give my best glittering 'give me the job' look at Tiff, who tips her head over to one side, and the lollipop stick wiggles from side to side. She takes it out of her mouth and I can tell she doesn't approve. But that's why she's here. Because she's been my best friend since, well, forever, and she's nothing if not honest.

It was Tiff who told me to apply straight away to the advert I ripped out of *The Lady*. Tiff who patiently peered over my shoulder and edited my CV, daring me to send it off. And Tiff who knew how much it meant when I got a call this morning asking me to come for an interview tomorrow. And so now she's here, to help me prepare.

'Isn't it a job interview to be a nanny? They don't want you to look like you're going to a nightclub,' she says. 'Don't you have anything . . . I don't know. Mumsy? Frumpy?'

Her words throw me into despair and I growl in frustration.

'This is my only good dress,' I moan. 'Scott bought it for me.'

Tiff's eyebrows rise, one more easily than the other, which is pierced with a small silver hoop.

'Ah, Scotty dog,' she says, knowing that particular nickname annoys me. 'I take it you haven't told him yet?'

I turn to face the mirror, away from her searching gaze and into my own deceitful one, letting my hair fall around my shoulders. I lower my heels to the floor.

'There's no point. I mean, I would if I got the job, but it's highly unlikely that someone is going to fly *me* to America,' I tell her, but I can feel a secret quickening of my pulse. This is so fateful, so – I don't know . . . *right*. Is that the word? The thought of jetting out of here to a new adventure on the other side of the world has filled me with a kind of longing I can't seem to ignore, no matter how hard I try. I won't think about Scott or what he might say.

'You wouldn't leave, though, would you?' Tiff says. 'I mean, if you got the job. You wouldn't actually go. Not really. You wouldn't give up all that sex, for a start. I mean, this is just to see if you *could*.'

I hear the hint of worry in her voice, despite her joke

about the sex. She's always astounded by how often Scott and I 'do' it. No wonder she thinks this is all a game. But it's not. At least, it might have started out that way – the whole application thing – as a kind of a fantasy, a kind of dare. But what if I really do get given an opportunity to make it all come true?

Dad saves me from answering, opening the door to my room and poking his head in. I wish he'd knock. He's grown a beard recently, which doesn't suit him. It's grey and makes him look even older than he is. Mum would never have let him grow it, if she were still alive. He has dark circles under his eyes, giving him a weary, hangdog look. The anti-depressants the doctor gave him were supposed to have kicked in by now, but I can't tell the difference. He still looks, well . . . sad. And seeing him this way – well, it breaks my heart.

'I'm popping out,' he says, but he doesn't look at me. We both know this is a euphemism for the fact that he's going to the betting shop and then to the pub. 'Make sure Ryan eats his tea.'

I can hear the noise of the PlayStation in the lounge where my little brother has taken up residence on the sofa. He'll be there for hours. Dad relies on me like this, more and more. But lately I've started thinking that me being here to parent for him half the time might be what is stopping Dad from getting better. Or getting over Mum. If I wasn't here, then he wouldn't be able to go to the pub. He'd have to look after Ryan and that might help him move on.

Dad suddenly clocks what I'm wearing. 'Going somewhere?' he asks.

I catch Tiff's eye in the mirror. She's kept all my confidences before. Even about Mr Walters. I know she'll keep the interview a secret and not throw anyone into an unnecessary panic, but in her eyes I see something I've never seen before. An acceptance. A sudden realization that I'm serious. And, with it, a willingness to let me go. I was quite mistaken; she wants this to happen for me just as much as I do.

'No,' I tell Dad, but as my eyes stay locked with Tiff's, I know that I will try my hardest to get this job. And that I'm going to do it, for me.

5

'This way, please, Miss—'

'Henshaw,' I remind the woman, as she walks surprisingly fast down a long corridor. She's carrying a clipboard and I look at her sturdy calves beneath American-tan tights, as I set off behind her. She's wearing those small blocky-heeled shoes with a gold square on the front that have never suited anyone in the history of the world.

She came to the reception area just now, where I'd been waiting nervously for half an hour, and introduced herself, but I didn't catch her name. It sounded German. Gunter, or something. Gunther? Did she notice that my hand was trembling when she shook it? She has a strange accent. Not English, but not American, either. European of some kind, for sure. Most likely she's German, I guess.

She's not what I expected. She's a po-faced, uptight-looking middle-aged woman, with grey-streaked mousy hair scraped back in a bun. She looks like she's never farted. Let alone laughed about it.

I tug self-consciously at the hem of my skirt. Tiff was right. I should have worn tights. My legs feel too exposed. Like I'm underdressed. I certainly am, compared to old

Gunter. She's wearing a tan-and-cream dogtooth tweed suit, which looks at once prim and expensive.

My high heels sink into the thick carpet as I trot after her, but I can't help being mesmerized by glimpses of the view I get from the glass panels of the offices on either side of the hushed corridor.

We're in The Shard, that huge building near London Bridge station. It's been so long since I've been to London that I didn't even know it had been built, so the address was a bit of a shock, and I had to check the piece of paper I was holding three times before I had the nerve to come in here. I've never been in a skyscraper before, let alone one like this. It's like I'm in a spaceship.

Ahead, at the end of the corridor, Frau Gunter opens a thick wooden door, which swishes against the plush carpet, and nods at me to walk inside. As I step over the threshold I take in the aroma of the stunning room beyond the door, and let satisfaction fill my lungs.

It smells of money.

Or of how I imagine money to smell, at any rate: of the best leather and of expensive perfume. Across the vast expanse of pristine cream carpet is a glass wall with a panoramic view. For a second, it takes my breath away. It's as if we're on top of the world. I can see the whole of London stretched out before me: thousands of buildings, their windows winking in the sunlight; red buses on the bridges, barges on the sparkling river. Seeing the pulsing, breathing city right there fills me with awe and a thrill of excitement that, for once, I'm part of it.

'Miss Henshaw?'

I turn to see the older woman gesturing to a soft fawn leather sofa and I quickly walk to it and sit down carefully, remembering to tuck my dress in underneath me and cross my legs. I lower myself, keeping my knees together, but the sofa seems to swallow me. I smile at her, but she cocks her head to one side and frowns.

'You don't look comfortable. Please. Stand.'

Surprised, and worried that I've already mucked the whole interview up through my lack of sofa etiquette, I get up – less gracefully. I think I've flashed my gusset, but she hasn't noticed as she's walking towards the other side of the room where there's a plush bar area. She drags a high stool towards me.

'This will be better, I think. Sit.'

With difficulty I hoist myself onto the stool, my back to the view. I feel a bit of an idiot, sitting on the high chair in the middle of the room. I notice now that in front of the bar area is a tripod with a camera on it, facing me. Gunter sees me looking at it.

'I hope you don't mind, but my clients asked me to record the interviews,' she says. 'They cannot be here, so I will send them the tapes later.'

I nod, wondering how many other people she's already interviewed. I'm relieved, too. She's not the client, then. I wouldn't be working for her. If she had kids at all, I imagine them to be frowning blond ones, in stiff lederhosen.

Gunter stands behind the camera, adjusts the angle so that it's pointing away from the sofa and directly at the stool, and then, referring to her clipboard, starts the interview abruptly, with no preamble. I tell her a bit about my experience, but I can't help my eyes darting to the camera occasionally. It's weird being recorded, and I feel judged in a way I can't put my finger on. I can see the tiny red recording light, and a miniature version of myself in the shiny black lens of the camera.

Who will watch these tapes later, I wonder? The whole set-up makes me think that 'the clients' (whoever they are) must be rich. As in super-rich.

Gunter nods as I speak, but her steely expression soon means that I'm exaggerating my qualifications. Trying to be light-hearted and amusing, I tell her about my initial desire to be a dancer/actress when I left school, which was quickly superseded by my love of children. How this is what I long to do. That I'm brilliant with kids, and kids *love* me. That I'm flexible, easy-going, yet strict, of course. Manners are my big thing. Isn't it awful when kids don't have manners?

I'm babbling a monologue, but I can't tell whether she's impressed or not. Eventually, when I pause, she says, 'And you exercise regularly? You're fit? You'd say you have stamina?'

For a moment I'm tempted to joke, *Of course I have stamina! You try going out with someone with Scott's libido.* But of course I don't. I lie instead; about how I don't mind working long hours and how I regularly swim to keep in shape. Although that's not true. I hate going to our local public swimming pool. All that body-piercing and tattoos on show makes me squeamish.

The truth is that I just have lucky genes from Mum. I seem to be able to eat loads without getting fat. People always used to tell her she was lucky, but there's nothing lucky about getting breast cancer at forty. Besides, everyone's thin when they die of cancer. Believe me.

'You don't have any commitments here, do you? I mean emotional commitments?' She glances down at her clipboard. 'You're single?'

'Yes,' I lie, backing up the fib on the application form that Tiff made me tell for my own good.

My cheeks colour as I wriggle in my seat and cross my legs with difficulty and sit on my hands, which I realize I've been waving around far too much. She glances up at me, her eyebrows drawing together. Is she some kind of body-language expert? In which case, she must know I'm lying. But it's too late now. I can't tell her about Scott. Yes, he's an emotional commitment, but not a 'forever' one, surely? But even as I justify my lie like this, I know I'm being unfair. Scott has hinted enough times that our relationship is super-serious, as far as he's concerned.

'You'd be free to travel straight away?'

'Uh-huh,' I say, biting my lip.

'And how are you in new situations? Would you say that you're an adaptable kind of person?'

'Oh yes. Totally. Completely flexible,' I tell her, with a little laugh, knowing that I've gone a bit over the top. 'No, seriously. I believe that you can only truly live life if you expand your horizons. That's why I'm here. Always do what you feel in your heart. Even if it scares you. That's what I always say.'

'And, Miss Henshaw, would you say that you're a discreet kind of person? I assume that you are. You don't appear to use your Facebook account ever, and you're not on Twitter, as far as I can see, but perhaps you prefer other social networks?'

I'm amazed that she's checked, although I realize that she must have, for me even to be sitting here. I don't tell her that this is not through choice. That I stopped going on Facebook when Ryan got cyber-bullied at school after Mum died. In a show of solidarity for Dad, I stopped writing anything at all about any of us online.

'That's not my thing,' I tell her. 'I think a person is entitled to a private life that stays just that. Private,' I add, putting as much gravitas into my voice as I can. 'In my opinion, people share far too much personal information about themselves that I'd rather not know.'

She nods in agreement. I seem to have got that right.

'I ask because my clients are often in the public eye and they do not wish to have any of their affairs – and I mean, *any* of their affairs,' she stresses, 'divulged in any way.'

They're famous, I realize. What if they're really famous? Brad Pitt and Angelina Jolie famous. What then? But no, people like that wouldn't even consider someone like me, surely? But then, I do sound good on paper. But what if I've sounded *too* good? What if I'm already out of my depth?

'It is of the utmost importance that they would be able to trust you,' she emphasizes, staring at me so forcefully it feels like she's pointing a gun. I spread my hands out in a gesture of submission.

'I'm trustworthy. I can keep secrets,' I tell her, remembering Mr Walters fumbling with his belt. Remembering how I cupped my hand around the hard bulge in his soft cotton pants and whispered that this was just ours. Our secret.

6

The monotonous hum of the plane throbs below me. When I open my eyes, I realize that my mouth has been open and someone has put a blanket over me. My tongue is thick from all the free champagne I have downed, and I have pins and needles in my left foot.

There's an intimate, hushed atmosphere in the business-class cabin. Everyone is asleep as we hover, seemingly suspended above the clouds. The smart air hostesses, who positively fell over themselves to serve me earlier, are all tucked away out of sight. I wanted to tell them that they'd made a mistake, that it was just me. Little old Sophie. That they didn't need to make a fuss. But I guess you can't say that kind of thing.

Besides, the facts speak for themselves: I am a paid member of the business class. I am going to work for some lah-di-dah people called Edward and Marnie Parker in New York. And they are paying for me to fly at this astounding level of luxury. And not only that, they will be paying me – wait for it – a staggering 1,500 dollars a week. That's more than I make in two months at FunPlex. 'Lucked out' doesn't cover it. And yep, I suppose champagne is the only appropriate drink, given the circumstances. So I had my fill and zonked out in a sozzled fug.

I needed it. After all, it's been an exhausting twenty-four hours. Saying goodbye to Tiff, Dad and Ryan was just awful. And then there was Scott. Oh God. Poor Scott.

Quietly, so as not to disturb anyone, I take off my headphones and ease myself out of my extraordinarily large seat and into the wide aisle. My eyes feel puffy and I need to wash my face.

I limp, with difficulty, up the aisle to the loos. They're free, but as I go to open the door, someone blocks it from inside and I jump back, startled.

'Hang on.' I hear a voice. The door locks and the green light goes on overhead with a muffled 'bing'. I hear hushed giggling.

Suddenly, there's a slap on the other side of the door and a gasp. I imagine someone's hand. More giggling and another low, male 'Shhh'.

I don't know what to do. I didn't think the mile-high thing was real, but obviously, if you're posh and fly business-class to America, it is very real. Every plane loo I've ever been in has been minging, but maybe this one isn't so smelly or gross. I suspect, judging from the sounds of the couple inside, they just couldn't help themselves – regardless of their surroundings.

I glance down the cabin, wondering who the couple could be, but I can't see any empty seats. I should go and find a different loo, but I don't. I don't want to draw attention to the couple inside.

There's another faint slap on the door and a high gasp.

My interruption has clearly not put them off their stride. Something about the noise makes me remember my own hand slapping the wall, my legs wrapped around Scott as we had sex for the last time. It was only hours ago, I realize, but it feels like weeks. As if he's already faded. Already dissolving in my head.

I'm not usually a voyeur, but the sensation, the vibration is undeniably horny and I can't help myself responding with an involuntary flip in my crotch. And the fact that I've so readily responded makes me feel like the traitor I am. I don't deserve to be horny. And anyway, I mustn't. I promised Scott.

Just like I promised him that this job wasn't a big deal. That I'd only be gone for a couple of months at the most. That I'd be back, only with more money. Which we could use as a deposit maybe, for a place of our own together?

I know I'm a cow for giving him false hope. The whole point of this adventure is that I don't know how it will end. That it's a chance at the unknown, an opportunity to take a different path, away from the inevitability of the one that my life has been on, which has led me here.

But I didn't say any of this to Scott. I'm a coward, of course, but I couldn't bear how rejected he felt. He blamed himself for me taking the job. He assumed it was because he hadn't shown enough commitment to me. It didn't occur to him that I was the one who wasn't committed enough. That no matter how much he's prepared to offer, I still want more.

I duck around the corner into the air hostesses' area, where they make the tea and coffee. It's dark and empty, cold rows of steel containers lined up like it's a morgue. I lean up against the wall, but from here I can hear what's going on inside the loo even more clearly.

I lean against the plastic wall, but then push back. Because I can feel them through the wall. They are thrusting up against it and, as I press the palms of my hands back against the wall, I sense the warm, rhythmic banging against them. It gets faster and harder, and she gasps and he makes a guttural noise, too.

I picture their bodies, her legs wrapped around his, dishevelled clothing, smeared lipstick, the wonderful escapism of a fast and hard screw; and, God, I wish it was me.

I feel myself pulsing now, as her voice gasps higher, the banging faster. He's panting hard, too.

'Come on, baby,' I hear him say.

Then they both do. The banging crescendoes, then stops. She sighs, then giggles and shushes him.

I imagine myself on the other side, the wet, delighted kisses, hushed groans of congratulation and pleasure. I feel a stab of jealous remorse, remembering how I clawed Scott's back, when we came, how we kissed and then cried.

Suddenly, I hear the door of the toilet opening and I step back further into the shadows.

'Shhh. It's fine, there's no one,' I hear a female voice say.

Then, to my horror, the couple – still embracing – fall into the dark area where I am standing. They kiss deeply, but it only takes a moment before they see me.

She's an air hostess, in uniform, strands of hair falling down from the otherwise perfect chignon. He's good-looking. In his thirties, maybe. He's in jeans and expensive-looking leather shoes, with his tanned sockless feet just visible. They turn their heads and stare at me, wide-eyed, then laugh. I blush furiously, not daring to speak, backing up against the coffee machines. They both know straight away that I know what they've been doing, and that I must have overheard everything.

'Awkward,' the man says, but he's laughing. He has an American accent.

'Sorry,' the girl says to me. She has blue eyes, long eyelashes and a pretty, upturned nose. She makes a grimace as she pulls at the front of her white shirt to rearrange her cleavage. 'You won't say anything, will you?'

I shake my head. Who does she think I'll tell?

Flustered, I walk towards them, to get past, to get to the cubicle.

'We should have invited her in with us,' the man says, winking at me, as I pass him. He raises his eyebrows up at me invitingly. His eyes spell out a clear question. 'She's a cutie.'

I'm so shocked, I rush inside the cubicle and close the door quickly. It smells of sex and the mirror is steamed up. How could they have done it in here? It's tiny.

But, like them, I too am now overcome. I lean against the back of the door and hitch up my dress. I push my hands down the front of my leggings to find my pants. Then I rub my first and second finger either side of my clitoris. I can't help myself, as I picture the air hostess and the good-looking guy.

I can imagine her more vividly now – her blue skirt hitched up, stocking tops, her white shirt open, her nipples falling out of her lacy bra. I imagine her pink lips pursed as he shoved her upwards with the force of his thrusting. I can see his hard cock sliding into her, and I imagine the hot, horny look on his face. I see him looking over her shoulder at me, to where I'm standing right next to them, watching. A sudden orgasm peaks, then drops me flat.

It's alien to me to orgasm alone, which is why the feeling ends so abruptly, I guess. Afterwards, I wipe the steam from the mirror and stare at myself, unsure whether to be ashamed or not, unsure *what* I feel. What am I doing? What have I let myself in for? How will this all end?

7

I yank my wheelie-case through the arrivals gate, more overwhelmed and close to tears than I'd like. You can tell we're in New York. Everyone is so loud, and I've never seen so many different types of people in my life. All of humanity seems to be represented here, and all of them are talking at once.

The queue through immigration took ages, even thought I was in the fast business track. I guess there was a problem with my open return ticket, and they questioned the idea that I was on a two-week probation period for my employers, so I may not, in fact, be taken on full-time at all, so wouldn't need the top-notch visa the Parkers have magicked up for me. I'm just as confused as the immigration officers were, and I guess it was my lack of clear details about my job that caused the hold-up. I feel a bit of a fool. I've flown halfway around the world for a job I know hardly anything about; to live with people I've never met. On paper, it sounds pretty reckless.

Ahead of me, a young girl in a denim jacket runs forward towards the barrier, flinging herself into the arms of an older woman with a squeal of delight. There's nothing like witnessing a family reunion to make you feel lonely and very far away from home.

As the crowd of expectant families thins out, I see the line of people holding signs. There are all sorts of names scrawled on bits of cardboard, and I study them all. What I don't expect is the man in a smart black uniform, wearing a peaked cap, who is standing slightly apart from the crowd at the end of the barrier. He's holding a clipboard with my name typed onto it in a large font. He must be in his fifties and is wearing designer shades and a grim expression, as if dealing with this common riff-raff is just, frankly, beneath him.

I approach nervously and introduce myself. He shakes my hand. He's wearing black leather gloves, despite the heat.

'Please come this way, Miss Henshaw. Welcome to New York.'

Outside, there's noise everywhere, honking cabs and large, colourful adverts for brands I recognize, but the air still smells intoxicatingly foreign.

The driver guy – I still don't know his name, and doubt very much that he's going to tell me – walks ahead of me, wheeling my bag. I wish I'd invested in better luggage. My case is neon-pink, and in his hands it looks like the cheap, tacky thing it is.

I hoist my fake designer handbag onto my shoulder and dig out my shades (also fake – but at least they're new and, as yet, unscratched). I shake my head, fanning my hair out of the collar of my leather jacket, trying to pretend that I'm important, but I don't feel it. I feel tired and grubby.

I hadn't expected it to be so hot in New York and I don't know how far we have to walk, but I'm already uncomfortably warm. I left freezing wintry drizzle in Manchester, but here it's most definitely spring. I suddenly realize that I have all the wrong clothes with me.

I hear a car lock beep and discover that our car – well, more of a limo – is parked right ahead of us, next to the kerb. It's black, sleek and shiny. It has tinted windows. The kind of car you expect to see celebrities in.

I wish Tiff could see this. Whenever we discuss our fantasy marriage ceremonies, a limo is always on the top of the hen-do list, but neither of us has ever been in one. Or has ever been likely to go in one. Until now. I wish I could be more excited, but I just feel very, very nervous. Like everyone must be able to tell the giant fraud that I am.

I sense raised eyebrows from the other passengers, and people waiting for the line of yellow cabs, as we walk directly to the limo and, in a second, my gaudy pink case has been swallowed into its vast trunk.

The driver guy opens the back door for me, like I really am a celebrity, and with less grace than I'd like, I step into the pale leather interior.

Then he shuts the door and I'm sealed in, the world outside immediately muffled. It's blissfully cool.

The car gently rocks as the driver, I assume, gets into the front, but there's a wall of black glass between us, so I can't see him. Can he see me, though? I'm not sure. I hear a clicking noise and then his voice comes through a speaker set into the door.

'Please make yourself comfortable, Miss Henshaw. It's

going to be a long drive. There's a refrigerator ahead of you, between the seats, if you need any refreshments. If you'd like to sleep, you'll find blankets and a pillow in the cupboard to the right of the fridge. If you need anything, please press the black button just at head height above your door.'

Then his voice has gone. Smoothly and with hardly any sound, we pull away from the kerb.

Oh.

My.

God.

8

No matter how exciting stepping into the limo felt, the novelty soon wears off. It just feels weird not having anyone to share it with. I have no signal on my phone, so my attempt to text Tiff a selfie doesn't work, and the driver wasn't kidding when he said it would be a long trip. I get excited as I get a brief glimpse of the famous New York skyline, but all too soon it's gone, and we're heading north and there's nothing worth looking at all – just lanes and lanes of traffic and industrial-looking buildings for miles.

Growing hungry, I finally pluck up the courage to raid the fridge and eat some odd-tasting crisp-type potato things, some Hershey's Kisses and a packet of peanuts, as well as having a full-fat Coke, for a treat, but I can't help feeling self-conscious the whole time. I'm not sure if the driver can see me.

I wish the glass wasn't there and he would talk to me. There's so much I want to ask, but somehow I can't pluck up the nerve to press the black button and start asking questions about our mutual employer.

Instead, I dig down in my handbag and pull out the brown envelope that contains all the info I have: flight details, the printed emails I've been sent, as well as all the information Tiff and I printed from the Internet.

The emails are from J. Gundred – I take it that was the actual name of the woman from the interview. She wasn't Gunter at all. Close, though. The emails are brief and to the point, and I get the feeling they were all written in haste, but then the Parkers seemed keen for me to start right away, and so Gundred has obviously worked around the clock to get my visa and flights sorted.

But I still don't know anything at all about the children. Even the barest, most essential facts, like how many there are, or how old. I did email back and ask her, but she told me the Parkers would introduce me to my specific job spec when they met me.

Now I'm wondering what I've let myself in for. What if they have problem children, or real delinquents? Maybe that explains why nobody has given me any details. Fuck! Or, worse, what if they have a brand-new baby? I fudged my baby experience on my CV. I haven't actually ever looked after a baby. Apart from Ryan, of course, but family doesn't count.

I wonder what type of parents the Parkers might be. There's certainly no evidence of any kids in their posh limo. No squashed biscuits or crusty car seats here.

Now something that has never entered my head hits me full force and I realize just how much I've been coasting along on the fantasy of all this. What if the Parkers are not only rich, but also very strict? Or really dull? What if they don't have a sense of humour – like old Gundred at the interview? What if she's their kind of person, rather than me?

I shuffle the papers and pull out the sheet from Wikipedia and the entries for Edward and Marnie Parker, the people who are now officially in charge of my life.

It's been hard to find out anything personal about them. From what I can gather, he's loaded, having accrued his fortune in the art world. He's some sort of cutting-edge curator, and there's lots of hyperlinks to cool young artists. There are words about art and architecture movements I've never heard of, let alone can actually pronounce, and paragraphs about how Parker has influenced this and that with his 'esoteric and eclectic tastes'. I imagine that he operates in a world of strict minimalism and sits on extremely uncomfortable chairs.

There is one picture of him. He's got a bit of a Robert Downey, Junior vibe going on, although he's younger. Late thirties, tops. He has greying hair and trendy black-framed glasses and is wearing a natty pinstriped suit in the photo, at some sort of red-carpet event. He looks like he keeps himself in shape, and his skin is perfect, although he's frowning, like he's annoyed to have his photo taken.

What, if anything, will we talk about over breakfast? That's if they're the kind of family that will let me eat with them. They may want to keep me entirely separate. But that might be just as well. I don't know anything about art. Although I do have a T-shirt from the market with a Damian Hurst fake-diamond skull printed on it, so that might count? But I doubt it.

She – Marnie – Mrs Parker owns an exclusive designer

boutique, but I'm not altogether sure what it sells. There's a picture of the shop front in an extraordinarily posh shopping street in Manhattan on Wikipedia, but no recent pictures of her. She used to be a model and there's a couple of shots from the Noughties, with her on the catwalk with some strange, angular costume on, slit down to the navel, and she's got crazy hair and blue make-up on (or at least the light is blue), so it's impossible to tell what she actually looks like.

There's also a link, but it's to a tiny blurry thumbnail of an oil portrait of Marnie Parker by somebody who sounds famous, as it was displayed in a big art gallery. It's difficult to make out, but she's definitely nude and lying on her side.

Maybe the super-rich don't worry about posing nude. I'd never do that, though. Not for anyone.

The other printed piece of paper was from a gossip site and the 'moving house' news:

The reclusive couple has recently relocated their family from their sensationally renovated brownstone overlooking Central Park to a mansion in Upstate New York. Their departure will be a loss to fashionable society, but a great gain to A.W.P. Gershbaum and Associates, who are accepting sealed bids on the property, which is expected to fetch in excess of 50 million dollars.

Fifty million bucks. Bloody hell! That sure is a lot of dough.

But I'm more interested in the details about the Parkers. It doesn't say how big 'the family' is.

There is only one further bit of information. Something

Tiff found. She's better at searching for stuff than me. It was a paragraph in a copy of the *Wall Street Journal* last year:

In the courts today, New York socialites Edward and Marnie Parker were successful in their bid to place a gagging order on Luca Weston, the chef who had lived with the family for three years. He had threatened to expose the Parkers in an interview. Weston had implied that the couple had kept him against his will, an accusation that Weston later denied. The Parkers, known for their highly esoteric taste and connections in the world of art and fashion, have been known to throw exotic parties, with a very high level of security.

A gagging order? I wonder what he knew? And I can't help wondering how a couple this wealthy and successful can have so little information available online about them. Maybe they've paid someone to keep all that from the prying public eye, too.

Should I be worried about what I might be walking into? Perhaps. But a part of me is more excited by the mystery of it all. What do I know about how the super-rich operate? Nothing. Nothing yet at all.

But I can't wait to find out.

Because that's what this is, right? An adventure. And it's way too late to back out now.

9

I'm engrossed in an offline game of *Candy Crush Saga* on my phone when the driver's muffled voice jolts me back to reality. It's not coming through the speaker, but I realize that we've stopped. Curious, I stare through the tinted window. The driver is talking to a guy whose face I can't see, in some sort of gatehouse. Ahead of us, there's smooth tarmac road leading over the brow of the hill. There are lots of tall leafy trees.

This must be it. This must be where the Parkers live. On a grass verge there's a very plush sign, carved from tastefully sawn-off tree trunk, saying 'Thousand Acres. Private Estate. Please report to the gatehouse.'

I quickly gather up all the papers strewn around me on the seat and shove them in my handbag, then scramble to tidy up the Coke can and stray peanuts. I press the button to open the window and stare out. We're moving again and it's lovely to feel the wind on my face.

I've heard of gated communities before and, let's face it, I'm used to the concept of estates – but only council ones, like the rough one where my school was, with its boarded-up windows, cheap booze stores and dodgy-looking junkies. In all my life I've never seen anything like this. It's as if the very, very rich have portioned off a private patch of paradise. Even the road is the most perfect road you've ever seen. It's so clean, you could practically eat off it. I think of Ryan. My God, how much would he love skateboarding down this baby?

On either side I can see driveways leading off, and get glimpses of the giant mansions at the end of them. There isn't a soul in sight, let alone another car. I can hear birds singing and the air is super-fresh. Even the manicured gardens look as if the flowers have been given a Technicolor makeover, like in those old movies.

We drive on for what seems like miles, the houses getting more and more spaced apart. I glimpse tennis courts, pools, Ferraris and four-by-fours. I can see only one person, way in the distance. As we get closer I realize it's a woman in a turquoise velour tracksuit with diamanté studs across the shoulders. She's skinny as a rake and is fully made up, despite looking like she's out for exercise, in pristine white trainers. She's walking four small shih-tzu dogs, but somehow it's obvious that she's someone's dog-walker – that, like me, she's staff.

Then there's a loud zooming noise and a black Porsche speeds towards us. I turn my head to watch it shoot up the hill, almost taking off at the brow. I guess speed restrictions don't apply here.

Finally, after what seems like forever, we turn off the road into what appears to be the last drive. The driver obviously has some gismo, because some tall iron gates open as we approach. They are black and ornate and look like they belong at Buckingham Palace.

There's no sign of a house, but the drive bends into the distance, lined on either side by wide strips of almost fluorescently green grass and dense oblong hedges.

I sit forward on my seat as, at last, the drive slowly begins to curve to the left and I finally see the house. I can't stop myself gasping in shock. And then I swear out loud.

'Fuck!'

It's the size of it, I guess. The sheer scale of it – and the wealth. The house must be modern, but it's made of the kind of pale sandstone they build stately homes out of, back home. It's like Downton Abbey's suave American nephew. There are two big towers on either side of the front, with imposing stone falcons at the top of them. There must be a hundred windows, most of them closed with white shutters inside.

The drive terminates in a vast gravel turning circle. There's a gushing fountain at its centre.

On the other side of the fountain, near the house, there's a removal lorry with gold lettering on its side and men in long brown overalls taking what looks like a giant guilt-edged canvas down the ramp and up the sweeping stone staircase towards the front doors, which are open.

The car comes to a stop some way behind the lorry and I can see lots of other workmen, shunting ornate vases inside the house. On the steps I notice a woman directing affairs. At first I think it must be Marnie Parker, but then I realize that it's old Gundred from the interview.

I wasn't expecting to see her here. She certainly didn't warn me that she would be here. She looks different from the last time I saw her. She's wearing slim-cut designer black trousers, with a thin, gold-chain belt, which actually show off what a taut figure she's got, and a black silky shirt buttoned up to her neck. Her hair is loose and I realize that she's probably a good ten years younger than I had her down for.

The driver opens my car door, but doesn't look at me as I get out and mumble my thanks. I make up the steps towards Gundred.

'Hello!' I call.

'Ah, you're here,' she says, but not in a friendly way. She sounds harassed, like I've turned up at an inconvenient time, when she's the one who's rushed me here.

She immediately continues to direct the removal guys, who are humping the heavy picture with extreme caution. She grabs my arm and forcibly moves me out of their way.

'How was your journey?'

'Fine, thanks,' I answer, turning to see the driver taking my pink case out of the trunk and putting it on the bottom steps, as if it might contaminate his hand. He doesn't look at me as he steps back inside the car, and Gundred doesn't acknowledge him. In a moment, the car crackles off around the drive and towards the back of the house.

'It's a bit busy here today,' she explains. 'As you can see.' She sighs, clearly anxious. 'Laura?' she calls out loudly towards the house. 'Laura!'

A girl comes rushing out of the house. I say 'girl', but she's older than me. She has her hair tied back in a ponytail and is wearing creased white shorts and a navy-blue polo shirt. It's a fairly unflattering and androgynous combination.

Oh God, is this the staff uniform? Will I have to wear it? It's hardly any better than the FunPlex uniform.

'Yes, Mrs Gundred? How can I help?'

She has chainmail braces on her teeth, like a fourteen-year-old. She looks like they occupy her entire mouth and she hates speaking. She squints through nasty plastic-framed glasses. Everything about her is awkward: from the way she stands all hunched up, to the way she wrings her hands nervously. Her fingernails are bitten right down.

'This is Miss Henshaw,' Gundred explains. 'Will you take her and show her room, please?' Then she adds to me, more kindly, 'Give me half an hour and I'll show you around properly.'

Laura, the girl, looks at me nervously, her eyes darting to the floor almost immediately, as if she's too embarrassed to look at me.

'This way, if you would, Miss Henshaw,' she says.

'Please, call me Sophie,' I insist, giving her my most friendly smile, but I catch a look between her and Gundred, who shakes her head. It's just a tiny beat, but an important one, I realize. There are strict rules in this place.

But surely – please, God – they're not going to insist on calling me 'Miss Henshaw' the whole time? It makes me feel like a crusty old ballet-school pianist, but I sense it'll take me a while to get to know how things work around here.

I go down the steps to grab my bag, but Laura rushes past me to seize it. She sees herself as lower down in the pecking order than me.

47

'Please, let me,' she says, but is obvious that I don't have a choice.

I follow her into the house, my eyes greedily looking around, waiting for the Parkers to appear. We're in a vast hallway with a black-and-white chequerboard floor, and a massive coloured-glass sculpture-thing hangs down from a glass dome. It's like the Venetian-glass one in the V&A Museum that we saw on a school trip. Only bigger. I guess you'd need fifty mill from a house sale, to afford a place like this.

I'm on tenterhooks, expecting any second to hear the kids running towards me. I have presents in my bag for them: sweets from England that I bought in Duty Free. I'm determined to make a good impression right from the get-go, but I can see now that this is not the kind of house where anyone is allowed to drop a sweet wrapper. Or eat sugar, even. Perhaps sweets were a bad idea.

But I can't help being distracted by the house. It feels more like an art gallery than a house. Off to the left I can see a glass wall and, beyond it, a room with a gleaming parquet floor. It's so shiny and so long I can immediately imagine doing a sock-slide right across it. I guess it's where the art must be going, from the lorry outside, as there are several canvases already stacked up against the wall.

There's a corridor stretching off to the right and a circular staircase spiralling up, with a black handrail going round and round, like a wheel within a wheel – Mum's favourite Dusty Springfield track flitting briefly across my mind.

Everything is perfect. And I mean perfect. There's not a scratch on the walls. It's extraordinarily clean.

'We'll take the service lift,' Laura says. 'This way.'

So, the Parkers aren't coming out to introduce themselves, I realize. I'm to be shown to my room. Not seen and not heard. Is this how it's going to be?

Laura takes me past the end of the staircase to the left and presses a button on the wall. A panel of the wall slides open and there's a carpeted lift inside, with mirrored walls. We enter in silence and Laura presses one of the unnumbered buttons.

Laura stares at the floor and I look at her reflection in the mirrors. I'm starting to feel paranoid. Have I got something in my teeth? Do I smell? Why won't she look at me?

'Do you work here?' I ask her, desperate to fill the silence as the lift moves off.

She nods. 'Sometimes.'

Her answer leaves me even more confused. 'Are the Parkers here?' I ask.

She shakes her head. 'Oh no. Not now,' she says.

I don't know whether she means that the Parkers aren't here now, or whether I shouldn't ask about them now.

The lift is so silent, I don't even feel it moving, let alone know it has stopped. But suddenly the door opens and we're on another floor. This time, it's like a house. There are windows overlooking the landscaped grounds, stretching off to a forest of trees in the distance. It's so English. Like one of those stately homes my grandparents used to take me to look round when I was a little kid.

'Just along here,' Laura says, stepping out ahead of me, pulling my case along the carpet, its wheel squeaking embarrassingly, like she's just run over a mouse.

It feels showroom-new. Like the cream carpet has never been walked on, the powdery grey-green walls just painted. I guess it must be, if they've just moved in. There are wires hanging from sockets yet to be fully fitted.

At the end of the corridor is a bay window with a life-size brass sculpture of a naked man. He's comically well endowed in the groin department. In fact, I would definitely say he has a semi. I want to giggle, but I stop myself in time.

Laura gets to a white wooden-panelled door on the left and stops. 'This is you,' she said.

She opens the door and wheels in my case and I step inside. Then, just when I've got inside, she shuffles out and closes the door, without a word.

I open the door and see her scuttling along the corridor. 'Thank you,' I call after her.

'You're welcome,' she says, but doesn't turn around.

God, she's weird.

I look the other way. The corridor is still empty. Apart from nudey brass man, who seems to be looking at me.

I smile and go inside my room and shut the door. Then I sigh and take it all in.

Wow! I've really arrived.

10

The room is prettily decorated in pale blue and white, and is filled with sunlight from the wall of windows. A long padded seat runs beneath them.

I flip off my Converses and pirouette across the carpet to the enormous circular bed. Then I flop down on it on my back. I gasp in surprise as the bed below me rises and falls with my weight.

At first, I feel seasick. I've heard of waterbeds, but have never actually been on one. Let alone a circular one. I pull up the fluffy eiderdown and sheet and mattress cover, and look at the mattress.

Bloody hell! It really is an actual waterbed. I lie on my back on it and rock my pelvis, smiling to myself as I ride the afterwaves. You could shag on here for hours and not have to move a muscle!

I roll over with difficulty, pressing my face into the sumptuously soft pillows. I've never smelt anything so clean. Can this really be all for me? This is like a proper guest suite. I expected a little box room. Or to be near the kids' rooms, wherever the hell they might be, but this is simply amazing.

I get up and trot over to the white door on the other side of the room.

'Get out of here!' I gasp.

There's an enormous white bathroom the other side, with an old-fashioned claw-foot bath in the centre of it, as well as a power-shower cubicle. It looks like it could be in the centre-fold of a *Homes & Gardens* magazine. It's like the poshest of posh hotel rooms that I could ever dream of. And it's mine. Just mine. None of Dad's shaving kit, or Ryan's toothpasty-gob on the side of the sink, no mouldy patch on the ceiling or noisy fan. No time limits on reading in the bath. It's just heavenly.

I rush back to my bag and grab my phone. I have to show Tiff this. She just won't believe it. But again, as I hold up my phone, I see there's no signal. Or Internet connection. I take a picture anyway, but it's so annoying I can't send it.

Damn it.

I loaf over towards the windows by the bed and peer out. The green lawns stretch away from the back terrace of the house in manicured perfection.

There's a vase of fresh flowers on the dressing table – tight buds of orange and coral roses – and a thick cream-card envelope propped up next to it. I sink onto the velvet stool and open it:

Dear Miss Henshaw. Welcome to Thousand Acres. I hope you had a comfortable flight. Sorry not to be here to welcome you, but looking forward to meeting you very soon. Please make yourself at home. MP

MP. Marnie Parker. That's nice of her. I sniff the roses. They smell of summer. Just then there's a buzzing noise and

I realize there's a phone on the dressing table. I pick it up. It's Gundred.

'Miss Henshaw, if you'd like to have a shower and freshen up, I'll show you around,' she says.

I get naked, stripping off my travelling clothes and chucking them in the corner of the room, and twirl into the bathroom. The sunlight through the blind catches my skin and I smile at myself in the full-length mirror, amazed by how different I look at this level of luxury. I look good, I think. Even though I say so myself. Surrounded by soft cream carpet and flattering lighting, my skin looks smooth and my eyes, despite the long flight, are shining.

I scoop up my breasts, admiring them, and then bend over the bath to reach for the soap and loofah.

'Oo-er,' I laugh out loud, catching my reflection, like I'm Betty Boop, before picking up the expensive-looking unused loofah and admiring the long, smooth brown handle.

Lewd thoughts immediately fill my mind and I realize that I have a residual horniness from the plane that I haven't shaken. Or perhaps it's more that this kind of luxury is an undeniable turn-on.

I wonder what kind of people Edward and Marnie Parker are. Whether they too have a bathroom like this. Whether they're used to it, or whether they get down to it on the bathroom floor every time they step into it.

The shower is filling the room with steam and I pull open the door and step inside. Jets assault me from all sides and at first I giggle, grabbing at the dial, until I've worked out how to control everything.

I grab onto a handle above in the tiles as the power-jets

assault me, blasting away the flight and the long journey and all my doubts. After a few moments of pounding, I turn the water to a different setting. Now tinkling jets of water squirt deliciously from below, catching me between the legs. I move, letting the jet rush against my clitoris. Beneath the rivulets of soap, I see my nipples stiffen. I rock against the jet, closing my eyes, letting the water massage me into sexual alertness.

In my mind, someone I imagine to be Edward Parker comes to me, stepping in behind me in the shower. I call fantasy-guy 'Edward', but the truth is, the guy is fairly faceless – a mixture of my dance partner in the club and Scott, and the guy on the plane and just someone older and rich, all rolled into one. Even so, it feels illicitly thrilling to steal my boss's imagined persona.

I imagine him naked behind me in the shower, soaping my breasts, our wet skin sliding together. I imagine pressing back against this thick cock. I think about how I feel for him to ease into me from behind. I watch us in my mind, as if I'm watching a film.

I feel my throat constrict. I see myself being pressed up against the wall in the steam, being filled up, as the shower jets send my nerve endings into overdrive.

The fantasy feels so real, but I yearn to be filled up. I grab the loofah with its smooth handle and ease it inside me, pushing it slowly in and out of me, as the water massages my clitoris.

'Oh Edward,' I mutter. 'Oh yeah, that's good.'

11

Half an hour later, after my sensational and unbelievably satisfying power-shower, I'm smothered in the free designer body cream I found, and I'm almost ready to explore with Gundred. I pull out my best jeans and a V-neck jumper and my pink ballet pumps from my case, before shoving my case in the closet. There's plenty of hanging space and shelves, and I resolve to unpack my stuff later.

I reach into my washbag for my deodorant and perfume and see the photo of Scott. He's naked in it, leaning back, with a smouldering 'come to bed' look in his eyes. I've had the photo for ages and it's always turned me on, but now I look at it, thinking that he looks almost like a stranger. I've just had the most sensational wank with an entirely fictitious person that I named Edward, and now I feel confused as I look at Scott's face. Should I feel guilty? Unfaithful even? Because I don't. I'm still high on endorphins from fantasy-Edward.

I suddenly remember Scott's bedsit and the grotty duvet. I put the photo back in the pocket of my case. I don't want to think about home now; I'm too excited about being here.

Outside my room I get a bit lost. Corridors lead off in

all directions, but eventually I find the grand staircase leading down.

'I'd prefer it if you'd use the service lift,' Gundred greets me, as I arrive downstairs in the hall. Can she tell, perhaps, that it took all my self-control not to slide down the bannister on my bum?

'Oh, OK,' I tell her.

The removal men have gone and Gundred looks exhausted.

'I'll quickly show you everything and then I'll leave you to it,' she says. Her tone, once again, makes me feel like I'm some sort of inconvenience. What is she? The housekeeper? The manager of this place? Just an agent for the Parkers? And where is she going? She's not going to leave me alone here, is she? I see now that she has her bag over her shoulder. She's not kidding. She really is about to leave.

I think of the friendly note from Mrs Parker upstairs and the lovely flowers, and try to calm down. There must be a plan.

Gundred pulls out a folded piece of paper from her bag and hands it to me. 'First, and most importantly, you'll need this.'

I look at the paper she's given me. It's a floor plan of the house. There are rooms shaded in blue and others in red.

'This will help you get your bearings,' she says. 'The red rooms are off-limits.'

Off-limits? Why, I wonder?

'Where are the kids?' I ask, trying to take it all in. *What the hell happens in the red rooms?* 'I mean, where are their bedrooms?'

'The kids are still away at camp,' she says. 'They'll be back in a week or so, but Mrs Parker wanted you to have some time to settle in first. Get acclimatized. As you can see, they haven't finished moving in themselves, which has somewhat delayed their schedule.'

I'm totally flummoxed by this news, my mind racing. Why the rush to get me here, if the kids aren't here? And what the hell am I going to do for a week without them? And how old are they, if they're at camp? Not babies, then. Phew.

Come on, Sophie, I tell myself. You're in five-star luxury. How hard can it be? When was the last time you actually had a break? Let alone a paid break?

'OK,' I say. 'Can you tell me anything about them, though?'

'Who?'

'The kids,' I tell her, confused.

She cocks her head on one side and then she smiles. I can't tell if she's amused by me or feels sympathetic. 'The kids? Oh, well, there are two boys. Twins. Luther and Tobias. Haven't I told you that already?'

'No,' I tell her. My tone is more petulant than I'd like.

She pauses. Then she seems to make a decision and, when she speaks next, her tone is reassuring. 'Oh, well, I really wouldn't worry about them. Just enjoy yourself this week. Believe me, you'll be busy soon enough.'

Relief rushes through me. Twin boys. Luther and Tobias. Nice names. OK. I can deal with boys. I'm used to Ryan. I'm a lot more confident now that I know what I'm dealing with.

I'm picturing the boys in my head as Gundred shows me around, and start to realize how easy it might be to enjoy myself. It's a busy, bustling home and I soon lose count of the number of corridors we walk down.

Don't panic, I tell myself. This is just like the first day at a new school. You'll soon know your way around like you've been living here all your life.

There's a swimming pool downstairs, with the giant sauna and steam room. In the kitchen I meet Mrs Janey, the cook, and there are lots of other people coming and going, too. They seem to be busy, either cleaning or decorating. It's hard to tell if they're permanent staff like me, or not.

Permanent staff. The thought trips me up. Is that how I see myself already? As permanent? As part of all of this?

England seems a very long way away.

12

Once Gundred has gone, I take myself off back up to my room and unpack and then lie on the bed and call Dad, but I can hardly get a signal. We have a ridiculous conversation of echoing feedback and half-sentences. I think I manage to get across the gist of my call – that I've arrived and I'm OK.

'Have fun. Love you,' he shouts, before the line cuts out, and I smile, although I can picture his face: I know he's missing me already.

It's all been so much to take in and I haven't slept for more than twenty minutes in nearly twenty-four hours. At first I amuse myself, trying to get comfortable on the waterbed, but there's no denying it's a ridiculous sensation. It's like being swept away in a boat and, when I shut my eyes as an experiment, I'm asleep in seconds.

It's dark in the room when I wake up and for a moment I have absolutely no idea where I am. I jolt upright, the waterbed lurching beneath me, and I yelp in shock.

I roll over cautiously and turn on the china lamp on the bedside table and yawn. A soft glow falls over the room and I get up and stretch and, as I do so, my stomach growls.

'Hello,' I call, as I retrace my steps along the dark corridor.

Ignoring Gundred's instruction, I get to the staircase, peering over. The bottom floor below me is in darkness.

'Hello?' I call again. My voice echoes in the stairwell.

I can't possibly be here alone, can I?

I run fast down the stairs and press all the lights on the panel at the bottom of the stairs. Now there's light, I feel slightly better, but it's still a bit freaky.

'Hello?' I call again. 'Anyone? Anyone here?'

I stare down the corridor towards the kitchens. It's dark beneath the doors. The silence is thick and conspiratorial.

I notice now that a row of uplighters has come on around the edge of the gallery room on my right, illuminating the walls. As I walk towards it, the glass door slides open and I walk inside.

Since I was here on my tour earlier, one of the large paintings that I saw being delivered has been hung on the wall. I realize, as I walk towards it, that it's the one I saw on the tiny thumbprint picture on the Internet. It is of Marnie Parker.

The splodgy oil painting dominates the whole wall. It must be at least five or six yards wide and as many high. Marnie Parker is naked and lying on her side, her hand on the gentle swell of her belly. It's an incredible painting – made more so by its sheer size. The oil paint is thick, like it has been trowelled on, but despite that, the more I look at it, the more detail I can see, like how the light falls on the upturn of her breast and nipple. I cock my head and gawp at it, but after a moment it feels illicit, like I'm prying. Her semi-closed eyes seem to stare right at me, challenging me. I look at the dark patch between her legs, then flush and deliberately turn away.

What kind of person poses for a painting like that, I wonder? Someone with a whole bucket-load of self-confidence, that's for sure. Will Marnie Parker be an intimidating boss? What will it be like to meet her, now that I've already seen her nude? Will she be embarrassed, or will I?

Me probably. She's had the painting hung on her wall, I remind myself. She obviously doesn't care who sees it. Not even the removal men. Let alone her young boys.

The parquet floor shines ahead of me. There must be fifty feet or more of clear space. There's not a blemish on it. The lighting in the room makes it intimate – despite its size. It's like a stage.

I remember earlier on, when I first saw this room, I wanted to do a sock-slide across it. I put my hand on my shoulder and rotate my arm. It clicks. I need to move my body.

I take off my pumps and, glancing around me to check that I really am alone, I tiptoe back over to the corner of the room, where I came in. I glance into the corridor. Nobody is there.

I haven't really planned this, but somehow I can't help it. It's just feels rude not to. With a quick run-up sprint, I cartwheel across the diagonal of the room. It feels astonishing – at once thrilling and shocking. I'm so out of practice that I'm panting by the time I come to a stop. But God, it's fun. I laugh out loud.

Revelling in the sheer space, I do a few twirls back the other way, a couple of arabesques, and all at once my dancing days come flooding back and I'm like a kid in class again.

I wonder if I can still *jeté*, I think, rucking up my jeans onto my thighs.

I run back to the corner and check again that I'm still alone. Remembering how I used to pretend I was Darcey Bussell, I focus on the far corner, then take a run up and spring like a gazelle into the air and land like a hippo. I turn and *jeté* again, trying for a softer landing this time. Then I try once more, and in no time I've crossed the room.

I come to a stop and lean forward, my hands on my knees, panting. Christ, it's been a long time since I did that.

Which is when I hear a sound like a whip, but it's actually one slow handclap. Followed by another.

13

It scares the shit out of me.

I yelp and turn to see that it's him: Edward Parker.

Of that I have no doubt. He's standing in the corner, leaning up against the door, like he's been there for ages watching me. He's wearing a cool grey suit with a collarless linen shirt.

Panicking, I try and control my breath. I know my cheeks are pulsing with embarrassment. Where the hell did he come from?

He looks different in the flesh. And very different from my fantasy shower-Edward. For a start, he's taller than I imagined and he's younger, too.

'Oh, I . . . I'm so sorry,' I gulp. 'I . . . I . . .'

I have no words.

I have totally and utterly fucked up.

Only then, as he pushes nonchalantly off the wall and walks toward me, do I see that rather than being stern, an amused smile is dancing on his lips. He has a dimple in his cheek.

'You must be Miss Henshaw,' he says. A smile plays on his lips.

Who the hell else would I be?

'Yes. Hi. I'm Sophie,' I blurt, as he reaches me in the centre of the room. I shake his hand.

'You're making yourself at home already, I see.'

'I'm so sorry. I . . . I . . . turned on the lights and I saw the picture and I couldn't help coming in to see it and then—'

I try and explain, but my words stall on my lips as I find myself swallowed into his eyes. He's not wearing glasses and he's staring at me so intently, I feel suddenly naked. His eyes are an extraordinary shade of light green, with speckled brown bits in his irises. He seems entirely without shame as he stares at me and won't let me look away. Heat rises in me. I know my throat has gone dry.

What can I tell him? I'm *jetéing* across his perfect parquet sprung floor because it's the most space I've had to myself in my entire life? That something about this room – maybe this house – made me want to dance? That I've never been somewhere so clean, or perfect, or posh?

I can't say any of that. It sounds too naff.

He breaks his stare suddenly and looks towards the painting.

'It's a beauty, isn't it?'

His voice is deep. Not too accented. The way he says it makes me feel as if I've already proffered this opinion and he's agreeing with me. The room, for him, is clearly about the painting, and not about me at all.

'I'm interested that you were drawn to it. What do you like about it, Miss Henshaw?'

I'm still slightly out of breath. I stand next to him and face the painting. He smells incredible, I notice. A deep, musky, spicy scent that is overwhelmingly masculine. A proper grown-up man's smell. Sexy. The kind of smell that speaks of a man with a fast car, expensive taste, oh yes, and a fuck-off great big oil painting of his beautiful wife.

'I like, er . . . the, um, size?' I offer. I cringe inwardly. I feel ridiculous for saying something so pathetic. The painting is clearly a masterpiece and must be worth a fortune. And this man – my new boss – is a world-renowned aficionado, for God's sake. It has many other qualities, other than just its size, obviously. Both good and bad, I realize. Like, for example, that it's a fairly inappropriate thing to hang in a house where young boys live. But they've grown up with an art-curator dad and a designer mother, I remind myself. Meaning that they're probably totally used to it, right?

'Ah, yes. You mean the way the proportions are all spot-on?'

'Yeah. And the light,' I hazard. He stares at me intently, waiting for more. This is a man who clearly doesn't entertain small talk. I glance again at the picture, desperately trying to summon up the most intelligent remark I can. 'And that sense that the artist has captured the essence of a woman. If that makes sense?'

'It makes total sense,' he says, and I know I've passed some sort of test. 'It's both brazen and vulnerable,' he says. 'Out there, and yet private. That's what I like about it, too.'

'Yeah, well, I like it that she looks comfortable in her own skin,' I add, wondering whether it comes across as astute and flattering, or whether it's too much.

'And, of course she was pregnant at the time, making her curves even more sensual,' he says wistfully. He says it as if it's a fact, but it feels conspiratorial. Like we're bitching about her behind her back, although, ironically, we're looking at her front. 'And she was then – and still is – so delightfully, as you say, *comfortable* in her own skin. She's not a scrap of a girl, but a woman. But of course artists have known for centuries that those are the only real women to paint.'

I'm humbled by his passion both for his wife and for the art itself. I feel stupid, too. Because, standing next to the painting, I don't feel anything like a real woman. And I suddenly want to be one very much.

'I'm embarrassed to say that I don't know much about art,' I tell him. The least I owe him is the truth.

'Is that so? Then perhaps I will teach you,' he says, smiling down at me. His eyes make me feel flustered and breathless.

He turns back and stares at the painting as if he's drinking it in and, in the silence, I can't help but sneak a peek at his profile. He really does have perfect skin. It's all I can do not to touch his cheek, to check he's real.

'Are you hungry, Miss Henshaw?' he asks. His eyes don't leave the painting. He knows I'm staring at him.

14

A few minutes later, and I'm sitting at the kitchen bar. Through a glass section of the floor I can see the swimming pool below lit up in green. The staff who filled the kitchen earlier have all gone and it's just him and me. I have no idea where his wife is and it somehow feels wrong to ask. If he wants me to know, he'll tell me, I guess. I've never met anyone like him before. He's making me feel like I need to be on the edge of my seat. I can't stop staring at him.

Is it because I know he's rich and successful, I wonder, that makes him have this aura? Tiff saw one of the Man. United footballers in a bar once, and she said that from the other side of the room you could tell he was famous, that he was wealthier than everyone else in the bar put together. But Edward Parker hasn't just got status, or wealth, like a footballer. That's obvious. No, he's got something else that sets him apart. Something I can't put my finger on. The magnetic thing that famous actors have.

I'm shocked by how good-looking he is. Not in a conventional way, but in a groomed, confident way. We were talking about the picture and how his wife is so comfortable in her skin, but he has the same thing, I now realize. Just the way his designer clothes fall around his body; his chunky designer watch and perfectly tanned hands. He could be a model. Seriously. He looks like the kind of guy they'd choose for a sexy older-man aftershave campaign, although he's not poncy or effeminate. He looks like what he is . . . a real man.

And as I watch him, I realize that I've never actually met a proper real man before. Not up close, like this. I mean, there's Dad, but he's scruffy and skint and sad. And Scott is a boy, by comparison. There was Mr Walters, who I thought was a man at first, but then really didn't turn out to be that manly at all. There have been men I've seen, on the peripheries of my life: Mum's rich uncle John, who lives somewhere in Spain; Lance, the guy who owned the bar I used to waitress in – but that's it. I've never actually chatted to someone who is, by the way he looks and the fact he's in this house, a multimillionaire. It's quite overwhelming.

The lights are low in the kitchen, making it feel warm and cosy, and there's lilting jazz music from invisible speakers, which I guess must be either in the ceiling or walls. It's hard to tell.

Edward has taken off his jacket and looks relaxed as he crouches nimbly by a drinks fridge and pulls out a bottle of wine.

Whilst I nervously jabber about my journey here and how much I loved the limo, I watch as he looks at the label appreciatively and then opens the bottle of wine with a corkscrew. The cork makes a satisfying pop.

He takes two large wine glasses, which are perfectly lined up, in a perfectly clean glass cupboard, and places one before me, his tanned fingers with their immaculately manicured nails delicate on its stem. He's treating me like I'm his guest, not like he's employing me. Like he's serving me, and I'm somehow the special one.

He pours a little bit of wine in his own glass, then lifts it to his nose and smells it. He's obviously a wine connoisseur and, once it has met with his approval, he pours some into my glass.

'Taste it,' he commands, standing back and looking at me. 'Tell me what you think.'

I'm lost. Like just now with the painting, I'm so aware that he knows so much and I know nothing. I'm entirely out of my depth, but he really has made it sound like he wants to hear my opinion.

To be honest, I'm not a big wine fan. Dad drinks lager, so we've never drunk wine at home. Tiff's mum gets in the occasional wine box, which we tuck into when we're round there for a Chinese takeaway, but it always tastes tinny and sour.

I take a sip and roll it around my tongue. It's light. Like nectar.

'It's delicious,' I tell him, meaning it.

'Good,' he says, smiling. His face lights up when he smiles. 'So, cheers – or what is it you say in England? Bottoms up,' he says, holding his glass up to mine. We kiss the rims of our glasses and they chime pleasingly.

There's a beat as our eyes connect. I feel like he's looking right inside me. I've never met someone with such an intense stare. It's like he has special powers or something, like he might be able to hypnotize me, just like that.

'About the dancing thing,' I say, brushing my hair behind my ear. 'Just now. I'm so embarrassed.'

His eyes stay on mine.

'I don't usually – I mean, it's very out of character for me to do that. It's just that it's such an amazing space, and I thought I was alone and I haven't danced since Mum died . . .' I try to explain. I don't know where this confession comes from, or what it is about him that has made me want to be so open and honest. He's my employer, for God's sake, but suddenly I'm opening up to him about something I *never* talk about.

' . . . and you took a chance,' he concludes. 'Always do what you feel in your heart, even if it scares you. Isn't that right?'

I stare at him, realizing that he's just repeated back what I said in the interview, word-for-word.

So he watched the interview Mrs Gundred recorded then. Of course he would have, but I feel so exposed. He knows so much more about me than I know about him. Perhaps he senses my discomfort, because he smiles at me and his eyes are kind.

'You never have to apologize to me for expressing yourself, Miss Henshaw,' he says. He stares right into me again. 'Never.'

I want to tell him to call me Sophie. But I can't. I'm still trapped in his gaze. And I know at that moment that this man is going to change my life. That something in me has shifted and the world suddenly has a different focus.

15

When it happens, it happens fast, taking me totally by surprise.

In two steps, he strides towards me across the kitchen and cups my face, brushing the hair away from it and, without saying anything at all, dips his head towards me and kisses me, like I've asked him to. Like this has been agreed between us.

And I think: *Yes. Of course.* It's shocking, yes. Exciting . . . absolutely, but above all it feels, well, *obvious.* Because this was going to happen, from the first second I saw him.

It's as if he's entranced me. Taken all my power.

I'm shaking, but his hand is on the back of my neck, his lips firm and confident against mine. I open my mouth and his tongue flits against mine, sending a shimmer of butterflies dancing through me. A deep, sexual moan escapes from somewhere deep inside me. Somewhere I never knew existed.

He lifts me off the kitchen stool, like I'm a feather, and I hitch my legs around his waist and our kiss is deeper now. Like I can't kiss him hard enough. My mouth is open, biting, gasping, my hair falling around us.

We're moving fast, but I'm floating, borne by his strong

embrace. I can't even think about what it means, but can only feel that I'm connected to him, that a force stronger than I can resist is pinning me against him.

He slides me back onto the breakfast counter. In a moment, he's hitched down my jeans and knickers, and he throws them with careless abandon on the floor. He stares at my nakedness, pulling my legs apart, his eyes glittering.

And I want it. I want to be bared to him like this. His thumbs start caressing my inner thighs. It's excruciating in its intensity.

I grab his hair, gasping, crying out, in exquisite pleasure, as he kisses me again, and then he bends down and buries his face between my legs. His tongue finds me – like he's always known which place to press, which way to flick. Like he knows me intimately already. Has always known me. I don't want it to stop. I can't help myself stop the soaring feeling that builds now . . .

The banging gets louder.

I wrench away from my dream and wake up. My heart is thumping. The intense sexual fantasy I've been having in my sleep dissipates and dissolves slowly. I try and grab onto it, but it's a cloud on a hot day.

I sit up and wobble from side to side in the bed. Bright daylight spills through the curtain.

My pulse is slowing, but beneath my pyjama bottoms I'm throbbing. And now a sense of horror and shame burns within me, as I hear the knocking at my bedroom door again.

My thighs are heavy with the beat of blood as I clamber out of bed and lurch towards the door, the heel of my hand over one eye, which refuses to open – mainly because it's glued together with mascara. I didn't take off my make-up last night, I remember.

Oh God. How drunk was I? We had . . . oh God, two bottles of wine. Was it two?

I open the door, expecting to see Gundred, but it's him. Edward Parker. My boss.

Him.

He looks immaculate in an artfully crumpled black suit and light-blue T-shirt. He has designer shades pushed up in his hair. He smiles at me when he sees me, his eyebrow arching up in question. His teeth are perfect.

'Hey,' he says, softly, with a gentle laugh. 'You're difficult to wake up.'

I've just been dreaming about him, and seeing him up close brings it all back so vividly, I can feel my cheeks pulsing. Can he tell? Does he know what my subconscious has been doing with him all night?

Jesus!

'I trust you slept well?' He's staring at me again and I can barely breathe. He looks amused. Like he's indulging himself in seeing me like this. I get a waft of his glorious aftershave.

I nod, hurriedly banning any thought of the dream from my mind, and instead forcing myself to piece together the events of last night. How he made me taste all the wines so that he could show me the difference between them, how he cooked me fresh gnocchi and truffle oil, which was so delicious I wanted to bury my head in the plate. How I told him everything – all about my family and Tiff – and how he listened like it was the most fascinating life he'd ever heard about. Only it wasn't. Isn't. Couldn't possibly be . . .

I didn't mention Scott once. I didn't *think* about Scott once.

He cocks his head to one side, staring at me through narrowed eyes.

I really dreamt about him giving me head. Oh my God. I can barely bring myself to look at him. I'm awash with pheromones and shame. This is altogether different from when I had an Edward-named fantasy in the shower. This was real – involving the real Edward. The real him standing here now.

'So, you remember that you agreed to come into town later?' he says.

I nod again, remembering now with a sickening jolt that he told me about his friend's art gallery opening this evening. In Manhattan. Proper central New York. Like I've only ever seen in the movies. How he invited me to join him, and I said I would, like it was no big deal. But, in the cold light of day, there's a million reasons why I don't want to – can't possibly actually *go*.

His wife, for a start.

He looks me up and down now. I don't want to speak. I know my breath must stink, but he's waiting for an answer.

'I said, didn't I . . . but I'm not sure . . . I mean—' I begin, flustered. 'I don't think I can. I'm not . . .'

'Do you have anything to wear?'

I pull a face, thinking of the black dress I wore to the interview, which I only flung in my case at the last minute just in case. And how Tiff told me that I was being ridiculous, and that I was staff and wouldn't be going anywhere posh.

He stares at me. He's obviously thinking what I'm thinking: that any cheap black dress that I've brought from England isn't going to cut it in Manhattan.

'I'm not sure if it'll be OK, though,' I say, lamely. Why are we having this conversation about my wardrobe? 'And I didn't bring the right shoes. I think maybe it's better if I don't—'

'That's no problem. How big are your feet?' He smiles and stares down at my bare feet. If feels like a funny question for him to have asked. I screw up my nose and follow his gaze, wiggling my toes.

'A thirty-eight,' I tell him.

He looks back up into my eyes, a smile in his. 'I really have no idea how your English sizes work. What dress size are you?' he asks. He's businesslike as he taps his lips, thinking. His soft lips. The lips I've already kissed like I wanted to devour him whole.

'A . . .' I croak. I clear my voice and shake my head, ineffectually preening my hair. 'A ten, I guess,' I try again.

'Turn around,' he says, pushing my shoulder gently. 'I know what to get, if I can actually get a sense of your proportions. But you wear such hideous baggy clothes, I have no idea of your actual shape.'

He's teasing me, I know, but it's still a shock that he's so rude. Are my clothes hideous? I thought they were cool.

'Can I see your back?' he asks.

'My back?' My mouth has gone dry.

'Uh-huh.' He says it so matter-of-factly, and then lifts

the hem of my pyjama top, and I pull it up a little more, crossing my hands over my chest. I try and look over my shoulder. 'I know about proportions from life drawing. Always start with the back.'

He's staring at my waist, like he really is sizing me up to do a drawing or painting. But I guess that's what he does. Did. Before he made squillions out of other artists.

'I see,' he says, as if he's just had some sort of big revelation. 'Don't you have lovely skin.'

He says it as a statement, then runs his finger along the curve of my back, as if he's painting it. Immediately my skin erupts into goosebumps. Fully awake now, my blood pounding, I look ahead in alarm and catch him staring at me in the mirror on the opposite wardrobe door. As my eyes meet his in the mirror, I feel a spark. Like there's palpable electricity fizzing between us. As if, in that one look, he's been able to tell every second of my dream and can see through me completely.

My pyjama top has ridden up and he must be able to see the bottom of my right breast. I hastily cover it up, and the moment is gone in a fraction of a second, but I'm still shaken.

He breaks my gaze quickly.

'Great,' he says, his voice breezy, as if nothing has just happened. He steps away, out of the room. 'I'll catch you later,' he says, as he walks away.

And then he's gone.

16

I'm rattled all morning, and I'm still trying to make sense of our encounter as I go downstairs into the kitchen and fix myself a giant bowl of cereal. Mrs Janey and Laura are in the kitchen too, but they're busy issuing instructions to three Hispanic-looking gardeners. Mrs Janey tells me to help myself to cereal, flapping her hand in the direction of the cupboards, as if I'm a big inconvenience. She obviously disapproves that I'm up so late, because she looked up twice at the big clock above the door and then back at me.

I feel like shit, and I know I look just as bad. I have a hangover and I'm jangled after my dream, and worried that I've made an idiot of myself. I should have protested more. I don't want to go to a party with Edward Parker. Not where I'll be on show. He said to have fun getting ready, but I have no idea what's expected of me, or what that means. Am I supposed to get dolled up in my black dress?

I hear a voice bellowing in the hall and turn to see a large black woman arrive in the kitchen doorway.

'Hello? Roberta Greerson.' Her tone and expression convey that she finds it impossible that she, Roberta Greerson, hasn't been given more special treatment.

She scowls at me eating, until I stop. She looks like she's

used to bossing lots of people around. She has shiny skin, and she's wearing lots of orange lipstick. Her eyes are green, accentuated by sparkly green eyeshadow. She takes her hair, which is a mass of tiny brown plaits, and puts it up in a band that she pulls from her wrist. Then she puts her hands on her considerable hips, like she means business.

'Which one o' you is Miss Henshaw?' she demands.

Mrs Janey, who moves away from the back door, shakes her head, nodding in my direction, and leaves us alone. She doesn't seem fazed by Roberta's presence at all, or ask her any questions. Was she expecting her? She must have been. How does this household work? I don't get it.

I slide off the stool and greet Roberta, who looks me up and down disapprovingly.

'Lord, what happened to you, girl?' she asks, scowling at my hair.

I pat it nervously. It's not that bad, is it? I go to work at FunPlex with my hair looking much worse than this.

She grabs my chin and thrusts my face into the light. 'You wearing some nasty make-up,' she exclaims. It's not a question.

These Americans really don't mince their words, do they?

'He said I'd have a job on my hands and, boy, he sure weren't wrong this time,' she continues, exaggerating this sentence, her eyes widening at me, and I think that this must be her attempt at humour.

I smile weakly, unable to finish my mouthful of cereal, as her strong thumb and fingers are pinning my jaw shut. Does she mean Edward, when she says 'he'? Has 'he' described me as an impossible case?

'We got work to do to get you in shape. Come on, girl. Hurry up. We ain't got much time to get you party-ready.'

I'm still hungover and desperately trying to figure out a way to wriggle out of the art-gallery party tonight as Roberta takes over my room, hauling in three enormous wheelie-cases, as well as a huge reclining leather chair, which she humps into the centre of the carpet with Laura's help. I'm told to sit in it, which I do with a thud, thanks to a fairly hefty push from Roberta's hand.

She spends a lot of time on her mobile phone taking calls and barking orders to other people. I get the feeling she's been dragged away from an important job to be here. She looks at her watch a lot. And swears even more.

I sit in the chair, but as I do so, an image of my dream flashes into my head, as vivid as if it had actually happened in real life. And then I remember Edward's look. His hand on my waist . . .

Stop, I almost say out loud.

I won't think about it, I resolve, banning my imagination. It's got me into enough trouble for one day already.

Roberta puts special hair-serum on my hair and then sets about massaging my face roughly. She tells me this is the latest beauty craze, which is all about cell-renewal, especially after drinking alcohol. She fixes me with a look. Like she knows all about last night.

The face massage is plain weird. It's rough and invasive, especially when she does my eyes, which makes me feel like she's going to pop my eyes out of their sockets any second. It really hurts, but my yelps don't stop her. She even gets inside my mouth, massaging my cheeks from the inside. It's bloody painful.

Afterwards she scrubs my face roughly, before applying a special mask, which dries like another skin, forcing me to keep still. Then she threads my eyebrows, which stings like crazy. She tuts at my hands, before painting my toenails and fingernails with the kind of precision and speed I have never encountered. If only the girls in the nail bars back home were like her, they'd triple their wages in a day.

Then she hauls me into the bathroom and washes my hair, puts on another face mask, daring me not to speak, and I can't help wondering if I'll have any skin left by the time she's finished with me. I'm tingling all over. And not in a good way.

She hands me a drink of something fizzy and forces me to drink her 'special tonic'. Then, once I've downed it, she puts pads of cool lotion over my eyes and tells me to relax, but it's hard to. I want to curl my toes up, but I can't because my nails are still drying.

'Who gave you this awful cut?' she demands, and I imagine her studying the ends of my hair between her fingers.

'My friend Stacey,' I counter, feeling defensive, but it's hard to speak with the mask on. I had my hair cut especially before flying here. I go to Stacey as she's an ace at waxing, and throws in a bikini, leg and armpit wax for the price of a haircut.

'Well, if you don't mind me saying, your friend Stacey don't know shit about hair.'

I do mind her saying it. I mind very much, but I'm not in a position to complain. It's difficult to move my face.

She sets about snipping my hair and I sit in terror,

wondering what the hell she's doing to me. After a while the snipping stops and, seemingly satisfied, Roberta sets about drying my hair, yanking it as she blow-dries it in sections and curls it. The room is soon filled with wafts of hairspray.

In the middle of this, there's a knock at the door and Laura announces herself. I can't see what she's got, but there is a moment of hushed reverence, before Roberta instructs her to put whatever she's carrying on the bed. Is this something Edward has sent for me to wear?

Eventually, my hair having been tugged, dried, curled and preened to within an inch of its life, Roberta removes the eye pads, wipes off all the gunk from my face, then rubs in a rich cream in luxurious circular motions and eventually instructs me to open my eyes. I'm so relieved that we're done, and the physical assault is over, that it takes me a moment to register the dress on the bed.

I guess it must be intended for me, but even the first second I lay eyes on it, I know I'll never have the nerve to wear it. It's made of this slinky silvery fabric, which catches in the light with shimmering golds and blues. It's the kind of fabric you'd expect mermaid costumes to be made out of.

Did Edward choose this for me?

I walk over to the dress and pick it up. It's so flimsy and insubstantial, it's going to show every lump and bump. It's also backless, so there's no way I'll be wearing a bra.

'Sensational, huh?' Roberta says, grabbing the dress from me and holding it up against me. 'Go put it on.'

'I can't wear that!' I squeal.

'Course you can, girl,' Roberta frowns. 'That's what you're supposed to wear.'

And you'll do as you're told. She doesn't say it, but her look does say it loud and clear. I'm going to wear that dress whether I like it or not. It's in the plan. Whatever the plan is.

The phone on the dressing table rings, making us both jump. It's Edward.

'Hi,' I say. And at that moment I catch sight of myself in the mirror and I almost drop the phone.

My hair looks incredible. As in . . . *in-cred-ible*. It's never looked so glossy and lush. My face is shining with vitality. I look like a completely different person. I almost have to do a double-take to check it's really me.

'Miss Henshaw, listen,' Edward says, and I spring back to listening to him.

Why does he keep calling me Miss Henshaw? Aren't we beyond that?

His voice is low, like he's trying to be private in a public space, as he continues, 'Trewin, our driver who you met yesterday, is going to bring you into town in the car and drop you at the gallery, where I'll meet you. I want you to promise me that you won't say anything to anyone when you arrive. Don't tell them anything, do you understand? Not your name, where you're from?' His voice is urgent.

'Oh . . . well, OK,' I stutter.

Why is this so important to him? I have no idea who will be at the gallery, so it's hard to imagine who I would talk to anyway. The way he's speaking makes me nervous. Exactly how many people are going to be there? Who would be likely even to notice me?

I've known from Gundred, right from the start, that

Edward Parker and his wife are intensely private, but this is the first real sense I've had of it. Perhaps it's all part of their mystique. Perhaps he likes to keep people guessing about him, but even so the words 'gagging order' spring to my mind.

'Under no circumstances tell anyone that you're my nanny, or that you are employed by me.'

'Sure,' I say. He makes our connection seem so formal, it wrong-foots me. Whatever closeness I thought we had is definitely one-sided. That dream has clearly skewed my view. I'm an employee, I remind myself. And nothing more.

'Also, it's very, very important that you don't give any indication of where we live. Any at all. Not even the smallest hint.'

'OK,' I repeat. 'Why would I tell anyone that anyway?'

He sighs. 'I'm sure you wouldn't, but we don't want the press all over us. It's happened before. And we're more exposed in Thousand Acres.'

Exposed to what, I wonder?

There's a pause.

'Can I trust you?' he asks, and I can see his eyes as he says it. Those eyes.

'Of course,' I tell him.

'Good.'

He rings off before I challenge him about the dress. Or ask him when I'm likely to meet his wife: the other part of the 'we'.

17

Everyone has their own so-called 'comfort zone' and mine, right now, is way, *way* on the other side of the planet. It's seven in the evening and I'm sitting on the edge of my seat in the back of the limo, watching the lights of Manhattan looming up ahead of me, and I don't think I've ever felt more jittery. Nerves and excitement are flooding my veins with adrenaline.

I'm dolled up in the dress and, even though I have a fake-fur stole around my shoulders – well, I presume it's fake, although it feels pretty damn fluffy to me – I feel excruciatingly exposed. I've never worn anything so sensual, or revealing, but the dress is so cleverly made, it's like a second skin and, considering its skimpy proportions, I have to admit that it's unbelievably flattering. I'm all curvy and cool, like that girl in the Chanel advert where she strips off.

There's no label, but I can't help thinking that someone who really knows about women made this dress. Despite my initial reservations, I have to admit that I don't think I've ever looked this good.

I stare down at the matching silver high shoes, turning my foot on its side to survey the spiked heels. They don't have a name or a label in them, either, or any markings at all, but I guess they must be designer, too. Will I be able to walk in them, though? What if I trip over?

I have no idea what to expect, or why I've been required to look like this, but as we snake through the traffic I want to pinch myself. Two seconds ago, I was in a dead-end job in FunPlex and now I'm here, looking like this, in Manhattan, in a limo. Tiff wouldn't believe me, even if she could see me right now.

I distract myself by staring out of the window at the buildings, the yellow cabs, the steam coming up through the sidewalks – just like it does in the movies. Only better. It's real. It's happening.

We drive along a wide avenue, snaking in and out of the traffic, and my face is pressed against the window as we go through Times Square and I see all the adverts lit up. It feels familiar and alien, and I wish I could stop the car and get out and look around. But I'm not exactly dressed to be a tourist.

Before long, we're in a wide block of swanky-looking brownstone buildings. They have tall windows and lots of shiny black cast-iron work. They were probably once warehouses, but they're done up now. I see trendy bistros and designer shops with grilles over them, the perfect mannequins lit up inside dressed in gowns and coats. I'm trembling with nervous excitement.

As we slow down, I can see that one of the buildings is open and a crowd of people is spilling out onto the sidewalk. The voice of Trewin, the driver, who once again has barely said two words to me, comes through the speaker in the door.

'This is it. You can leave your coat in the car,' he instructs.

Coat? My stole isn't a coat. But maybe he's right. Maybe the dress should be seen.

Quickly I rummage in my handbag, which I will also leave in the car. I grab the see-through make-up bag stuffed with my essential 'top-up' kit that Roberta gave me. I check my eyes in the shiny black compact. They're still perfectly made-up. They look clear and bright, my lashes sculpted to perfection.

I wave a wand of lip-gloss over my lips and twirl one of my bouncing curls over my shoulder. Then I shrug off the stole and check the top of my dress. It's a halterneck, but is so cleverly cut, it somehow supports my boobs in a perfect way, even though I'm not wearing a bra. Suddenly I remember Scott and how he used to cup my breasts.

Scott. Oh . . . *shit!*

I still haven't messaged him – or emailed or rung – as I promised I would. I didn't have enough reception at the house, though I must have here. But it's too late to call him now. I'm so rubbish only to have just thought of this now. The last contact we had was when I texted him from the plane just before we took off. He'll be worrying about me by now.

I'm amazed by how distant he feels, like he's from a different life altogether. What would he say if could see me now? I wonder, seeing my gaze staring back at me in the mirror.

I wouldn't want him to see me, I decide. I wouldn't want

his small-minded, small-town judgement ruining how I feel right now. Which it would. Besides, Scott – for all his bravado and reputation with his mates – would never have the nerve to do anything like this. To step out into the world. To feel the fear and do it anyway, as the poster on my bedroom door says. I may fall flat on my face, but at least I'm willing to give it a go. And that, I realize with a sad sigh, is why I left.

The limo slows and stops by the sidewalk. I see the faces outside staring at me. They can't see me through the tinted glass – I know that – but I still flush.

Behind them, standing in the doorway, I see Edward. He steps forward onto the sidewalk. He's wearing a skinny-cut blue silk suit, which makes his tanned face look amazing.

'It's OK,' he mouths. I know he can't see me, but it comforts me that he knows I can see him. That he knows I'm looking for him. He smiles at me. There's that dimple in his cheek. There's no sign of Marnie Parker. No sign of his wife at all.

I hear Trewin getting out of the driver's seat. I shove my bag and stole into the shadows and take a deep breath to calm my nerves.

And then the door opens.

18

I take Trewin's hand as he helps me to step onto the pavement. And I swish out the skirt of my dress and smooth it over my curves as I stand, trying to stop my legs shaking.

It's just as I feared: everyone is staring at me. I swear there's a sudden hush as I stand by the car.

In a second, Edward is in front of me. I can't tell what he's thinking. Does he like my dress? Do I look OK?

'Hi,' he says. His eyes don't leave mine as he leans forward to kiss me. I'm expecting a polite kiss on the cheek, but to my surprise, his lips touch mine.

It's the smallest kiss, but it's so unexpectedly intimate, I feel my breath catch. I smile back at him. As long as I'm in the bubble of his gaze, nothing else matters. My nerves reduce down from a code red.

I've been telling myself all day to drop my stupid fantasies about him, to stop the ridiculous crush I've developed in just one meeting, but standing here, his kiss still tingling on my lips, I know I can't do it. I feel lit up by him.

Edward's hand slips around my waist, his warm fingertips grazing my flesh and, once again, goosebumps arpeggio up and down my spine. I am careful with the front of my dress, which has a slit down the front to the middle of my stomach.

I don't want any boob blunders, but before we left Roberta and I had a practice and she assured me that it was virtually impossible to fall out of it.

Edward guides me, so that we both turn in unison. 'Smile,' I hear him whisper under his breath, although we're both already smiling. A man with a big camera crouches in front of us as we walk towards the gallery. I thought Edward was photo-shy? I thought he didn't like publicity, so why are we being photographed like we're a couple? Where is his wife? What's going on?

'That's great,' the guy says, briefly checking the view on his camera. 'And another.'

But Edward is being pulled away, to shake a man's hand. He's an effusive young guy with a shaved head and piercings all up his ears. He has an elaborate tattoo on his neck.

'It's such an honour, man,' the man says, pumping Edward's hand. 'I can't believe you're here.' He must be the artist.

Edward winks at me and lets go of my hand and steps away, so that I can be photographed alone, but I know I haven't lost his attention. I gaze at him confused, but he gestures to me to turn around in a slow circle and I do. The photographer snaps away at me. I've never even considered modelling for a second. I'm not quite tall enough and have far too large a chest, but I can suddenly see the appeal, although they're snapping away at all angles.

Ignoring the photographer's request for more pictures, Edward dispatches his fan with a clap on the top of his arm, and puts his arm once again around my waist and guides me protectively towards the doorway of the gallery. Just the way he is with me makes me feel more special than I've ever felt. It fills me with confidence.

As we walk inside, a girl in a short orange dress stands aside for us and I have a jolt of recognition. She's that actress in *Spider-Man*. The one Scott thinks is hot. She's minute in the flesh, but she has a kind of star quality and I smile at her. She smiles back, like we're mates already. Wow!

The gallery is rammed and it's hot inside. Music pumps out. The open-plan space is lit with lasers, which occasionally illuminate the metal walkways high up, criss-crossing the warehouse. It's the most exceptionally cool place I've ever been.

And this, I realize, is actually what it's like to be in the centre of things. And it feels . . . magic. Because all my life I've been waiting for this. To be somewhere this happening.

On the walls are huge, dramatic black pictures, like photograph negatives that have barely been exposed. Waiters and waitresses walk around carrying trays of champagne and sumptuous-looking canapés between the groups of people. I see people turn to look at Edward and me. I keep my head held high.

'You've got a small job to do,' Edward says in my ear.

'Oh?' I ask. A job? What does he mean?

'Go straight ahead and up those stairs. That's all.' His eyes smile into mine. 'When you're halfway up, put your arms up on the rail and turn round. Look over your shoulder,' he tells me. 'There'll be more pictures. Then the guys will leave you alone. Whilst you do that, I'll get you a drink.'

He fondles a long curl of my hair, and then nods

encouragement at me and I walk alone through the gallery, but I can't help feeling that I'm parting the crowds. That everyone is staring at me.

Without Edward by my side, I feel like an imposter. A fraud. I concentrate on my instructions, keen not to disappoint him, but – surrounded by all these beautiful people – I'm terrified that I'm going to trip up any second. I scan around to look for Edward, but I don't see him.

I know now why he doesn't want me to speak. Because I don't – and won't ever – fit in here. This, I realize, is a performance. One for which I've had specific instructions. And until I know what's going on and what the nature of the production is, all I can do is play my part. I focus on the metal staircase ahead of me, imagining that it is a stage. I can do this.

Anyway it's impossible not to sashay in these shoes, which give my stride a confidence I don't feel. I hold my chin up, as I keep going. I reach the stairs and start to walk up the steep metal steps, putting my hands up on the rails. Halfway up I stop, as I've been instructed, and look nonchalantly over my shoulder. Below me, looking up, are two cameramen, their shutters flashing furiously. They must be getting a hell of a rear-view. This dress splits up the back almost to my bum. I don't smile; I just raise one of my newly shaped eyebrows, like I'm a prize diva.

Then I see a man in a scruffy brown suit standing to one side. He has rumpled, curly black hair that looks like he's just got out of bed, and a shadow of beard on his chin. He sucks a drink through a straw.

He stares at me and, when my eyes meet his, his own

eyebrows rise up in such a way that I realize I haven't fooled him for a second. That he thinks I'm ridiculous. I quickly look away from him and turn, continuing up the steps.

I see some people above waiting to come down, but they're going to let me pass first. I smile at the girl. She has blue-black raven hair, cropped in a brutal fringe. She puts her hand over her mouth and whispers to her Japanese-looking blonde friend, who looks at my dress and nods.

Do they like it? Don't they? Do I look ridiculous? It's impossible to tell.

I carry on, as fast as I can manage, away from the photographers and that off-putting man. At the top of the steps there's a walkway, and I see Edward on the other side at the bar. He puts his chin up, his eyes telling me to walk towards him. My eyes don't leave his. It's a long way down on either side of the walkway, and I don't have a head for heights. Halfway across, he nods again, and I realize he wants me to stop.

How many times have I misinterpreted Scott? I think. Dozens. Half our arguments have been over me misreading his body language in clubs and pubs – when he wanted to stay, and I thought it was time to leave – and yet here I am being controlled by the gaze of a man I hardly know.

I wait for Edward, putting my hand on the bar of the walkway. Up here, I have a view over the whole gallery. Looking down on the crowd, I realize this must be the 'eclectic' crowd that Edward hangs out with. I looked it up in the dictionary after reading Edward's Wikipedia entry, but whilst there's an arty sort of vibe, the people all look similar to me. Most people are wearing black and, with the black pictures on the wall, I feel like I'm a shimmering light.

Edward approaches.

'Try this,' he says, holding out a clear drink in a Martini glass.

I take the drink. My silver-blue nails look stylish against the glass. Roberta did an amazing job. I'm never going to take these nails off. That is seriously my favourite nail-polish colour of all time. I look at the big costume ring I'm wearing. It's a large, round, sparkly knuckleduster on my middle finger. Of course I assumed it was costume, but now, as it catches the light, it dawns on me that the hundreds of diamonds might well be real. I glance down at the stringy diamond necklace that hangs down the slit of my dress. Is that real, too?

'Are you OK, Miss Henshaw?' Edward asks. This time, his leg touching mine, the way he says my name feels intimate. Like it's a pet name and we're way closer than we actually are.

But that's not true, I remind myself. That's just what happened in my filthy imagination. This is purely a business arrangement.

I nod, smile and clink glasses with him, and take a sip of the drink. It's neat vodka, by the taste of it, and it's ice-cold. But it's not bitter or acrid, but rather delicious. I take another sip. Edward's eyes sparkle at me as he watches me. I suck the liquid off my bottom lip. My nipples are hardening beneath the thin fabric of the dress, as if he's staring at them, but his eyes don't leave my face.

He leans in, his mouth close to my ear, to speak above

the music. I feel his hand on the curve of my waist. And in this half-embrace, every nerve tingles. I close my eyes briefly, trying to steady myself. I breathe in his delicious scent.

'You look sensational,' he says.

As I open my eyes I look ahead to the bar, where people are staring at us. There's a photographer with a long lens pointing at us.

19

As the evening wears on, I notice Edward occasionally scanning the crowd. Is he waiting for his wife to show up, I wonder? What will happen if she does? He makes no mention of her, and neither do I. I think about bringing her up, and try and find a way to chat about her, but each time I do, the words feel all wrong to say and then I give up.

Despite the fact that everyone in the room knows exactly who he is, Edward stays close to me all night. At first, I think it's only for show, but I get the impression that he's enjoying talking so intimately in my ear. I don't mind. I like his arm being around me, or his leg being pressed against mine. It's like we're playing a game, pretending to be a couple.

I've never had the undivided attention of someone who is clearly the most important man in the room and, to my eye at least, the best-looking by a mile. I can't stop staring at him. Just the way his eyebrows are fascinates me. I just want to touch his face and press my finger into that dimple on his cheek. I can see the start of some hair on his chest above the top of the button on his shirt. The more intimately he talks to me, the more of him I want.

I start to enjoy myself and stop being nervous. And after a few more of those delicious vodkas, I start to feel perfectly protected by him, like his rare plant. If people are talking about us, let them. I don't care.

He gives me a private low-down on the various people in the room, secretly pointing out agents and artists, salespeople and critics. He has an opinion on them all. Most of them make me smile. He seems so serious, but actually he's got a great sense of humour.

'See that guy? Over there? With the bushy eyebrows. Two o'clock. Man, he has a serious breath problem. Agent. Nightmare. Always fleecing me.'

Edward is approached endlessly, but as soon as anyone comes near us, he seems to freeze him or her out and, when he pointedly doesn't introduce me, they quickly leave.

I like monopolizing his attention. Like I've got one over on everyone else in the room. I feel like the 'It' girl – a feeling I've never had before, but have always wanted.

'So, how come you're in this whole art-world thing?' I ask him.

'The art-world thing,' he says, repeating my accent. Amusement dances in his eyes. Then he shrugs. 'I wanted to be an artist, once upon a time,' he admits. 'I loved drawing. It was my passion for a while.'

'So why didn't you pursue it?'

'There are other far more talented artists than me,' he says. 'And I realized that my talent is actually bringing out the best in other people.'

He stares right at me as he says this, and then he looks

at my lips. It's as if he's suddenly thought about kissing me and, for a nanosecond, the rest of the room shrinks.

'Come, let's look around,' he says. He holds my hands tightly as we negotiate the walkway downstairs.

He's holding my hand.

When we get to the bottom of the steps, I don't want to let him go, but he does, putting his arm around my shoulder and leading me over to the paintings. Several people come up to him and greet him, but his arm stays around me. A couple of clearly affluent women look me up and down enviously.

'So is this guy one of yours?' I ask Edward, nodding to the giant black canvas ahead of us.

'No. This isn't to my taste. He's talented, but I don't agree with the direction he's taken.'

I get the sense that Edward is a difficult man to please. He's also someone who knows what he likes.

'So what is your taste?'

He turns to me and smiles, and there's the dimple again. 'Simplicity,' he says. 'Beauty.'

'Real women,' I remind him, with a wry smile. I can't help remembering his passion about Marnie and right now, with this sexual energy building between us, I feel that it's the right moment to remind him about it.

'Real women, of course,' he says. 'But I like most of all to find something unexpected.'

Is he talking about me? Am I unexpected?

'And then I have no control. I have to have it.'

My heart is pulsing as we carry on walking through the

gallery. My head is light from all the drinks, but also from what he's just said.

We've reached the back of the gallery now, where the crowd is thinner. There's a kind of side-room enclave to our right where there are smaller paintings.

We're just about to walk into it together, when Edward's phone rings in his pocket. He takes it out, looks at the caller and then excuses himself. He nods at me to go into the smaller gallery space and wait for him.

He smiles at me and points at me to stay where I am, as he backs away, and I want to bend my knees and do a little victory jig.

Bloody hell. He is just utterly gorgeous. Never in my wildest dreams did I imagine that tonight would turn out like this. I try and figure out how long it's been since I've actually been in the country, but it can't only be thirty-six hours – that's ridiculous. It feels like I've been here forever, and I'm loving every moment.

I can't begin to think about what it means, but surely this isn't all one-sided. He must get this crazy connection, too, right? You don't just meet someone and click the way we have, surely?

I walk further into the small gallery and take an audible exhale, cautioning myself to calm down. Edward Parker is married. Married, *duh*. And he's my employer. Nothing is going to happen between us . . . as in, ever.

But even as I think that, I can't help remembering the way his eyes connected with mine in the mirror this morning, or how it felt when he leant right up against me and told me I looked sensational. It felt like he was lighting me up from the inside. And I want to feel like that more.

I stare at the smaller pictures on the wall in this space. I can't say that I can make out what they're of. If anything, they look like the photos you see of star constellations, mainly with black backgrounds with shimmering, jewel-coloured splodges across them. There are a few sketches, but they're literally just a couple of lines. I lean in to see the label on the painting. 'WOMAN RECLINING,' it says. I stand back and try and see how those two lines could possibly be a woman reclining? Is this whole art world just total bollocks, as I've always suspected?

'So. You and Edward Parker?'

I turn to see that someone has joined me in the small gallery. It's the guy from the stairs in the crumpled brown suit. The one who was looking at me when the photographers were taking pictures? There's a sly insinuation in his tone, which is backed up in the look he gives me now.

I stare at him, not hiding from my expression how offended I am.

'Oh, don't get me wrong. He's an interesting guy,' he continues. His eyes are full of questions and he's scanning me, taking in every detail of my attire. I feel self-conscious as he stares at my cleavage. 'I'm Harry, by the way,' he says, as if he's suddenly remembered his manners, and he retrieves his hand from his pocket to shake mine. 'Harry Poulston.'

'Hi,' I put my hand up in a limp wave and look over my shoulder for Edward.

Harry cocks his head, expecting me to exchange pleasantries, but I suddenly remember my promise to Edward not to say anything or give anything away. As the obvious silence lengthens, I stare down at my glass again and press my lips together.

He nods, as if realizing something and smiles. 'Oh I get it.' He nods again and points at me. He smiles, but it's not a friendly smile, like Edward's, but a sneaky one. 'The cat's got your tongue, right? Or are you a mute?' He pretends to think, putting his finger on his lips. 'Or have you been subjected to a gagging order, too?'

He knows about the gagging order? I stare at him, wondering what this is all about, but my gesture has given me away.

'Ah, yes,' he says, still sizing me up. 'Quite a little show you've put on tonight. Quite a show indeed.' He watches me again. 'But those are slippery people, the Parkers. Between you and me, you should be careful what you're getting yourself into.'

I glance around more desperately this time, wanting Edward to come back. I don't like this guy. He gives me the creeps. I give him my best withering look, but he seems to take strength from my discomfort.

'Strange, don't you think, that they've moved from Manhattan to the middle of nowhere? Although no one seems to know why? Or where, for that matter.'

'That's because it's none of your business,' I blurt out, feeling defensive. This is exactly what Edward warned me about. People probing, asking questions. This guy is probably a journalist. A snooper.

'Oh. A Limey,' he says, taking in my accent and grinning widely. 'Well, well,' he says, as if this makes sense to him.

'I bet you know where they've run to, don't you?' he says, leaning in close to stare into my eyes.

I recoil away. I wish he'd just fuck off. Where is Edward?

'Funny they went right after that business with the missing painting . . .'

He lets the comment hang in the air. I look at him. What missing painting?

I back away and he realizes he's gone too far. He puts out his hands in surrender. 'Listen. You seem like a nice girl. I just don't want you to get mixed up in anything, you know . . . ?'

'No, I don't know,' I snap. 'I don't know what you're talking about. Please leave me alone.'

He smiles, disappointed, and nods. 'OK, Princess,' he says. 'Have it your way. But here's my card. I will get to bottom of the mysterious Parkers, with or without your help. But if you ever want to talk, then please . . .'

He thrusts the cards towards me, so that I have no choice but to take it.

And as I hold it in my hand, I turn and my eyes connect with Edward's.

He's across the gallery in a few quick strides and takes my elbow as he quickly escorts me away from Harry. He's going too fast and I almost trip. I turn back to see Harry raising his eyebrows again. He's clearly delighted that he's made Edward so angry.

'What did he say?' Edward hisses when we're out of earshot. He takes the card out of my hand and crushes it in his fist and drops it on the floor.

'Nothing. He just had questions.'

'So *not* nothing,' Edward counters back, as if I'm being stupid. I'm frightened by his tone. I want nice Edward back.

'He was snooping round, wanting to know why you moved, where you lived.' I don't tell him about his comment about the missing painting.

'Fuck!' Edward swears. It's weird to hear him swear. He's not the type. He's clearly cross. *Really* cross. He stops suddenly, when we're back in the large gallery, and turns to me. His eyes are blazing. 'And what did you say?'

'Nothing,' I tell him, talking loudly over the thumping music, the beat of which throbs with my cheeks. 'Nothing at all. I promise you.'

He leans in closer, his eyes boring into mine, like he can rewind the experience by the sheer force of his stare and replay it to his own satisfaction. For a moment I'm really scared. I glimpse now that there's something lurking inside him, something deep down and scary that I don't want to unleash.

'I promise,' I tell him again, but I feel shaky. Suddenly, I want to cry. I'm way out of my depth. 'You can trust me. I told you that.'

He nods and exhales, like he's deflating. His flash of anger suddenly shuts off, as if he's slammed the door on it. Then he embraces me in a tight hug. 'Sorry. I'm sorry,' he says, stroking my hair. 'I didn't mean to upset you. I just can't stand guys like him. And it annoys me that he honed in like a vulture, the second my back was turned.'

'It's OK. I understand,' I say. But I don't. I don't understand anything at all. But all I can think of is the relief of his embrace.

'Let's get out of here,' he whispers in my ear.

20

The journey back home seems to take no time at all in comparison to the time it took to drive from the house, but maybe that's because I have Edward to occupy me. We sit in the back, the low light on, and he tops up my glass with champagne. He has his legs stretched out and I'm propped up with pillows, my feet on the seat and I'm covered in a soft check blanket.

I have my phone plugged into a cradle that's popped out of the door and I've had my playlist on. He has different taste from me, but I'm surprised at our mutual love of The Killers. He's got a great voice. We're laughing as we sing along. I don't care about Trewin. He's behind the glass. I'm just so relieved to be out of the gallery and alone with Edward. Nice Edward. Not angry Edward. I don't ever want to incur his fury again.

'I've been meaning to ask you. This phone is useless at the house,' I tell him, as I lean forward to change the song. I take a slurp of champagne. I feel giddy and pissed – but in a great way, not in a slurry way. The kind of pissed you always want to be when you have a drink – like you're on sparkling form. 'I have no reception or Internet. Is that something we can sort out?' I ask casually, peering at the screen to put on another playlist.

'I'm sure we can,' he says, but when I look up, he's frowning. 'That's more Marnie's department than mine. She'll help you. Ask her.'

Marnie. It's the first time he's mentioned her tonight. I'm suddenly nervous. Like we've hit on a taboo subject. I don't know how she'd feel if she could see me now, drinking champagne with her husband. And, yes, I can't deny it – flirting with him.

Having never met her, I really can't imagine what they're like together. I've put thoughts of her entirely on hold this evening, but now it's as if she's here in the car with us. I shrink back in the seat, wrapping the blanket around my legs.

'I haven't met Mrs Parker,' I say, keen to make her name just as formal as he makes mine.

'Oh? Haven't you?' he asks. He sounds genuinely surprised by this news. 'Wasn't she at the house when you arrived, yesterday?'

I shake my head. A will.i.am tune comes on, and Edward's face clouds in displeasure. I pick up the phone and quickly change the song. I put on Ed Sheeran, an album that Tiff and I love, but that Scott says meanly is 'period girl music'. Edward seems to relax.

I can't work out what he's thinking. He leans forward and takes out the champagne bottle from the fridge. He tops up my glass. I replay our chat yesterday, when he caught me dancing by the portrait. Did he think I'd already met his wife then? This knowledge tilts my memory of everything we discussed in the kitchen and gives it a different edge that I can't quite grasp.

'You just missed her then. She went to LA for a meeting. I'm sure you'll meet her soon enough,' he says. 'I thought she might be there tonight, but I guess her flight must have been delayed.'

Again, I'm confused. Why would he pay for me to be all dressed up and to be photographed with him, then spend the whole evening with me like he has, when his wife could have shown up at any second? Not that we were doing anything wrong, exactly.

'So who do you want to call?' he asks, sitting back. His eyes narrow at me. 'On that phone of yours.'

'Family. Just family. I should tell them I'm here and everything is OK.'

'OK?' he mocks me and smiles. And again, there are his eyes, boring into mine.

'OK. Better than OK.'

'What about your boyfriend?'

He knows. Of course he knows, I realize. I exhale and look up at the ceiling of the limo. I feel like I've been busted. He watched the tapes, and someone as discerning as him must have realized I was lying.

'It's none of my business, of course,' he adds, but we both know that somehow it is. 'Doesn't he mind you being here?'

I picture Scott's bloodshot eyes. The way he begged me not to leave. And suddenly, out of nowhere, my eyes fill with tears. Shocked and annoyed at myself, I press my knuckle into the corner of my eye.

Edward leans forward and puts his hand on the blanket and squeezes my knee below it. I long to grab his hand and hold it in my own.

'I'm sorry. I didn't mean to pry. It really is none of my business.'

I exhale and smile and flap my hand in front of my face. This is stupid. Why am I crying? I hate myself, that I'm suddenly like this. I guess the booze has made me maudlin. I've always worn my heart on my sleeve. That's what Dad always says, like it's a good thing, but it's not. It's just embarrassing.

'I'm sorry,' I tell him. 'I don't mean to be emotional. I did have a boyfriend – I mean, I *do* have a boyfriend. Scott,' I tell him. I feel like a child all of a sudden. Caught out. 'I know I said I was single in the interview, and on my application. I didn't . . .' I sigh and take a sip of champagne and focus my eyes on the ceiling to try and wash down my tears. '. . . I didn't want you to think I wouldn't want the job because of him. Because I do.'

I'm all too aware that the Parkers specifically wanted someone with no emotional commitments, and here I am, tearfully admitting to Scott. What if Edward sends me home? What if I've failed already? Before I've even met the kids?

'Sorry,' I say, rolling my eyes at myself. I blow out a slow breath.

'It's OK. I'd rather you were honest,' Edward says. His hand stays on my knee. I glance down at it.

'I just . . .' I take a deep breath. If he wants the truth, then here it comes bubbling up in me. '. . . I just wanted more. More from life. Does that make sense? I just wanted to grab an opportunity to do something new. See the world, you know?'

'Of course,' he says. His eyes twinkle. They're swallowing me up again. I've admitted something so personal, but he makes me feel so safe. 'I know exactly. I felt the same at your age.'

'And I felt . . . I don't know – I know this sounds mean, but I felt like Scott was suffocating me. Through no fault of his own,' I add. 'It's just that I felt defined by our relationship, not for anything I'd done on my own.'

Why am I talking about Scott in the past tense? Just the realization of this makes me even sadder. But I've known it deep down, since the minute I stepped on the plane. But right here, right now, it's a relief to set these words free.

'Were you close?' Edward asks, sitting back, breaking contact. I long for him to touch me again.

I nod. 'We were once. He thinks we still are.'

Edward pulls a sympathetic smile, like he understands what a shit I've been, but forgives me anyway.

'Oh,' he says. 'That's tough.'

Why is he being so nice to me? How can he possibly understand? And yet he does. He does, more than anyone ever has. I'm suddenly so grateful that I've told him this. That he knows this about me.

'I couldn't explain to him,' I confess. 'I tried. He thinks everything is perfect between us, you see. We have sex all the time and—'

I suddenly gasp and stop. I laugh, shocked that I've said something so outrageously intimate to my employer, but Edward only smiles at me and nods for me to carry on.

'I mean, sorry. You don't need to know about that.'

'You'll find out that your definition of a great sex life, Miss Henshaw, may need some adjusting over time.'

His eyes twinkle over the champagne glass. What does that mean, I wonder?

'But you're right. A girl as stunning as you should have a man's devoted attention. You're obviously a sensual person. You mustn't ever settle for anything but the best.'

He thinks I'm stunning? I'm reeling from this casual admission. I need to finish the Scott conversation, though.

'So now you know. That's why I left,' I say, relieved that he understands. Because that's it. He's hit the nail on the head. I don't want to settle. 'Sex isn't everything, right?' I tell him.

'No. It's not. Well, not until you've properly experienced sex, that is.'

And at that moment his eyes meet mine and I feel a kind of shuddering thrill that it takes me a moment to recover from.

21

The house is shrouded in darkness as the limo crunches onto the gravel drive, but the grounds are lit up in silvery moonlight.

We walk together up the steps, although I'm holding my shoes in one hand and the skirt of my dress in the other. I'm glad of the fur stole. I've been parading around all night with my navel out, but suddenly it feels inappropriate to have so much flesh on show.

Edward opens the door with his keys and then chucks them on a marble table in the hallway. He puts on the lights.

'Marnie?' he calls. 'Marnie, are you home?'

I hold my breath. I've been waiting all this time to meet her, but after our chat in the limo, I feel a closeness with Edward that I don't want to break.

Silence greets us.

'Damn it, I thought she'd be back by now,' he says, but he doesn't sound particularly cross. Guiltily I feel my stomach flip at the clandestine knowledge that we are all alone.

'She's not here?' I check. I watch as he punches in some keys on the security panel by the front door. The tiny lights, which look very complicated, change. This must be the automatic door-locking system for the internal doors, I realize.

'She'll turn up when she wants to,' he says. He doesn't look at me.

I can't fathom out his elusive answer, as I head inside with him and follow him down the corridor. What kind of weird marriage do they have, if they don't keep track of where each other is? Maybe they're not close at all. Maybe they have some kind of hostile 'arrangement' marriage, where they both do their own thing. I get the impression that Edward is a man who has been starved of female attention. Perhaps Marnie Parker is some kind of powerhouse bitch who emasculates him and doesn't listen to him.

He heads towards the kitchen, but on the way opens the door into a room I've never been into before. This is one of the 'red' rooms opposite the kitchen. He reaches inside and quickly flicks a switch on the wall and some low lamps come on, making the room seem inviting and warm.

Maybe the red rooms are red because they are out of bounds to the kids. That's what old Gundred means, I realize, as I walk inside. There's nothing sinister going on at all, because it's so beautiful, I can understand why the Parkers might not want it to get messed up.

There are two fancy-looking silk-and-brocade sofas hugging a glass table with an elaborate and fragile-looking glass sculpture on it. No, this is definitely not a room for little boys.

'I won't be a moment,' Edward says, nodding for me to wait in the room.

Through the French doors in the large bay window I can

see a terrace lit up with subtle lighting in stone flags. There are fancy-looking wrought-iron chairs and a table with lots of pots of blooming hydrangeas. Edging the terrace is a stone balustrade with a lawn stretching out beyond, the trees casting long shadows on the silvery grass.

I walk towards the set of white shelves along one wall. They are less shelves, though, than individual art spaces, each displaying ornaments or books. I run my fingers over the heavy, glossy art books at the end.

One falls down with a thud and I jump, worried about upsetting the perfection. I look behind me towards the door. Then I lift the book to replace it, but, intrigued by the black-and-white photo on the cover, I pick it up and open it. I notice it's signed on the inside front page in large, scrawly writing.

'To Edward, with my love from Robert.'

I sit on one of the low ottoman stools and pull the book onto my knees. I flip through the photos.

All the pictures are of flowers. Petals, black on white, but they look so astonishingly like a woman's vagina that I feel myself blushing. I've never seen such pornographic art. I turn the pages, the images becoming increasingly out-rageous. Is this nature, or is this sex? It's hard to tell. That's probably the point, I guess.

I hear Edward coming and snap the book shut, putting it back on the shelf quickly. I'm still high from all the champagne, and maybe a little more turned on than I'd like from the images I've just seen. My legs shake slightly as I make my way quickly to the corner of the room, where there's a record player on a stand.

I busy myself, riffling through the record collection next to it. Dad used to have a record player – a family heirloom from his own father – but when Mum died, he gave it and all his records away. I didn't know he'd done it until it was too late. We had a row about it, but he said we needed the space, although the truth was that he just couldn't stand the memories.

I select Al Green as a safe option and flip it out of its cover and put it on the turntable. I love the way the needle crackles at the start of the record. Something about putting on a record in this room makes me feel sophisticated and powerful. Like I actually live here and I'm in charge. I hope it'll be OK with Edward. I hope he won't mind.

'Would you like a nightcap, Miss Henshaw?' Edward asks, coming into the room and going over to a glass cabinet on the other side of the sofas, which contains lots of expensive-looking bottles. I'm used to him calling me 'Miss Henshaw' now. It feels like a tease and I like it.

He's taken his jacket off and he's wearing navy-and-leather braces over his white shirt. It's an old-fashioned item of clothing, to my mind, but on him it looks sophisticated and cool. I wonder what it would be like to put my fingers on the wide elastic straps and push them off his shoulders. I picture them hanging by his hips. How he'd look down at me, knowing that this is the first crucial step. That it would be the button of his trousers next. Then his fly . . .

He glances at me, waiting for an answer. Can he tell what I'm thinking?

The only nightcaps I'm used to are Jägerbombs, but I don't think he'd have the ingredients, and it would be far too uncouth to suggest something like that in a room like this.

'What do you have?' I ask him.

'Anything you desire,' he says, his eyes staring at me intensely. I feel the way he says 'desire' resonate through me. Like I'm a violin string, or something, and he's just plucked me.

My hips start to sway as I glide across the room towards him. I love the way the fabric of my dress moves against my skin. I know I'm showing off, but suddenly I don't care. There's music and moonlight and it would be rude not to dance.

'I'll have what you're having,' I tell Edward, smiling as I kneel on the sofa. I'm so relieved we're here. Like a child allowed to stay up, I'm so relieved he hasn't sent me to bed and that the night is still ours. Once again, I feel the silence of the large house cocooning us, like it did last night. Was it only last night that we were in the kitchen? It feels like weeks ago. It feels like we've known each other forever.

'Then it'll be a fine whiskey,' he says, turning decisively back to the bottles. I stare at his back-view, liking the way his trousers are cut and how great his bum looks. He must work out a lot. It's all I can do not to reach out my hand and touch him.

'Do you have yours with water?' he asks, his back still turned to me. 'I think it's sacrilegious myself, but you may prefer it.'

'I've never had it,' I tell him, getting off the sofa and moving to stand next to him.

'You've never had whiskey?' he repeats, as I start to inspect the fancy bottles in the cabinet. There's a silver ice bucket. I see my warped reflection in it and turn to look at Edward.

He seems surprised by me, but I like the feeling he's giving me, that I'm a blank canvas. If someone is going to draw on me and create an impression, I can think of no one I'd like to do it more than him.

'Taste,' he says, staring into my eyes. He hands me a cut glass and his fingers brush mine as I take it from him. The electricity from his touch seems to run up my arm.

I sip the whiskey and it burns my throat. But I like the sensation. I like even more the sensation that he's staring at me. My eyes don't leave his.

'Try another. See which one you prefer,' he says, preparing another glass with a cube of ice, which chimes in the glass. I watch his steady hand as he pours the golden liquid over the ice. Al Green croons in the background. I think of the black-and-white orchid I saw in the book.

Edward hands me the second glass. As our eyes meet again and I don't look way, the atmosphere between us feels so charged that I can barely breathe.

I take a sip of the second whiskey. It's smoother than the first.

'You like this one more, right?' he says.

How does he know? How can he read me, like I'm a book?

He tops up the first glass and clinks it against mine. Again, we're staring at each other as we both take a sip.

I know this shouldn't be happening, but now my dream last night and tonight start merging. *It wasn't a mistake. He wants me. I can see it in his eyes.*

'Come,' I urge him, the whiskey-burn giving me a surge of confidence. 'Come and dance with me.'

I grab his hand and, laughing, pull him towards the rug by the doors and the criss-crossed oblong of moonlight.

He puts down his drink on the cabinet, and then mine. He smiles and takes my hand in his and pulls me into his embrace. It feels so grown-up. So romantic. His hips sway against mine as I lean against him. I put the side of my head on his shoulder, thinking how much I'd love to dive into his smell.

I want to stop time. I feel so exquisitely alive as I move against him. I feel him touching my hair. And I know then that he wants to touch me. All of me. And I want him to. More than I've ever wanted anything in my life.

I pull back and stare up at him. Our faces are just inches apart.

I lean in, closing the gap. I already know how his lips will taste. I stop breathing and close my eyes. I feel my heart beat . . . one two . . . one two . . . as I wait for our kiss to start.

And then he's gone.

He steps quickly back from me. He coughs, putting his fist over his mouth. He grabs his whiskey from the bureau where he put it down, and grips it tightly. He puts his hand in his pocket.

He doesn't look at me.

And I understand, of course, that this wasn't supposed

to happen. He's employed me as his nanny. But the fact is it has happened: this insane connection, this unbelievable chemistry. He can't deny it now.

I want to tell him this, but the words stall on my lips as his eyes meet mine. His gaze is hooded and unreadable, like he's retreated. Gone. I can see it straight away.

I catch a glimpse of myself in the mirror on the wall. I'm blushing. All my former cool, my borrowed allure, I now see – the allure the stylist gave me – has gone.

'I think it's time to call it a night. Before one of us does something we'd regret,' he says.

He means me. Not 'us'. I'm the one in the wrong here. I feel a new flush of humiliation wash over me. My breath catches in my throat. I want the rug to swallow me up.

'I suggest you go to your room now,' he says, sternly.

And I do. I do as he says, and I leave feeling like I've just made a complete fool of myself.

And Edward Parker does not call me back.

22

I feel like crying, but no tears come. I don't lie on my bed, but sit on the chair by the dressing table, staring at the carpet. I guess the whiskey has hit, and I feel exhausted, drunk, humiliated and ashamed all rolled into one.

I feel deflated. Punctured like a balloon. I can barely move my limbs.

After a while, I get up and battle my way out of the dress, which clings to me like a rubber band. Furiously I fight my way free, scrunching it up and throwing it into the corner with a yelp.

I pull off the necklace roughly, annoyed that it gets caught in my hair. I yank off the big sparkly ring, and dump them both on the dressing table.

I can't go in the bathroom. There are too many mirrors and I can't face my shame. Instead I grab the fluffy robe on the door and pull it tight around me; then I sit on the floor by the bed, my knees pulled up, my forehead resting on them, and try and work out what the hell I've done wrong, but it's hard because my head is spinning – all of the incalculable units of alcohol that I've consumed this evening finally taking their toll.

How could I have misread the signs so badly? Why have I screwed up this chance? Why do I screw everything up?

I lurch drunkenly to the cupboard and pull out my case with a dry sob. I guess I'll have to start packing. There's no way I'll be employed after that little scene just now.

Oh God.

I picture Edward's dark gaze. The way he sent me to bed. I thought . . .

What the hell does it matter what I thought? What I thought was wrong.

I yank out the horribly neon-pink case and fling it open. The photo of Scott falls out of the pocket in the top. I pick up the picture of my naked boyfriend, his stiff cock just out of the shot, but we both know it's there and he has his hand around it, waiting for me to jump on.

But I never will again. I know that now. I stare at Scott, my eyes burning as I feel the depth of my betrayal for the first time. Not just because tonight I tried to kiss another man – really *wanted* to kiss another man – but because of all the things I said about Scott. How I admitted that he wasn't good enough for me.

I let out a tortured laugh at the irony of it all. All this time I thought I was so much better than Scott, but he's not the one running around half-naked making a fool of himself. You can bet on that. He's only ever been loyal and loving.

And I'm just a stupid girl looking for trouble.

I turn the photo over, then I pick up the teddy bear that Ryan gave me and hug it close.

23

I don't know what wakes me, but I'm suddenly alert, although the house around me is silent. It must be a few hours since Edward sent me to bed, but it feels much longer. I'd fallen into a deep, low-down miserable sleep.

I groan, lurching up, trying not to vomit. I have a stinking, hideous hangover, the size of Texas. I lurch into the bathroom and run my hand under the tap, then shovel water into my mouth. I look up at myself and see my face in the mirror, my eye make-up streaked down my cheeks like a horror clown. I try and rub it off, but only make it worse.

Then I hear it. The sound of a woman's laugh. It's very short and then stops, immediately muffled. I can't tell if it came from outside, or inside the house.

I go over to the window and stare out, but the garden is dark. Don't they say that the hour before dawn is the darkest? I'd never believed it, but now it really is pitch-black out there, the moon having gone. It can't be long until the sun comes up.

Is Marnie Parker back? Or is there someone else in the house? I thought I was here alone with Edward, but maybe Gundred and Laura are here. Or maybe I just imagined it. I think I must still be pissed.

I go back to the sink and spit some more water out and, feeling lousy, retreat to bed. I lie in the dark, wondering what Edward is doing. Whether he's still downstairs drinking Scotch. Or whether he's gone to bed. And, if he has, is he with Marnie? Has she returned from LA? Could that be Marnie's laugh I heard?

Maybe he's telling her all about our evening together. Maybe that's why she's laughing, because he's describing how the stupid English nanny made a pass at him.

Or maybe I just imagined the whole thing. There was no woman laughing. It was just in my head.

I pull the pillow over my head and roll onto my side. I have to get some sleep and work out what I'm going to do.

Then I jolt upright. There's something outside. Right outside my room. I'm sure of it. Has someone just knocked? I listen, head half-raised from the pillow, my ears straining for a sound.

Could it be Edward? Has he come to apologize? Has he changed his mind? I scramble off the bed. I tiptoe-run to the door and quickly open it.

But there is no one there. I walk out into the corridor. Everything is still.

Then I see a shadow pass across the nudey bronze man at the end, as if a door has been opened further along the corridor, around the corner.

I creep soundlessly along the carpet, pulling my robe tighter around me. I'm not sure why I'm investigating. I'm in no fit state to introduce myself to Marnie Parker, if she's here, but I just want to know where the light is coming from.

I press myself against the wall, like I'm in a spy movie, and surreptitiously peek around the corridor to my left. There's a room at the very end and the door is slightly ajar, a thin sliver of light crossing the carpet.

I tell myself I'm being ridiculous, but even so, I check my reflection in the glass window opposite and make an attempt to smudge away my make-up again. I don't have time to go back to my room and tart myself up, just in case I do bump into Edward.

I stare back towards my door. I should go back. I should. I should just go back to bed. There's nothing to be gained from investigating. What if someone catches me snooping around? I've already got myself into enough of a scrape tonight.

But then again, what if it is some kind of sign from Edward? What if he's given me the choice to clear the air?

I creep along the corridor, my heart racing. I look behind me, checking I'm alone. I feel absurdly frightened and yet adrenalized with excitement.

As I get nearer to the room at the end, I can smell cigarette smoke. I stop and sniff the air to make sure, but it's definitely a cigarette. Why haven't the smoke alarms gone off? It can't be Edward, I realize. He is most definitely not a smoker. So who would be smoking this late at night?

The door is open just a tiny fraction and I tiptoe silently towards it. I can hear sounds now. Sounds from inside the room. I can hear two voices. A couple. A couple having sex.

My pulse races. I have accidentally stumbled on something that is none of my business. I have to run away before

I get caught. But I don't. Because my brain is working overtime.

Who is behind that door? It can't be anyone other than Edward. Edward and Marnie. In which case, this can't be an accident. Edward must have wanted me to see this. To know that he's with his wife. If I needed proof, here it is. He wants her. Not me.

Still, I step towards the door. Closer and closer.

Do I *want* to see? Can I bear to see him with another woman? With his wife? But I can't seem to find the strength to turn away. I'm just too curious.

In the room I can hear the couple now making out with a totally careless abandon. They are really going for it, judging from the oohs and aahs she's making. She clearly has no qualms about the door being open. The woman makes an orgasmic sigh and I feel myself throbbing in response. It's the horniest sound, and I'm instinctively responding in a way I can't stop.

I press up against the door, putting my eye against the slit. I need to see them for myself.

But the room is empty.

There's a perfectly made-up large bed with a gold brocade cover, a cigarette burning in the ashtray on the bedside table. On the wall opposite the bed there's an enormous television screen, and on it a tastefully lit porn movie is playing.

I stare at the screen. It's a close-up shot. I can't see the woman's face, just a bit of her dark hair. She's naked apart from a suspender belt, and she's arched back over a low ottoman, like some 1920s diva, her ample breasts pointing towards the ceiling. Her nipples are puckered and hard. She gasps in desire as the man, side-on to the camera, slides his large, plump cock against her glistening slit. She's neatly waxed with a ruffle of dark pubic hair. He is glorious, his manicured thumb flexed against his straining curved cock, which trembles as the smooth head disappears and re-appears.

He is kneeling and I see his taut buttocks flex. He groans and my insides flip over. I can't move. I'm leaden with desire. She pulls her stockinged feet up and lifts up her pelvis, so that her arse is bared to the guy. Tantalizingly slowly, he slides the tip of his cock down and dips it into her perfectly puckered pink arsehole.

'Like that,' he mumbles, his voice heavy with passion.

A voice I recognize. That isn't . . . that can't be . . . oh my God. Is it Edward?

Now the camera pulls back and I realize that this is a proper movie, not a home movie. There's a cameraman operating the camera. Still the camera pulls back and I see more of the woman, but her face is turned away from the camera. Is it Marnie? Or someone else? Has Edward filmed himself having sex with someone else?

I stare. Unable to breathe. My legs are trembling uncontrollably.

It's Edward. I'm sure it is. Younger, but my God, he's gorgeous.

I watch his face, his eyes closed, his hands coming to the side of his head, his stomach rippling and flat as his long shaft slides into woman's arse.

Then I hear a sound along the corridor. I gulp. Terrified

I'm going to get caught, I take flight, running along the corridor, my robe flying out behind me, like a ghost.

A voice. A woman's voice I don't recognize. A door opening and closing. Has she seen me?

Jesus!

24

I feel bone-tired the next morning. I've dozed on and off since the discovery of the porn room, but it took me ages to stop shaking. I still can't make any sense of it or what it means. Was it Edward in that movie? It can't have been. And if it was, then who was he with? And who was watching it? Who did the half-smoked cigarette belong to?

I feel deeply jangled that I perved in on something I wasn't meant to see. Even more jangled that I nearly got caught.

In the cold light of day my humiliating pass at Edward when we got home last night comes flooding back in vivid bursts, my shame doubling and trebling, the more I think about it.

I study the map Gundred gave me and see that the room is a red room. Even so, when I get dressed, I go down the corridor to check it out. Laura is cleaning the windows at the end.

'Whose room is this?' I ask her.

She turns, surprised by my tone. I cough, embarrassed that I've been so abrupt.

'No one's,' she says with a shrug. 'Why?'

'I . . .' I begin, but run out of words. What can I tell her?

That I stumbled on a porn movie in the middle of the night? I've already been warned off the red rooms. They are out of bounds and none of my concern. If the Parkers want to play porn in the middle of the night, then that's their business. They didn't leave the door wide open. They – whoever they are – thought they were alone. It was totally wrong of me to spy.

I still feel deeply unsettled and scared of what I'll find downstairs, but soon I can't put it off any longer. If I see Edward, I'm going to be contrite and apologetic and try and clear the air, if at all possible.

As for the porn movie? I'm just going to pretend it was a dream, and park it. I was drunk and confused. I can't be sure of what I saw. There's no point in even trying to analyse it any more. Because if I ever dared mention it to anyone, then I have no doubt that I'd be instantly dismissed, and I'm on thin enough ice as it is. Maybe they've already decided to fire me.

I hope not, because I can't face the shame of having to go home and explain what I did wrong, or that I didn't even get so far as meeting the kids. I can't face Tiff's disappointment, or Dad's joy that my foray into the outside world didn't work out. But most of all, I can't face Scott. The dreadful certainty that I will have to break up with him for good this time and that I have no reason to break his heart, other than my own stupidity and vanity.

But grovelling to stay isn't exactly an easy alternative. However, I have practised my speech to Edward. About how I overstepped the mark and foolishly misread the signals; that the glamour of the evening went to my head and I got completely carried away. How I understand if the Parkers want me to leave, but that, on my life, nothing like that will ever happen again. It's no excuse, but I was a lot drunker than I realized. I know that now, from how colossal my hangover is this morning.

I take a breath, trying to stop my spinning head and fighting the nausea down as I walk into the kitchen.

I brace myself, expecting to find Edward, but a woman is sitting at the kitchen counter. She laughs as she stares at the screen of an open MacBook laptop, peering through trendy black-framed glasses on the end of her nose.

It's her.

It's Marnie Parker.

She has short spiky blonde hair and the most incredible high cheekbones. She's not wearing any make-up, but her skin has the kind of radiance that can never be bottled or bought. She could have had work done, of course, but she's naturally youthful, like she's in her early thirties, although I know she must be older.

But my overriding shock is that, in the flesh, she's just plain beautiful. Jaw-droppingly beautiful and, in the sunshine-filled kitchen, she sort of radiates this aura.

But *of course she's beautiful*, I mentally kick myself. Why wouldn't she be anything other than beautiful, if she's married to a man like Edward? Seeing her throws the humiliation of last night into even greater relief. My mountain of shame just trebled in height. I'm now experiencing Himalayan humiliation.

It *can't* have been her in the movie. The woman in the movie had dark hair. Actually, it can't have been a movie of the Parkers at all. I've been so obsessed with Edward, I realize that my whole judgement has been coloured. I feel myself blushing furiously. Oh God, I'm such a fool.

'There you are,' she hoots in delight, clapping her hands as I shuffle into the warm, sunny kitchen, shrinking inwardly. Unlike Edward, she has a thick American accent.

I grip the cuffs of my woolly cardy and pull it tightly around me and approach her. I feel shivery and cold in the heat of her presence. I smile weakly. I want to die.

She takes off her glasses and slides off the stool. She's wearing a white sleeveless vest, which shows off her impressive cleavage, as well as her long, toned arms, which host wristfuls of cool bangles. She's wearing ripped skinny jeans and her feet, with their perfectly manicured pink nails, are bare. She has a pretty silver ring on her second toe.

She's possibly the sexiest woman I've ever seen. She's not thin, but kind of peachy, in a curvy, womanly way. She reminds me of those old pictures of Marilyn Monroe. She's a *real woman*, I realize. The kind Edward was talking about. I bet there were a dozen artists falling over themselves to paint her.

'Let me see you. You *darling* girl,' she says, grinning widely at me. Her teeth have a slight gap in them in the front, but somehow this little imperfection only adds to how flawless she is.

She stands in front of me and grabs my shoulders. She's taller than me and she kisses me warmly on both cheeks. She smells gorgeous, too. A fresh, zesty scent that tingles my nose.

Then she pulls back and looks at me more closely.

'Oh, my poor baby,' she soothes, her eyebrows knitting at me, clearly some kind of realization dawning on her.

Do I really look that terrible?

She protrudes her bottom lip in sympathy. 'Did you get Edwarded?' she asks.

Edwarded. Like that's a thing.

Not waiting for an answer, she puts her hand on her hip. Some rings sparkle and her bangles jangle. She puts the other hand up to her face and pinches her eyes.

'Don't tell me, don't tell me,' she says, as if she's divining a memory. 'So, probably – let me think . . . ? Margaritas or Martinis. Oh my God, yes, Martinis for sure. Daiquiri, probably. Champagne, *definitely*. Am I close?'

She opens her large Persian-cat grey eyes and stares at me. She's not being horrible, but quite the reverse. The fact that she knows how dreadful I'm feeling, and seems to be implying it's not my fault, feels so comforting.

I nod. 'And whiskey.'

She slaps her forehead dramatically. 'Whiskey! Oh my GAHD. That, too.'

She gasps and grabs the top of my arms. 'Sweetie. Lesson one. Nobody can drink with that monster at his speed. Nobody on this Earth. He has a liver from the Devil alone.'

I smile weakly, warmed by her kindness.

'He wasn't mean, was he?' she asks, peering into my eyes and stroking my cheek tenderly. 'He's a old shark for trying to wrong-foot people.'

She doesn't know. She can't possibly know what happened. Which means *he* can't have said anything. Which means that maybe it's not so bad after all.

I shake my head. It's all I can do not to throw myself into her arms. I just want to cuddle her. I'm so grateful that she's being so nice.

'I'm sorry,' I tell her. Because I am. About everything. About making a fool of myself with her husband. About being a hungover wreck, when I wanted to make the best first impression. 'I wanted to be—'

'Oh, darling, darling, darling,' she interrupts, smoothing my hair, shaking her head to refuse any confession I'm about to make. 'You, sweetie-pie, are my star. My *star*,' she gushes, leaning in and grabbing my cheeks and planting a huge kiss on my forehead. She pulls away, all wide eyes and teeth. 'Come see! Come see!' she says, grabbing my arm and pulling me over to the counter.

What the fuck?

She twists around the laptop. There's a full-length picture of me at the gallery last night. I'm on the stairs, looking over my shoulder. It looks like the kind of shot they use in the glossy mags after Oscar night. Except it's me.

She claps her hands together and presses her forefingers against her lips, watching me closely for my reaction. 'Isn't is just fantastic!'

She's obviously beside herself with excitement, but I can't see why. I stare at the picture, hardly recognizing myself. I've been to hell and back since that naive girl was photographed. I was expecting Marnie Parker to be upset, so I don't understand at all her overtly joyful reaction at seeing me.

'You don't mind?' I venture. 'You don't mind that I was

there?' *With your husband*, I nearly add, but before I can say it, she cuts me off.

'Mind?' she guffaws loudly. '*Mind?*' She shakes her head at me as if I'm crazy. 'You, my darling girl, are a genius.'

I don't feel like a genius. I feel like an idiot. What's going on?

Marnie slides her perfect vintage-jeans-clad buttocks onto the seat. She smiles at me and laughs, astonished that I haven't cottoned on.

'That dress is the centrepiece of my secret collection,' she says, tapping away at the keys on the keyboard. 'And Edward knows – I mean, he *knows*, right . . .' she glances at me over the top of the screen, in a show of seriousness, 'how stressed I've been about it. So when I went to LA, he got Roberta to *steal* the dress,' she says, giving me wide eyes. 'And then got *you* to out it at the gallery. He told them that you'd run away from my private show!' She claps her hands and laughs. 'It's a PR triumph.'

She twists around the screen. This time, it's split into four. Four different images of me. But I see now that she's not looking at me, but at the dress.

Oh.

It was always about the dress.

I stare now at the screen, but I'm not looking at me, but at Edward in the next picture. The one where he's just given me a Martini on the high bridge. I thought he was being intimate, but actually, in each shot, he looks like he's being a protective bouncer. Like he's waiting to be caught out any second.

He was playing along with the ruse, too. He was staging it all.

I feel a lump in my throat. What an idiot I've been. I have no claim on Edward. What must he think of me? No wonder he cut the evening off, the second it looked like it was getting out of hand. He used me all along, and I was too stupid to realize it.

'He is so naughty,' Marnie continues, her voice high with delighted mirth. 'You wait till I see him.' She raises her eyebrows in mock-threat. 'The phone in the office has been ringing off the hook. I have twenty orders already.'

'He's not here?' My voice cracks.

'*Gahd*, no. He left – I don't know . . . early . . .' she says, flapping her hand dismissively and turning back to the laptop. 'I was fast asleep.'

So she wasn't watching a porn movie. And neither was Edward.

She must have been here last night, then. When we got back. Perhaps she was asleep, whilst I was trying to get off with her husband downstairs.

What happened? Did he go upstairs and crawl into bed with her? Did they talk about me?

But no, they couldn't have, if this revelation on the Internet was his romantic big surprise for his wife. The realization hits me with full force. They haven't discussed me, because I don't matter. As in, *at all*. I am nothing to Edward Parker, except a naive clotheshorse. And nothing more.

'Sweetheart,' Marnie says, suddenly gauging my non-reaction to all this. 'You look terrible.'

I nod. I'm fighting back tears.

She claps her hands together twice, as if she's made a decision.

'OK. Sit,' she commands, taking my shoulders and forcing me into her place on the stool. She taps my shoulders decisively with her fingers. 'I'm going to fix you.'

Five minutes later, she's got a juicer out and she's piling vegetables in it until she's concocted a sludgy brown smoothie, into which she tips sachets of powder. I know she's going to make me drink it, but even the thought of it makes me want to puke.

I can't take my eyes off her, though, as she gushes about the collection and how clever Edward has been, and how she'd never have agreed to such a ruse. I thought she'd be – I don't know – some sort of ice-queen. I expected her to be mysterious and intense, but instead she's the warmest, most confident person I've ever encountered. I can't imagine anything fazing her at all. She seems to be so gregarious and full of laughter, and she's talking to me like we're old girlfriends and I've popped in for a catch-up.

I watch her shimmy between cupboards, knocking the drawer shut with her hip. She's all toned curves and womanly softness. If I thought she was comfortable in her own skin when I saw her in the oil painting, it's nothing to how she actually is in the flesh.

'I knew I'd love you, as soon as I saw your interview in London,' she says, pouring the smoothie into a glass. She licks her finger with the mixture on it. 'There were others of course, but I said to Edward, "She's the one. She's perfect."'

So it was Marnie who chose me, not Edward. This only

makes me like her even more. And feel even shabbier about last night.

'Here.' She puts the drink down in front of me and grins, raising her eyebrows. 'Do it down in one. It's the only way. Believe me, after nearly twenty years with Edward, I know the only way to cure the morning after.'

She leans against the counter, watching me drink. Then she shakes her head in self-congratulation.

'The boys will love you when they arrive.'

I don't know whether it's the smoothie, or her warm smile, or the relief that I'm so clearly not about to be sacked because of what happened last night, but I feel myself relaxing. I'm so relieved we're back on familiar ground and talking about my job.

But I'm not kidding myself, either. It is still going to be horribly awkward the next time I see Edward.

'When will the boys be back?' I ask her.

Marnie pulls a face. 'Oh God, well . . . soon, I hope. There's so much to talk about, but let's do it when you're less hungover, right?'

I nod gratefully and she smiles again at me.

'Step one is the juice. Now for step two,' she says.

'Step two?'

25

In a moment she's dragged me towards the front door, and I squint into the morning sun.

It's warm outside. Marnie jogs down the front of the house in some cool designer sneakers that she roughly shoved on in the hall. She's got a spring in her step – like she's up to something. Even in my hungover state, it's impossible not to be swept along by her.

On the driveway at the bottom of the steps, gleaming in the morning light, is a convertible sports car. I know nothing about cars, but doesn't Prince William have one like this? As I reach the light-blue shiny car, I realize it's an Aston Martin. And it's new. As in brand-spanking-new. There's not a scratch on it. The tyres are completely black. It must be worth a fortune.

'This is step two,' Marnie tells me, with a grin.

'It is?'

'Yep,' she says, jogging around to the driver's side. 'Get in.'

She doesn't even need a key to start it, but presses in a code with a confident punch. She takes some Ray-Ban shades that are in the tray between the two seats and puts them on. They're too big for her, but she manages to rock them anyway.

She laughs gleefully as the car starts. The roar of the engine is thunderous beneath me. She revs it like she's one of the boy racers on the estate by my old school. As I sink into the passenger seat I'm engulfed by the smell of sunshine on leather. The tortoiseshell dashboard gleams. I reach out and run my fingers over the dials. It's so beautiful.

'Where are we—?'

I don't get a chance to ask where we're going, though, as we're off and I have to grab onto the pale-grey leather handle on the door with one hand, and the seat with the other, as she shoots off around the driveway and accelerates down the drive. My hair is flying around my face and I am thrown back in the seat by the G-force.

I see the electric gates at the end of the drive parting and wonder if they'll be open wide enough in time, and I grit my teeth, flexing my feet, but Marnie expertly changes gear and revs up. I hold my breath as she shoots through the gates, which are still not fully open, and we skid out onto the tarmac road.

'Mrs Parker, please,' I whimper, but Marnie just glances over at me, raises her eyebrows and grins.

'You ready for some speed?' she hollers.

More speed? That was enough! I'm ready to throw up. The smoothie is yo-yoing.

'Let's do this thing, baby,' she cries as she thrusts her foot to the floor. The wheels spin. There's smoke and the acrid, choking smell of burning tyres and then we're off, careering up the road. Her leg is flexed as she pushes on the accelerator.

It feels like I'm on a fairground ride, but Marnie is loving it. She whoops with delight, keeping her foot to the floor. The car is singing fast up an octave, as it revs to the max, the spoke on the dial straining right around towards six o'clock.

As we approach the top of the hill, Marnie throws both her hands up in the air, with an almighty whoop. We're about to take off at 120 miles per hour over the brow of a blind hill.

And her hands aren't on the steering wheel.

I scream and grab the wheel as we crest the hill. For a moment we're suspended in mid-air. I'm still holding the wheel and screaming as we land with a bump on the other side, like we're in a movie shot.

The car careers down the hill towards the gatehouse. Marnie puts her hands behind her head, grinning at me to steer. We're going to hit the gatehouse if she doesn't take control. I stare at her wildly.

'Fuck!' I scream. 'For fuck's sake.'

She laughs and takes the wheel at the last possible moment, tearing past the gatehouse and the bemused guy inside. Is this a joke to her? Is she getting some sort of thrill from my terror?

We scream out onto the public road and I see her arms flex as she spins the wheel to turn the right-angle needed to set us straight. The back end of the car hip-wiggles terrifyingly as we get straight on the road. A truck is coming towards us, but we're still out of control.

I scream again, covering my face, waiting for the impact.

26

When it doesn't come, I look through my fingers. My heart is in my throat and I'm out of breath, panting furiously. I've never been so scared in my life.

Marnie whoops, then raises her middle finger high up in the air as the truck driver honks his horn, the tone changing as we pass at full throttle.

'Slow down,' I shout.

Marnie stares at me, as if genuinely surprised by my reaction.

'Stop the car,' I scream hysterically at her.

She slows and pulls down into a lay-by. We lurch forward as she applies the brake to make us stationary. Once we're at a standstill, the car purrs, like the savage beast it is.

'Are you fucking crazy?' I shout at her. I don't care that she's my boss.

She tuts, like I'm making a big fuss, and laughs, running her fingers through her hair to ruffle it up. She's had a serious kick out of that.

What the hell is wrong with her?

'You nearly killed us,' I continue, but I can see she's not bothered in the slightest. In fact she ignores me and looks at her nails, in a kind of teenage gesture of nonchalance.

Growling with rage, I clamber of the car and slam the door. I walk away and try and calm down, but I'm shaking like a leaf and I'm out of breath.

'Jesus Christ!' I mutter under my breath, the image of the gatehouse and the truck imprinted on my retinas. I've never, ever been so scared.

Slowly, like it's no big deal, Marnie gets out of the car, too.

I turn to face her, still furious, but her look is confused, like I'm overreacting. And suddenly a thought crosses my mind. Did she do that deliberately? Is her friendliness all just a facade? Maybe she does know all about last night, and how I behaved with Edward. Perhaps this is her sick way of revenge.

'OK,' she says, putting her hands up in surrender, then akimbo on her slim waist. 'OK.' Her tone is placatory. 'I scared you,' she says deliberately. 'But that was the whole point of step two,' she says, cocking her head at me.

'What?'

'Well, your hangover's gone, right?'

I do a mental scan of myself. She's right. My hangover has gone. She's terrified it out of me.

'I cleared it with Tom in the gatehouse, so we'd have a fast run up the private road. I wasn't expecting the truck, I'll admit that,' she laughs, 'but actually we were perfectly safe. I've done a lot of driving in my time. I used to race – you know – professionally.'

I stare at her and feel myself calming down. I didn't know that about her, but then I hardly know anything about her at all. I guess I would have reacted differently if I'd known.

Even so, I find her level of overfamiliarity disarming. It's like she's pretending we actually know each other – like this is something she might do with a friend – but we've only just met.

'Well, your idea of "perfectly safe" and my idea of "perfectly safe" are very different.'

I sound like a school matron, even to myself. Marnie picks up on it.

'Sorry, Miss Henshaw,' she says in a sing-song voice that makes me furious. How dare she take the piss out of me? Only Tiff gets to take the piss like that. 'It was supposed to be funny.'

Funny? *Funny?* She's serious. Jesus Christ! No wonder her children need a nanny, if their mother behaves like this.

I growl with frustration. I turn away and fold my arms, completely stumped. I don't want to look at her, let alone speak to her. I certainly don't want to get back in the car with her. Everything about this encounter has shaken me up. I don't know where I stand with her at all. She's behaving unlike anyone I've ever met.

I swallow hard, determined not to cry.

'So . . . all right, I'll admit it. I'm an adrenaline junkie,' she says, softly, and I realize she's come round the car to stand next to me. 'I can't help myself. Edward says it's exhausting that I love living on the edge, but that's why I was drawn to you,' she says, prodding me playfully on the shoulder. 'Because I think you're the same. I think you like to challenge yourself. Try new things. Feel the fear and do it anyway.' She raises one eyebrow at me in a challenge. She's quoted me, too. I'm totally cornered.

Her tone soothes me.

'I wouldn't let anything bad happen to you. You've got to know that, right?' she says, her eyes searching out mine. They are filled with sincerity. She reaches out and cups my face. I stiffen. It's weird that she's touching me. 'I only wanted to have some fun. And get rid of that pesky hangover.'

I swallow and nod. I can't do anything but believe her. And even though I didn't exactly have a choice, I did follow her of my own free will into the car. As she continues to stare at me, I feel like a jerk for overreacting.

'And now for your reward,' she says with that wide-eyed smile, obviously relieved that I've softened. She turns and gestures to the car. 'Ta-dah!' she sing-songs, walking backwards away from me. 'It's your turn. You can drive.'

I put my hand on my chest as she goes to the driver's door and opens it, waiting for me to get in.

Is my driving licence even valid in the States?

'Come on,' Marnie coaxes, seeing me hesitate. 'You won't get to understand unless you get to feel the buzz yourself, will you?' And she eyeballs me in such a way that I know that if I don't get in and prove myself, I'll have made a liar of myself and everything I impressed her with in my interview.

27

She's a good teacher. I'll give her that. She's patient when I kangaroo-jump the car away from the lay-by and forget that I have to drive on the right.

I'm squinting into the sun, wishing I had shades on, as I grip the wheel, but after five minutes of Marnie's gentle coaxing I've got the hang of it.

I hate to admit it, but she's right. Boy, it's a kick, to drive such a powerful car. It's like taming a wild beast. Egged on by Marnie, I up the speed, feeling all-powerful as we gun it down the open road. I can't help but whoop loudly as my hair flies around my face. This is *epic*.

There are fields on either side of the road and it feels like we're in the middle of nowhere. The Thousand Acres estate is entirely surrounded by farmland, and I see a huge red combine-harvester-type tractor way off in the distance. I guess this must have been a huge landowner's estate at one time. All this land must be worth a fortune, though, I reckon. And I suspect that the Thousand Acres development has taken steps to ensure it remains cut off from the usual sprawl of urban development.

The buzz of this car keeps on giving and soon I'm squealing with delight, too. It's part-hysteria, of course. This can't be legal. If I crash a car this valuable, I'll be in serious shit. That's if I'm not dead.

But, God, it's fun being given permission to let my hair down. All the anxiety of last night flies away, driven out by the speed we're going at. I can only think about right now, right this minute.

We turn around eight miles later, when we hit the outskirts of the next town and its giant mall. I see drivers stop and stare at us, as we drive in through one end of the car park and out the other side with a throaty roar. Their looks only prove to me what a cool thing I'm doing. We're doing. That we're two hot chicks in a kick-arse car.

I look at Marnie, thinking she'll want to swap, but she lets me drive back towards the house, putting her feet up on the dashboard, like it's no big deal.

When we arrive back at the entrance of the estate, though, Marnie makes me stop. She gets out and I see her lolling by the window of the gatehouse, talking to the guy inside. I see her flip her hips to one side, her toe pointed on the ground behind her. She's like a flirtatious fourteen-year-old and a sex goddess, all rolled into one.

I watch the guard as she speaks. He's probably fifty or so, with thinning hair and a bushy moustache. He's the kind of guy who I can imagine in *The Simpsons* as a corrupt lazy cop, but right now he looks as if all his Christmases have come at once, as Marnie chats to him. When he speaks, I see her laughing, rocking her head back. If she was in trouble, it's absolutely smoothed over now. She blows him a kiss as she flicks her head for me to get out. Then she jumps back into the driver's seat and puts on her shades.

This time we drive at a more sedate pace up the road and, on the crest of her hill, she wiggles the back of the car somehow, in a final salute to the security guy. I had thought she was out of control, but now that she's driving slowly, I can see that she's not only totally competent, but unbelievably skilled. What else can she pilot, I wonder? A jumbo jet? I wouldn't put it past her.

The tall iron gates open as we approach the house and, all of a sudden, I feel an overwhelming urge to confess. I feel like I should tell her what I did with Edward. That I tried to fling myself at him. But just as I'm about to, we reach the house and the moment passes.

It feels weird as we stop in the drive. I feel as if something has fundamentally changed, but I can't put my finger on it. Perhaps it's the fact that I didn't know Marnie Parker half an hour ago, but now she's made me more furious than anyone I can ever remember making me, whilst simultaneously making me feel special and included.

'So I want you to promise me something,' she says, turning in her seat. She takes the shades off and puts them back where she found them. 'About today.'

Her expression seems serious, even though laughter is dancing in her eyes. She presses her hands on my thigh. I like the way she touches me. I like it that she's so tactile.

'Sure. Of course.' I smile back. I can't believe how much better she's made me feel.

'I don't want Edward to find out that we went for a drive, OK?' She is suddenly serious. 'You OK with that, baby?'

'Uh-huh,' I say, although I'm not sure what I've just

agreed to. But my acquiescence has obviously been the right thing, because Marnie nods.

'Good. Then it'll be our little secret,' she says.

28

The second we step out of the car, the magic is broken. As we get through the front door there are two phones ringing, and Mrs Gundred is there, giving Marnie one of them. She looks harassed, and annoyed that Marnie has gone out. She gives me a filthy look, as if it's my fault. She seems horrified that we've been out in the car.

Maybe it was Gundred who was watching the porn. Maybe she suspects that I caught her. That I know her guilty secret.

Trewin is there with the limo, clearly waiting for Marnie. He doesn't even acknowledge me.

'See you, sweet pea.' Marnie waves to me as she takes the phone and I suddenly feel deflated. I liked being with her and, now that she's gone, having dismissed me with just a wave, I feel strangely rejected.

I hang around in the hallway near the service lift as she talks on the phone.

'Yes, I've met her,' she trills. Is she talking about me, I wonder? I watch her as she starts jogging up the stairs. 'She's a delight. Just as you said.'

I feel myself flushing with relief. Then I hear her laugh. 'Yes, honey, your car is here. It's magnificent. Oh, Ed . . . as if I would! Of course I'm not going to drive it. Relax.'

Her voice trails away, but I'm astonished by how easily and convincingly she's lied to her husband. She's taken out his brand-new car, against his instructions, and *I've* driven it, too. And now I'm complicit in her lie, because I've promised to keep our drive a secret.

As I get in the lift, I look at myself in the tinted mirrors, but I know I look pale. I feel wobbly and worried. What have I just done? What if something terrible had happened in the car? What if I'd crashed it? What if Edward finds out about today?

And then I remind myself that Marnie is a self-confessed adrenaline junkie. But if she does that behind Edward's back, then what else does she do? I suddenly remember Harry at the party last night telling me that the Parkers are slippery people. Have I got myself into something here that I don't understand?

Telling myself to stop being ridiculous, I go upstairs to my room, but as I open the door, I see that my bed is covered with bags, some of which are tied up with ribbons.

I see a cream card propped up on the dressing table. The writing on it is in proper fountain pen and is loopy and flamboyant:

Miss Henshaw. Thank you for your assistance last night. I took the liberty of having a new wardrobe delivered. I hope some of these items are to your taste. Edward

Oh my God. Edward Parker has sent me an entire new wardrobe. Is this a peace offering then? Does it mean he's forgiven me for last night? But how has he arranged all this?

Unless he arranged it yesterday and left the note for me this morning.

Was that why Gundred looked annoyed? Because she had to arrange for all of these bags to be brought to my room? Because she disapproves of me being spoilt?

Who cares, I tell myself. Forget Gundred. Edward has forgiven me. That's all that matters.

I feel breathless with girly excitement as I open all the expensive carrier bags and take out the clothes, admiring myself in the mirror. There are jeans, plain T-shirts, but like proper designer-cool ones, some vests and sweaters, and a couple of sweet cocktail dresses and some funky red shorts, but everything kind of matches. I read once about how women are supposed to have a 'capsule' wardrobe. And this is it.

I am so stupidly overwhelmed and grateful that I see tears in my eyes as I parade in the sexy blue sundress with the matching bikini. It's divine. I've only had cheap bikinis, but this one is lush, and I feel like I could flounce into a snooty club in Ibiza in this get-up. If only Tiff or Lisa could see this. They'd both die of jealousy.

I need to get a grip and put last night behind me, and embrace this opportunity and be the best nanny the Parkers have ever had. I won't be alone again with Edward and, now that I've met his wife, I can see how stupid I've been. I shall make myself indispensable to them both.

Downstairs, I search out Gundred, whom I find in the hallway, and ask her if she can sort out the Internet connection for me.

If she knows about the clothes, she doesn't let on. She

doesn't mention my pretty sundress, sandals or new shades. I get a perverse thrill from parading them in front of her.

'I'm not authorized to help you with that, Miss Henshaw,' she says. She's wearing a formal beige suit today and her hair is scraped back. She is busy with an iPad and doesn't look at me. She's got an Internet connection. Why can't I?

'But I asked Mr Parker, and he said Mrs Parker would gladly help me.'

'Then ask her.'

'Well, I will, but she's not here, and I really should contact my family. Perhaps I could use the laptop in the kitchen?'

She looks at me aghast.

'No,' she says harshly. 'Please do not touch any equipment in the house. It is strictly out of bounds. Is that understood?'

'OK,' I tell her in surrender. She's being so strict and touchy.

I shake my head and take off up the stairs, remembering too late that she told me to use the service lift.

'Miss Henshaw. If I find out that you've touched a computer . . .' she calls out after me, a threat implicit in her voice.

Then what? I want to ask. I'll be put in the stocks? I ignore her and jog on out of sight. Just because she's working in a place like a stately home, she doesn't have to behave like I'm the wayward governess. Do the Parkers know what a harridan they've employed?

I decide to tackle Laura, when I bump into her in the upstairs corridor. She's still vacuuming. I get the impression that the staff leap into action the second the Parkers leave the premises, and make it all tidy. She jumps in fright when she sees me.

I repeat my plea to get some Internet access, and she is just as terrified of me touching any computers as Mrs Gundred, although she tells me that the gardener's phone signal works at the bottom of the garden.

'Thanks,' I tell her.

We're standing by the nudey-man brass sculpture. I catch her eye and nod at it.

'What do you think of that?' I ask.

She blushes bright red.

'Don't ask me,' she says and I hear a hint of panic in her voice. She picks up the vacuum cleaner and scuttles in the opposite direction.

Man, she's odd.

29

I can't help turning my face up to the sun as I walk to the end of the garden, marvelling at the efficiency of Marnie Parker's two-step hangover cure. I felt like shit when I woke up, but now I feel fine. More than fine.

I wish now that I'd had more time to savour the car. I wish I'd taken some pictures. And, most of all, I wish I hadn't overreacted when she drove like she did. Looking back, I was a bit prissy. Not cool. Certainly not as far as Marnie was concerned.

Right at the end of the grass where the lawn runs out, there's a wooden kissing gate and a path leading down to a row of weeping willows and a lake. As I approach, I see there's a slatted wooden diving platform in the middle of it and on the other side a sort of Scandinavian summerhouse. It's so idyllic; with the birds tweeting and the water reflecting the trees above, it looks like the kind of scene that should be on the front of an architecture magazine. No wonder the Parkers fell in love with this place. I can see a long rope tied to one of the trees at the far end by the summerhouse. I can't wait until the boys are here. I can already picture them in my mind's eye, swinging into the lake – boyish limbs flailing in mid-air, braced to hit the water.

I walk to the end of the jetty and sit down, dangling my feet so that my toes just touch the water. I watch the birds in the trees and the shadow of the branches in the water, and the concentric circles as the fish beneath break the surface. It's so beautiful here and I experience something I've never felt before. A sense of satisfaction in my solitude. I realize that I never get to be alone. Not really. I'm always at work, or with Dad and Ryan, or with Tiff or Scott. I honestly can't remember the last time I had a day to myself, stretching out ahead of me. It feels like the most heady of luxuries.

Time seems to have done something odd to me. It's as if I've had ten years' worth of emotions and experience condensed into barely three days. I feel so different from the girl who left Manchester.

I feel solicitous about all the exciting things I have to analyse, now that I'm on my own. Part of me longs for Tiff to be here, so I can tell her everything. And yet, at the same time, I can't deny I like the fact that all of this is just mine. Besides, I couldn't explain it to Tiff when I can't explain it to myself.

I can't comprehend exactly what my relationship is to either of the Parkers and, with things unresolved with Edward, I feel more scared than ever that he and Marnie will talk about my behaviour last night.

Perhaps it doesn't matter? Marnie is so obviously thrilled about the dress and the impact I made at the gallery, and we laughed so much when I finally relaxed about the car, I can't imagine her taking Edward seriously if he did tell her that I tried to kiss him.

I was so sure that I'd be fired and sent packing; and now, lying here, I'm so grateful that I've got a second chance. Because I'm pretty sure I have, now that I've met Marnie. I laugh to myself, both thrilled and baffled about the drive this morning.

I'm sweating now and I squint up at the hot, bright sun in the sky. The water looks so cool and inviting that I quickly make my decision. Sod it! I'm here on my own. I'm on holiday, and I'm damn well going to jump in.

Quickly I strip down to my bikini, then laugh at myself when I realize how much I don't want it to get wet. I check once more that I'm definitely alone. Then I quickly take the bikini off and, holding my nose, jump into the lake.

It's absolutely glorious. The water is cool and smooth, and I swim a few strokes into the middle of the lake and then lie on my back, looking at the sky through the trees. I feel my nipples poking through the surface of the water, and look down at my body and think how wonderful it feels, after the winter in England, to be warmed by the sun.

And then I think of Edward and, as soon as I do, I picture how his eyes were when he made me wait for him on that walkway. I see it, as if I'm watching a film. Me in that astonishing dress, him walking towards me, his eyes devouring me. I think of how he felt when I was dancing against him, how he gripped my hands.

My legs kick in the water as I picture his lips, and how he looked at me. Somehow the clothes he sent me feel like an apology as well as an admission of guilt. Is he feeling bad about what happened, too, I wonder?

I know logically that last night was all about me being

photographed in the dress, but there weren't photographers in the car, were there? There weren't photographers when he came to my room yesterday morning.

Was I really that wrong to try and kiss him? Surely I can't have misread the signals that badly? He wanted me, too. I know it. I know it's wrong, because he's married to Marnie and she's amazing, but they obviously have a weird relationship. After all, she keeps secrets from him – like that car. What does he keep from her, I wonder? He resisted me last night – and rightly so. But only just. Maybe he wasn't angry with me, but angry at himself.

And then there was the movie. The movie playing in the empty room. I can't for the life of me work out what it means.

I'm swimming in the clearest of lakes, but Edward fills my mind. I kick my legs out in breaststroke, feeling the water caress my naked body. I get to the steps on the other side of the lake from the diving board near the summerhouse and grab onto the bottom one, which is just concealed in the water, and swing round to sit on it.

I smooth my hair back, looking at the rivulets of water dripping down over me to my wet stomach sparkling in the sunshine.

I lean back and close my eyes, feeling the sun on me, feeling the water lapping against my hips. It's so sensual and such a turn-on.

As the birds sing in my ears, I start to fantasize. I imagine Edward standing in his suit as he was last night, his hand in his trouser pocket. Then I picture him standing on the diving platform, looking across at me right now.

I suck the moisture off my bottom lip, imagining him staring at me from across the lake. I open my eyes a tiny way, but I'm looking into the sun and I imagine I can see him through the droplets of water.

What would I do if he stripped off now and dived into the water? What would I do if he swam across to me as I sat here, waiting for him? I picture him sliding up against me and how his wet body would feel against mine.

Under the water I reach down and press my fingers against myself. I feel a longing to be filled. For it to be him that fills me.

30

Afterwards, when I'm dressed again and sit dripping on the diving platform, I feel like a fool. It's ridiculous to go around fantasizing about my boss, when nothing is ever going to happen. But maybe, after last night and all that pent-up sexuality, I just needed to get that out of my system.

I look at the phone in my hand and the reception bars, which are now filled in. I have no excuse. I have to call home. *Come on*, I tell myself. *After this morning, how hard can it really be?*

I brace myself to call Scott and am secretly delighted when I get his voicemail, but even his jokey, laddish greeting seems tacky and annoying. I leave a neutral message, telling him I'm fine and that I've arrived safely and I've been busy.

Busy? Busy is such a pathetic word to describe what I've been up to. Busy is how I usually describe a double-shift at work, followed by an Asda weekly shop for Dad. That's 'busy', in my world. Not flying business-class halfway around the world, or riding in limousines wearing a cutting-edge designer dress. Busy doesn't usually involve midnight dances, or driving at 120 miles an hour in a brand-spanking-new Aston Martin, or swimming naked in a clear-water lake and nearly giving myself an orgasm as I fantasize about another man. Except that, perhaps now, it does.

My message sounds lame even to my ears. I add a hurried and chirpy, 'Love you, miss you, bye.'

I press the red button and wince. I think of Edward's hand on my knee in the back of the limo last night, when I told him about Scott. When I told him the truth. And now I've gone and made a liar of myself again. It's as if the Parkers have called me out – to be a better person – and lying now feels worse than ever.

I look up at the expanse of blue sky between the trees. As I dial Dad's number I think of home, in the rain, our cramped flat, the noise of Ryan's PlayStation, and I realize just how much I don't want to go back. How they could never understand how different this world is from theirs? How everything can change in three days.

'So what are the kids like then? You got them licked into shape?' Dad asks, after I've given him the details about what I ate on the flight. I don't tell him about the couple shagging in the toilets. He's trying to be jolly, but I know from his tone that he's just attempting to be nice and that he's missing me dreadfully.

I explain about the Parkers being in the process of moving, and how the kids are still at camp.

'That's weird,' he says. 'Surely that's the reason they wanted you there right away.'

'It's kind of nice to be having a break, though.'

'How the other half live,' he jokes. 'Ryan, come and say hi to Soph.'

Ryan is monosyllabic as usual. I tell him that I'm looking

after twin boys and that he'd love it here, but he's not impressed.

'Have they got any good computer games?' he asks.

'I'm not sure yet,' I tell him. 'I'm sure we'll have lots of fun, though – you know, being outdoors.'

Being outdoors is not Ryan's thing at all and he knows I'm teasing him.

'Look after Dad, OK?' I tell him.

My conversation with them both leaves me feeling unsettled. Perhaps Dad is right. It is weird that the kids aren't here. I determine to search out their rooms. To hell with Gundred's red-room policy. I need more information about what I'm getting myself into.

31

Neither Edward nor Marnie arrives back that afternoon, and Gundred is too busy with another lorryload of packing cases that arrives to be able to answer any questions. As it gets dark and the staff leave, I start to wonder if I'm entirely alone in the house. I walk around in a circuit, trying to find someone, and return each time to the kitchen. I rummage in the fridge and hastily make myself a peanut-butter sandwich, remembering the delicious gnocchi that Edward rustled up.

Will he be back soon, I wonder, to conjure another Michelin-starred supper? Will he be back with Marnie? Will it be awkward to see them together? What will the eating arrangements be in the evenings? There's so much basic stuff that I still don't know. My head flickers with questions.

But as the minutes tick into hours, I start to think they must both have forgotten me. I'm a grown-up, I remind myself. An employee of theirs. I don't need them to come home and cook for me, but even so, I'm unsettled and unsure what to do with myself. And the house is so quiet.

Maybe I should explore some more. I don't want to sit in my room all evening. Maybe there's a sitting room with a TV? I can hang out in there.

I turn on all the lights, determined not to freak myself out, or get caught out again by Edward lurking in the shadows. I hunt down the corridors, turning each door handle, and find loads locked. There are no keyholes, though, so I guess they must be centrally locked. It's an unnerving concept. What if the system goes wrong and I'm accidentally locked in my room? What then?

Finally I find a sitting room with a sofa and a TV, but it's full of packing cases and an unassembled table-tennis table on its side. I'll be hanging out in here with the boys a lot, I guess.

I make my way up the stairs and look along the dark corridor of the first floor. I haven't been in these rooms before, or come to this floor. I turn on the corridor light and see cream carpet stretching off into the distance.

I walk along it, examining the art that has been hung on the walls, each picture with a light above it. There are oils, mainly. I study each one in turn. There are still-lifes and old-fashioned-looking portraits of women. I think of that man Harry in the gallery, and his comment about the stolen picture. Could he mean one of these? Any one of them wouldn't look out of place in the National Gallery back home.

I really hope Edward comes good on his promise to teach me about art. That's once we've got over the initial awkwardness about last night. I think I just won't mention it. Not if he doesn't. I think it's best if I pretend it never happened.

As I stare at the paintings, I can't help feeling that I wish I wasn't so ignorant. I wish I knew more, not just about art, but about everything. This whole place so far gives me the feeling that there's so much I can't quite grasp.

Marnie and Edward are so cultured and have such fine tastes. They are proper grown-ups, like I always imagined I would be one day. But the gulf between my experience and theirs is huge. Even if I went to night-school every night for the next ten years, I could never catch up.

It never seemed to matter at home – my lack of further education. I've always thought it funny that my cultural knowledge extends to the entire back-catalogue of *Coronation Street* and no further. But what might make my team win in a pub quiz counts for nothing here, and I feel it keenly. I feel like I should be more. That I should be properly living, like the Parkers are; with money and a career and taste. I don't want to be somebody who just gets by, like Dad does. Who scrapes through life, never getting to see anything beautiful. Who sees it all as a horrible challenge, instead of an opportunity. Being up close to wealth and class, like I have been in these past few days, has opened my eyes. It's filled me with a kind of ambition I didn't know I had.

There are rooms along the right-hand wall and I turn each door handle in turn, but each one is locked. I'm not exactly sure what I'm looking for – I'm just curious, I guess.

The corridor stops at a T-junction, and another corridor snakes off left and right. I turn to the right, figuring that I'm probably below my room here, which is on the floor above. This house must have twenty bedrooms at least, I reckon.

There's antique furniture in this corridor. A dark wooden armoire and a couple of intricately carved chairs.

Again, I try the door handles. They're all locked. I see a window and glance out of it, down to the back of the house. There's a garage part that I haven't noticed before, but no sign of the limo or the Aston Martin. Where *is* everyone?

I retrace my steps and decide on a whim to go and look out of the furthest window, back along the corridor the other way. My tread is silent along the carpet. This corridor has modern art on its walls: a long, splodgy glass piece going along the entire length of the corridor. I want to touch it, but it looks fragile.

At the end of the corridor there's a bay window with a small, empty bookcase in it. I stare down onto the lawn. I see a shadow on it. It must be coming from the room on my right. I reach out my hand for the handle and it turns. I push the door handle and peep around the door.

32

Marnie Parker is standing inside, on the other side of the bedroom, her back to me.

Oh God, I've accidentally found her bedroom. And she's in it!

For a second I freeze with shock. Then she turns around, but she doesn't see me. She's wearing a pair of large black headphones and has her eyes closed. She looks like she's enjoying some intense music. She's wearing a floppy silk, red kimono, which gapes open at the front as she sways her body in the silence. I stare at her for a second, deliberating whether to back out.

I had no idea she was in the house. I feel a childish stab of disappointment that she hasn't sought me out. That I've been wandering around like Billy No Mates and she was here all along.

Suddenly, she opens her eyes and sees me. Her eyebrows knit together. She's obviously confused that I'm standing in her doorway. I feel caught out. I'm snooping. She knows it, and I know it.

I don't need to even ask: this is definitely a red room.

But then her face lights up into a smile, flooding me with relief.

'Hey, speed-freak,' she shouts, like she's delighted to see me. She gestures me towards her with a big arm movement, which makes her kimono sleeve flap around, like she's a matador. Is she drunk?

I walk into the room and shut the door and, as soon as I do, I feel like I've been sealed into an inner sanctum. No wonder I didn't hear her. The whole room feels cut off from the rest of the house.

The walls are decorated in a swirly dark-green wallpaper, which would be revolting anywhere else, but makes the whole room have this louche, chic designer vibe. There's lots of low silk furniture and fluffy rugs, and a row of scented candles on a recessed shelf in the wall. Those expensive ones you get in glass jars, which fill the air with a musky smell and cast shadows up to the ceiling.

The huge bed to my left is on a raised area and has shallow cream-carpeted steps leading down into the room. The bed is one of those teak Indonesian carved ones and has a deep bottle-green silk eiderdown on it and lots of embroidered cushions. It makes me want to flop down face-first on it.

Marnie is on the other side of the room in the corner, by a carved arched doorway, which looks like it leads into a brightly lit dressing room beyond. The door is partially blocked by a large wooden packing crate. I can see an ornate Chinese-style lacquered chest of drawers, the top of which is open.

Along one wall, just like in my room, there's a line of windows with a window seat below them, and padded cushions in pretty Chinese silk. On the other side of the room, in the opposite corner, is a silk chaise longue and an armchair. It's like the kind of ridiculously cool apartment I imagine you'd find in Shanghai. Somehow, though, it fits Marnie.

I could be wrong, but it feels like this is just her room. There's no sign of Edward or any of his stuff.

'Listen, listen,' Marnie says, smiling at me as I approach nervously across the cream carpet, waving her arm again for me to hurry up. She takes the headphones and puts them on my head. Her eyes are wide and excited.

I'm assaulted by music. The beat somehow transports me straight into an imaginary club. It's got a sexy, cool kind of vibe. It makes me want to shut my eyes and wave my arms around, just like she was earlier.

Reluctantly, I take the cans off and hand them back, smiling. 'Cool,' I say, immediately regretting it. It sounds pretty lame.

'We'll both enjoy it,' she tells me, grabbing a remote control from the window seat. She presses a button and soon the same music fills the bedroom with sound. She turns it down a little. 'I like it loud,' she says, swaying her hips to the music. Her robe gapes more. I see the full swell of her breast, but Marnie hasn't noticed. 'It's my latest mix,' she says, chucking the cans down on the window seat.

'Oh?'

'I DJ sometimes,' she says. 'I used to be serious about it, but now it's just a hobby.'

Motor racing, DJ'ing, modelling, designing . . . is there anything she *can't* do? She can also magically transport herself without a car, so it seems. How comes she's here? Does that mean Edward is here, too?

'I like it,' I tell her, smiling and nodding to the music. I feel like I should move – dance a bit – but I feel awkward and geekish.

'That's how Edward and I met. In a club. Years ago. I still do a set occasionally, when I'm asked to, but I don't know . . . It's not really an old lady's game.'

'You're not an old lady,' I reply with a laugh. Because she's not. She's impossible to place. She's at once wise and girlish. And she's just cool. I've never met anyone so cool. I can't stop staring at her.

I feel relief, too. She seems so friendly. Edward can't possibly have told her about what happened when we danced. As the day has gone on, the horror I felt first thing has changed into something else – a kind of euphoria that I might have got away with it, which is only confirmed now by how nice she's being.

Marnie grins at me and goes to the window seat and I notice that the diamond-leaded window is open. As she sits, she crosses her legs and stares at me, the robe falling open to reveal the length of her very smooth, toned legs, but she seems entirely unselfconscious. Her toenails have changed from this morning and are now painted in green glitter paint. What has she been doing all day, I wonder? Where has she been?

'What have you been up to?' she asks me.

'Nothing,' I lie. 'Well, just a bit of exploring.'

'Find anything?' she asks. She doesn't look at me. She knows I've been snooping. Is she going to tell me off about the red rooms? Does she know about me discovering the porn movie?

She can't possibly.

'No,' I say, putting my hands into the front pockets of my jeans and shrugging. 'Only you.'

I've found her by accident, but she's making me feel like I've come here on purpose. Perhaps I have. Perhaps I've been looking for her all this time. I can't deny how good it feels to have found her and not be on my own. I can't read her mind, but I see her leaning back and pushing open the window a bit further. What is she doing?

'It's such an amazing house.'

'I'm glad you think so.'

'I'm just curious, though,' I ask, stuffing my hands into my pockets. 'Why are there no photos of the kids?' I say photos, but I mean signs. Of any kind. Because there haven't been – in this whole search.

The moment I say it, I realize how peculiar – and yes, offensive – it sounds. She looks at me, her eyebrows knitting.

'What an odd thing to say,' she remarks.

'Sorry. It's just . . . I'm so desperate to meet them. I saw the lake today and thought how wonderful it would be to see them on the rope swing.'

'I know, darling. I'm sorry about this, and all the delay.' She rolls her eyes. 'You must be tearing your hair out, but believe me, this move has been hellish. They lost all our stuff. Can you believe that? I mean, they lost *two* containers. Big ones. How do they do that?'

'I'm sorry,' I tell her. 'I had no idea.'

'You can't imagine the stress of it. And the chaos, when we've both got so much on. We had to send the boys away to this amazing adventure-camp in Canada, which they'd been begging to go to. I don't want them coming here until it feels like a home, you know. It's not fair.'

'Of course,' I stutter, feeling like an idiot. I'm just a minute cog in the giant juggernaut of their lives, I remind myself. I have no right to demand any special attention when they're in the middle of moving. The timing of my arrival was probably the last thing on their minds.

'Anyway,' she says, shaking her head, 'please don't remind me of the kids. Not right now. I can't do this when they're here, can I?' she says, and I see now that on the windowsill is a long joint, which she now retrieves and brings inside the room. She takes a deep drag of it.

'Don't look so shocked, Miss Henshaw,' she laughs, pointing her fingers at me and exhaling the smoke. 'You're young. I've heard of that Manchester-scene thing. Don't tell me Miss Prim-and-Proper has never had spliff?'

She thinks I'm prim and proper? I feel my cheeks flush.

Of course I've tried a spliff. I've had a few Ecstasy pills, too, but I went off the whole idea of getting off my head when Mum died. Besides, Scott has a mate, Derry, who smokes weed all the time and he's such a loser, we both agreed that we'd never smoke with him.

'I don't, I mean . . .' I stutter. She's still staring at me. I can't believe she thinks I'm such a bore. She wouldn't, if she knew what a fool I made of myself with her husband last night.

'Here,' she says, handing it to me. 'Have it. You'll like

it. It's not that strong stuff. I just use it to help me relax. Although Edward hates the stuff. I told him I'd given up, so don't tell him, OK?'

Another secret.

I nod and take the joint from her, and take a drag and cough. It's strong and tastes different from anything I've smoked before.

Marnie takes the joint back and has another luxurious puff, as if I've offered it to her. As if this bonds us somehow. She watches me, amused, through narrow eyes.

'So now you're here, you can make yourself useful,' she says, suddenly grabbing my arms, like we're about to have a big adventure.

33

Making myself useful, it turns out, means helping Marnie to unpack the crate. The top part is full of clothes, and I stand in her dressing room, which has mirrors all along one side and hanging rails and built-in compartments along the other.

I feel stoned, in a slightly giggly, fun way, and I can't help dancing a bit along with her as she passes me each tissue-wrapped package from the crate. Soon it feels like Christmas, to be carefully ripping off the tissue paper, until I'm ankle-deep in it, like it's snow. As she speaks and I hang up the sculptured jackets and smart pencil skirts she passes me, I can't help marvelling at the quality of each piece. I've never been around designer clothes, and yet she has a shopload for her wardrobe. And this is only a fraction of her stuff, she assures me. No wonder she found moving stressful.

It feels thrillingly intimate to be handling her clothes. To be chosen to help out. And it feels great to have a purpose at last. To actually be doing *something* in return for all this money they're paying me.

'That I wore to Sydney Opera House at the Millennium,' she says, sighing as I unfurl a long midnight-blue velvet number on a hanger. 'I was going to give it away. Auction it. But then I changed my mind, right at the last minute.' She takes another drag of the joint. If she's worried about the smell, or Edward catching us out, she seems to have forgotten all about it. Even so, the windows are wide open. 'It's been hell moving. But great to clear everything out, you know.'

I nod, but I don't know. I have the same tiny wardrobe in my bedroom in the flat at home that I've had since I was eleven. I cannot imagine owning a walk-in closet, let alone all the clothes to put in it. Clothes that I've chosen to wear in places all round the globe.

'Oh, right,' she laughs after a while, when the rail is half-full. '*That*'s where it all went.'

'What?'

'Check out this baby,' she says, pulling out a black silk corset from the bottom of the crate. She laughs. 'That was one of my first designs. Still cute, though, huh?'

She puts the strapless corset up against herself and shimmies her hips, so that the beading-loops on the bottom of it jiggle.

'It's beautiful,' I gasp, unable to stop myself running my fingers over the silk panels. 'I've never worn a corset.'

'What?' Marnie's laugh is shrill. 'Are you *serious*?'

I feel myself blushing.

'I know people who do,' I say, thinking of Tiff and that Ann Summers corset she wore to a hen-do, 'but it's not the same. We just have tacky underwear shops where I live.'

I don't tell her about Scott. That he says he likes me best naked.

'Well, believe me, honey, this stuff isn't tacky. Between you and me, my intimate collection and lingerie line are what keeps this whole ship afloat.'

This nugget of information surprises me. I thought Edward made a fortune. That they even need to keep anything 'afloat' astounds me. But perhaps I haven't grasped her meaning. What is an intimate collection, I wonder?

'I had no idea you designed lingerie,' I tell her, thinking of the picture of the shop on the Internet. So that's what it sells. Of course someone as brazen and clearly shameless as Marnie would front a high-end business like that. It makes perfect sense.

'Didn't you?' she asks, surprised, but I don't really know anything about her, except that she's constantly surprising me. 'I designed a whole bunch of costumes for Dita. That's how I got into it.'

'Dita?'

She explains about the famous burlesque star, and a distant light bulb clicks on. I've read about her in *Hello!* magazine. I picture her dark hair and red lips.

'Here,' Marnie says, pressing the corset towards me. 'Try it on. I'm sure it'll fit. That's the great thing about these corsets. They're adjustable.'

'Oh no, honestly, I couldn't,' I gasp, stepping away, laughing.

'Why not?' she says, genuinely surprised.

There are so many reasons why not. I'm not going to get half-naked in her bedroom. She's my boss. But her eyes say differently. She challenges me. Just like she did in the car this morning.

'Go on, it'll be fun. In fact, do the whole lot,' she says, suddenly lighting up and throwing up her hands, as if she's just had the best idea of her life.

34

The *whole* lot, in Marnie-speak, is the full burlesque get-up. Before I know it, she's rooting around in the crate and handing me items to lay out on the bed.

I laugh as she produces each new piece, retrieving more and more outrageous items from the depths of the packing crate. Soon there's crispy tissue paper flying through the air. She's completely thrilled with the idea of me dressing up, and I can't help catching her infectious enthusiasm. We're giggling like kids, but that must be the joint. I've never felt this stoned.

The underwear is simply, well . . . astonishing. I take it in armfuls to lay out on the bed. Getting to look at everything, and touch it all, feels so deliciously illicit. It's like when I was little and I used to watch my mum put on her make-up, copying the way she smudged her lipstick against her lips, feeling the buzz of her dressing up to go out.

Even now, quite often dressing up to go out is still the best bit of the night for me. But this is *that* feeling times one hundred. It's the feeling of being in a boutique full of silk and lace, all wrapped up with the knowledge that it's just me and Marnie in her inner sanctum. It feels so deliciously feminine. I don't give Edward a second thought.

I gorge my eyes on all the pieces. There's a headdress with a huge, fluffy black feather on it. The first black silk corset has flesh-coloured lace panels and sparkly fringing, then there's a red one with black ribbons, a pretty cream-and-pink one and a bawdy purple one. They are each a work of art. There are also long, black silk gloves to match each of them, and seamed silk stockings with lace garter tops.

It's impossible to choose between them, but I opt for the first one – the black one.

'So, you have to put it all on in order,' Marnie instructs matter-of-factly, but there's a childish sparkle in her eyes. 'Starting with these.' She flicks a tiny triangle of silk at me and I realize it's a thong. She grins. 'Go on,' she urges.

I swallow hard. I feel stoned and embarrassed when I realize just how small the thong is and that she's expecting me to put it on. Right now. In front of her.

'You don't think I've seen it all before?' she drawls, with a throaty guffaw.

Of course she's seen it all before. She's a model. She designs underwear. Besides, I don't want her to call me Miss Prim-and-Proper again. I can do this, can't I? I'm not a prude. If she doesn't care, then neither should I.

She turns away, to collect the joint from the ashtray on the windowsill, and I strip off out of my new jeans. I fold them quickly and put them on a low velvet chair near the end of the bed. I feel embarrassed by my white knickers and cheap T-shirt bra. I feel like a schoolgirl and I bite my lip.

I turn away, with my back to Marnie – even though she's

staring out into the night – to put on the thong. The contrast between it and my nasty bra couldn't be greater. Thank God I had a proper wax before I came here.

'No wonder you looked so goddamned hot in my dress,' Marnie says from the other side of the room, folding her arms. 'You, darlin', have a magnificent ass.'

I quickly glance over my shoulder at my bottom. I've never described it as great before, let alone 'magnificent', or even an 'ass', but I laugh anyway, feeling absurdly flattered.

'Now then. Next are these,' Marnie says. She has the joint in her mouth and she's peering through the trail of smoke into a small wooden box. 'Take that hideous thing off,' she instructs, without even looking at me, flapping her hand at my bra. 'It's a disgrace to womankind.'

I laugh and dutifully slip off my bra, crossing my hands self-consciously over myself at the front as I do so.

She walks towards me, and now I see that inside the box is a pair of black sequinned nipple-tassels.

'Oh my God,' I laugh, peering into the box. 'Seriously?'

'Sure,' she says, with a grin. 'These are my favourite bit.'

I can't believe I'm standing practically naked in front of her, but Marnie has made it feel so normal, like such a giggle, I suddenly don't care. Hell, I want to try on nipple-tassels, and this could be my only chance.

'Hold this,' she says, giving me the joint, forcing me to expose one of my breasts as I move my arm. I take a deep drag. I'm conscious that I'm now bare in front of her, but she doesn't react. *This is cool*, I think. *She does this all the time. Don't be a prude.* I let my other arm fall to my side, my chest completely exposed now.

'So. You have to put the glue on,' she says, leaning down. She takes a small plastic tube from the box and unscrews the lid. Her face is close to my breast. I can feel myself shaking. She puts the tiny nozzle of glue against my nipple and a drop of cold liquid comes out. My nipples immediately stiffen.

I look down at them and at her.

'Sorry,' she smiles, raising her eyebrow, 'it's cold, right?'

She takes the nipple-tassel out of the box and carefully sticks it over my flesh. It's weird, but I like it. The heel of her hand resting against my breast feels so intimate. I've never been touched there before by a woman. I start to tremble in the cold draught from the window. My skin goosebumps all over.

I watch as she does the other breast, concentrating hard, but now I feel something else as she touches me. It's so intimate. So strange to be so close to her, but I can't help feeling excited, too. The fluttery, shaking feeling increases.

She cups her hands under my breasts and stands back to survey her handywork, checking the nipple-tassels are in line.

'Aren't you darling,' she says, almost to herself. 'Just perfect.'

I flush at her compliment. I felt cold before from the draught from the window, but just standing here in my thong and two nipple-tassels, a wave of heat washes over me. I smile at her and raise my eyebrows, and then look down at myself with an excited grin. I want to wiggle, but she can tell this.

'No, no, don't move,' she cautions. 'Not until you've dried.'

She takes the joint from me and parades to the other side of the room, dancing a bit to the music. I turn round to face the bed. I guess the corset is next. I can feel my legs trembling.

I pick it up and, having ditched the joint, Marnie is back.

'That's it,' she says. 'Put it over your front. I'll lace you up at the back, but when you take it off, you undo the front, see?'

I nod, examining the intricate hooks. Will I be taking it off? I'm more interested in how you put such a boned contraption on.

I feel her close to my back, and the strings wrench me in and I yelp and laugh. I feel like Scarlett O'Hara, but a naughty version. I put my hands on my tiny waist. It feels great to be so cinched in. It feels nice to know the nipple-tassels are below. I see our reflection in the mirror, Marnie at my back bending over. I see the curve of her bum beneath the gown.

'Edward loves all this,' Marnie says, in a confidential tone. Her face is near my hair now. I feel the silk of her robe on the top of my arm. 'He's a sucker for a girl all dressed up.'

There's an edge in her voice that I can't place. Does she know about last night? Is she talking about me? Or have there been other girls?

But at that moment she spins me round and her face is

so open and sweet, I dismiss the thought immediately. I can't think about Edward. Not now. Not after last night. Not when this is happening, right here and right now. She pushes my hair back away over my shoulders. It's such a motherly, proprietorial gesture. She's loving this.

She licks her bottom lip.

'You look fabulous. But hitch up a bit,' she says, still surveying me with a professional eye.

She grabs the soft flesh of my breast and pulls it up inside the corset, careful not to dislodge the tassels. I feel my crotch flicker and twitch. My breath catches. Her hand is warm.

'Wow,' I joke, covering it up by looking down at my impressive cleavage. 'Look at that.'

'Look at that,' she agrees, impressed. She squeezes the peachy tops of my breasts and makes a jokey, lewd guffaw, but her eyes are somehow serious as they meet mine. Then she strokes her hands over the curve of my waist. 'How do you feel?'

Her eyes are narrowed now.

'I feel . . . I don't know. It's so sensual and sexy,' I confess.

She stares at me again, appraising me. I feel so flattered that she likes what she sees. I wish now I had make-up on, and heels and perfume. I wish I could be even better.

'Put the stockings on,' she says, flicking her eyes to the bed. 'Roll them carefully, or they'll ladder.'

I like the way she gives me the instruction – like she's this experienced big sister or something. I suddenly want to learn everything I can from her. I want to shine for her.

I turn and put on the exquisite stockings, carefully rolling them up one at a time, but I'm so aware of Marnie. I glance at her on the other side of the room. She's studying an iPad. What's she doing? She's not going to take photos, is she?

In a moment she's back, then she kneels down on the carpet. Her face is just inches from my barely covered vulva, but she's concentrating solely on fixing my stocking tops with the suspenders. Even so, I can feel the heat of her breath as she fiddles with the attachments, her warm hand brushing my inner thigh.

The quivering feeling inside me only grows. I guess this kind of get-up is designed to make you feel sensual, but I'm dismayed by how horny I feel. Maybe it's just the music and the joint.

Then, as she's fixing the back stocking, she puts her hand between my leg to straighten the stocking at the front. The side of her hand accidentally slides against the silk of the thong. Everything beneath twitches. I feel an almost orgasmic flush rush through my abdomen.

When I look down in panic, to see if Marnie has noticed, I glimpse the full swell of her breasts in her open robe and my mouth goes dry.

Finally, after she's put my feather headdress on, I'm done.

She claps her hands, surveying her handiwork. I can see my own reflection in the dark glass of the window opposite.

I can't deny that there has always been an inner showgirl inside me. But my eleven-year-old dreams of one day being on the West End stage always remained a closely guarded secret. The gruelling dance lessons Mum took me to taught me that I would never have the stamina or self-discipline to make that dream happen. But standing here, all dressed up, I feel a remnant of inner hope coming alive. This feels like it might be the performance of my lifetime.

'Now, it's time,' Marnie says, arching one eyebrow and staring directly at me. 'You dance, right?'

And at that moment I realize that she knows. She knows everything. Because otherwise why would she ask in such a loaded way if I dance?

35

I fight down my panic and don't look at her as she picks up the iPad.

I'm being paranoid, I tell myself. She can't know, can she? If she did, she wouldn't be this nice to me. *Would she?*

The music changes. Marnie throws her hand up in the air and wiggles her hips, a coquettish Marilyn Monroe move that makes us both giggle.

'Oh yeah. Here it comes, baby,' she cries as music fills the room. It's a bawdy tune I've never heard, all trumpets and trombones, sliding and suggestive. Its hip-bumping, boob-thrusting rhythm surges through me.

'Go on, dance for me, baby,' she shouts over the music. She grins at me and claps her hands.

I sigh and roll my eyes and flap out my hands. 'I can't. I don't know how.'

'Yes, you can. Fuck it, who's here to judge?' she shouts over the music. Thank God it's so loud. 'Do what comes naturally. Go on. Have a go.'

She shimmies her shoulders at me to encourage me. I see her breasts jiggle. I reach up and feel the length of the feather through the silk glove on my hand. I feel at once ridiculous and excited, and I can't fight the power of the music.

I want to perform. I cock my hips out to one side. I run the glove down the smooth curve of my bum. Marnie wolf-whistles, slides back onto the windowsill and watches me. She claps her hands and laughs. 'That's it.'

I like it that I can make her laugh. I waggle my fingers in the glove and stretch my arm out, imagining I'm some sort of Wild West hooker. I'm performing as much to my own reflection as I am to her. I strip off my glove, then twirl it around my head and throw it at her.

The gesture is so confident, it gives me courage.

'Oh yeah,' she says. 'Give me some high kicks.'

She whoops with joy as I high-kick, then turn around and waggle my bum.

She wolf-whistles again. 'You're one hot lady,' she catcalls.

And I feel it. Slowly, with her encouragement, I start to strip. It feels brilliant to perform for her. I don't know if I'm doing it right, and I'm certainly no Dita Von Teese, but I feel sensual and horny and in my power. I get it now. This is what Marnie is all about. This – this sexual, womanly quality that makes her so attractive. Because right now I feel like I have it, too.

And it feels great.

I run over to the chaise longue on tiptoes and twirl seductively on its seat, before putting one leg up and undoing my stockings. I'm hamming it up, but Marnie is loving it, and the more she does, the more I enjoy myself.

I dangle the stocking over her, running it along her face. It's a ridiculous gesture.

'Baby, you're a natural,' she says.

I nimbly skip, turn and flirt my way back to the carpet steps, then fumble with the front of the corset, still twirling along my carpeted stage, then I pull the open sides together and slowly reveal my breasts. I feel sexy, like I've never, ever felt.

Eventually I'm back as I was before, in just the thong and tassels, but now I don't feel naked, or vulnerable. I feel clothed in something invisible. Something that's womanly and powerful.

Marnie is standing before me now, staring at me. In fact she hasn't taken her eyes off me, but I don't feel embarrassed. I feel thrilled to perform for her. I like her seeing me like this. I know she gets what I'm feeling.

'So what next?' I grin. I'm out of breath. I look down at the tassels. I don't want to stop. I don't want this to end. And there's something about the tassels. I've never really properly celebrated my breasts before, even though they are so fundamental to my sexuality. And here they are. Dressed up for Mardi Gras.

'You sort of bounce on your heels,' Marnie instructs. She stands in front of me to demonstrate. Her robe is open now, but still covering her. She's only wearing simple black knickers beneath. I watch her ample breasts bounce, and suddenly I long to see them. I want her to be doing this with me.

'That's it,' she laughs, as my nipple-tassels spin. 'The trick is to do it in both directions.'

She sort of comedy-wiggles her shoulders, but I can't. I stick my tongue out of my mouth, trying to coordinate my nipple-tassels swinging the other way, but it's impossible. And very funny.

I'm laughing and Marnie is laughing, too. I'm stoned and giddy and dressed as a burlesque dancer, learning from my boss how to tassel-waggle. The absurdity of it couldn't be funnier. And then I stumble forward on the step, just as I've got the tassels to go in a circle. I fall into Marnie's arms.

She doesn't pull away, and all I can see is her lips.

'Hey, you,' she whispers, suddenly serious.

And I can't breathe. Because she says it like you'd say it to a lover. An equal. In those two words she acknowledges our nakedness, or sexuality, our attraction. She doesn't pull away, and neither do I.

I feel a kind of thrilled terror of the kind I've never felt before. Because with those words, she's made this real.

She's made me hers. But I'm not.

But then her smile kind of freezes. And then I hear it. What she's obviously picked up on first.

'Marnie?'

The voice is faint, but it's obviously Edward downstairs.

I gasp, coming to my senses. Edward is here and I'm in a sensual embrace with Marnie, wearing only the skimpiest of G-strings and nipple-tassels.

Marnie's eyebrows shoot up.

'Oh God. You look so funny,' she says, registering my panic as I spring away from her. The nanosecond of serious intimacy is broken by her laughter. Like it never happened.

I grab my clothes from the floor, wrenching my jeans on

and hopping into them. I pull on my hoodie, not bothering with the zip, and scoot for the door.

I can't look at her.

I can't bear this.

She lolls against the door frame as I charge along the corridor, like a frightened rabbit, to the service lift, praying that Edward is using the stairs.

36

I get to my room and press myself against the door. I'm panting, gasping for breath. I'm trembling all over. Marnie's laughter is ringing in my ears.

I can't believe that Edward is here and he nearly caught us just now in her room. What would have happened if he had? Why was Marnie so unflustered? Why did she think it was *funny*?

And that moment.

That moment.

Hey, you. I can't get it out of my head.

But then it was gone so fast, maybe I imagined it.

I feel sick with the thought that she might think I was coming on to her. That my seductive dance was somehow real.

There's a whole load of lines that seem to have blurred, and my actions and feelings don't make sense at all.

And that's what makes me feel so angry. Because she doesn't mind. She doesn't care. She gets off on that kind of thing happening. She admitted it herself to me earlier. She's an adrenaline junkie. She likes living on the edge. She made it very clear what makes her tick. She must have known all along that Edward was on his way home. She must have

187

been smoking that spliff, knowing that any second she might get caught. She must have dressed me up and made me dance, knowing the same.

It's all very well for her to live like that, but it's not fair that she used me like that. For a thrill.

How fucking dare she, I think, omitting a low growl. I've been duped again.

But it was *my* thrill, too. I went along with it, didn't I? It wasn't as if I checked where Edward was, or when he'd be back. I just got sucked into Marnie's world, like I was this morning. I feel like I did when I was in the car, all over again. Sick and angry and cross.

I groan again and bury my head in my hands.

You look so funny. Her taunt rings in my ears.

I'm annoyed that I feel like this. Like a fool for running out of there, like I've condoned her impression of me as a prude. She clearly enjoyed me being embarrassed, but now, having run away, I'm upset I reacted like I did. Once again, I feel completely wrong-footed by her. I feel stupid and young and immature, like I was only playing at being the kind of mature woman Marnie is.

Did she expect me to stay? Be cool about what was going on?

Clearly, the answer is yes.

I think of all the models she must have seen. All the private clients she referred to: world-class women who have the money and sex appeal to dress up in the classiest underwear money can buy. And here am I, scuttling around like an idiot.

Again, I think of the film I discovered last night. Now

I know that Marnie smokes, I can't help wondering whether she set up the film for me to find. She's such an exhibitionist, I wouldn't put it past her.

Is she testing me, I wonder? Could I really have carried it off, if we were found together by Edward? Edward saw me last night in that dress Marnie designed. He wouldn't have been shocked to find me in her room helping her unpack, but now I've gone and made it a huge drama.

What's happening now, I wonder? Is Edward in her room? Are they discussing me? In the silence I strain my ears, hoping for clues, but the house is silent. Or maybe I'm too low down on the list of things they need to discuss? After all, Marnie hadn't even told me she was in this evening. Maybe the minute I was out of her sight, I was out of her mind.

Perhaps she'll pretend it never happened. Knowing her, even just a tiny bit, I can imagine her right now, sweeping all the corsets into the crate, stubbing out the spliff, facing Edward after his day . . . where? Where has he been? I can't even make the most basic of guesses, I know so little.

Or maybe she's getting dressed up in a corset herself. She told me that Edward likes a girl all dressed up. Perhaps she's seized the moment and is dancing for him to that music right now. Just the thought of it feels like a dull ache in my chest.

I go into the bathroom and move to the sink, washing my face in cold water. Away from the candlelit bedroom and Marnie, I feel dizzy and nauseous. I've smoked more in the last two hours than I have in my entire life. I shouldn't have pretended I could keep up with her. I was showing off. Hoping to impress her.

But what will she think of me now?

I can't stop thinking about how she looked just now in her gown. How sexy I found her. I'm so ashamed by how much. If Edward hadn't called out right then, I might have kissed her. Is that what she would have wanted, too?

What's happened to me? What's happened to my self-control?

I get up and quickly change, ripping off the nipple-tassels and getting into my pyjamas, as if the whole act of making myself normal will distance me from the burlesque dancer I was just a few minutes ago, but it can't.

I lie in the dark, shivering. My head spins, the repercussions going round and round in my head. I see Marnie laughing – her head thrown back, her red gown flapping. I see Edward in the gallery, remember his leg pressed against mine. I see myself shimmying whilst Marnie claps her hands, the feather on my head nodding. I see her eyes in the car, hear her crazy laugh . . .

Eventually I doze off, but in the dead of night there's a knock on my door and I'm instantly awake. Is it him? Is it her?

I stumble across the carpet and fling open the door. I don't know what to expect. What on earth will happen next?

37

What I don't expect is empty space.

There's nobody there. Except the bronze nudey man, who is shadowy in the darkness, although I know he's still slyly grinning. I look down: on the carpet outside my door is a shiny cream box with a pink ribbon wrapped around it, on top of a package wrapped in tissue paper. Marnie's tissue paper. The same paper everything was wrapped in. I step into the corridor and pick up the bundle, looking both ways, but the corridor is empty.

I slide the ribbon off the box and lift the lid. Inside is a cream card – the same card that came with the flowers from Marnie. The same handwriting reads:

You were beautiful tonight. I thought you might want to keep the corset. Don't worry. It's our little secret. The enclosed might help with how you're feeling . . .

I push aside the tissue paper and gasp.

It's a vibrator. There's a slim instruction booklet attached as a label. The front of it reads 'Intimate Collection' in pink script. So that's what she meant. She designs sex toys as well as underwear. It makes sense, but I'm still shocked. Shocked that she's so brazen about it.

Guiltily, I take the box back and the tissue-wrapped corset inside the room and lock the door. Then I run to the bed and put the box on it and pull out the vibrator. I let out an astonished laugh as I hold it in my hand. Marnie Parker, my boss, has given me a vibrator.

It's not cock-shaped, as you would imagine, but kind of flat and curvy. Womanly, like I imagine the shape would be if you moulded a bit of wax against a female's parts. It's made of smooth latex and it's warm and sensual, not cold and gaudy like the pink Rabbit that Tiff won at the hen-do.

There's a tiny silver button on one end. I press it and the whole thing starts to vibrate with a low hum.

I stare at Marnie's note, trying to fathom out its meaning: it *might help with how you're feeling.*

How does she know how I'm feeling? Because she's feeling the same? Was she as turned on by what happened as me? Is she into women? As in *really* into women, I suddenly think? What if that's her thing?

Is she bisexual?

Surely not?

Because if she is, then does that mean I am? I've never been turned on by a woman before, or had a lesbian relationship of any kind, although I know plenty of girls in school who experimented.

Marnie's note seems to imply that she knows how I was feeling when I fell into her arms. It's one thing to have had a crush on Edward and to have overstepped the mark, but feeling like I did about her seems altogether more dangerous. It makes me feel out of control.

I put the vibrator down and stare at it. If I accept this gift – if I do anything with it – then it's acknowledging the secret feelings I had just now for Marnie. She knows that.

But then, at the same time, she's been sweet enough to worry about my embarrassment. Her note has let me off the hook. I don't need to panic about her saying anything to Edward. Or losing my job. Perhaps, as far as she's concerned, what happened just now between us was perfectly normal and innocent. That kind of thing probably happens to her all the time.

I sink back on the bed and it rocks beneath me, then seems to cocoon me, as I lie back with a sigh.

I don't know if Marnie's gift has made me feel better or worse. I can't imagine that she would have discussed me with Edward and then written that note.

I think of her dancing in her red kimono. I think of Edward watching me, like he watched me dance in front of Marnie's portrait in the gallery downstairs.

I grab the vibrator and push the button. Then, not giving myself time to think, I push it underneath my pyjama bottoms.

The smooth hardness slides against me. It feels warm, unlike the ones I saw in the sex shop in town with Tiff, which looked cold and painful and not a turn-on at all. In fact this one feels surprisingly like the real thing. I wriggle my pyjama bottoms off and let my knees fall apart, then I push the tip of the fat end inside me a little way and gasp.

I think of Edward in the doorway of Marnie's room. I

think of him finding Marnie and me in our almost-naked embrace. Then I think of him on the bed, lying there, Marnie watching us from the window seat, smoking a spliff, her red gown open as I dance for them both.

I gasp, sliding the vibrator out again, thinking of Edward's eyes, as I let the buzzing drift against my clitoris. I feel sweat breaking out on my forehead.

Marnie's right. This does help.

38

I don't see Marnie Parker the next morning. Or Edward. They must have left the house at the crack of dawn, because I was up, listening out for sounds in the house, as soon as I was awake.

I have a long shower and try and make sense of the previous evening. In the clear light of day I decide that it's stupid to read too much into that moment I shared with Marnie. We were both stoned. Nothing happened. We were mucking around, that's all. I have nothing to be ashamed of.

I won't mention the vibrator.

Laura is in the kitchen alone. Once again she won't even so much as look at me, let alone engage in conversation.

'Where is everyone?' I ask her, going to the sleek white unit and filling up the kettle at the sink.

She flinches at the sound of my voice. 'Mr and Mrs Parker won't be back until the day after tomorrow. Mrs Gundred is away in town, too, so I'm afraid you'll be on your own.'

'Isn't there anyone else who stays here? A groundsman or something?'

She looks at me and shakes her head, like she's scared. She turns away, busying herself with a pile of napkins that she's folding and putting in one of the spotlessly neat drawers.

It's weird Marnie and Edward have left when there's still so much unpacking to do. I thought Marnie wanted everything sorted.

'Laura, do you know anything about the boys? About when they'll be back?'

She turns away, so I can't see her face.

'Laura?' I ask her again.

'Don't ask me,' she says. It's as if I've threatened her. She really is the oddest person I've ever met. She's so jumpy and timid. It's like I really could scare her to death.

'But . . .'

She turns around then, suddenly, shocking me with the aggression in her tone. 'I said don't ask me. I don't know anything about them. Anything at all, OK?'

I watch her go, feeling slack-jawed at her reaction. I only asked!

I don't see her for the rest of the day. I think she's making herself scarce. With nothing to do and unable to go anywhere at all, I feel completely useless. I wish I had just a small bit of information and could prepare myself for the boys' return. I resolve to try and discover their bedrooms, but as I go around the house I find that most of the doors on the upper two floors are locked.

The afternoon is hot. There's a barometer on the back terrace against the wall and I study it. Grandad had one in his allotment and taught me how to read it when I was little. It looks like there's going to be a heatwave.

I walk along the back terrace and cup my hand against

the bay window, looking at the patch of carpet where Edward and I danced. Nothing is out of place. The room is stylish and modern. The drinks cabinet is closed. It's as if we were never there. It's just odd being in a huge house alone like this. Especially when so much of it is out of bounds. Don't they trust me?

I look at the bookshelves and see if I can see the photography book, but I can't, although I'm sure I left it on the end of the shelf.

I make myself a sandwich, grab a towel and a magazine from the downstairs loo and make my way back down the garden to the lake for a swim. I'm too creeped-out to use the indoor pool by myself.

It's a glorious day and the sun beats down, making it too hot to step in bare feet on the platform. I go to the other side of the lake and try to explore the summerhouse, but it's locked. I sit on the wooden slats of its porch and turn my face up to the sky, guiltily remembering my fantasy about Edward.

Which is when the phone in my pocket buzzes and continues to buzz. I'd forgotten – there's reception here.

There are ten messages from Scott. The first he's made from work and he's talking in a hushed whisper. Alfie, his sales manager, is big on personal calls. That is – not making them.

The second and third are from the car, back-to-back, as Scott runs out of space. He tells me how he's missing me. How Derry has finally given up weed (ironic, since I've just started smoking it) and how he was seeing Derry, to play Xbox. The fourth is from the pub. His voice takes on that whiney tone. He's missing me, but he's also annoyed that I'm not returning his calls. The fifth message is aggressive. He's taken it personally that I haven't called him back. I sigh and brace myself to continue listening.

The sixth, as expected, is apologetic. It's late. He's in bed alone and just wants me home. As he speaks, his voice cracking with emotion, I picture his bedsit, the traffic outside. I scan myself for a physical reaction, for some lurch of my gut that would make me know that I'm missing him, too. That I want to go back to his bed. But there's nothing.

The seventh message starts with heavy breathing. He's masturbating. I can tell.

I hear him grunting on the phone, the staccato 'Ah' as he comes. Once, the noise of that would have turned me on, but now I feel slightly soiled that he's been masturbating on my answering machine. He's so immature.

The ninth message is a giggly, gleeful one. He's delighted at his phone message. 'That was for you,' he says. I know that he's probably already told his mates.

The tenth message, the last and most recent, was from a couple of hours ago, just before he would be leaving work. He's five hours ahead of me here. If I call him now, he'll probably be at home, but having listened to the gamut of emotions on his phone messages, I'm not sure what there is left to say.

I dial his number quickly, not giving myself an excuse to back out. I feel breathless and nervous.

'Where the FUCK have you been?' Scott demands. He sounds really cross. I'm sure he is, after his messages.

'I'm sorry. There's no reception in the house.'

'You could have emailed, or Facebooked. I've been writing you messages on your timeline.'

'I mean there's no connection. I can't get online. I think they'll sort it out, but they've been busy.'

They. The Parkers. Two people who are so vivid in my mind. People I'm talking about like it's them and us. But it's not. Scott's the one who is the outsider. Even being on the phone to him feels alien.

He lets out a small growl of frustration. He hates things being out of his control. 'So when are you coming home?' he demands. He doesn't sound like he believes me about the phone.

I know this kind of mood of his. This petulant mood where he behaves all stroppy and I stroke his ego, calm him down, bring him back to me. It's all part of the game we've always played: me soothing the big, moody bear. Me making all the right noises until everything is OK. I can tell that he's expecting me to do it now. To tell him how much I'm missing him. But I don't.

'I'm not sure. And I haven't met the kids yet, so I don't know whether I'll be staying on long-term.'

I picture his ear tips going red, like they do when he's angry. He hates me being vague. I can tell my answer has confused him.

'So . . . so what are you doing, if the kids aren't there?'

I bite my lip and look up at the sky through the trees. What have I been doing? A very good question. How can I even start to tell him?

And right then and there, I know that too much has happened for me to be the person I was, who left Manchester not even a week ago. I've already seen too much, felt too much, experienced too much.

I think of Edward, and how he was in the back of the limo when I told him about Scott. Just the thought of his face makes my tummy flip over.

A girl as stunning as you . . . mustn't ever settle for anything but the best.

'How long are you expecting me to wait?' he snaps. I swallow hard. Leave the pause too long. 'Soph?' His voice goes up. We both know something's coming. I hear the catch in his voice. The fear.

I have to be brave. I have to take this leap of faith into the unknown. It's the only way.

'Scott,' I say, quietly. 'Scott. I don't think it's a very good idea if you wait for me.'

39

I feel bruised after my conversation with Scott, and it's even harder having to process these feelings all alone. He was furious, of course. Then upset, then angry, then dismissive and then nasty. He called me a bitch several times, and I am. It made it so much worse that it all happened somewhere so beautiful.

I call Tiff straight away and, in typical Tiff style, she presents me with a long list of Scott's faults and how delighted she is that I've finally seen the light. I don't tell her about Edward, or what's been happening to me here. I know as soon as I hear her voice that she wouldn't understand; and it's that, rather than the conversation with Scott, that really makes me cry. I've never felt so cut off or alone.

Exhausted, I return to the house and mooch about, feeling at an utter loose end. I root around in the fridge, but I'm not really hungry. The heat doesn't help.

In the evening I turn on all the lights. I try not to get too scared, but I can't help going through a whole psychodrama about what might happen if someone breaks in. I picture myself in all sorts of scenarios in which I'm tied up and forced to answer questions about the Parkers, for which I have no answers.

I'm anxious that the Parkers think it's perfectly OK to leave me all alone in the house like this, with no means of contacting the outside world. Is this how it's going to be when the boys are here? We'll be all alone here? Will I ever be allowed to take them out? And if so, will they give me a car? But even if they do, where would I go? I think of the drive I took with Marnie – how far it was until the next town. There's nothing around here at all, except the other houses along the long road to the gatehouse. But I can't imagine any kind of neighbourly scenario in which I pop round for a natter. People are in Thousand Acres because they want to be private. Besides, even if I wanted to go and visit a neighbour, I'm not sure I'd be able to get out of the big gates guarding the drive.

Telling myself to be grateful for what I have, I retrace my steps to Marnie's room. I don't know if I'm searching for her, or if I'm just searching for someone to talk to, but her room is locked and the corridor remains dark.

In the main gallery, the light comes on and the door automatically slides open, as if it's been waiting for me, and I stare at Marnie's portrait. Now I've met her in the flesh, she seems even more enticing. I stare at her breasts, remembering how she touched me and applied the nipple-tassels. How she stared right into my eyes as I fell into her embrace and our flesh touched. Her eyes stare at me, as if she knew, even then, what she was doing. That she has the power to undo people.

By the wall there's a stack of pictures, waiting to be hung. Curious, I flick through them. There's one at the back with a thin strip of tissue paper over it. Carefully, I peep beneath.

It's a framed black-and-white photograph of a man. He's naked except for leather chaps, which show off his glistening, smooth buttocks. He has a concave, muscular dancer's body and he's leaning over a square counter and resting his nakedness on it.

I immediately feel the heat rising in my cheeks as I gawp at his impressively large, semi-erect cock and plump balls beneath it. It's so brazen, yet such an unashamedly beautiful image that I feel a spasm in me as I stare. This is art, of course. Of course it is, but it still feels pornographic. Is Edward really intending to hang it on the wall in here? Is this what he and Marnie are all about? People who like to shock? Am I supposed to play along with their game?

I stare again at the photo and it stirs a sexual longing in me that feels scarily out of reach.

I think of Scott and how I've exploded my life back at home. What if I never have sex again? What will I do if I never get to see a cock again? Not that I've ever seen one as large or perfect as the one in the photo. As I stare at it, my mouth starts to water. I just want to feast on it. Take it in my mouth.

I back away. Marnie smiles at me from the wall.

40

Edward comes home the following evening, by which time I'm emotionally exhausted. I'm so starved of actual in-the-flesh human attention that the moment I hear a car on the gravel drive, I shoot downstairs and pretend to bump into him.

He's friendly, but tired, he tells me as I follow him into the kitchen. He doesn't meet my eye.

Seeing him for the first time since I danced with him, and then he told me to go to bed, makes me feel breathlessly nervous. Is he still cross with me? If he is, will he mention it? More to the point, has Marnie said anything to him? About me dressing up? Does he know she gave me that vibrator? I feel the weight of the secrets I'm keeping pressing against my chest.

He's wearing a cool blue jacket, jeans and smart leather shoes, and I'm reminded of the man on the plane. The man who was fucking the air hostess. Except that Edward is much better-looking and I can't imagine him doing that kind of thing for a second.

'How are you?' he asks, as he flips through a pile of papers on the side. I lean against the counter, waggling my foot. I feel caught out.

'Fine, thanks,' I tell him, but my breath catches. I cover it up quickly. 'Thank you for the clothes,' I say, quickly. 'I love them all.'

'You're welcome,' he says, like it's no big deal. Which I guess it isn't for him. He doesn't look at me.

I so want everything to be OK. I desperately don't want him to hate me, but standing here, I feel wobbly. My whole world has changed since I last saw him. I've dumped Scott, my boyfriend of three years, and in doing so upset all the security I have at home. I have untethered myself, and this free-floating feeling is so scary. I want desperately for Edward to catch hold of me, hold on and stop me floating away.

I've been telling myself all day that my decision to be honest with Scott has nothing to do with Edward. Because nothing is going on between us – or ever will be – but seeing him again makes me realize that my heartache of the past twenty-four hours or more has actually been *entirely* to do with him. Because of that night. Because of how he changed me.

He looks up then. My stomach tumbles over itself as his green eyes bore into mine.

'Seriously? You don't look OK,' he says, although I can tell he's not being unkind.

'I'm fine.'

'I hope you didn't get lonely here by yourself?'

I shrug nervously. 'A bit.'

I don't tell him that I cried myself to sleep last night. That I felt bereft this morning, and more at a loose end today than I've ever felt in my life. That I really don't know what I'm doing here – or why it's such a big deal that I can't seem to relax.

Then he puts the papers aside and looks at me properly. 'What's happened?' he asks, walking towards me.

How can he know? How can he tell, just by looking at me, how I'm feeling? Nobody has ever been able to do that before. Am I really that easy to read? I think of him at the art gallery: how he watched me, how we seemed just to be able to communicate. Except that I got it all wrong, I remind myself.

I can tell that he's offering a shoulder to cry on. Not that I will ever be putting my head on his shoulder again. But even so, his soft gaze melts me. I have to grip onto the counter to stop myself from taking the three steps needed to be in his embrace.

I shrug and take a shuddery breath. 'I spoke to Scott,' I tell him. Up until I saw him, I hadn't intended to tell him this news at all, but something about the way he is – his intensity – makes me feel that I have no choice but to tell the truth. 'I told him it was over between us.'

'Ah,' Edward says slowly, as if he understands everything. 'Well. You did the right thing.'

Did I? I'm not so sure. I nod, fighting back tears. 'I know. But he was angry and . . .' I blow out a long, pent-up breath. 'He said some things that weren't very nice.'

Edward smiles sympathetically and searches out my eyes, but I'm determined not to cry. I don't want him to think I'm the crybaby, out-of-control nanny.

'Huh. Well, I guess that's understandable. If I were Scott, I wouldn't want to lose you. And men . . .' he shrugs and gives me a cute smile, 'we say dumb stuff when we're cornered.'

And as he looks at me, I suddenly realize that he's apologizing about the other night and that we're not talking about Scott at all.

I nod and bite my lip. And right there and then I realize I don't want to discuss Scott with him after all. I don't want to bore him with the details of my calls with Tiff, and how she tried, but failed, to understand what's going on.

The important thing is that I've severed myself from home. Cut them all off like a limb, and seeing Edward has now staunched the flow of pain. It's all been worth it because he knows I've been brave.

'Drink?' he asks.

'One,' I say pointedly and smile shyly. I'm speaking in code, too, and he knows it. I'm talking about the other night and how drunk I was.

'Sure,' he says, smiling more broadly this time. It feels like the air has been cleared in the gentlest, most subtle way possible. He looks at me again. 'Actually,' he says, rolling his shoulder, 'I've been in back-to-back meetings all day and I need a stretch. I fancy a swim. Will you join me?'

41

I'm first in the indoor pool. I went upstairs to change, opting for my black swimming costume from home rather than my new bikini. As I bicycle my legs in the perfectly clear water at the end of the pool, watching the reflection of the water dance against the ceiling, I remind myself that I am to be strictly professional. There must be no physical contact whatsoever. Edward is with Marnie. I am their employee.

End of.

But this little inner lecture is cut abruptly short when Edward appears from the corridor. He's wearing dark-navy swimming trunks, which don't look daft like Speedos, or pikey like swimming shorts, but are somewhere designer and chic in between. They show off his tanned, muscled legs and his astonishing swimmer's physique. I check him out, comparing him to the memory of the guy in the movie.

It wasn't Edward. I see that now. Edward is slightly stockier than the man in the film. But even thinking of it – making the comparison – ignites that forbidden horny memory. I try very hard and shut the door on it.

Seeing him practically naked only proves what a great figure of a man he is. He drinks heavily and eats gourmet food, but his waist is trim and there's no sign of a pot-belly.

He's hairy, too. But in a good way. Scott always used to wax his chest, preferring himself smooth, and lamenting old men with hairy chests, but Edward's chest and stomach are covered in soft, dark hair, which just makes me want to touch him even more.

He jumps nimbly into the pool and gasps a little at the temperature of the water and laughs, and I look at the dark, intimate hair of his armpits as his palms recoil from the surface of the water. I want to tell him that, compared to the pools back home, this is a bath.

He strides towards me at the end of the pool. I can't help my eyes darting to his nipples. I see them pucker and stiffen. I wonder what it would feel like to flick my tongue over those sensitive buds.

Stop it, I yell at myself silently.

'So you swim a lot, right?' he says, pulling the black goggles around his neck up towards his face. I suddenly remember the lie I told in my interview about how I swam to keep in shape.

'Probably not as much as you,' I say, nodding at him. I'm referring to his perfect swimmer's physique and we both know it, but somehow the compliment is too personal. He ignores it.

'First to twenty then, Miss Henshaw,' he says, ducking under the water.

It's no contest, of course. He's faster and has a much better technique than me. He cuts through the water in an effortless crawl, his body streamlined, his feet hardly breaking the water. I feel a childish urge to wave at him or pull a face as he passes me in the water, but he's concentrating hard. Like everything he gets involved in, he seems completely absorbed. I long to be the focus of his attention again. I get the impression that he's forgotten I'm even here.

He wipes me out on the first ten lengths, but then he slows down and I start to catch up. As I swim, trying to remember my best technique, I remember how good it feels to do serious exercise.

I've been lolloping around the house for two days, moping in my relationship-ending blues, but what I should have been doing is swimming.

But I'm like this, I remember. Whenever I exercise, it feels so good that I vow I'm going to repeat the experience daily. That I'm going to exercise *all the time*. It's the same with sex.

Don't think about sex, I caution myself, but the pornographic image of the black dancer in the photograph taunts me, all mixed up with the man in the movie.

Edward wins by a length. I thought for a moment he was going to let me win, so I try extra-hard to beat him. I'm panting, and my cheeks are pounding, when we finish.

'Not bad,' he tells me, completely unruffled. 'You're fast.'

'You're faster.'

'You thought I'd let a girl beat me?' he teases.

I flick him playfully with water. 'You would, if you had any chivalry,' I tease back.

He grins at me and hauls himself out of the pool, his biceps flexing. He grabs a towel and dries his hair, making it go all spiky. He looks boyish and coy. Even so, I try to rip my eyes away from the rivulets of water that run between the dark hair on his stomach.

He walks towards the side of the pool, where I'm still in the water, trying to catch my breath. He's holding out a light-blue towel to me, shielding my body, as if he doesn't want to look. I clamber up onto the side, inelegantly failing to do so in one, and levering myself up with my knee.

For a second, as I walk towards the outstretched towel, I think he might wrap me up in it, but instead he lets go of one side and I grab it, wrapping it around myself, feeling self-conscious.

'I'm going in the sauna,' he says, as I wipe my face. 'Come, if you like.' It's not an actual invitation as much as a factual piece of information, as if he's trying very hard to keep everything on a strictly professional basis.

I nod. 'I will in a minute. I just want to shower first.'

It's a lie. I want to check my face. I don't want to realize later that I've got panda-eyes from where my make-up has smudged.

In the small toilet cubicle I hitch myself up in my swimming costume, remembering Marnie doing the same thing the other night with the corset, but the effect is not nearly the same in a swimming costume. I look at myself in the mirror and give myself a hard stare. Maybe it's the exercise, maybe it's being with Edward and everything being OK after the other night, but I feel better. More than better. I feel excited.

I rinse my hair in the shower and take a deep breath. Then I head for the sauna. This is good, I tell myself. This is professional, yet fun. I can do this. There's no harm in being in a sauna with him, is there?

42

Edward is sitting on the top slats, his eyes closed. He has a small blue towel wrapped around his waist, but I see a sliver of flesh running from the top to bottom of the edge of the towel. He's taken off his swimming shorts.

He's naked beneath the towel.

I stare at that intimate stripe of hip, then deliberately rip my eyes away.

I creep in, not wanting to disturb him. He looks like he's meditating or something, surrendering himself entirely to the heat. I lie down on the bottom bench, my head as far away from him as possible, near the door, and stare up at the pine ceiling. From where I'm lying stiffly, I can only see his lower legs. Through the pine slats I glance over at the stripe of blue towel.

In seconds I can feel my heartbeat in my skin. My swimming costume dries out and sticks to me. I try to get comfortable, turning over and lying on my front instead, feeing a bead of perspiration trickle between my breasts.

There's a low gasp and I sense Edward leaning forward. I peek over my shoulder. He's got his elbows on his knees. His head hangs down.

'This is the best bit,' he says, with a low sigh. 'There's nothing like a sauna.'

I don't tell him that this is very different from the saunas I've ever been in. There was one that Tiff and I went to once, in a holiday park in Whitney, but the man in it was clearly a pervert and so smelly we had to retreat. I've never been in a private, pristine sauna like this before.

My temple is wet where it's leaning on my forearm. I watch the rivulets of sweat drip down my other elbow. I feel every pore of my skin. The heat throbs. I hear my breath booming in my ears.

Through the tiny gap, under my arm, I look at Edward's leg. Is his towel still on? I imagine what's below. I imagine him hanging down over the edge of the wooden slats. I picture his semi-erect cock and plump, juicy, suckable balls . . .

Stop it, I tell myself, forcing the thought away, but something about the heat just makes me horny. I can't help it.

I can feel the blood pulsing in my abdomen now, and lower, between my legs. I've never been this close to anyone so sexually attractive and not been able to touch them.

Suddenly, Edward gets up. He's naked and, although I've been expecting it, it's still so shocking, it's like a slap. He's standing near the coals with his back to me. He's naturally naked, though, not showing off, as if this is perfectly normal. I guess it is, in a sauna.

Secretly, I feast my eyes on him. I know I should close them, but I can't stop staring at the swell of his buttocks, the smoothness of his back. He has a line where he's been sunbathing. But somehow that only makes it more wonderful to see this intimate part of him. I picture my hands clawing the pale flesh, pulling him closer inside me . . .

I can't breathe – especially as now he chucks some water on the coals and there's a hiss of steam.

'Do say if it gets too much,' he says. His voice is low and soft. 'I like to go as far as I can stand it.'

Is he talking about the sauna?

He turns and I close my eyes. I can't bear to look. I can't trust myself to look at him fully naked. What if he has a hard-on?

This is sauna etiquette, I remind myself. People go naked in saunas all the time. But knowing he's there, just inches away from me, excites me in a way I've never felt.

'You look very tense, Miss Henshaw,' he says.

I can't even trust myself to reply, worried that my voice will betray the tension I'm feeling.

He's standing next to me and he's naked. If I turn over I'll see him. His cock will be inches from my face. My mouth is completely dry.

'Shall I massage your shoulders?'

I remember how he made me lift up my pyjama top the morning of the party. How I felt powerless not to obey his command, and it's the same now. His tone is neutral. Like it's a perfectly reasonable thing to ask and not flirtatious at all. How can he do that? Ask if I want a massage, when he's naked, and make it sound like he's asked if I want sugar in my coffee?

'OK. That would be nice,' I manage.

'Here, pull these down,' he says, tapping the top of my swimming-costume straps.

Dutifully I lift up onto my elbows and, careful not to reveal any flesh, pull down the top of my costume.

'You should really take the whole thing off,' he says. 'It's bad to wear fabric against your skin in the sauna.'

I can't look at him. I can't open my eyes. If I do, I'll give away what I'm feeling.

I can't work this out at all. Is he being serious? Is his deadpan delivery all part of some sophisticated game? Does he really think I'm going to strip off and that'll be just perfectly normal and fine?

But maybe he does? He sounds like he's genuinely telling me off about my costume. Like I've foolishly transgressed a basic social rule.

I have several choices. To pretend I haven't heard him, which is ridiculous and out of the question. To make a joke of it – but I really don't think I can pull it off. Or to scramble out of my costume and pretend it's no big deal to be totally naked.

I opt for the last.

Except that it's a *huge* deal.

I quickly swivel and sit up too fast so that my head spins. Edward has already turned away, pretending to respect my modesty – except that he's naked himself.

It's so confusing and I'm so unsure of the rules. Does he often massage people in the sauna?

Is this just one enormous tease? Or is this the start of our affair?

Is it?

'I think massages in the heat are the best,' he says, like it's no big deal, quashing my racing thoughts. 'I see this brilliant Swedish guy, Sven, sometimes and he works his magic in a heated room.'

How can he chat like this, when we're both naked? I lie back down on my front on the towel on the slats. I squeeze my thighs together and rest my head on its side, my arms above my head.

I'm laid out before him, naked.

Naked.

My mind swims in the heat about what it means. Each second seems to stretch out, as if we're in slo-mo. The stifling temperatures seem to be loaded with the promise of what will happen next.

Edward is next to me, staring down at me. I feel heat all over my skin in a wave – not just from the steam, but because I know he's looking at me. Does he like what he sees? Is he looking for imperfections? Of which there are many, I'm sure.

He opens my ankles so that my legs are slightly apart, and I feel him kneel with one knee on the bench between my shins. My breath catches.

He is in between my legs. Can he see me? Can he see up my thighs, between them?

He leans forward and I feel him place his hands on my lower back just above my bum. He makes a few exploratory squeezes, then massages quickly and firmly either side of my spine. His touch says that this is professional, that this is a sports massage. Except that it's not.

Sven isn't here.

It's just us.

'There,' he says, quietly. 'I thought so. You're storing all your tension just in here. Breathe and relax,' he says, as his hands work the base of my spine.

There's nothing flirtatious in his tone, but his hands say something different. My skin sings as he touches me.

I keep entirely still as he starts to move up my spine and reaches my shoulders. When he does, I can't help a low, lusty groan escaping my lips.

After a while the heels of his hands come back and grind in confident, knowledgeable circles at the bottom of my spine. I can feel the flesh on my buttocks rotating. From where he is above me, I wonder if he's looking at them.

I squeeze my lips together. This is torture. Exquisite torture. To have a gorgeous naked man leaning over me, telling me to relax, when every fibre of my being is urging me to lever back on my knees and impale myself on him.

But God, his hands feel good.

He's leaning right over me now. The hair on his thigh tickles my leg.

He only has to move slightly and he will be able to see all of me. I fight the urge to turn over with every ounce of self-control I possess. I ache to be below him. I picture it, as if it's actually happening, and yet, despite how close he is, I can't do it. I don't have the nerve.

I can't face being accused of overstepping the mark, or of throwing myself at him, like he did the other night. I know instinctively that if he wants anything more than a massage to happen, then it will have to come from him. I sense he knows this, too. He might as well have put me in chains.

And then he moves down.

He leans against my buttocks, flattening his hands against them, pressing, kneading. It's so intimate – so shocking – and yet . . . On the other hand, maybe this is what any professional masseur would do. Perhaps *he* gets this done all the time.

But all I can think is: *How is he feeling? Does he want me, too? Is he staring at me now, growing hard?* Blood pounds in me. If I were a cartoon, there would be kettles of steam coming out of my ears.

His fingers are lower now, splayed out against my hips. His thumbs massage the crease of my thighs and buttocks, slipping inwards, just inches from me. I can't breathe. I am inwardly trembling, my nerve endings screaming.

Is he going to touch me?

Is he going to touch me where I need him to?

I can't bear the tension. I feel myself aching, screaming.

I can't believe this is happening. He's intimately massaging me. We're millimetres away from this straying into proper sex. But then he breaks the crackling, sizzling silence.

'So, I hear you met my wife.'

It's a statement, not a question. His tone betrays nothing of what he feels about this fact. We could be chatting in the kitchen. Even more alarming is that his tone doesn't give any indication that he's noticed what he's doing to me.

'Uh-hnn,' I croak. I'm breathless. Dying of heat, unable to breathe, uncontrollably turned on, but now we're talking about Marnie. His wife.

I picture her watching us, like she watched me dance for

her, but that somehow only ups the sexual tension crackling over me, like I'm live with electricity.

What has she said? Did she tell Edward that she dressed me up? That he almost caught us together? *Edward is a sucker for a girl all dressed up.*

I think of her note and of the vibrator she gave me, and how she assured me it was our little secret. Was she telling the truth?

But I can't think about Marnie as his hands now move down, massaging lower, but somehow this is even more of a turn-on. His thumbs circle my inner thighs – not somewhere I ever thought of as an erogenous zone, but suddenly he touches somewhere halfway down on the inner edge of my thigh and it's like he's found the key to somewhere I never knew existed. Who knew I had an erogenous zone that specific, right there? I gasp, astounded, and I know that I'm going to come and nothing is going to stop it.

I'm trembling. I can't help myself. He must know what he's doing to me, but I don't care. I can't think. I can't concentrate on anything apart from his thumb on my thigh.

'She told me you were really helpful. Thank you for that. Poor Marnie. She's got a lot on.'

Is that all she said? I can't tell, but I don't care. His thumb is still circling, higher and higher, the erogenous zone stretching with his touch.

'It was nothing,' I manage in a mumble. But it wasn't nothing. THIS isn't nothing.

I want to scream, but instead, wide-eyed and staring forward, on total red alert, eyes popping, I stop breathing as his thumbs reach the top of my inner thighs. I tremble violently in the silence that follows, waiting for the final millimetre, waiting for him to discover how wet I am. For him to make this moment flip from the pretend to the real. I'm nanoseconds away from pushing myself onto this thumb. I ache and strain for the release I know will come.

But then his hands move away. He grabs both of my thighs with both of his hands and, in a powerful, sudden movement, runs them down the length of my legs in one glorious, smooth wet stroke. It's so unexpected and so strong, it's as if he's pulling the orgasm out of me. I open my mouth and gasp, my head exploding in a thousand stars as his hands move down past the backs of my knees and my shins.

He does the same thing to my legs three times and then flicks the sweat off the bottom of my soles, as if he's flicking away energy, and each time my orgasm rolls over me like a wave. A giant tsunami of a wave.

'There,' he say, satisfied. 'Better?'

Does he know what's just happened? Does he know that he's just given me the most extraordinarily intense orgasm? Of a kind I've never, ever had before?

I can't move. My mouth presses dumbly into the towel.

'That's me done,' he adds. His voice is hard to read. 'You look less tense already.'

He's got to be kidding, right?

That's it? Just like that, he's going? Is he really going to pretend he doesn't know what just happened?

I turn slightly and see him grab the towel. He ties it around his waist and tucks the end in, before turning towards me, but he can't hide the huge bulge beneath the towel. My throat is completely dry, my insides clenching with desire. I just want to rip the towel off. I just want to see his huge erection. I want to hold it, lick it, taste it, fuck it. The proof is right *there*, but so out of bounds.

'Take your time,' he tells me. 'You can stand it more than me.'

And then he opens the door and he's gone, in a blast of cold air.

I hit my forehead on the wooden slats.

43

The next morning I'm still trying to work out what happened. I've been in a headlock of confusion all night. On the one hand, there's the quite overwhelming fact that Edward Parker massaged me naked in the sauna and gave me the best orgasm of my life. And on the other, that actually, as far as he's concerned, *nothing happened*. Except everything did. My head goes: we had sex, no we didn't, we had sex, no we didn't. It's exhausting.

As I make my way downstairs, I glance at the nudey bronze man and the framed artworks on the wall and try and put my finger on how it can be that Marnie and Edward Parker live like this. How can they function normally with such a crazy undercurrent of sexuality going on all the time?

But then, maybe I'm just not used to Americans. Maybe my Englishness makes me naturally more uptight. Maybe their art holds the key. Maybe their sensuality is just part of them, part of their artistic nature, and I'm just picking up on it, like the cultural novice I am.

What is increasingly clear to me is that they live their lives on a different level from anyone I've met before. People like Dad and Scott and Tiff are of an altogether different class. And it's not just to do with money. It's to do with an aesthetic. The mundane level of life that my people settle for and call happiness isn't even on the bottom of the Parkers' radar of enjoyment.

I hear voices as I approach the kitchen.

'There you are,' Marnie beams, as I come into the kitchen. She marches over to me and claps her hands, then gently strokes my cheeks, back to her usual tactile, lovely Marnie ways. Her eyes sparkle as they stare into mine, as I try to cover my shock. I can't help but smile at her.

I had no idea she was back in the house. Was she here last night when I was in the sauna with Edward? I couldn't find him, after I'd come out of the sauna and doused myself in a shockingly cold shower. I guess he must have gone to one of the 'red rooms'. His study, perhaps. Or maybe he was with Marnie all along. This house is just so weird. The way it can swallow people up and hide them.

I glance over to where he's sitting at the breakfast bar, sipping a coffee. He munches a piece of toast and doesn't look up from his iPad. Just seeing him sitting there in a white T-shirt makes me flush. I can't stop thinking about his naked bum and his hands. Oh my God. His hands.

'Morning,' I say to them both.

It's the first time I've seen Marnie since I danced for her, and even though she's being so friendly now, I can't help remembering her laughing as I scuttled away along the corridor in my half-undress, tripping over myself. I'm determined to try and regain my professional status with her. She's not remotely embarrassed about it, so I guess neither should I be. Certainly her wide-eyed, innocent grin betrays nothing of what happened between us the other night.

'You're OK?' she checks.

As I meet her eye, I'm pretty convinced her comment is not loaded and that she has absolutely no idea what happened in the sauna last night. But why would she? Edward didn't know either, did he?

'Uh-huh. Fine, thanks,' I reply, with a deceptive smile. This is all just so weird. I cover up how freaked out I feel by opening the cupboard where the cereal boxes are kept.

She's wearing a blue leather pencil skirt cinched in at the waist and a printed T-shirt with a kind of rock band-thing slogan on it and a collarless leather jacket. She has heavily made-up eyes and pale lips, and she looks like she could step right into a magazine.

She grabs her coffee and takes a quick sip. She's obviously in a hurry.

'So, will you get there at around eight?' she says to Edward, going over to the breakfast bar. She leans down behind him and kisses his cheek, expertly commanding his attention.

From behind the door of the open cereal cupboard I spy on them. I realize, with a jolt, that I've never actually seen them together before. I haven't let myself imagine it, but now that I see them here, in this mundane domestic setting, I see something I hadn't expected: they're perfect. Portrait-picture perfect. Side-by-side like this, they're bizarrely matching: a male and female version of the same beast.

And right here and now, I see what I haven't wanted to believe, that *of course* Edward is innocent. He didn't *intend* to give me an orgasm at all. It was all my own stupid fantasy again.

He has Marnie. Desirable, sexy, amazing Marnie. Why

would he even look at me twice? Why would he even consider me, a lowly employee, in a sexual way at all? I'm a clotheshorse, at best, I remind myself. Someone who drunkenly threw herself at her boss.

He jolts out of reading, and almost subconsciously lifts his hand to stroke the side of Marnie's head, a gesture so familiar it makes my heart ache.

'Huh? What's that?' he asks.

'Ed,' Marnie chastises. 'I've told you ten times . . .' She stands back, puts her hands on her hips and then rolls her eyes at me, as I shut the cupboard and put the cereal box I'm holding on the counter. 'The party. You remember. The party. My set . . . ?'

Edward sighs and rubs the bridge of his nose, then pulls an embarrassed face. 'That's tonight?'

'Uh – yeah,' Marnie says, not amused.

'Shit, shit, shit!' he swears. He's genuinely annoyed with himself. 'Sweetheart, I can't,' he implores her.

She cocks her head at him, exasperated and disappointed.

He makes a helpless noise. 'Lloyd's in town. We have dinner at the club with the investors. I totally . . .' He puts his hands out. 'My screw-up. I'm sorry. I'll make it up to you.'

I can tell from the crestfallen look on Marnie's face that it's a big deal. He stands and takes her in his arms. They fit like a pair of lovebirds. He whispers something in her ear and I watch his hand ruffling the back of her hair, like he loves the feel of her neck. The same hand that massaged my inner thigh, just hours ago . . .

I turn away, my cheeks pink. I tip some cereal into a bowl, but my hand is shaking.

'I know,' I hear him say, his voice loud and bright. 'Why don't you take Miss Henshaw?'

I look up to see that Edward and Marnie are both staring at me, although Edward's look is dark and unreadable. 'You'd like to get out of here for a while, wouldn't you?' he asks me.

This is such a loaded question, I don't know how to answer.

'Yes, God, yes,' Marnie says. 'Of course. Of course you must come.' She strides confidently towards me with a grin. 'Poor Miss Henshaw. I feel like we've totally neglected you. Like you're a little bird we haven't fed. You come with me and let loose a while.'

A caged bird. Is that how she thinks of me?

'Where?' I ask.

'Baby, you're coming partying with me. We'll leave Mr Boring behind.' She playfully sticks her tongue out at Edward, then pushes the bowl away from me. 'There's no time to eat. You can grab something in town.'

She links arms with me and sweeps me out of the kitchen. I feel Edward watching us go.

44

I do need to get out of the house. The second we get through the gates, my sense of claustrophobia lifts and I realize that Marnie's description of me as a caged bird was more accurate than I thought.

At the last minute Mrs Gundred comes with us and we both sit in silence as Marnie talks on her mobile. Gundred's an odd fish. She rattles away on her laptop and entirely ignores me.

I focus instead on Marnie and, as I hear her talking to a friend on the phone about the party and how she's been practising her set, I start to feel part of something cool and exciting. I'm so grateful she's brought me with her. I'm so grateful that I have something to occupy my mind, other than my obsessive thoughts about Edward. As I look at Marnie laughing, watching her reflection in the window of the limo as she laughs, I feel such a huge sense of retrospective shame about my secret orgasm. What would Marnie think if she knew how desirable I find her husband?

I think about Edward at home alone in the house right now. Did he deliberately want me to go with Marnie today so that we wouldn't be alone together? What would have happened if we were? Would we be able just to hang out together? Pretend nothing happened last night?

As we arrive in the city, I make a resolution. I'm going to stop my stupid, girlish crush on Edward and focus on the future and my role as the Parkers' nanny. I will avoid any situation in which I'm alone with Edward and keep our relationship strictly formal.

I owe it to Marnie. Sweet, kind, attractive, bubbly, vivacious Marnie. I will not let her down. I won't do anything to jeopardize her marriage or complicate her relationship with Edward. My crazy, abandoned moment in the sauna with him will remain a secret.

So. Decision time. My crush on Edward stops right here and right now. I'm so excited by my resolve, I almost blurt it out to Marnie.

We stop on a Manhattan street that seems vaguely familiar. And then I remember. This is where Marnie's shop is. I look expectantly through the limo's window for the shop front, my attention caught by the crowd of fashionable people on the street. I want to pinch myself. I'm in New York but, unlike the other night when I was meeting Edward, this feels much more real and tangible. I'm actually going to be able to get out and take a look around.

Mrs Gundred leaves the car, without a word to me or Marnie, and walks inside a dark doorway. Is that the lingerie and 'intimate collection' emporium? I would have thought someone as uptight as Gundred would be shocked, but she's obviously something to do with Marnie's business. I wonder if she's ever had a go on one of Marnie's vibrators. I sincerely doubt it.

'OK, listen up,' Marnie tells me, when she's finally finished her phone call with a flurry of ciaos and air-kisses. She takes out a wallet from her handbag and grabs a bundle of notes. 'Take this,' she says, pressing it into my palm. 'My treat. Although *don't* tell Edward. Go to José's boutique in the Meatpacking District. You'll find it. Everyone knows José's. Tell André, or JoJo, that I sent you and they're to find something for you to wear tonight. They'll understand.'

I stare at the money in my hand. 'Really?'

Is this my pay cheque? Is this the money for the first week? I want to ask.

'Take it, take it,' Marnie implores, wrapping my fingers around the notes. Then she takes a leather pad from her handbag and rips out a cream page. In fountain pen she writes an address and a mobile number. She smiles at me. She looks like she feels sorry for me. 'Listen. I want you to take the day. You don't need to be back here till much later on. I'm going to be tied up all day. Take in the sights. Do the tourist thing, if you want.' She grins at me.

'But . . .'

'Here's my number and the address of the shop,' she interrupts, handing me the piece of paper. 'Call me if you get lost or need anything.'

I stare at the note and the money in my hand. She wants to get rid of me, I can tell, but she's being so generous, I can't help grinning.

'Go go go, little bird.' She shoes me away, opening the door. 'Go explore the city. Go have fun.'

And right there and then I realize that I am like a little bird, and at last I'm free.

45

New York is simply dazzling, although I have to admit that it's quite overwhelming on my own.

The day is so perfect, I hum that Lou Reed song I love on a loop. The sun is shining, the trees are in bloom, the city is breathtakingly beautiful and I can't help but soak it all up – the street buskers, the pigeons, the yellow cabs, the subway signs. It's all vaguely familiar from TV and films, but the vibrancy, the feeling that everyone is on the move here, everyone is living an interesting life, a million stories being played out all around me, takes my breath away.

I take a cab to Central Station, just to look inside, then go to the Empire State Building and queue up to ride in the elevator to the top and chat to an old couple from San Francisco who are here on their Golden Wedding anniversary trip. I write a postcard to Ryan and Dad when I'm at the top of the tower looking out over Manhattan, watching the cruise ships in the distance on the Hudson. The Statue of Liberty looks tiny. Like a piece on a board game.

It's a sweltering day and I take a break in Central Park on a bench in the shade. I consider calling Tiff, even though I know it will cost a fortune. Being on my own, surrounded by tourists and regular New Yorkers going about their business, has made me feel more normal than I have done in days. It makes me remember that this is the holiday at the start of my new adventure, and she'll be at home wondering what's happening to me. I want to share New York with her, but I feel too overwhelmed to describe it.

I stare at the phone in my hand. I know what will happen if I call. She'll fill me in on the fallout from the scandal of me dumping Scott. She's bound to know, from the crowd down the pub, what's going on. I bet he's been slagging me off and I know she'll be desperate to tell me if he has, but I don't want to hear it.

What I want to tell her is about Edward and my orgasm in the sauna. If I manage to tell her what happened, it might stop being such a big deal, but even as I think about describing it to her, I realize how wrong I'll sound. How deluded.

I buy a burrito from a stall and the Mexican lady chats to me. She asks if I have a boyfriend, as she loads up my burrito with pickles. When I tell her I'm newly single, she says that being alone in Central Park is a perfect way to start a romance with a total stranger, but even as she says it, I think she probably tells everyone that.

I take a horse-drawn carriage around the park with some Japanese tourists who have a spare seat, but all the while I feel entirely separate, like I'm watching a film montage of myself in New York and I'm not actually here at all.

In the afternoon I buy a guide and find my way to the Meatpacking District, asking directions in three cafes until I reach the brightly lit, open windows of José's boutique.

It's achingly cool inside. Even the shop assistants look

like they've just stepped off a catwalk. Music thumps out, while the shoppers feign total disinterest as they browse the minimalist rails. Everything I look at has a chunky security tag on it.

I find JoJo at the back of the store. I thought I would be finding a woman, but JoJo is a man. He has a Mohawk dyed blue, and a shaved head and pierced nose, and he's wearing three-quarter-length brown check trousers with DM boots. He should, in theory, look like a clown, but he looks totally hip.

He surveys me up and down in my white T-shirt that Edward gave me and the red shorts. I'm wearing my Primark pink pumps, as I knew the sandals would give me blisters. Just from one twitch of his eyebrow stud, I can tell it's a huge fashion faux pas.

When I explain that Marnie Parker sent me, his eyebrows shoot up.

'Is that so?' He has long, languid, slurring speech. I get the impression that he is wondering what the hell he can do with me. 'Come out back. I have some pieces to show you.'

Out of the glare and glamour of the shop, amongst the boxes and hangers in the storeroom, there's a makeshift changing room with three outfits hanging up. Two I turn my nose up at immediately, as far too grungy. The third is a purple leatherette dress. I guess the style would be 'prom queen meets cavewoman' if you had to describe it. There's a strapless bodice and tight-fitting skirt with slashes and kilt pins. There's no way I can wear a bra with it, so I don't think it will work, but JoJo forces me to try it on.

I shuffle out of the changing room in my bare feet and he looks at me, before bunching in the material under my armpit and putting a pin in it.

'We can work with this,' he says. 'Definitely. The colour's great with your hair.'

Working with the outfit means altering it to fit entirely to my shape. Half an hour later, I'm laden with purple platform shoes that perfectly match the dress, a kind of diamanté-studded neck choker and a leather wristband thing.

It costs nearly the whole amount Marnie gave me, but then I had a feeling it would.

I swagger down the street with my designer shopping bags, pretending that I'm in *Sex and the City*, relieved that my outfit for tonight's party will work.

I'm so absorbed in mentally working out what I have to do in order to be ready for the party that it takes me a second or two to realize that someone is calling out to me from the other side of the street.

46

It's him. It's that guy from the party the other night with Edward. The reporter. Harry.

Fuck!

It looks like he's been dining at the restaurant opposite José's at a table outside. I look up to see him waving wildly, before wiping his face with a napkin, chucking some notes from his pocket on the table and running after me.

I hurry down the street, away from him, my head ducked down. I don't want to talk to him. I have nothing to say to him.

Edward's face looms in my mind. How he was at the party when he found me with Harry. How furious he was that I'd talked to him. And I remember Harry, too, and his crazy, inaccurate insinuations. The Parkers are lovely, kind and generous, artistic people. How dare he try and put poison in my mind.

'Taxi!' I yell, putting my hand up, and a yellow cab swerves across the lane of traffic to stop next to me. Relieved, I open the door and chuck in my bags. I'm about to close the door when Harry appears, panting next to me on the kerb. He holds the door.

'I thought it was you,' he says with a grin.

'Please go away,' I implore him.

I catch the cab driver's eye in the mirror.

'Don't be like that, Princess,' Harry says. He leans forward and claps the cab driver on the shoulder as he clambers into the back of the cab. 'We're all fine here,' he assures him.

We're not fine, but the cab driver is moving away from the kerb.

'Where to, Ma'am?' he asks.

I stare at Harry.

'Tell him,' he shrugs. 'I'm going where you're going.'

I dig out Marnie's piece of paper, positioning my body away from Harry's, so that he can't see it. I mumble the street name on the piece of paper she gave me.

The cab driver squints at me in the rear-view mirror, concerned.

I sit back in the seat and bite my lip.

'Well, this is nice,' Harry says, grinning at me. He's the kind of guy who likes to be deliberately annoying.

'What do you want?' I ask him in a hushed whisper, getting as far away from him as I can along the sticky black seat.

'There's no need to be hostile,' he says, turning in his seat to face me and spreading his arm out along the back of it towards me. 'I thought it would be nice to catch up.'

'I don't know you. I don't like you. I don't want to speak to you,' I tell him. I need to be clear. Set my boundaries.

'Fair enough. You've had your briefing. I understand that,' he says, not in the least offended by my rudeness. 'I'm just concerned for you, that's all.'

'I don't need your concern,' I snap, but I still feel a shiver of alarm. My *briefing*. He's right. I have been briefed.

'But that's where you're wrong,' Harry says. 'You do. You don't know what you're messing with, Miss . . . ?'

He stares at me expectantly, wanting me to say my name. I fold my arms and stare out of the window.

'Oh, come on,' he says, 'gimme a break.'

He puts his hands out and appeals to the cab driver, who smiles at him, clearly both confused and amused by the scene playing out in the back here. I get the impression that he's on Harry's side, not mine.

'Henshaw. Sophie Henshaw,' I say quietly.

'Sophie. I like that,' Harry says.

I shake my head and grit my teeth, annoyed that I've given him this piece of information. Annoyed that I'm in this situation at all. I don't know a living soul in the whole of America, apart from the staff at Thousand Acres, Edward and Marnie Parker and him. And yet here he is. What are the chances? He knows it, too. He looks like the cat that's got the cream.

'You made quite a splash in the press the other night,' he says, sitting back in his seat. Despite myself, I hear it as a compliment. He saw the pictures then, but why is he so interested?

I don't say anything. The cab drives on another block.

'I'm surprised you're back in town so soon. Must be a special occasion if you're shopping in José's,' he says, nodding to the bags at my feet.

'I have a party to go to,' I tell him, before I can help myself.

I regret it immediately, but tell myself that I haven't given too much away.

'Is that so,' he says. I can tell he's absorbing the information, using it, like the rat he is.

'Please. Can you just leave me alone?' I ask him, hoping to appeal to his good side.

He stares at me, frowning. 'You really have no idea, do you?'

'No idea about what?'

'Listen, I don't know what your connection to Edward Parker is. You might be his mistress, you might not be. But let me tell you. You're playing with fire.'

God, he's irritating. If he has some beef with the Parkers, why doesn't he come right out and say it? Why be so cryptic and annoying?

'And what business is it of yours?' I snap. 'Exactly?'

'Trust me. I know things that you don't know.'

'What things?'

He gives me a sly smile. 'Not so easily done,' he says. 'I'll tell you my secrets, if you'll tell me yours. If I snag the kiss-and-tell on the Parkers, it would make my career.'

I stare at him, astounded by what he's just said. What he thinks I might do.

'Can you pull over, please?' I ask the cab driver.

'Ma'am?'

'This man is getting out just here.'

I glare at Harry, hoping he'll take the hint. How dare he suggest that I would betray the Parkers? How dare he think I'm the kind of person who would even consider it? How desperate does he think I am?

'Goodbye,' I say pointedly, opening the door onto the sidewalk and gesturing for him to get out.

He grins at me as he climbs over me. I pull my knees around to the side, like he might contaminate me if he touches me.

'I'll catch you later, Sophie Henshaw,' he tells me with a grin.

'I hope not,' I say.

He closes the door and taps the top of the cab.

'He sure has the hots for you,' the cab driver says.

47

Marnie's offices aren't like offices at all. I don't get to see the shop, but go straight up to the open-plan space where the designers hang out. I'm early, but it doesn't seem to matter and I'm glad to get a sneaky peek into what Marnie actually does.

I meet Kay and Brendan, two of her designers, who seem entirely unfazed by my presence. I watch them as they work on large desks, discussing fabric samples and a photoshoot that is coming up. There are mannequins everywhere in various lingerie outfits. Some have normal underwear, others Marnie's burlesque-style collection. To me, they look wonderful. If I could afford it, I'd have every single piece on display.

Not that I'd ever have cause or occasion to wear them, I remind myself. But how amazing would it be, to be that rich and have the kind of lifestyle that you could treat yourself to lingerie like this? I try and fast-forward into my fantasy future and visualize myself in a swanky penthouse somewhere, but just as soon as the image forms, it pops with my thorny self-doubt. This is *me* we're talking about. How would *I* ever get to be like *that*? But that's the whole point of the lingerie, I guess. The promise it captures.

There's a palpable buzz about the photoshoot. I help to move desks out of the way, when some guys arrive to deliver the most amazing velvet furniture, which Marnie is delighted with. Then lighting crew arrive and put up a grid, wiring it up from the ceiling. There are workmen everywhere.

There's a runner, Keilan, who is cute; and then there's Marnie herself, who around nine o'clock suddenly remembers the party. She shouts to everyone to get ready soon, and shortly afterwards there's a bottle of Grey Goose vodka out. Her whole crew in the studio are coming to the party and, as the music thumps, I can tell it's going to be a crazily fun night.

I see Roberta, who made me up for the party with Edward, who gives me a big hug and fixes my make-up. It feels like one big, happy family and I forget all about Harry. No wonder Marnie often stays in town. This feels so far removed from Thousand Acres and her life there.

The party is only a few blocks away, but after we've got ready, Marnie makes us all pile into the limo to get there, and I feel like we're in a Katy Perry video. Marnie's wearing tiny shorts and a cropped T-shirt with a diamanté slash on it and a tiny top hat. She's so excited about her set, it's hard not to get pumped up too. Before we arrive, Keilan takes out a little pillbox and gives everyone in the limo a little white pill.

'A little livener?' he grins.

Marnie takes one, so I take one too, when he offers them to me. I have no idea what they are, or what they'll do to me. I'm vaguely aware of how irresponsible this it, but I'm with Marnie and her staff. How bad can it be? For all I know, they're breath-fresheners. Except, as soon as I swallow it, I know they're not.

The party is in full swing when we arrive. It's in a big club and there is an infrared-lit tunnel leading into it, which makes everyone's teeth go purple. Marnie grabs hold of my arm, teetering in her high-heeled patent boots. I glance at her white T-shirt and see her breasts clearly outlined below it, her nipples dark shadows beneath the white cotton.

As we arrive in the roaring noise of the club, she throws up her arm and whoops with delight. I hear a whoop from the crowd below. Marnie has arrived, and everyone knows it.

It feels great to have her arm looped around my shoulder, like I'm her partner in crime.

And she thought she was old! She's a total diva, more like.

In the DJ booth I sit and watch her wait her turn. I lean up against the speaker, feeling the bass of it throb through me. Keilan arrives and hands me a tall vodka drink and asks me to come to the private table he's got downstairs, but I'm suddenly high and I want to dance.

I join the crowd in the middle of the floor and stare up at the DJ booth as Marnie comes on. We shout and whoop and hop around, like we're her most ardent groupies, and soon the whole place is rocking out. She plays her ambient music, but with a big beat and it's so much fun to dance to. I've never, ever had so much fun. I feel so honoured to know her. So flattered to be part of her tribe, especially when she gives a shout out to us on the PA system and points at me. She's pointing at me from the booth, and I blow her a huge kiss and punch the air.

I'm sweating and entirely lost in the music when I spot that she's left the DJ booth, and I wonder where she's gone; and then I see her arrive on the dance-floor.

The crowd parts for her and she throws up her arms and dances. I see her wriggling her hips and I'm amazed by how young she looks. She could be a teenager. My God, if I get to look like her – be like her – when I'm her age, it'll be incredible.

Friends and fans greet her, and Marnie screams with delight when she sees each one. I carry on dancing, but I can't take my eyes off her. I see the curve of her waist, as she wriggles and writhes. She's so sexual, and sensual, too. A kiss here, a hug there, a hip-grind and smooch. She's loving every minute.

Finally she reaches me and beams at me. I look at the tiny gap between her teeth. Her eyes are dramatically made-up, but even so I see myself reflected in her giant dilated pupils as she squeezes up against me.

'Hey, baby. How's my little bird?' she asks.

'You were brilliant,' I tell her. I mean it, and she knows it.

She smiles, pressing herself against me as we dance. I feel her hot leg sliding against the inside of mine. I know people are watching, but I don't care. It's fun to be raunchy-dancing with Marnie Parker. I feel completely abandoned, like we're the hottest chicks in the club and everyone knows it.

She puts her arms over my shoulder and stares down at

me, like she owns me. Then she leans in, her mouth against my ear.

'I like watching you dance. I liked it the other night.'

I'm so surprised she's mentioned it that I blush. I remember how she spoke to me when we were last pressed together like this.

Hey, you.

I remember her saying it. How she looked. How I thought afterwards it wasn't real, but it was. Because, as she pulls back and stares at me, she looks the same now. I see the question in her eyes.

'Did you get my gift?' she asks me.

Somehow she's shrunk the room. I can only stare into her eyes. I forget the crowd, the DJ, the drinks, the dances. I only feel myself in her arms.

'Did you like it?'

I nod. 'I loved it,' I tell her. I feel brazen saying it. I want to tell her what I did with it. How I thought of her when I made myself come.

Suddenly, she grabs my hair and pulls my head back and stares right into my eyes, like she's trying to see inside my head. For a second I think she's going to kiss me, and I feel a sharp stab rush through me. I don't move. I can't move.

'Are you brave enough?' she whispers.

For what? I want to ask, but I know. I think I know, anyway. She's asking if I'm brave enough for what she's offering me. Whatever that is. But it's something unknown and forbidden. I know that much. I know that's what she means. I want to tell her yes. I feel 'yes' screaming through me, although

I feel terrified in a way I haven't ever felt before. Because she's asking me to be a different person and she knows it. But even in not replying I feel she's dragged me a little way down an entirely new path with her. That she's opened a door.

And then the moment is gone as quickly and momentously as it arrived.

She smiles then. 'Not quite brave enough,' she says. 'Yet.'

Then she winks and breaks away from me, leaving me trembling.

48

I watch her go, feeling the deliberateness of how she's teased me. I feel her delight radiating out of her, as she ignores me. I watch her dancing away from me, swallowed by a sea of bodies and arms, a swirling, thumping, rocking mass of bodies, and I feel hot with jealousy.

I don't know what to do. It's too late now to follow her and, after what she said, I can't, without it being some sort of statement. Some big acquiescence to . . . what? I don't know. But something. Something scary between me and her.

But at the same time I don't stop hoping that she'll come back. I scan the people dancing around me, longing to see her blonde hair. Longing for her to appear through the crowd with that grin on her face.

But with each passing second, her look – her question – continues to burns through me. I dance, crushed up against strangers, but I feel all alone and shaky. Like something has happened, when nothing has. It's 'the strange disquiet of a shaken conscience' – a line from a poem I read, bouncing around now in my mind, as I jig to the music, but I'm hardly listening.

She'll come back, I tell myself over and over. She'll come

back and make everything normal. She's just playing with me. She doesn't really want me *that way*, surely? That's just Marnie trying to shock me.

But is it? Is she suggesting that she and I get it on? It's a laughable, preposterous idea and yet, when I'm with her, it seems so real. And that's what scares me.

She's right. I'm not brave enough to answer her question. I've been so freaked out by my feelings towards Edward, but they are innocent compared to the hot confusion Marnie makes me feel. And it's all so frustrating and intangible. It's like she can suddenly flip into being this other person – who is nothing to do with everyday, normal life. And when I get a glimpse of that, I'm like it, too. Like I forget everything: that I'm her nanny, I'm her employee, living under her roof, eating her food . . . fantasizing about her husband.

When I do see her next, she's back up at the DJ booth. I stare up at her. She's with a young black guy, and immediately I think of the picture I saw by the wall in the gallery back at Thousand Acres. Is it the same model? He looks like a model. He's wearing skinny sexy trousers and an open shirt, and even from down here I can see his six-pack stomach glistening. She has her arms around his neck and she's staring at him. All I can think about is the picture.

I stop dancing in the middle of the dance-floor and stare upwards, watching her. Watching her reeling him in with her eyes. He's staring right at her. I see him physically pulling her towards him, his hands on her bum, and I know from the smile that she can feel his erection through his trousers and that she hasn't pulled away.

I feel my heart pounding as I watch him bend down and his lips kiss hers. They stay there for a long moment, then she pulls away and laughs, putting her arm up and dancing away from him, but he's entranced. He grabs her, circling her from behind, pressing against her. She's squashed up against the bars at the front of the DJ booth. I see her eyes narrowed, smouldering.

Then she opens her eyes and stares down into the crowd below and her eyes lock immediately with mine. It's like she knows I was there all along, watching her.

She smiles at me and winks, then puts a finger to her lips, like she's telling me to shush. Like this is our secret.

Then the black guy is pulling her away and she's laughing as she's swallowed into the dark shadows.

I go to the bar and have a bottle of water to try and sober up, but my pulse is still racing.

What did that little display just mean? Why did she put her fingers to her lips to tell me to shush? To tell me to keep her secret, because that's what she was doing.

And the guy she was with? There was no mistaking what he wanted from her. What she'd promised him in that long kiss.

I'm totally confused and so shocked, but I can hear Marnie taunting me in my head that I'm little Miss Prim-and-Proper.

Does that mean she has an open relationship with Edward? Does he know that she's unfaithful to him? Is that why he's been flirting with me? Does that make what happened between us in the sauna OK?

I'm so lost in thought that I don't notice until too late that there's a guy standing next to me at the bar. He's staring at me.

Oh, for fuck's sake. It's him. It's Harry.

49

In the mass of sweating, half-naked dancing bodies he looks out of place in a black sweater. When I notice he's there, he grins at me and lifts his bottle of water to me in salute.

'I've been looking for you,' he shouts over the music. 'I thought you'd be here.'

I remember now that I told him about the party.

'Are you having a good night, Sophie?'

I'm annoyed that he's calling me by my first name. That he's presumed some kind of intimacy. I think of him telling me earlier that the Parkers are not what they seem. He's certainly been proved right, from what I've just witnessed, but even so, I still feel fiercely loyal.

'I heard Marnie was playing. I remember the old days, of course,' he shouts, a nod of his head, like he's one of the old-school cognoscenti.

What old days is he referring to, I wonder?

He nods his head to the music, pretending to enjoy it. I desperately scan the crowd of faces, looking for a familiar one, but all of Marnie's staff seem to have vanished. And now that Marnie has disappeared with that guy in the booth, I feel a stab of sobering fear. What if they've just left me here? What if Marnie has abandoned me on my own in New York to fend for myself?

She can't have done, I tell myself. She'll come and find me, I'm sure. I'm just going to have to wait it out. But in the meantime I'm stuck with Harry.

'I'm going to dance,' I tell him.

I dance until my legs ache. I find a group of people in the middle who are truly off their faces and, even when the music changes to some thumping techno that I normally hate, I don't stop dancing. I can't stop. Harry is sitting at a small table in a booth and doesn't stop watching me. If I stop dancing, he'll corner me. It feels like hours go by, but he still sits and watches me, and even though I try very hard to ignore him, his sly smile makes me know that he knows I'm not getting away with it.

Eventually I dance away out of his direct eyeline and, running to the corner booth, retrieve my tiny clutch bag. I get to the loos, where I dial Marnie's number, but I get a voicemail.

I realize that I don't have a number for Edward, or any real clue how to get back to Thousand Acres.

In desperation, I sneak out of the toilet cubicle and, checking to see that Harry isn't looking, slip outside.

To my colossal relief, Trewin is parked further along the kerb. He gets out of the driver's seat when he sees me, and I run on trembling legs towards him, worried in case Harry is following me.

'I think I should wait for Mrs Parker,' I tell him, breathlessly.

'That won't be necessary,' Trewin says.

'But . . .'

I stare out of the back of the limo window and see Harry coming out of the club and looking along the street for me.

Trewin pulls off from the kerbside as I duck down in the back. I sneak a peek and see Harry staring after the car.

There's no sign of Marnie.

50

There's no sign of Marnie the next morning, either, but Edward is home. When I arrived late last night, all the lights were out and I crept upstairs alone, but Edward is whistling when I go downstairs, and I pass Mrs Gundred in the corridor, who gives me a cold smile.

I hesitate before I enter the kitchen. Should I tell him? Should I tell him what I saw? Should I tell him about how flirtatious Marnie was? How I saw her kissing another man? How I lost her in the crowd and came home alone?

But I'm hardly an innocent snitch. I was involved in her deception of him, too. I think of Marnie, how I danced so suggestively with her and how she held my hair. I can't stop thinking about her eyes. The question she asked. The question I didn't answer, but the one that still makes me feel guilty. Like I've done something wrong. Like I've already somehow strayed somewhere forbidden.

'Good morning,' Edward says brightly, when he sees me.

He's wearing shorts and a pale-blue Fred Perry shirt and has shades in his hair. He looks refreshed and groomed and in an exceptionally good mood, which only makes me feel worse. I haven't had enough sleep and I'm feeling the effects

252

of all those vodkas. My feet are killing me from dancing in those purple shoes all night.

'I hear it was fun last night,' he says.

I'm confused. How would he have heard that, I wonder? Did Trewin tell him that he drove me back at four o'clock this morning? That I crashed out like a baby in the back of the limo?

I avoid his eye. I don't want him to ask me about Marnie, or where she is, when I have no answers. I don't want to land her in it, but in the cold light of day her betrayal feels monstrous. Why would she go off with that guy when she has someone as wonderful as Edward at home? I can't help the feeling that she only did it to annoy me, even though that makes no sense.

He is packing a straw bag and I watch him as he goes to the fridge to select some wine. Is he going on a picnic?

'Marnie said her set went well. She was nervous, although I guess you'd never be able to tell, if you didn't know her.'

'You've spoken to her?'

He looks at me, confused. 'Of course. She told me all about it when she got back last night.'

'She's here?' I ask in astonishment. 'She's back here?'

Edward laughs. 'Of course she is. She's in bed.'

'Is she? Are you sure?'

'Don't you believe me, Miss Henshaw?'

His tone makes me flush, but I deserve it. I did sound very rude.

'Of course, I'm sorry. It's just that I waited at the party . . .'

'She said you were having fun dancing. She didn't want

to drag you back home, so she left the limo for you and came back with me in my car.'

Marnie drove home with Edward, and left me at the party?

I know it shouldn't matter, but it does.

'I didn't realize,' I say, my voice catching. 'I waited. I thought . . .'

I shake my head. I don't know what to think now.

'But Trewin was there all along. You were perfectly safe,' Edward replies. 'She wanted you to have a good time. She says the boys will be here soon enough, and then there won't be any nightclubbing for you.' He laughs at me, like I don't know what's about to hit me, but I can't think about that now. About my impending responsibility.

Marnie really is home. I think of her dancing. I think of her on the balcony with the black guy, and realize it was all a facade. She came home with her husband.

Did she sit in that big green bed surrounded by candles and tell Edward about me dancing? The thought makes me irrationally furious.

'Did you meet anyone interesting?' Edward asks.

I can't work out the tone of his question. I wonder for a second if he knows about Harry.

'Not really. There were so many people there. I danced a lot.'

I sound surly and unfriendly, even to myself.

'I heard. Marnie says you're a great dancer.'

Does she? I wonder what else she's told him. I catch his eye and he smiles at me. Does he know about me dressing up in Marnie's room and doing a burlesque dance, or is that still our little secret? Just like Marnie kissing the guy last night is 'our little secret', I suppose.

I can't look at Edward. Instead I busy myself making a cup of tea, although I don't want one. I don't know what I want.

'It's a beautiful day,' Edward says.

I haven't even noticed, only having just got up. I want to go back to bed and pull the covers right over my head, but now I glance out of the open back door and see that the sky is a deep, clear blue. The green grass of the gardens is blindingly bright.

'I've got the day off,' Edward says, as I dunk my teabag in the hot water.

The day off what, I wonder? I look up at him, unsure of what he means and whether it has anything to do with me, but with the next sentence he crushes the vague glimmer of hope I have.

'I'm going sailing.'

'Oh. That's nice.'

'Do you like sailing?'

'I don't know. I've never tried it.'

Edward laughs. 'My goodness, Miss Henshaw, you're so green. There really is so much you've never experienced.'

I flush again, feeling foolish. I want to tell him to stop teasing me. That it's not my fault I come from where I do, that we never had any money, that my parents couldn't afford to drive us on holiday to the seaside, let alone give their children sailing lessons.

Edward sees that he's offended me. 'I'm sorry, that sounded

rude. I only meant that it's so wonderful to be young. To have so much ahead of you.'

I shrug. I should go, but somehow my feet won't move.

'Marnie hates sailing. She lets me indulge in my hobby occasionally, though.'

I wonder what else she lets him indulge in. I wonder why she hates sailing with him. I wonder why everything is so separate with them.

'I'm leaving soon for the coast. Would you like to come with me, Miss Henshaw?'

'Me?'

'Yes, of course you,' he says and then he smiles right at me. That smile. That intense, right-to-my-bone-marrow, attentive smile that sets loose and hot and fluid again all those feelings I'd resolved to harden into stone.

I clear my throat. 'Won't Marnie mind?'

'No. She says it's fine.'

So he's cleared it with Marnie, then? They've discussed me. They've discussed this . . . this plan?

'Ah. Sounds like our lift is here.'

And right at that moment I hear the sound of an engine and, staring through the kitchen window, I see that a helicopter is about to land in the garden.

51

As I run and grab my bikini and sun cream, I'm sure the noise of the helicopter must wake up Marnie. That is, if she's here. But I'm still not convinced that Edward is telling the truth.

As I run down the stairs, though, I hear Marnie in the hallway talking to him. I arrive downstairs, and she's make-up-less and wearing her red kimono.

'Have you got a hat?' she asks me, as I get to the hallway. The helicopter is loud through the open doors.

As she meets my eyes, she shows nothing. There's no mention of last night. No sign that just hours ago she was taking pills and grinding against complete strangers on the dance-floor, let alone kissing that lithe black man. She looks like a mum, asking a logical mum-like question.

'You sure you won't come?' Edward asks her. 'It's the perfect conditions.'

'*Gahd*, no. You know I get seasick.' She turns to me, pressing a large cotton hat into my hands. 'I can't stand it. And Edward is so bossy. Do you have sea legs?' she asks me.

'I don't know. I've only ever been on a ferry.'

'Well, you'll find out soon enough,' Edward says, laughing.

'You go. Have fun. I've got a ton of stuff to sort out here.'

'I can help. I told you,' Edward says, and it's like he could back out of the plan at any second.

'I'll be quicker without you here. Don't mind me. Don't forget Becca and Angelo are over later for dinner.'

'I'll be back. I promise,' Edward says.

He leans forward and kisses Marnie on the cheek. He squeezes her shoulder and she grabs his hand and kisses his fingers. It's such a sweet gesture, I turn away.

Oh my God. He has no idea. No idea what she's like when he's not around.

'Good luck,' she calls, but I don't know if she means for me or for him.

We get into the helicopter and I watch Marnie shielding her eyes on the terrace, her kimono flapping around her legs as we rise into the air. The house behind her seems much larger than I've even pictured in my head. I look down and see the willow trees and the lake. Further out, I see that Thousand Acres is surrounded by a high wall.

The wall's hidden from the house by the trees, but I'm shocked to see the scale of the fortified perimeter. They certainly have gone to some lengths to protect themselves.

I smile over at Edward, who is sitting squashed next to me. I have to clench my fist to stop myself reaching out to grab his hand, as the helicopter nose dips, then soars high above the fields and away to the east. I feel my stomach fall in that thrilling way it used to when Dad drove over the humpback bridge near Granny's house when we were kids, but I'm not sure if it's just the helicopter that's making me like that or because Edward is smiling back at me.

52

It takes about forty minutes before the helicopter lands near the coast. I stare out of the window down at the blue sea and the strip of yellow beach, the surf breaking onto it and the cars on the coast road, and grin over at Edward, excitement bubbling up in me.

I can see a big marina surrounded by low buildings and palm trees. It looks very exclusive. I'm nervous about landing and laugh about it with Edward, but we land with hardly a bump.

Running under the rotors, my hair whipping around me, my shirt flapping, we sprint over to a guy in a golf cart, who slaps Edward on the back and hugs him warmly. He's in his fifties and has that rugged outdoorsy kind of look that people who are on boats all the time must get.

The guy – I think it's Roly, but I don't catch his name properly, as there's such a racket from the helicopter – is obviously old friends with Edward and, as they bend their heads together to chat, it occurs to me that I haven't asked about the plan for the day. I've slept so little, and been so swept along with the excitement of the helicopter, that it didn't occur to me to ask. But Edward was already going sailing before he asked me. He must be meeting friends.

What if I'm just a spare part all day? How will he explain what I'm doing there? And will Roly be sailing with us?

I quell my childish disappointment. For one heady moment, I thought I might be alone with Edward for the day. But that is not going to happen. And even if it did, after the sauna incident, could I really trust myself with him?

We set off in the golf buggy towards the boats in the marina. Edward chats to the guy in the front and I hear them laughing, whilst I sit in the back with the picnic bag. I watch the helicopter rise into the air, and the ripples on the water.

Ten minutes later, we're bumping along a wide-slatted harbour jetty and I gawp at the power-yachts lined up on either side of us. I watch a small boy on one of the yachts fishing. Seagulls cry in the distance. It smells briny and of petrol, too.

Edward's yacht is moored at the end. It's a proper sailing dinghy with neatly folded navy sails and lots of shiny wood. Two deckhands are polishing the gleaming handrails on the deck. They jump onto the jetty and greet Edward warmly. I think they're going to come with us, but then I watch as Edward pays them both in cash and they stay on the jetty.

I get out of the golf buggy with the help of Roly, who respectfully takes my hand. He has kind, twinkly, sea-dog eyes.

'Have a great day,' he tells me.

'You're not coming too?'

'Oh no,' he laughs. 'There's been a change of plan.'

Has there? He nods down towards Edward.

'You'll be in safe hands, don't you worry.'

Edward is already on the yacht. I take off my flip-flops, seeing that his yacht-shoes are still on the jetty. He holds out his hand and I jump down towards him. I feel the hot teak boards beneath my feet. Edward waves to the deckhands as they throw up the rope that's mooring us. I sit in the small cockpit with the bag, marvelling at how competent Edward is, as he starts the engine and takes the tiller.

Oh my God. It's just us.

53

The breeze blows in my face as we move away from the jetty.

'Miss Henshaw, would you mind putting the wine in the fridge?' Edward calls to me, nodding to the door in the cockpit.

I open the small gates and negotiate my way down the three wooden steps into the galley below.

I know nothing about yachts, but I can tell this must be an expensive one, from the plush finish. It's all pale wood and there are blue-and-white cushions on the little benches next to a table. I search through the built-in cupboards until I find the fridge and unpack the picnic Edward has brought. I see that there's a lobster salad in a Tupperware pot. It looks delicious. There are also two bottles of white wine. I make a mental note not to get drunk, but then, who am I kidding? Against all my expectations, I'm alone with Edward in the sunshine for a day.

I can't even begin to work out how I'm feeling about last night and what happened with Marnie, but again I got the wrong end of the stick. I made a huge assumption, when everything was perfectly innocent.

And now we're here. I've been whipped away into a

different environment and all the rules have changed. I think for a second of FunPlex and how boring my life was back at home, how I longed for a changed to my routine and for something to happen. I've gone from that to this. It's ridiculous. I can hardly catch my breath, but it feels amazing. It feels like I'm fully alive for the first time.

This is so sweet of Edward to bring me sailing. I tell myself that I'm just going to enjoy myself and stop worrying about what it all means. Or, for that matter, what's going to happen, because clearly nothing is going to happen. This is perfectly innocent.

Back on deck, I hold onto my hat as we motor between the harbour walls and then we're out on the open sea.

Edward may be 'bossy', according to Marnie, but I'm fascinated by how the yacht works and what all the bits are for. Before long I'm winching in the sails and watching the wind fill them as the boat rocks over the sea. It's thrilling that we're moving on air power alone, and I yelp as the boat keens towards the sea's shining surface and grab Edward's shirt.

'Don't worry,' he laughs. 'We're not going to capsize.'

Even so, as the wind picks up, we both put on harnesses and I sit next to him at the back of the boat on the rail, our weight counterbalancing the boat as it slices across the waves. A plume of spray soaks me, but I don't care. It's exhilarating and I'm loving every minute of it. It feels like him and me together, battling the elements. Everything about Thousand Acres, Marnie, the boys, Scott, Tiff, Dad – everything is wiped clean out of my mind.

After an hour or so, the wind drops a little and we tack

in back towards the coast. Edward lets me have a go on the tiller and explains how the sails work, and before long I'm sailing by myself. It's the most incredible feeling.

Soon, though, the wind drops more and I look up at the cliffs as we head for a rocky cove, where the water is a deep aquamarine.

I loosen the sail and it flaps in the wind, and I laugh breathlessly as Edward shouts at me to put my back into it and winch in the sail. Finally, it's in and tied off, and Edward puts the engine on and we chug into the secluded inlet and weigh anchor.

Out of the wind, just us, the sun scorches my cheeks as I turn my face up to it. We could be in Greece or somewhere, the sun is so hot and the sea is so blue.

'Well done. You deserve a break,' Edward says, once the anchor is down. He jumps down into the cockpit. 'You're a natural sailor.'

'I love it.'

Edward swings down into the galley, missing the steps, and I watch him land, looking at his tanned feet from above. It's such a boyish gesture and I feel privileged to see him so much in his element.

He comes back up with the wine and two glasses. He grins at me as he hands the glasses to me so that he can pour the wine. Behind him, the water sparkles in the sunshine.

'So what do you think? Fun, huh?'

'Amazing,' I tell him, clinking wine glasses with him.

'You're a fast learner.'

'Do you sail by yourself? Isn't it a bit dangerous? I mean, I know you're experienced, but even so . . .'

'I usually sail with the boys or with Roly, who picked us up, but he couldn't make it today.'

I think back to the guy in the golf car – Roly, with the twinkly eyes. Was he busy? Or did Edward tell him not to come with us? I suspect it was the latter.

'You feel safe, don't you?' he checks.

'Of course.'

I do feel safe. This morning I thought it would be weird being alone with Edward after the sauna incident, but I'm so relieved to be away from the house and away from Marnie.

Once again, I think about Marnie last night and how she kissed that guy and how she was this morning, and I feel a surge of protection towards Edward. I watch him go back down to the galley and I hear him clattering around preparing lunch. He's so wonderful. How could Marnie possibly betray him?

'Do you like lobster, Miss Henshaw?' he calls.

'Why do you call me Miss Henshaw?' I ask, laughing and leaning down into the cockpit.

'You're my employee,' he says. 'Those are the rules. Rules are rules with employees,' he shrugs. But I'm wondering who made up the rules. And if *they* did, whether us being here alone on a yacht is breaking them.

'Fair enough,' I tell him.

But even as I say it, I suddenly get a flash of Mr Walters – or John as I later knew him. And how we broke the rules. How I deliberately made him break the rules. Because that's what I do.

54

The lunch of lobster salad and crusty French bread is delicious. We eat on deck, sitting casually, our legs up on the benches in the cockpit.

'It's getting hotter. We might have to have a swim soon,' Edward says as he spoons the last of the lobster salad onto my plate.

I nod, remembering him in his swimming trunks. I have my bikini with me today, but suddenly I feel nervous. I'm not sure I trust myself to be half-naked with him again.

We eat and chat and laugh easily, and soon the conversation turns again to last night.

For a moment I'm tempted to blurt out everything about Marnie. About how it felt like she'd propositioned me and how frightening I found it, but I don't. It's more complicated than that, and I don't think I could bear cross-examination on that point.

'It was good fun. We had fun,' I tell him.

'Marnie likes to be shocking,' Edward says. 'It's who she is.'

Did she tell him about dancing with me, then? Is that what he's referring to?

'She's very talented,' I venture.

'Isn't she? In so many ways.' He says this in such a resigned way that I suddenly think her behaviour last night is the tip of the iceberg. 'And very competitive. Especially with me.'

There's a pause. I watch the beads of sweat on his wine glass and how his finger lazily strokes them away. I wonder what he means, but I'm not sure how to ask him to clarify exactly how she's competitive with him.

'Marnie thinks I'm very prim and proper, but I'm not,' I tell him.

He laughs. 'I don't think she does. She thinks you're adorable.'

His eyes meet mine over the top of his sunglasses and I flush. Does *he* think I'm adorable, too? He doesn't say it.

'I think she thinks I'm a prude.'

I'm know I'm half-saying this for effect, because I like chatting like this. I like being the centre of his attention and making him laugh. Because part of me wants to deny Marnie, to make her out to be someone with a false impression of me, although the truth is she's got me spot-on.

'Well, I can't imagine you doing anything very shocking,' he says.

It's a challenge. I hear it as a challenge. I forget that I'm employed as his nanny. That being a safe pair of hands is why they've chosen me. Instead, I long for him to know that I can be daring and dangerous.

'I can be shocking,' I tell him, sipping my wine and looking at him over the top of my glass.

'Really? Then go, ahead, Miss Henshaw, shock me.' His

eyes dance with laughter. 'What's the most shocking thing you've ever done?'

I look at him. Actually the most shocking things I have ever done have happened to me in the past week. The orgasm he unwittingly gave me in the sauna was pretty shocking. I don't tell him this. Instead I shrug.

'Well . . . I had an affair with my teacher once,' I tell him, as if it's no big deal.

'Did you?'

I nod and pull a face. I feel foolish now for telling him.

'Go on . . .' he urges. 'What happened?'

'You don't want to know.'

'I do. I'm fascinated.'

So I start opening up. I give him the edited highlights of that summer. It seems lame in comparison to this, and what's happening right now, but I still spin a convincing yarn. I tell Edward about John Walters and how he was lost in the teaching profession. That he'd sung in a band once and I found his stories so appealing; how I identified with the fact that he felt misunderstood. As I'm telling Edward, though, it sounds clichéd. How can it not? I see amusement dancing in his eyes.

'The bottom line, though, was the danger. The fact we might get caught. I think that's what turned us both on.'

'And did you?' Edward asks. 'Get caught, I mean?'

I shake my head. 'No.'

'So what happened?'

'He couldn't handle it. He sort of fell apart. In the end we both had to walk away.'

'Were you heartbroken?'

'I thought I would be, but when it happened, I wasn't. I felt stronger, braver, because of what happened. People are so judgemental about that sort of thing. You know, the age difference,' I tell Edward. 'But the fact of it was that I was seventeen. I knew exactly what I was doing. I didn't get coerced into it.'

'Did you tell anyone?' Edward asks.

'Only Tiff, my best friend. And now you.'

'I won't tell anyone,' he says. 'Promise.'

Then he smiles at me and it's a smile that takes my breath away. I busy myself with sipping the wine, but I feel that hot electrical spark again. The same one I felt when I looked in the mirror in my room, that first day he inspected my back. The same one in the gallery. The same one we're both ignoring.

'How about a swim, Miss Henshaw?' he asks. 'I could do with cooling off.'

55

We jump off the back of the yacht in unison.

The water rushes up to meet me and it's surprisingly cold. I gasp for breath, start swimming on my back away from the boat, then tread water and wait for Edward. I look down at my legs. The water is so clear I can see shoals of fish below us.

A speedboat crosses the entrance of the little cove we're in, in a flash of white and foam. I'm reminded that we're not alone. A few seconds later, the swell in the water comes towards us, taking me unawares. A wave washes over my head and I gulp in water and cough.

Edward grabs me in the water and I'm suddenly pressed up against his chest. I can feel his legs moving below us and there's something about this – about his strength, his manliness – that makes every fibre of my being tune into this moment.

I'm fine, but he swims with me for a little way in his arms, then grabs onto the metal steps at the back of the yacht and guides me towards them, but I don't want to let him go. I feel his strong torso against mine. I feel my calves on the back of his thighs, where I'm clinging onto him. I feel the heat of his body, his muscles, the hair on his legs.

We've both reached the steps, but I'm still clinging onto him. I can see the water droplets on his cheek and the freckles on his nose.

And still I don't let go.

I feel his arm loosening, guiding me, but I just cling on tighter. He stares at me then, his eyes meeting mine, in surprise.

Our faces are inches apart. I can feel his breath.

'Miss Henshaw,' he says and my insides melt. 'Don't.'

Don't.

In that one word, my heart soars. In that one word, he acknowledges that there is a choice. That if I don't stop clinging onto him, everything will change. The choice will have been made.

So I make it.

I don't care any more. I don't care about anything other than this moment. That there's just the two of us, pressed together, in the whole wide blue ocean. Two individuals locked together whilst the rest of the world – the whole rest of the world – is somewhere else. Out of sight and out of mind. There are no consequences, only survival. And right now I might die if I don't find out what it's like to kiss him.

I dip my face towards his and close my eyes. I close the gap and feel the delicious fusion of my lips on his, feeling the heat of our bodies in the cool water.

I pull away after a second and stare into his eyes. I have no idea what he's thinking, but he doesn't let me go. He looks into my eyes and then at my lips, as if he can't believe I've just kissed him. I hear his breath catching.

For one second, I think he's going to pull away. That he's going to be horrified. The water swells around us, moving us. I brace myself to pull away, too, to deal with the avalanche of embarrassment I'll feel, and the consequences of doing what I've just done. But I don't regret kissing him. I don't regret taking the risk.

'You told me never to apologize for expressing myself,' I whisper.

It's too much. A step too far. I can see that as his eyes close.

I tense, starting to pull away, but then I feel resistance and his arm clamps around me. Fiercely. Possessively. And I know then that he's made his decision, too.

56

I hear him moan as we are carried on the swell and our kiss deepens. I wrap my legs around his hips and instinctively he presses against me. I can feel how hard he is beneath his shorts, and I gasp, pulling at his hair, my lips against his, desperate for him. And just as it was that first night I dreamt of kissing him, it feels so right. My mind is screaming . . . *Yes, yes, yes.*

But compared to my dream, this is a million times more vivid. A million times more wonderful.

He swings round to grab hold of both the steps and I'm crushed between him and them.

'Go up,' he breathes.

He turns and lifts me then, under my arm, to hoist me onto the steps, and I scramble up the three steps onto the ladder and up to the boat. My legs are shaking too much to stand up. Instead I sit down, scrambling backwards on the hot teak, waiting for him.

He follows quickly behind and slides off the top step onto the deck on top of me, and then I'm beneath him, and Edward Parker fills my vision.

I drink him in. Even having been swimming, he still has his distinctive scent and I'm enveloped in him. I've imagined him so many times this close to me, but now that this is happening – now that it's so thrillingly real – it's like everything that has gone before has been in black-and-white, and right now I'm experiencing colour for the first time.

Slowly now, he pushes my hair over my ears and stares at me. Then he lowers his head and kisses me again. I arch against him, desperate to feel as much of him as I can. I love the way he kisses. How his tongue flicks against mine. I grab his lip in my teeth and gently tug.

I hook my legs over his calves, hungry for the most contact that I can make, and grab his head, my hands in his hair. I feel the tops of his ears, wanting to kiss them, too. Wanting to kiss every part of him and claim him as my own.

He leans up on me, his elbows by my head, and stares down at me, his hair dripping onto my face. I can feel his hardness against my bikini bottoms.

He strokes my face.

'Sophie,' he says. 'Oh, Sophie.'

He's never said my name before and it's that, more than anything, that makes me realize in a sudden rush that this is as real for him as it is for me. That this isn't in my head or just a fantasy.

'At last. You said my name,' I murmur. Then I kiss him, deliciously, deeply and with absolute abandon.

And then we're both in a frenzy.

He moves down, gasping as he rips off my bikini top and sucks my nipple, and I'm lost. It's so erotic, like he's ignited a touchpaper and I'm burning up. I claw my hands into his hair, desperate to feel him. He kisses down my wet navel, pulling down my bikini pants in one easy move, and then his tongue is upon me, lapping at me, like he can't get enough of me. I lie back, my eyes flickering, watching the blue, blue sky, as waves of pleasure crash over me. I nearly come as I feel his fingers inside me. He knows exactly where to press, exactly where to stroke. I feel his thumb trace up the inside of my thigh, just like he did when he massaged me.

I don't want to come yet. I tear myself away, pushing his shoulders. He smiles up at me between my legs, then kneels up. I kiss him again, tasting myself on him, then slide my hand confidently inside his shorts and grip his thick girth. He feels so hot and smooth and gorgeous.

I take my hand out and undo the tie on his shorts and push them down, staring as his proud cock stands to attention against his flat, tanned stomach. It's even more beautiful than I'd imagined. Typical of Edward to have a model-perfect cock, I think, as I grip it tightly and lean forward, starting at the salty base and staring up into his eyes, as I flick my tongue up his length. He stares at me, his breathing a ragged hiss as I reach his tip and flip my tongue over the smooth, wet, delicious pinkness. It honestly feels like the most glorious thing I've ever put in my mouth.

I plunge my mouth over him, taking his shaft deep in my mouth, letting him fill me as far as I can. He leans forward, splaying my buttocks. I feel sun shining on me as he reaches for me. I'm dripping, desperate.

I slide back and forth, feeling his hot cock straining, then he gasps and pulls away. He pushes my shoulder gently and

I lie back, waiting for him. He leans down on me slowly and, as if it was always meant to be there, his cock is right at my opening. He brushes the hair out of my face and stares into my eyes as he pushes inside me. All I can see is his face, his huge, beautiful eyes and, behind him, the blue sky. It's as if every sense I have is fizzing. I gasp, reaching for him, holding his face and kissing him – snogging him – like it's the last snog of all time. I wrap my legs around him, pushing my heels into his buttocks, feeling him fill me up completely. It feels like every part of me is fusing with him. And I want him. All of him. Every last part.

He kneels up, still inside me, and smiles. Lifting one of my legs, he takes my foot and sucks my big toe, his eyes never leaving contact with mine. I can feel his balls against me, his cock right inside me, but the toe thing – that's all new. It's a whole other dimension.

'You are so goddamned gorgeous,' he says, as he runs his tongue in between my toes. His thumb presses into a point on the bottom of my foot that sends my pelvis involuntarily shooting up towards him. He smiles, knowledgeably. Then it's the turn of the other foot and I'm in raptures. I can hardly breathe.

'Not yet,' he whispers, gently lowering my foot.

He pulls out of me. His cock glistens in the sunlight. He stands and, for a moment, he's like a mirage. Like some kind of sea god, holding his hand down to me. I feel the sea, the sun, the glittering heat of it all blinding me.

I wonder where we're going, but wherever it is, Edward changes his mind, as if overcome with desire. He turns me round and grabs me, and I hang onto the metal rail at the side of the boat. I can see our reflections in the water as he bends his knees and then enters me from behind. His head is next to mine, his hands reaching around to cup and fondle my breasts. I think I might topple over, the boat gently swaying beneath us, but he's got me. I reach up behind me, stroking his hair, looking at our faces side-by-side in the watery reflection. I wriggle backwards onto him, wanting him, wanting him to fill me up. I gasp, lifted off my feet as he thrusts into me. Then one hand stays on my nipple, squeezing tightly, just as I like, as the other reaches down. I feel him rub his fingertips against my clitoris. I grab the back of his head, crying out as he speeds up and we both come.

57

Afterwards, an hour or more afterwards, when we're finally burnt out, I sigh as I look at the sky. As I lie naked in the sun in Edward's arms on the soft cushion of the cockpit, he traces the outline of my shoulder with his finger and stares at me as if I'm the most beautiful thing he's ever seen. I feel his eyelashes whisper against my cheek.

I stare at his nakedness, tracing my fingertip down the contours of his stomach, and look at the smooth skin of his now-soft cock, loving that I now know it. Loving that, after our frenzied first fuck, our second was so sensual. How we both watched, both trembling as I knelt over him and his shaft entered me, the base of it straining, my lips folding around it. How I felt his tight balls against my buttocks. How he sat up with an agonizingly pleasurable sigh and buried his face between my breasts, before kissing me and biting my nipples gently until I cried out. How I clasped my hands around his neck and rocked back on him.

It's been such a revelation, but I've discovered something so fundamental about Edward. Because now that I've shared my body with him, he makes sense as a person. That undercurrent of sexuality I've been feeling at the house is real. Because he exudes it from every pore, and I've seen how alive he becomes when he's making love, like every single part of his attention, his skill, his desire is focused. As if he, as a person, has been designed for lovemaking, and everything else that he does is a mere distraction.

It's so vivid in my mind that I still feel its aftershock, as I lie here naked in stillness, feeling like a goddess. I'm exhausted and spent, my mouth still sore from our non-stop kissing, but as the boat rocks gently on the waves I'm filled with a kind of peace I've never felt. I feel physically, emotionally and spiritually connected to him in a deeply profound way and I know that he feels it, too.

We're silent for ages and then he takes a breath in and slowly exhales. 'Oh, Sophie,' he mutters.

'I'm sorry,' I tell him, but my voice isn't sorry. I smile at him, tracing the line of his delicious lips. 'I started it. I couldn't help myself—'

He silences me with a kiss. 'It's not your fault,' he whispers. 'Do you think I haven't wanted you from the first second I saw you dancing across the room?'

'You have?'

'Oh my God, you've been driving me crazy, and then the sauna . . .'

I laugh. 'You knew? You knew what you were doing to me?'

'Sophie,' he says, like I'm being ridiculous. Like there's no need any longer for pretence.

'I was desperate for you to touch me.'

'I went as far as I could go. If you'd only turned round, you would have seen how ready I was for you.'

And I see now that he's been waiting for me. Waiting for

me to make the first move. That this always had to be my decision.

He kisses me as we laugh. Eventually, he pulls away.

'Stay there,' Edward says and quickly moves into the galley. I love watching him naked. I love the way his body is so natural and that I am seeing this amazing, intimate knowledge of him that nobody ever sees. He grins at me, his eyes sparkling as he disappears inside. 'Don't move,' he says, suddenly turning back and pointing a playfully stern finger at me.

I watch the space where he's gone, waiting for him to come back, and I resist the urge to punch the air. Because I feel like I'm triumphant. I've won, after all.

He does care. He does feel about me like I do about him. It wasn't all in my head. The relief, the elation, is indescribable.

He comes back with a bottle of water, which I drink greedily. He's got a pad and a pencil. I know Edward feels it, too, because he keeps glancing at me and smiling. A deep, satisfied smile that just makes me want him all over again.

'I want to draw you,' he says. 'I've wanted to since I caught you dancing.'

I settle into what I imagine, and hope, is a classical pose and I stare out to sea, feeling his attention as he stands, leaning up against the wooden wall of the cockpit with the pad and pencil. I want to speak, but there are no words to describe how brazen and wanton I feel. Like I'm Eve and I've just eaten the apple for the first time.

I want to savour every secret second of it.

I feel the breeze tickle across my nipples, making them hard. I breathe in the smell of the sea and the pungent smell of sex emanating from my skin, and the glorious moment lingers on and on.

Edward's forehead is furrowed in concentration as the pencil moves across the pad. He looks boyish in his intensity and, even though he's so much older and more sophisticated than me, right now I feel the power balance is all my way. It's a heady feeling.

When he's busy shading, I move, but he doesn't notice, he's concentrating so hard. I creep forward along the padded bench on all fours, and duck underneath the drawing pad and take his cock in my fist.

'What are you doing?' he says, laughing.

'If I see something unexpected, then I have to have it,' I tease, quoting him and remembering how he was in the gallery.

Edward laughs and then sighs as I lean forward and run my tongue around the soft edges of his balls. I feel the soft skin pucker against my tongue. He's hard now, his cock stiffening. I run my tongue up the length of it.

'Oh God, that feels good,' he says and I take the fat, delicious tip of him in my mouth, letting my lips caress and kiss him, like I'm snogging his cock. I make a low groan, running my tongue over the smooth, hard edge leading to his tip. He's too delicious.

I feel the pad fall away and I look up at him.

'What are you doing to me?' he whispers and smiles a soft smile down at me.

'Everything. I want to do everything with you,' I tell him,

resting him against the side of my mouth. I can see the blue sky behind his head. He has never looked more like a god.

58

When the wind picks up, the temperature drops and we hurry down below and squeeze up together in the shower cubicle in the cabin. He lathers up my hair and washes me.

He holds me close as the water dribbles over us.

'I'm sorry about that night,' he says, softly, stroking suds along my back. The way he touches me makes me feel like he's trying to memorize me. I've never felt more cherished.

'What night?'

'When I made you go to bed. I felt terrible. I realized that night what was happening. What was happening to me? How I felt about you and . . .'

I kiss him then. I'm so touched by his confession.

'It doesn't matter,' I tell him. Because it doesn't. Not any more. We are right here, right now in this moment. Together. That's all there is.

I remember then, him telling me that I would have a different view of sex once I had sex that had changed my life.

As I rest my head against his chest, clinging onto him, I know now what he meant.

And then it's happening again. I feel him stiffen between us and I caress him in my hand.

He twists me around and I lean up against the shower wall as he enters me from behind. I gasp as he fills me up, holding my arms up, his fingers entwining with mine. He bites my earlobe and I know that his is the only body I ever want next to mine for the rest of my life.

But already I know that the stopped clock has started again. That the delicious pocket of time we've had is over. That we're already racing towards an unknown future.

59

We don't talk about what has happened as we sail back, because the journey is rougher. The boat bucks and dips, like it is refusing to go back to reality, too.

Back in our clothes, I guess we look as if everything is as it was this morning, and yet everything has changed.

Now my body knows his, it's as if I can hardly bear the clothes against my skin. I want to be naked with him all over again. I put my hand over his on the tiller, running my fingers over his knuckles, memorizing the shape of the freckles on the back of his hand.

I sense our connection being broken as the harbour comes into view and I feel him tense. He starts issuing instructions about the sails.

When the last sail is in and the motor is on, and the boats come fully into view, I see the golf buggy coming along the jetty and I suspect there'll be the same efficient journey back to Thousand Acres, but I know it's going to take every ounce of my strength to step off the yacht and back onto land.

I think of the house, and of Marnie waving us off and of my room there, and I feel a sudden chill.

'What are we going to do?' I ask him. 'I mean, how will it be?'

He looks deep into my eyes. 'Oh, Sophie,' he sighs, but something in his tone sets alarm bells ringing. 'You have to know that this afternoon was magical for me. But I think we both know that it can't happen again. You understand that, don't you?'

I hear him say the words, watch his mouth move, but I can't believe him. I refuse to believe what he's saying.

'No. I don't understand anything any more. I don't understand how I can feel like this, when I've only just met you.'

I stare at him, my eyes welling with tears, and I see that he looks emotional, too.

'I'm sorry,' he whispers and I know he is. But that doesn't stop it being unbearable.

Surely it can't just be a one-time thing? It feels too monumental for that. And he knows I'm thinking that, because he leans forward and puts his forehead against mine.

'I feel it, too,' he says. His voice is husky. 'But we can't ever be together like that again. There's too much at risk. There's . . .'

He doesn't have to say it. He can't say it, and neither can I. There's Marnie, his kids and the fact that I work for him. And I know that he's saying it, but I refuse to believe it.

I refuse to believe that he can't ever be mine. That this is end, when it feels like the beginning.

60

The journey back in the helicopter is excruciating. I can't bear to be next to Edward and not able to touch him. He's stressed about the time, and that we're late back to the house. He speaks to Marnie on his mobile and I pretend not to listen, but he's his usual affectionate, charming self and she doesn't suspect a thing. His voice doesn't betray even the slightest hint of what has happened.

He sits in the front next to the pilot. We don't speak at all and, as the helicopter lands on the grass at the back of the house, I know I've missed my chance for any further communication. I can't look at him, as the pilot opens the door for me to get out and Edward offers me his hand as I jump down.

I see some people wave at us from the terrace. A couple. He has a pink cashmere jumper draped around his shoulders and she's wearing a proper cocktail dress and heels. She holds onto her skirt and her champagne glass, as the rotors of the helicopter cause a windstorm. I can tell they are laughing – thrilled by the novelty of their host arriving like this.

But, then, I guess they're used to it. These sophisticated people are Edward and Marnie's friends. The kind of moneyed, cultured people who inhabit their world. Seeing them here makes the dream of this afternoon shatter like a mirror.

'Hurry up, Ed,' Marnie chides him, as we run in through the kitchen door. She's wearing a light-blue translucent lace dress, which hugs her curves. She looks elegant and sexy at the same time. She's got a tray of hot canapés that she's about to plate up and the kitchen is filled with a delicious smell of roasting chicken. There's no sign of Mrs Janey. Marnie, the perfect hostess, is doing this all herself.

'Angelo's got the most hilarious story about the auction in Singapore. You'll die when you hear who was there,' she says to Edward, before reaching up and kissing him on the cheek.

I glance through the kitchen to where a door I've never seen open has been pulled back to reveal a chic dining room. The candlelit table has been laid up with immaculate china set for four. There's a beautiful flower arrangement in the middle and yet more fine artworks are illuminated on the wall. It's breathtakingly sophisticated. Another red room, then.

'You both look so sea-swept,' Marnie laughs, looking at us both.

My cheeks sting from sunburn and from something else, too. Something much more painful that she can't see. My eyes are tired from all the salt, and from the strain of not letting my hot tears fall.

'Do you want to join us?' she asks me. 'Dinner is nearly ready.' Her smile is open and friendly. She doesn't suspect a thing. But why would she? Why would she ever suspect that Edward would betray her with someone like me?

I shake my head. She's just trying to be polite, but I know she doesn't want me there. Besides, I can't sit around that table making small talk with Edward, Marnie and their friends. Not after what happened today.

'Thank you, that's really kind, but I'm going to take a shower.'

'What have you done to Miss Henshaw?' Marnie says, punching Edward playfully. 'She looks exhausted.'

'All that sea air. Miss Henshaw is a fine sailor,' Edward says. He doesn't look at me.

'The boys will be thrilled at that news,' Marnie says, with a knowing look at Edward. 'Rather her than me.'

But already I don't want ever to go back on that yacht, unless it is a repeat of today.

'I'll catch you later then,' I say, lamely, watching as Edward steals one of the delicious-looking canapés from Marnie's tray. He puts his arm up to wave at me, but still doesn't meet my eye.

Then he puts his arm around Marnie's shoulder and walks with her towards the terrace, calling out a friendly greeting to his friends.

61

I take a long bath and carefully sponge down all the places where Edward kissed my body today.

I take in a shuddery breath as I lie back in the steaming bubbles, picturing myself as he made love to me in the sunshine, and then in the shower. And now we're back and he's downstairs with his guests and Marnie, like it never happened. I feel a tragic sense of loss that I can't deal with.

I've really gone and done it this time. I've really gone and got myself into one hideous, enormous scrape. What am I going to do? Am I going to stay here and look after the boys, and pretend this afternoon never happened? Can we both really keep such a momentous secret?

My mind skitters about, trying to grab onto something solid, trying to relive this afternoon, but then make sense of what it all means, now we're back here at the house and have crash-landed into reality.

I'm still amazed that it happened. Amazed that I was brave and confident enough to make the first move. Looking back on how the event played out, I can't blame Edward. It's my fault. I kissed him first.

Maybe it was telling Edward about Mr Walters that did

it. Perhaps it was my very trustworthiness, my ability to keep a secret, that clinched it for him.

But I don't know if I *can* keep this a secret. It feels too big. It's all-consuming. As if it's already taken me over and fundamentally changed the person I am.

But I have no choice. I can't tell a soul. And even if I could, who would I tell? I can't tell anyone at home. What would Tiff say? She'd be horrified. She was shocked enough at Mr Walters, but she'd be disgusted with me if she knew about Edward. That I might have screwed up my one decent chance of employment because of my stupid crush.

I can't confide in anyone here. There's nobody to confide in. Mrs Gundred would fire me on the spot, and everyone else would blab straight away. Of course they would. They'd tell Marnie.

Oh God. Marnie. What if Marnie suspects, or ever finds out? She'd hate me and feel so betrayed. I dread to think what she would be like if you crossed her. I dread to think how it would feel to incur her wrath, which I would, if she got even one tiny hint of what I've done. What we've done.

What we *did*.

Because, according to Edward, that's it. It will never happen again.

And the worst bit is that I now see that for myself. I refused to believe it on the boat, but just seeing Marnie, being in the house, seeing how complex his life is, I realize what a stupid fantasist I've been.

Having an affair under Marnie's nose? In her house? It's unthinkably dangerous.

I should leave, I tell myself. I should get out of here. But what excuse would I give? I can't just leave, when they've been so nice to me. When they've tried to bond with me and make me feel at home.

But if I stay, then that little agonizing scene I witnessed just now will be a daily torture.

I groan and cover my face with a hot flannel, but I can't escape all these feelings. I know all of this, but still my heart aches for Edward. It can't really be over, just like that, can it? Not now I know he hasn't been able to resist the force that has pulled us together, either. Which means there is a slim chance that he might not be able to again.

Perhaps he is just as shell-shocked by what happened this afternoon. Perhaps it's ten times worse for him. Maybe he's eaten up with remorse and guilt. I picture him downstairs, with his brooding, dark gaze, trying to hide his secret from Marnie. Is it as unbearable for him as it is for me? Maybe, just maybe, it is.

Or maybe he's taken it all in his stride. Maybe I'm not the first affair he's had. Maybe he's had loads of women before me, and managed to keep them a secret from his adoring wife. Maybe, maybe, maybe. I can't bear this mental torture.

I get out of the bath and apply moisturizer and wrap myself in the dressing gown, but I feel at once too hot and shivery, like I have a fever. As Elvis used to sing from Dad's record player, 'I'm all shook up.'

It's getting dark now, and soon it gets late. I don't hear anything from downstairs and, restlessly, I toss and turn in the bed. But the waterbed just reminds me of being on the boat, so I get up and sit on the window seat, staring out into the garden; but somehow it doesn't feel quite so romantic any more, now that I've seen the big wall. The big wall that is imprisoning me here, trapped with this secret.

I hug my knees, watching the clouds cross the moon, thinking of the yacht, but already the memory of it is sailing out of reach. I smooth out the picture Edward drew of me, which I insisted on taking, just before we left the yacht.

Is that really me? Is that how he sees me? I look at the curve of my spine and waist, and how he's captured the expression on my face. I'm so touched that he drew me like that. That I was beautiful for him. It feels so private to have a token of his creativity, a tiny part of him.

I clutch the picture to my chest, my heart aching for the touch I know will never be mine again.

And then I hear it.

The knock on my door.

For a second, I just stare. Is it Marnie? Does she know? Has he told her? Has she come to slap my face and tell me to leave?

My pulse racing, I creep across the carpet and open it.

62

He's right up against my door, like he's leaning on it for support. He's not drunk, but he looks broken.

'I just wanted to check you're OK,' Edward says, but his voice catches. His eyes are pleading with me as they meet mine. I can see straight away that he's fought a battle with himself, and lost.

I'm so relieved to see him, I want to cry. I wrap my arms around myself, trying to hold myself together. I stare at his shirt.

'Sophie?' he whispers, and I let out a small, gasping sob that comes from somewhere inside me.

I close my eyes. This is unbearable. I reach out and put my hand on the front of his shirt. Then he takes my hand and kisses my palm.

'I'm sorry,' he says in a low voice. 'God, it's hard. Hard for me, too.'

And I know then that he's telling the truth. I open my eyes and stare into his. He looks like a little boy. He looks like I feel: emotionally wrecked.

'You're OK, then. That's good,' he nods. He looks as if he's about to turn away.

'Edward,' I whisper.

He turns back to face me.

'Don't go. Please stay. Just for a minute,' I beg him, and then I grab him and pull him inside the door. He doesn't resist.

As the door shuts, he's already folding me into a frantic hug, as if we've been reunited after months apart. Not hours.

He puts his hand into the back of my hair as he kisses me.

'Oh God, I can't stand it,' he whispers between kisses.

His words make my insides molten with a mixture of desire and triumph. He can't resist this thing between us, just like I can't. For all his declarations this afternoon, it's taken just hours for him to crack.

I claw at his hair and he lifts me, my dressing gown falling open. He lifts me up, my legs wrapping around him, and he carries me to the bed, where we both flop down.

Edward laughs at the movement of the bed and somehow that breaks the tension. I stare into his face, stroking his cheeks. He's here and with me, and the overwhelming ache I've been feeling all evening finally goes. The release is so powerful, I want to cry.

He kisses my neck, and I gasp as he takes my breasts in each hand and squeezes them against his face, as if he'll never be able to have enough of them.

Then he's moving down and kissing across my stomach.

'All I could think about at dinner was this,' he tells me, kissing the small mole on my hipbone. 'This delicious, perfect mole of yours that I love.'

I feel my whole abdomen shaking and I strain up towards him. And then he's between my legs. His thumbs circle my thighs again, but this time I know he's not going to stop. I lie back, wide-eyed, staring at the ceiling, gasping, as his tongue flicks across me, and he makes a low, guttural moan that sends goosebumps shooting over me.

He presses his mouth into me, as if he's devouring a peach. And then there are his thumbs, still circling, upwards . . . upwards . . . like I told him drove me crazy in the sauna.

I gasp as he lifts me up by my hips, his fingers pulling apart my butt cheeks, and he licks me deliciously, pulling back to look at me.

'I want all of you,' he breathes. He licks me again. I shudder uncontrollably. I feel bared to him, like he's making the most intimate study anyone has ever made. I get the feeling that there is no part of me he'll leave undiscovered. And that's just fine by me.

I feel his tongue inside me, pressing as far as it can go, then he sucks my lips, deliciously, and then he's circling my clitoris, flicking across the erect nub, and it's almost unbearably intense. My breath is ragged, every nerve ending on fire. He's in control of me and he knows it. He knows *exactly* what he's doing.

I feel him slowly press his finger inside me as he sucks on my nub and I'm so close now.

'Come to me, baby,' he whispers as I teeter on the edge.

Then I'm cascading down, shattering, thundering, plummeting . . .

63

Afterwards, I'm speechless. My legs shake uncontrollably as he places them on the bed. Then he tucks my dressing gown around me and I can't help laughing. He can't cover me up or tuck me away, like what just happened isn't a massive deal.

He stretches and flops onto the bed beside me.

'This is hopeless,' he tells me. 'All my resolve . . .'

I lean over and kiss him. 'Don't feel bad. I wanted you to come. I'm happy you did. Oh God, you don't know how happy.'

'But now, I have to go,' he says, putting a finger on my eyebrow and tracing a line to the corner of my eye.

'Don't.'

'I have to. Becca and Angelo are still here. They're having nightcaps. I said I was getting a painting to show them. Marnie will be looking for me.'

The mention of Marnie makes me shudder. Our eyes meet. We both know how wrong this is. That our borrowed time is over.

'Go then,' I say, covering up the moment and half-teasing him. I push him off the bed and he falls on the floor, laughing.

'What's this?' he asks me. He reaches under my bed and pulls out a black sequinned nipple-tassel.

I jolt upright, recognizing it.

He holds it in his hand. His look is dark. Not cross exactly, more confused.

I shift upwards in the bed and take it out of his hand.

'Oh that,' I say, as if it's no big deal, but my heart is hammering. 'Marnie gave it to me. She gave me some underwear.'

He seems to consider this for a moment. 'Did she.'

It's not a question, more a statement. Like he's trying to figure out what happened. And I know then that I should come clean and tell him everything. I feel the secret of that evening, of my dance, of our embrace so forcefully I think he must be able to tell. I brace myself for his fury, but then Edward does something unexpected. He smiles.

'I'd like to see you all dressed up one day,' he says quietly. He strokes my cheek. 'That would be something.'

As quickly as it came, the moment to tell him about Marnie – about Marnie and me – passes. He hasn't suspected and I'm not going to tell him. I can't risk anything coming between Edward and me. I can't risk losing this.

'I'd love that, but how can we . . . I mean?'

He gets up, then leans over me. He holds my face and, bending down, stares into my eyes. 'Promise me you'll hold your nerve. Promise me you won't say anything. To anyone. Ever.'

'I promise.'

'I don't know, either . . . how any of this can work. We will just have to take it one minute at a time.'

'OK.'

'Marnie must never know.'

'I know. I understand.'

'She mustn't even suspect, OK? It would break her.'

I nod. I feel bad, like the scarlet woman I am, but Edward forces me to look at him, searching out my eyes.

'Can I trust you?'

'Of course.' I reach up and kiss him, my lips lingering on his soft lips. I want to kiss those lips forever. I can smell myself on him. I know it's wrong, but there's some primal monkey-like part of me that feels triumphant that I've claimed him. Marked him as my own.

64

I'm terrified the next morning about seeing Marnie and Edward together, but Marnie is alone in the hall when I sneak downstairs. I can hardly bring myself to smile when she waves at me and grins. I feel wretched about the lie my life has become.

Her husband wants *me*. And she has no idea.

She's laughing on the phone. It takes me a moment to realize she's talking to one of the boys.

'OK, baby,' she says. 'She's here now. Daddy took her sailing yesterday. Oh yes, he's been licking her into shape.' She raises her eyebrows at me, her eyes dancing, but her words have such a unintended double-meaning, I feel sick. 'Yes, she's a brilliant sailor, apparently. She's desperate to meet you guys.' She listens for a while and laughs, her eyes misty with affection. 'OK, I understand. Tell Tobes it'll be fine. Daddy and I are having the party at the weekend. So maybe after that? OK, OK, I'll call her and organize it. You have fun.' She blows lots of kisses. 'Love you. Love you, too. Be careful,' she stresses, but I get the impression that her son has already rung off. She presses the phone against her chest. 'They are having a ball,' she says. 'But God, I miss them.'

'I'm sure you do,' I mumble, but after everything that happened yesterday, I realize that I've hardly thought about the boys. Seeing the force of her maternal bond only makes me realize that Edward must feel the same.

Marnie fixes me with one of her sympathetic stares. 'Aw, poor Miss Henshaw. I know you are hanging around here like a spare part. But they'll just be in the way if they're home when we have this party at the weekend. I told you about the party, didn't I?'

I shake my head.

'Didn't I?' she says, as if she can't believe it. As if we've talked and talked and it's unbelievable there's been such an omission. 'Oh, well,' she gushes on, 'we're throwing a little house-warming bash. Some of Ed's investors are in town, so it's one of those two-birds-with-one-stone things, you know?'

She looks at me, like I honestly might know. That I have these kind of social conundrums myself. I shrug, unsure how to respond. I wonder where Edward is. Edward, who made love to me all day yesterday. Edward, who came to me last night.

Edward, who is imprinted on my mind.

My lover.

Her husband.

'Now Ed's gone upstate on business until tomorrow, and Mrs Gundred's away at the weekend. I'm going to tear my hair out organizing it, and then there's the shoot today. Gah! Why does everything come at once? Thank God the boys aren't here, too.'

But I hardly hear the last part of her sentence. Edward has *gone*? He's gone upstate on business . . . just like that?

I think of him last night in my room. How I fell asleep with a stupid grin on my face. I wouldn't have done if I knew I wouldn't see him today. Or tonight.

I fight as hard as I can to hide the crushing sense of hurt and disappointment that threatens to swamp me. Why didn't he tell me he was going? How could he leave me to face Marnie alone, after yesterday?

Suddenly, she looks up at me and frowns. 'Are you OK, honey?' she asks. She sounds so sweet. So innocent.

I make an incoherent sound in the affirmative, then cough. 'I can help,' I offer. 'I'm not doing anything.'

I might as well. If I stay around here I'll go out of my mind.

'That's sweet of you. I sure could do with an extra pair of hands, although I warn you, it's going to be a long day.'

I smile at her and shove my hands in my pockets. 'Just tell me what I need to do,' I say, trying to sound reassuring.

65

'OK, bring that forward. Two steps,' Marnie calls to me.

Marnie is standing next to the photographer, Marshall O'Kieffe, in the middle of her studio in Manhattan. I know that Marshall is famous and the absolute best in his field, as his three assistants, Tara, Lee and MacKenzie, have each whispered the news in revered tones.

Marnie doesn't look at me as she ushers me closer. Her concentration is intense and I'm careful to do the right thing. I'm carrying a large silver reflector, which I'm angling in the lights, so that the light falls on the model in front of me. My legs are screaming. I'm desperate to sit down. It's been non-stop since Marnie and I arrived at the studio this morning, and I've lost track of time.

It's been fun chatting to the models, most of whom are younger than me and have already worked all over the world.

I can't help feeling smug, though. I feel my secret lighting me up from the inside.

Edward.

His name chimes through me like a bell.

Every few seconds my mind goes back to the yacht . . . To Edward's hands. To how his body felt against – inside

– mine. With time giving me perspective, I expected the experience to fade, but my retrospection only makes it more amazing and more profound.

I wish I had some means of calling him, but I don't have his cellphone number and I have no idea where he is. I hope Marnie is telling the truth and he is away on business, and not back at the house waiting for me, when I'm here.

There's still so much I don't know about his life: where he goes, what he's working on, who he sees. But I guess I will soon enough. My mind loop-the-loops on all the possible scenarios of what will happen next. Edward said we'd just have to take it second-by-second. But with each second that passes I just want him more, not less.

Is it the same for him, I wonder?

And how exactly will it be when we're back at the house? Will he come to me in the night, like he did last night? And what will happen when the boys are there? What if we get found out? What then?

I can't think about what then. It's too dangerous, when everything is at stake.

As Marnie flits around the studio in a blur of action, I watch her from my still poses and see how amazing she is, and the thought of hurting her feels terrible. Like a physical sting.

Of course I know how the facts look. That I'm cheating with her husband, behind her back, but somehow what has happened between me and Edward feels as if it has nothing to do with her. Just as their marriage has nothing to do with me. I know that.

I also know that I'm trying to justify my behaviour to myself, but no matter what the risks, I have still crossed a line and I can't stop now. I can't call it off, or pretend it isn't happening. It's too big for that.

And that's why this affair I've started with Edward has to stay a secret forever. It will be locked away and will be private. But knowing that, and keeping it to myself, just makes the facts of the secret even bigger, even more amazing. I'm surprised nobody can tell. It feels like I'm bursting with it. And, annoyingly, the one person I really want to tell is the one person I can't.

'Come forward,' Marshall calls and I realize, jolting out of my reverie, that he means me. I carry the reflector forward, closer to the bed.

Since I was here the other day Marnie's studio has been transformed into what can only be described as a hall of decadence for her lingerie shoot. It's how I imagine an opulent opera set might look. There are red velvet drapes and chandeliers, as well as an antique iron bed. Music thumps out and the patient, half-naked models, with their flawless make-up and stunning hair creations, courtesy of Roberta and her team, hang around on the edges, drinking black coffee out of Styrofoam cups.

I'm so used to seeing everyone in lingerie now, it has become normal. I've also got a brand-new kind of respect for models. I've been amazed by how much work there is to do to get the shots right, and it's not helped by the fact that both Marshall and Marnie are utter perfectionists. Each shot has taken an age to set up and this one, the most complicated of the lot, is still in the process of being created.

I look up at the model as I step closer. Her name is Karen, and I see her eyes flick down towards me and she winks. She keeps her pose still, though. I try not to stare at her, but it's difficult not to. She's got the most beautiful pale skin and she's dressed in a rose-lace bra and thong from Marnie's collection. I can see the muscles on her stomach and the downy skin of her thighs, and the dark, dusky pink of her nipples through the lace.

Karen isn't the only model waiting in an uncomfortable pose for the lighting to be perfect. Marshall's three assistants fuss round in the background, whilst Xanda, the make-up assistant, comes in for touch-ups.

I glance behind Karen to the iron bed, where a male and female model lie semi-naked in a sleepy-looking embrace, although they're both wide awake and fully posed. Behind them, in silhouette, are three more models at the edge of the set, in various combinations of Marnie's underwear.

Marshall chats quietly with Marnie, then walks over to Karen and gets her to bend over further towards the camera. Then Marnie is there, arranging Karen's ample cleavage in the bra. I see her touch her breasts, the way she rearranged me in the corset in her room.

So it was normal then. She does that to everyone.

I'm just remembering the last time I dressed up in underwear when Marnie, who has been too busy even to speak to me all morning, catches my eye.

'Oh God, that reminds me,' she gasps, as if she's just

remembered something vital. 'I'd like to do a close-up cleavage shot in black, for the inset, but I don't want anyone to leave the set, now it's nearly there. There's so much to remember.'

'Do you want me to help?' I ask, although I have no idea how.

'Would you? That's a perfect idea. You are a doll. So just slip one on in black, OK?'

Shit! She means . . .

Me in a bra?

That's not what I meant *at all.*

'Keilan.' She snaps her fingers and Keilan arrives. 'Take Miss Henshaw and find her the rose collection in black. Tell Roberta I don't need face, I'm just doing a pack shot. We're seriously running out of time.'

Keilan takes the reflector from me and props it up, then takes me off the set to the wardrobe space squeezed in behind the fake brocade walls.

'It's hectic, right?' he says, grinning at me.

'I don't know how this has happened. I'm hardly an underwear model,' I tell him as he races through the boxes to find my size. 'Does she really want me?'

'Marnie gets what Marnie wants. I wouldn't argue, if I were you. Today, it's just about getting the job done. We can only have Marshall today for these shots.'

I guess he's right. It would be churlish to make a fuss. Marnie has enough on her plate, and I did offer to help out.

After I've put on the bra, I feel self-conscious as I parade around to the make-up section in my jeans and bra and pink sneakers, but nobody in the studio bats an eyelid.

Roberta applies foundation to my chest and dusts me down with the most glorious-smelling, faintly sparkling powder. Keilan's right. It's just about getting the job done.

Claudia, the costume assistant, checks the bra on me, adjusting the straps and pulling at the front.

'It's just going to be here,' she says, framing her hands around the very front of my peachy cleavage. 'OK. Nothing else. So don't worry.'

Back on set, Marnie pulls me into a lit area and fusses around me. She cups the bra and jiggles me around in it, until my breasts look perfect. Then Marshall's assistant, Lee, sets up the camera on a tripod. He's a tall black guy and he's wearing a back-to-front baseball cap and waistcoat. He exudes a kind of serious cool vibe. He's totally professional and into this. I try not to think of the nude portrait in the gallery back at Thousand Acres.

I can't help giggling nervously as he comes in for a close-up. It doesn't feel like I'm being photographed at all. It's all about the details of the bra.

'You're a star,' Marnie says, grinning at me. I smile back, glad that I didn't back out. Glad that I've manned up for the task.

'Keep still, keep still now,' Lee drawls from behind the camera. I watch him bend over in his perfect designer jeans.

Marnie squints at the monitor. 'That's good with that lighting. We'll use it for now, just in case,' she says, and that's that. It's over. 'Actually, can you just put the briefs on, hon?' she calls over her shoulder to me. 'Do you mind? I might need you at the back in the next shot.'

I want to protest, but I've already been coerced into being photographed. I guess being in the background won't hurt. As I go back to find Claudia, I want to laugh.

Oh my God. I'm in a lingerie shoot in New York.

66

Marnie calls a break at seven and we all stand around and drink champagne. The caterers have been, and I watch Marnie scoffing down a burger, but Violet, one of the models, says it's best just to drink – rather than eat – until the shoot is over. I try and get into the models' mentality, but my tummy growls. I down a couple of glasses of champagne, which takes the edge off.

The music changes into something clubbier, and the lighting suddenly makes a more intimate mood in the studio. Props are brought on and off. Some of the models leave and others arrive.

'So let's do intimate shots next,' Marnie says. 'We just need the mood shot.'

Karen strides over towards us. She's in high heels and smoking a cigarette. She's changed and is wearing a see-through negligee, which strains against her curves. Her lids are heavily made-up and she has this air of a starlet about her. She loves the way she looks, she says, and we all admire how Marnie's underwear has made her look so deliciously slutty.

'Perfect,' Marnie says, as Karen bends over the bed. The thin black gauze stretches across her naked buttocks, but she doesn't seem self-conscious, as Marnie looks at her from behind. She looks very, very hot.

'Keep the Dietrich-vibe going for the others, Roberta,' Marnie calls out. 'This section is going to be all black-and-white shots,' she informs me.

I'm still reeling from how she casually mentioned 'intimates' in her last sentence.

'So . . . do you mean . . . um – the vibrators and stuff?' I ask, but it comes out as a squeak. I sound ridiculous.

Marnie laughs at me. 'Yeah, stuff. The fun stuff.'

She suddenly turns on tiptoes and strides over to Marshall. She puts her head close to his, pointing at the bed. Above the bed I see a lighting grid move down closer. It has various cameras and lights attached.

'I think Carmena on the bed, like this,' Marnie says, jumping on the bed. She kneels up. 'But over someone. Miss Henshaw, lie here a second.'

She pats the bed and I dutifully go over and lie back stiffly on the bed. Then she kneels on either side of my torso, facing away from me. I look down at the frayed strands on her shorts and the back of her toned thighs. I feel an unexpected sexual shiver rush through me.

'Yeah, this will work. Stay there,' she says and looks over her shoulder at me and winks.

67

Marnie is soon busy arranging everyone around me on the bed, and there are so many bodies and she's so busy that every time I try and get her attention, even if I can move, I miss the opportunity.

Then Carmena arrives. She's the model who will be straddling me in Marnie's place. She's wearing a riding hat with a veil over her face, with extraordinarily red lips. But that isn't the shocking bit. She's wearing crotchless fishnet tights and high stilettos, and a strapless bra that barely covers her nipples. I try not to look at her nudity through the slit in her tights as she hooks her leg over me. The spikes of her heels look terrifying as they face towards me.

I look at the back of her and her mass of swishy dark hair, cascading down from the hat. She's from Brazil and she has the most incredible skin. Her thighs are solid and muscular. She looks like she runs a lot. Underneath her, I feel like a white, flabby whale. Where the hell is the model who is going to replace me?

'So here's the samples for everyone,' Keilan says, arriving next to the bed with what looks like a very heavy cream box. The same kind of box my vibrator came in. 'Let's see what we have today in Marnie's box of tricks, boys and girls.'

There's laughter as he starts to hand out a whole array of sex toys, much to the glee of the models.

'Oh yes, this is my favourite,' one girl called Lexie squeals, picking up a double-ended dildo.

'Give me that,' Karen says, grabbing it. 'Oh my God, it's fantastic.'

'And so versatile,' Lexie jokes.

The models pass around the toys and bend the dildo in different directions. It's kind of jokey and fun, but still pretty shocking, from where I'm lying down. They all look like they're familiar with Marnie's 'intimates' and aren't at all embarrassed about them, but I feel like I've come out in a full-body blush. I try and hide it. I don't want Marnie to call me Miss Prim-and-Proper in front of all these people.

Marshall fusses around, flashing lights in everyone's faces. Soon he's discussing the dildo with Karen and Sean, and they bend it and put their heads close together, taking an end each in their mouths. I feel a deep stab of something sexually exciting, even though they're just mucking around.

Marnie comes over with a black silk eye-mask. I'm still waiting to be replaced in the shot by a model, but as Marshall poses everyone, it dawns on me that Marnie is going to make me stay in the shot.

'Do you want me to stay like this?' I ask.

'Uh-huh, you're fine as you are – just keep still is all,' she says, but that wasn't what I was asking. 'Put this on, like this,' Marnie adds. She demonstrates, putting the mask over her head and covering her eyes. Then she removes it and offers it to me, but I'm so flustered I drop it. I am close up against her. She smiles down at me gently as she takes the silk blindfold and puts it over my head herself. 'Don't look so scared,' she says.

'I can't do this,' I stutter. 'I'm a not a model, I mean . . .'

'You're hardly going to be seen. Look, there are bodies everywhere. It's all atmosphere and close-ups. The shots will be blurry. Don't worry, little bird.'

I can't back out now without looking ridiculous. And I don't have the nerve to stand up to her.

I feel myself trembling, as the blindfold really does block everything out. I know I shouldn't be nervous. I know there are other models around me, but now, as I can't see what's going on, all my other senses are on red alert.

Suddenly, I feel something soft shoot across my stomach and down to my thighs. It makes me jerk with shock.

'You like that, huh?' I hear Marnie's voice. I feel the soft, ticklish sensation again and Marnie laughs. She's got a feather. 'Just . . . here,' she says, trailing the feather along my thigh.

I jerk my leg away.

'You only move when I tell you to move,' Marnie tuts.

There's a sound of rustling.

'How do you feel about the handcuffs?' she whispers, but she's already got my wrist. It's not a question. She's going to handcuff me up, whether I like it or not.

'Mrs Parker, please,' I beg her. 'I'm not . . . I mean . . .'

This has all got out of hand.

'Hush, little bird,' she laughs. I feel something soft gripping my wrist and a click as she tightens the handcuffs.

'But this isn't my kind of—'

'How will you know how you feel, unless you've tried it? This is just a photoshoot. It's not real. It's just for fun. Nothing bad is going to happen. I promise,' Marnie says in a soothing voice. I feel the handcuff clamping me to the bedstead. I feel panic rising, but then I feel someone pressing against me.

'You know Edward loves all of this,' Marnie whispers. 'What would he say if he could see you now, huh?'

I feel a hot-and-cold chill rush through me. Is she telling me because she knows what happened with Edward and me yesterday? Is she telling me because she suspects, and she wants to show me that she's still in charge? But she laughs and moves away.

There's flesh on my flesh. Carmena is above me again, straddling me. Then I feel Marnie kiss me on the cheek.

'Don't be scared, darling. You look beautiful. Peachy.' I feel her hand squeeze the flesh of my breast and plump it up in my bra. I gasp.

I try and think about Edward, but he's slipped away. Being on the boat, so natural and free, feels just about the opposite of this, which feels claustrophobic and scary and new. But still, the overwhelming sensation of sex is all around me and, despite everything, I feel hot between my legs.

I lie trembling on the bed as I hear others getting on the bed next to me. There's a jumble of voices in hushed whispers. I feel a bare leg press up against mine. My temperature rises.

I sense Marshall moving around, the camera click-clacking.

'Hey, sweetie,' I hear someone say. It's a girl. I feel something sequin-like graze my shoulder and a hot body pressing up against my side. 'I'm just going to squash in here.'

'Oh God, you haven't tried these, I bet,' Marnie says. I hear a buzzing. 'Nice, huh?'

She runs something buzzing over my collarbone.

There's a laugh. 'Yeah, try that. Karen and Joe. OK. You take it.'

The buzzing goes to the other side of the bed. I feel movement beside me on the bed.

'OK, how about this?'

The buzzing comes back.

'Stand above her,' I hear Marshall say, across the bed. 'Legs more open. That's it. Maybe in the mouth . . .'

I hear one of the models giggling, 'We'll do it together . . . hmmm.' I hear some wet kissing-type sounds. My breath is ragged.

My mind is going crazy. What is happening all around me? Is this a porn shoot? I feel Carmena move forward and laugh in a lusty way. I know that if I didn't have a blindfold on, I would be getting a full view of the slit in her tights. The thought of it sends me into a state of unexpected horniness.

'So, we're going to try something here,' Marnie says quietly next to me. 'You'll like it. Open. Lee, over here.'

I sense that Lee is close. Lee, Marshall's assistant. The one I thought reminded me of the photo I saw in the gallery. I hear him laugh gently. There's rustling. I feel fabric on my face as he leans over me. He's taking a picture of my wrist against the bedstead. I smell his aftershave. It's musky and manly, mixed with a kind of primeval male pheromone that I feel myself responding to, despite myself.

Then he moves away and something presses against my mouth and, instinctively, I open my lips. There's something that is warm and soft, but hard, too. It must be some kind of phallic-shaped toy. It has a weird taste, but it feels like the real thing. Very, very much like the real thing. Except it's huge.

'Oh yeah, that's good,' I hear Lee whisper.

Oh my God. Is it Lee himself? Is he in my mouth? What's happening? But as quickly as it happened, he moves away. It moves away. I feel blood pounding in my cheeks. What's happening? Being blindfolded and tied up is so terrifying, but I can't deny the deep, lusty thrill that courses through me.

'Take it over here, to Karen,' I hear Marnie say.

I hear Marshall's camera snapping some more. Above me, Carmena sits down briefly. I feel the nakedness between her legs against the bare flesh of my stomach.

'Oh yeah,' I hear. Something is buzzing and I sense she's holding it. 'Like this?' she checks.

'Uh-huh,' Marnie says.

'We've got it with the negligee,' Marnie says, and I hear Marshall snapping. 'Let's do it with the briefs.'

Then, quite suddenly, something is buzzing against the outside of my knickers. The vibrations shoot through me. I sense Marshall is close, taking a close-up of the vibrator against the silk that is straining over my vulva.

I shudder as the vibrator jangles all my aching nerve endings. It's so intense. I long for it to be beneath my knickers, against my flesh, but Carmena is pinning me down, holding the vibrator against me. She gyrates her hips, her thighs squeezing my sides. I feel her wetness, and feel my own beneath the silk knickers.

'You like that,' Carmena says to me, with a hushed laugh in her voice.

I feel someone pulling my legs wider. I feel the vibrator right between my legs on the very edge of my knickers.

I'm completely pinned to the bed, tied by handcuffs and, with Carmena on top of me, I can hardly move. The vibrator is exquisitely close, but not close enough. Every fibre of me strains towards it, silently begging for the release that might come.

The atmosphere on the bed is quieter. I hear a deep moan from the other side of the bed and more licking noises, but I can only concentrate on the vibrator. I grab onto the bedstead, trying to strain against it.

'Hush, hush, little bird,' Marnie says. 'Don't get carried away. It's all over now.'

68

I don't think she's serious, but quite suddenly the atmosphere changes.

'Brilliant, that's great, everyone,' Marnie says, clapping her hands. 'What do you think, Marshall?'

'They're terrific shots. I think we've got more than enough. It's a wrap, people.'

Everyone starts clapping and moving off the bed. The vibrator leaves me abruptly. Carmena hooks her leg over me and her weight disappears.

Is this a joke? Is this really happening?

I feel like I've been left dangling and, pulling myself together, retreating takes everything I've got.

There's laughter and chatting, and I hear more champagne bottles popping.

Eventually I realize that I've been left alone. And I'm still handcuffed and blindfolded.

'Hello?' I call out. 'Over here.'

I strain against the handcuffs. I really can't move.

I hear Marnie's voice coming closer, then suddenly I feel her bounce on the bed next to me, making me jump. She undoes the handcuffs and I take off my blindfold, my eyes adjusting to the bright studio lights.

Marnie's eyes are shining. 'That was fun, huh?' she grins, jumping off the bed again to join the models.

Everyone is in a celebratory mood, but I don't know what has happened to each of the models, so I can't look at them. I certainly can't look at Lee.

I feel shaken – ashamed and worried about what just happened. Why is everyone laughing? Didn't they get horny, too? Or was it just me? I feel embarrassed that I've obviously transgressed some shoot rule. Maybe it was just acting, for them.

'Come and see,' Marnie calls.

I get off the bed and go over to the massive Mac, which the models crowd around. I look at the shots as they arrive on the screen. They are all grainy and shadowy. There are lots of close-ups of the sex toys. Nothing explicit. It's all just suggestion.

Then I see the vibrator against the stretched fabric of my knickers.

'My God, Ed will love these when he sees them,' Marnie says. 'Look at that.'

I stare at the picture. My mole – the mole that Edward claims to love – is visibly on show. If he sees the shots, then he'll know I've been here. Panic engulfs me. If he thinks I was tied up on the bed with Marnie, then what else will he think?

And then I see the shot of my lips. And there's something that looks alarmingly real between them.

Oh, fuck! What have I done?

69

I can barely function, I'm in such a panic, although I try my best not to show it. The models get dressed and swap numbers, and there's lots of air-kissing. They all seem completely fine about the shoot, but then I can see why they would. They all trust Marnie. She treats them like they're all family. And she pays them well, too.

'You were brilliant today,' Helen says to me, kissing me. 'Come to the bar with us, if you like. Now you're one of us.'

Am I one of them? Do they mean: now I'm a model? Or: now I'm complicit in the secret shoot? I'm flattered to be part of Marnie's tribe, but at the same time I can't help feeling that I've betrayed Edward in some fundamental way I can't put my finger on. As if Marnie's shoot has blotted out everything that happened. I try and remember our day on the boat together, like I could earlier, but now the memories are as illusive as smoke.

'I'm going to help Marnie clear up, then maybe we'll come down.'

I find myself blushing as Lee kisses me goodbye. It can't have been him, can it? He can't have actually been in my mouth? Everything tells me that I'm being ridiculous, but the photograph looks so realistic.

Eventually it's just Marnie and me in the studio. She turns down the music and puts on something soft and soothing, and the whole atmosphere and frenetic energy of the day finally go.

She sits on the bed and lights a spliff. For a second she looks exhausted as she inhales.

'What a day!' she sighs. Her eyes crinkle as she smiles.

'It went well, didn't it?' I ask her.

She picks a bit of tobacco off her tongue and blows out some smoke. I see her cleavage in her vest. A flash of the bed comes to me – Carmena over me, the slit in her gauze pants . . .

'You were sweet to help out.'

'It was fun,' I tell her with a shy smile. She pats the bed next to her and I sit down. She hands me the spliff and I take a puff. I don't inhale too deeply. I remember what happened last time.

'You seemed worried. Are you OK, baby?' she asks me.

'Just . . . it's just . . .' I glance across at her, feeling like a fool. 'I'm worried about that shot. That one of my mouth. I don't want you to use it.'

I hand the spliff back to her.

'It's wasn't . . . it wasn't – you know . . . real, was it? It was so difficult to tell. It wasn't . . . Lee?'

Marnie hoots with laughter. She puts her hand on her chest and rocks back.

'Oh, poor Miss Henshaw. You are so innocent.'

Innocent? If only she knew.

'It's not funny,' I say. I feel oddly close to tears. She curtails her laughter and then goes across the studio and roots around in a box. She comes back with a thick black object.

'This baby? I guess it's done it's job if you thought it was real.'

She's holding a big black dildo with ridges on it. She sticks out her tongue and licks the end of it, her eyes fixed on me. Then she puts it in her mouth and lets it push out her cheek, just as it did mine. From where I'm standing, it looks absolutely real and extremely rude. Her eyes narrow and smoulder. She's enjoying teasing me. That was what I did to her husband. Seeing her with the dildo in her mouth makes me imagine her doing it to him as well. I feel blood rush to my cheeks.

Then she stops and hands it to me.

'Wow,' I tell her, meaning it. I'm so relieved that it's not real, but Marnie being so sexual with it has set me more jittery than I can make sense of. 'It . . . it felt so real. Not that I've . . .'

'Haven't you?' she asks, and then she smiles softly. 'Of course not. My innocent little bird.'

I blush again. Deeper this time. I can't meet her eye.

'It's horny, huh,' she says, but it's not a question. 'I like it, too. I always design my sex toys with my own fantasies in mind.'

'Oh,' I mutter, taken aback that she's admitted something like that.

'Oh, don't look like that,' she teases me. 'Like I've embarrassed you. Surely we're beyond that, after today.'

She's got a point.

'Fantasy is entirely normal and healthy. Haven't you ever fantasized about being filled up by a great big one like that?' she asks me, nodding to the dildo in my hand. 'Of course you have,' she answers for me. 'Every girl has. A lot of men, too.'

I don't know how to respond. I think about the picture I saw in the studio of the male model. I feel slightly sweaty as I hold the large dildo. She hands the spliff to me again and this time I inhale on it greedily.

She takes the dildo from me and holds it up like a trophy.

'I think it's magnificent,' she tells me. 'Some of my finest work.'

And I can't help but giggle. Maybe it's the spliff hitting.

I force myself to be brave. I have to ask her. I have to find out the truth.

'So talking of black men . . . The other night . . . when you left me in town?'

She turns her head and raises her eyebrows at me. She's clearly surprised I've brought it up.

I force myself to continue, even though her look unnerves me. 'The guy I saw you with . . . ?'

'Alain? The dancer?'

I nod. 'The guy in the booth?'

Marnie stares at the dildo, following my train of thought. 'Oh, did you think . . . ?' She looks at me sympathetically. 'No, sweetie. He's one of my oldest friends. He sometimes models. In fact he was going to come today, but he had a Calvin Klein shoot.'

'Oh,' I say. 'But, I saw . . .'

My words fizzle out. What did I see? Her dancing and flirting – a long kiss. Nothing more.

'Sorry,' I mutter. 'I just thought . . .'

I can't tell her what I thought. I feel anxious that I thought it; even more anxious that I wanted to tell Edward about it.

Edward. My Edward. But he's *her* Edward, too, I realize as she starts to speak again.

'Honey, you have a lot to learn,' she says. She puts the dildo down and takes another puff of the spliff. 'I flirt with guys like Alain, only because it's so safe to flirt with gay guys like him. I would never cheat on Edward. He's the most jealous guy in the world.'

Is he? That's news to me, but I suddenly feel like I'm on quicksand. How have we managed to start talking about Edward and Marnie's relationship with him? I don't say anything. If I say anything, I know I'll give myself away.

'I'm sorry. I didn't mean to pry. I just . . .'

'I got carried away. It was just so exciting to be back in Manhattan. To be back home. I miss it so damn much.'

'Why did you move then?' I ask, surprised.

'To get away. To make sure we got time on our own at home. You know, proper family time with the boys. It was so hectic when we lived in Manhattan. Always people around. And things . . .' she sighs, 'got complicated.'

Suddenly, I remember the court case and the gagging order. I remember Harry and the secrets he claimed to know about the Parkers. Is Marnie going to let me in on the mystery?

'It's easy for you,' she sighs. She picks up a strand of my

hair and runs it through her fingers. 'You're young. Everything is simple. Things get more difficult as you get older.'

What's difficult about her life, I wonder? 'How?' I ask.

'Life is tricky. *Relationships* are tricky,' she says with a sad laugh.

She's still holding my hair and, as her eyes meet mine, my heart thumps very hard. She's talking about her and Edward. She's talking about the fact that he is unfaithful to her.

Oh my God. I feel panic sweep over me in a wave. *She knows.* She's telling me she knows.

'Edward's a very special man,' Marnie says, seriously. 'One of a kind. It takes a lot to keep him, you know?'

I don't know. I don't know what she's had to endure to keep Edward's attention, but now my confidence wavers. If she hasn't been able to keep him, what hope in hell do I have?

'And I will do anything I can to keep him happy,' she says. She doesn't look at me, but stretches away and puts the spliff down on the side table next to the bed. Her vest rides up and I see the curve of her waist.

Is she threatening me? Is she telling me to back off?

I will do anything I can to keep him happy.

What does she mean?

But when she turns back I see that she's not being threatening at all.

'Look at you. You're just a girl. Look at your lustrous hair and your bright eyes. You have no idea what it's like to get older. To be older.'

'You're not old. You're amazing. You're the most attractive woman in the world.'

She laughs and strokes my cheeks with the back of her hand, like my skin is the most precious thing she's ever felt. I remember Edward stroking my cheek almost in the same way, but somehow with Marnie it's different. This feels more intimate. More . . . new. Like she's taking me somewhere forbidden and I've already started following, before I realize what she's doing.

There's a moment of absolute stillness between us. I retreat, freeze.

'I think you're incredible, anyway,' I tell her. 'I'm sure Edward does, too.'

'Thank you,' she whispers and I feel a surge of affection towards her. I smile back, then reach out and hug her and we embrace, sitting on the bed. It feels so good to give something back to her. Even if it is only a hug. I sense she needs one, after today.

'You're so sweet. You have no idea what a breath of fresh air you are,' she says, smiling softly down at me; then she leans down and kisses me gently on the lips, like it's the most natural thing in the world. And, oddly, it is.

She doesn't say anything, but pushes me over and we lie side-by-side on the bed and she laughs. I feel her hand take mine.

We lie watching the shadows on the roof of the studio. I feel stoned and giddy, but next to Marnie I feel so safe. I feel connected to her. Like it's her and me against the world.

'Are you going to tell me off for kissing you?' she says.

'No,' I tell her. 'Of course not.'

She moves then and leans up.

'Then I'm going to kiss you again,' she whispers, as if we've just decided this together.

And before I can say anything, her lips are on mine. This time the kiss is different. It feels different. She doesn't move away, and neither do I, and after a couple of moments I feel her mouth open and a spark of electricity jolts through me as our tongues touch.

It's horny, yes, like I've been with Edward, but it's so unexpected and so forbidden, it has an edge to it that is thrillingly new. I know I should stop and pull away, but somehow I can't seem to. It's like being kissed for the very first time – ever. Well, it is for me, by a woman. The knowledge of this throbs through me. Is this how women kiss? Wow!

Finally, she pulls away and smiles, like she's delighted. I see the tiny gap between her teeth that I adore. I'm shaking uncontrollably and she trails her fingertip down my stomach.

'You're such a sensual little thing, aren't you?' she whispers.

I feel molten hot as her hand reaches my jeans and she squeezes me. 'I saw you on the bed. You got very hot and sticky, didn't you?' she says, a slight tease in her voice.

I reach out and touch her face, then her hair. She stares intently down at me as I feel her hand over my jeans, her fingers pressing into me through the fabric.

'Maybe we should finish that off?' she whispers. 'What do you say?'

No, is what I should say. No, because I'm not bisexual and I'm in love with her husband – and I'm pretty sure the feeling is mutual. But Edward and me: that relationship, right now, feels like it belongs to another land and time. And God, yes, I'm curious. Curious as hell. Because I want to know what it feels like to be with a woman. All those feelings I had on the shoot, when Carmena was on me, come rushing back. Only this time with the knowledge that Marnie and I are alone, and this might be my only chance ever to answer her question. Edward has nothing to do with this – with me and Marnie. This is about women, I tell myself. How will I ever know how it really feels to be a woman if I've never felt one – experienced one for myself.

I take the plunge. I can't find any words. Instead I slide my hand under her top, lifting up her vest. I want to feel her flesh.

She makes a low, guttural sigh that makes my insides flip. Like she's been waiting forever for me to touch her.

She pulls away quickly and takes off her top, her hand leaving me.

This loss of contact sends a shockwave of reality. What am I doing? What are we doing?

But it's all moving too fast and I don't want it to stop. It can't stop now.

She doesn't say anything as she takes off her thin bra and then, apart from her jean shorts, she's naked.

Her breasts, now that I've finally seen all of them, are larger than I expected and her nipples are puckered and already erect. I've seen them, partially of course, when we were in her room, and I've seen them in the portrait, but now they are here in front of me, it feels more intimate than anything I've ever witnessed. I reach out and cup one of her breasts. I can't believe this is happening, I can't believe I'm touching her, but I can't help myself. I draw her towards me and kiss her lips, my shaking hand exploring the shape of her, feeling the weight of her breast. She is so soft. So womanly. So wonderful.

Then I stop kissing her and, feeling brave, lean down and flick my tongue against her nipple. She moans. And in that noise, all the power shifts. She wants me and I want her. And suddenly I need to explore as much of her as I possibly can. And I won't stop until she's taught me everything she knows.

70

We are silent as Trewin drives us through the dark night back to the house. Marnie doesn't look at me, but sits next to me, her hand over mine.

I can still taste her. I feel shaken and ashamed and thrilled at the knowledge of what we've done. I know she's feeling the same. I feel the silence fizzing with the knowledge of what we just did.

Does she feel undone by the passion we shared, too?

Because it was passionate. All of it, but especially once we were naked together. I can't stop remembering how it felt to lie together, how it felt to be engulfed in her softness. How it felt more sensual than anything sexual I've ever experienced with a man, but it was open, too. Because we talked and laughed as we explored one another and it felt so private, being there on the bed with her, just me and her and the toys.

Oh my God. The toys.

And it was *me*. I instigated it. I told her to show me everything, teach me everything. I told her to explain and demonstrate her work, and oh, how she loved it. How she loved exploring me, showing me, leading me forward to feel more, think more about my body. How she called a sexual honesty from me that no one ever has.

I can't breathe as I think of myself splayed handcuffed and naked, and how we slid together in the oily lubricant she rubbed over me, and how she slid that large black dildo into me and licked me.

I still feel the rocking aftermath of my orgasms that came time and again.

'Don't look like that,' she whispers when we arrive at the house and stand on the steps.

'Like what?' I ask her.

She turns to me and strokes my face. 'Don't be scared. There's nothing to be scared of. You explored your body, your sensuality, fully for the first time. It's a wonderful thing. Some people go through life never finding out. Never exploring their sexual self. But you have been brave enough to begin that journey. It's a wonderful thing, my darling. The sharing of the start of your journey.'

I nod, feeling oddly close to tears. I'm so grateful to her for making it OK, and I hug her close.

'Thank you,' I whisper. 'Thank you for everything.'

'Let's not talk about it, or analyse it. It was too special for that. It's just ours.'

71

I sleep like a baby. When I wake up, I don't even remember straight away. And then I do. And it's like I've been shot.

I sit bolt upright in bed.

Marnie and me. We had sex. Forbidden, amazing, illicit, thrilling sex.

Fuuuuck!

If I thought I'd got myself into a scrape after having sex with Edward, it's nothing to what I feel now.

Edward. My Edward. What have I done? How could I betray him so soon?

I get dressed quickly and get downstairs as fast as I can. I can't bear to be alone with my thoughts. I'm shaking so much, I just need to see people and be normal. Because if I see people, speak to people, then hopefully I will regain my balance, because I feel like I'm teetering on the top of a very tall building.

I'm unprepared for the scene that greets me. I'd totally forgotten about the party, but the rest of the world hasn't. The whole ground floor is swarming with people, and I see catering vans on the drive through the open door. A huge dining table is being set up in the gallery.

Marnie is in full operations mode, barking orders to

everyone. When she sees me, she immediately dumps a load of heavy tablecloths in my arms.

'It's all hands on deck, today, Miss Henshaw,' she says. She doesn't mention yesterday, but she doesn't look at me, either. How has she got the energy for a party? The woman is superhuman.

The hours whizz by, and I help Marnie dress the table and watch her make decisions about the food, and some of the time I completely forget about yesterday. And then, suddenly, I remember and I feel hot and dizzy. Is she thinking about it, too? It's impossible to tell. She doesn't look at me directly once all day.

I'm feeling jumpy, too, as I'm expecting Edward to walk in at any second.

Edward.

Oh God. Edward.

I keep thinking about the yacht, but the whole experience has been warped and changed after what happened with Marnie yesterday. I know it's crazy, but I feel like I've been unfaithful to him and that he'll know the minute he sees me.

But then, at the same time, I know that what Marnie and I shared has nothing to do with Edward. It was just about her and me. I feel about Marnie and me like I feel about me and him.

God, it's all so confusing, but I know that until I see him and find out how he's feeling, I won't be able to think straight.

Around four o'clock Marnie announces that the house

is ready. 'I'm going to change,' she says. 'Oh, where has Ed got to?'

I go to my room and take a long shower.

When there's a knock on my door, I'm so skittish I almost kill myself slipping out of the shower. I'm convinced it'll be Marnie, but it's Edward.

He's standing by my door, looking absolutely stunningly perfect in a dress suit. His white shirt has gold studs up the front, but he's not wearing a tie. He looks like he's just stepped out of a James Bond movie.

'Hi,' I squeak, trying to tame the pile of towelling on my head.

His face lights up and, all of a sudden, my insides melt.

'Marnie sent this for you to wear,' he tells me, revealing that he has a hanger hooked on his forefinger. 'I'm in the doghouse because I'm late.'

'Thank you,' I tell him, taking the carrier case from him, my towel slipping off my hair. I feel like a total mess, but his hand brushes mine and then he stares at me and it's those eyes – those amazing eyes of his. My pulse starts to race.

'I missed you,' he whispers. 'How have you been?'

'Fine,' I tell him. But I haven't been fine. I've been something entirely other than fine. I've been somewhere so far away on the outer reaches of my comfort zone that seeing him now, hearing that he has missed me, pulls me back as if I've been on a bungee jump.

All the craziness of yesterday – the shoot, everything that happened with Marnie – suddenly feels like a distant dream. Like it happened to someone else. It's such a relief that I am still the me that I was with Edward on the yacht. It feels like I've just landed in a safety blanket. In his gaze, I'm safe.

I smile stupidly at him.

And suddenly I don't care about Marnie, or the party, or the risk I'm taking. I just pull him roughly into my room and, dropping the carrier, press myself up against him. Then, holding his face, I kiss him deeply. Claiming him once again, just for me. It's so wonderful I feel giddy.

He is a man. My man. And I need him right now.

'There's no time,' he murmurs through his kisses, but he's already pulling off my robe and I'm untucking his dress shirt.

He pushes me back against the door, wrapping my legs around his waist. We press our heads together and laugh with relief and delight. He kisses me deeply and hungrily.

Then he's undressing, his trousers falling away and, in a second, he's fucking me hard against the door, his hands clasping my buttocks. I claw at his hair as he thrusts, filling me with pleasure.

And it feels like he's claimed me again, and everything that was so scary and new that happened with Marnie last night is at last erased. From this moment I can put it behind me and lock it away. I will never mention it. Never think about it ever again.

Afterwards, he lowers me to the floor and gently laughs as he kisses me, but as he pulls away from me, I can tell he's stressed about the time. He goes into my bathroom and I watch as he washes his face and fixes his hair and quickly re-dresses.

I stand naked in the doorway, watching him. He catches my reflection in the mirror.

'Tomorrow I'll take you to the Hamptons and we'll be together. I promise. Just us. I'll come and get you early,' he says. 'OK.'

He draws me to him I press my head against his shoulder, feeling the tender heartbreak that in a moment our embrace will be over. I breathe him in. That smell I love.

72

Edward hardly looks at me later as I come down and mingle with the guests who've arrived on the terrace. It's a warm evening and the lawns are dappled in the soft evening light. It's like a perfect party of the most perfect people you've ever seen. I feel like I've stepped onto a film set.

I like the dress Marnie has given me. It's a demure cocktail dress with yellow roses on it. I feel very 1960s retro in it, and I've tied up my hair to match. I feel as if there's a neon sign above my head, though. Can't everyone tell that Edward and I are lovers? Isn't it so *obvious*? It feels so obvious to me.

Gundred and Laura are serving canapés, and I feel awkward. I feel out of place. I'm staff, I should be helping, too. I'm not sure what my role is, or what I'm supposed to do. I'm being treated like a guest, but I don't feel like one of these sophisticated people, who all seem to know each other. I wander through them, hearing snatches of conversation. 'He's got Nicole for the shoot. She wasn't his first choice, but I think it's a great casting.' 'Did he get the Picasso? I knew he would.' 'And then Anthony insisted, and we got the whole of the frescos reinstated, but planning in Venice is a nightmare.'

I hear Marnie's familiar laughter on the other side of the terrace and I look up and catch her eye. She looks stunning in a strapless black sheath of a dress. Her blonde hair is greased back, which only accentuates her incredible bone structure even more. She's wearing some stunning sapphire-and-diamond dangly earrings that almost graze her shoulders.

She looks me over and I can tell that she approves of what I'm wearing. She flicks her eyes at me, and I assume she has some kind of errand for me inside. I follow her, going into the house through the French doors where Edward and I danced that night.

'You look divine,' she says. She reaches out and strokes my cheek. 'Positively edible.'

I flush at her reference. Her reference to us.

'Thank you for the dress. I love it,' I manage, pretending to ignore her remark.

'Keep it,' she says.

She doesn't look around, but simply stares at me, then, taking me quite by surprise, she leans down and kisses me.

'I can't stop thinking about you,' she breathes, kissing me again more fully.

Despite everything that has happened, and all my resolve about Edward, I feel a deep sexual tug inside me, along with a rising sense of panic. I might try and forget what happened between us, but she's not going to let me.

I pull away, terrified that she's being so brazen. What if someone saw us? What if Edward saw us?

I thought last night was a one-off thing, but then I look at her and I remember who she is. An adrenaline junkie.

I see the risk she's just taken blaze triumphantly in her eyes. She can see I'm shaking.

All at once I remember her taste in my mouth. I remember being naked in her arms, her sex against mine . . .

She raises her eyebrows at me, like there's been a dare and she's won.

I can't breathe as she strides out of the room, away from me.

73

I just about manage to regain my composure, but I can't concentrate at dinner. All I can think of is Edward earlier, and of Marnie kissing me just now. Just when I'd put it all behind me. Just when I thought it was simply Edward and me again, Marnie kissed me. And I didn't repel her. How could I, when she knows me like she does?

My mind struggles to cope with what it means. How can I be involved with them both? How can this be happening? Under their roof? I'm in way over my head. I don't look at either of them. It's too confusing. Too scary. I feel tied to both of them, as if by elastic, pulling me in different directions, as if the power of the secrets I hold will rip me in two.

In the gallery at dinner I'm sitting opposite the nude painting of Marnie, and just seeing her like that reminds me of her on the bed in the gallery. Has she positioned me here on purpose, so that she can taunt me with her nudity?

Edward is opposite me, below the painting. His look is dark and unreadable as he catches my eye, but he is the perfect host. He introduces me to a German guy and his wife, who are sitting on either side of me, as 'our English friend'.

'You're from Manchester,' the woman, Hilda, says. 'What a great city.'

I like her. She's got rosy cheeks and drinks like a fish. She has flawless English and is a Professor of Art History. It sounds like she has a very high-profile academic career somewhere very important. She mentions several art books that she's written, but their significance is lost on me. As she talks on about her achievements, I feel more and more uncomfortable. I have nothing to offer. Nothing to share. I feel like an ill-educated fool. Edward comes to my rescue.

'Miss Henshaw is a part-time model,' he tells Hilda, in a low whisper.

For one hideous second I think he must know about the shoot yesterday. Has Marnie told him about what happened? Can she have shown him the shots? But then his eyes bore into mine.

'She quite inspired me back into life drawing.'

'Anyone who gets Edward back at the easel gets my vote,' Hilda says. 'He was the prodigy at the Sorbonne when we were there, a million years ago,' she laughs.

I smile at her and at Edward. I'm touched that he's made me sound like his muse. I feel a pang of jealousy that Hilda knows his history. Were they lovers once, I wonder?

I glance over at Marnie, who is blissfully unaware of this conversation taking place. She's holding court at the end of the table, but she too is talking about a world I know nothing about. I listen, as if I'm observing myself from the corner of the room, as she tells anecdote after anecdote about her own and Edward's life together, and he chips in, charming his guests.

At one point she comes down the table, insisting that all the men move around for the next course. She talks quietly to Edward and then he laughs.

I stare at them, watching how connected they are. I see Marnie lean up and kiss him. He closes his eyes and kisses her back.

'Oh, you two, you're always the same,' one of the guests next to them teases. 'Get a room!'

Some others around the table laugh. 'They are insatiable, those two,' a woman opposite me crows. 'I don't know how she does it. How you can keep a man loving you that much.'

Marnie trills with laughter, her hand on Edward's chest. 'You're just a jealous old divorcee, Anna. Get over it.'

The woman, Anna, laughs. 'And you're always sickeningly happy and in love.'

I can't stand it any longer. As soon as I can, I make my excuses and go to bed, announcing that I have a headache. I don't give Marnie or Edward the chance to persuade me to stay, as they are with their guests. Neither of them can leave the table, and I don't look at them as I leave the room.

It feels like I've made a statement to them both, but as soon as the glass panel slides back, I feel ejected and shut out in the cold. I glance back at the warm ambience of the table and long to return. But it's too late.

Up alone in my room, I open the window and listen to the music and laughter downstairs. I keep wishing I had the nerve to go back downstairs and join in the fun. I know I've rather backed myself into a corner with my jealousy, but it's so difficult to see Edward and Marnie together like that, knowing what I do about them both. Knowing that what they're presenting to the world isn't the truth.

I am the truth.

The party goes on until the small hours and, eventually, the first of the cars starts crunching on the gravel drive, taking its occupants back to their amazing lives and their exceptional homes elsewhere.

When the house is finally quiet, I lie, tense in the dark, waiting for the knock on my door. I'm convinced Edward will come to me, but he doesn't.

74

He finally knocks on my door just before seven the next morning. He's just had a shower, but he looks sleepy. But then again, that's probably because he is. I doubt he's had much sleep. He was with Marnie. His wife, whom he clearly loves. Did he have sex with her last night? I bet he did. Did he enjoy it? Did either of them think about me?

'You OK?' he asks. 'I missed you last night.'

I'm wrung out, chewed up with jealousy, but I'm also so relieved to see him. That he's remembered his promise.

'Are you ready?' he asks me, his eyes boring into mine. 'Come on. Let's get out of here. I need some fresh air and to clear my head.'

Up until he said those words I wasn't going to go. I was going to make an excuse about how difficult I'm finding all of this, and that I can't cope with him and Marnie and what might happen.

But the words stall on my lips. His eyes plead with mine.

And God, I want it, too. I want to get out of here and clear my head. The thought of being on the yacht with him, just on our own, fills my mind and it's all I want.

Downstairs, the caterers are already clearing up and there

are a couple of vans outside and some men packing up tables and chairs. It feels illicit, like we're sneaking out.

Edward tells me his car is near the garage. We walk in silence together through the back door and round the corner, and suddenly my heart lurches.

Marnie is leaning up against Edward's blue Aston Martin. She's wearing a red miniskirt and has a stripy beach bag over her arm. Her eyes are hidden by huge shades.

'There you are,' she says, with a big grin. She doesn't mention that I'm with Edward. 'We thought you'd forgotten.'

We? What 'we'? And forgotten about what?

It takes a millisecond for me to realize. She's coming, too. She knows all about the trip. She clearly doesn't think Edward and I are in the process of sneaking off together. Quite the reverse. She's in on the whole thing.

'Isn't this fun! Ed is so clever, thinking of going to the Hamptons. I hate clearing up after a party,' she smiles, opening the passenger door and getting in.

Edward doesn't look at me, or say anything. He lifts up the driver's seat to make way for me to squeeze into the joke of a back seat. I baulk, wanting to back out, but he senses this, because he stares hard at me, and I know I have no choice. Marnie has found out about our plan, and now I have to live with the consequence. And so does he.

I squeeze into the small space as he clicks his seat down, sealing me in. There's nowhere to put my legs. I feel wretched. Like a lapdog.

'You still not going to let me drive?' Marnie teases Edward, pulling down the sun visor and smoothing her lipstick. She looks at me over the top of her glasses in the mirror and winks.

'No,' he says.

So he still doesn't know, then. That she stole his car for a joyride.

'Miss Henshaw, I swear my husband is a tyrant,' Marnie says. 'He knows I love cars, buys my favourite car, and then won't let me drive it. What is a girl to do?'

I feel myself blushing. She's reinforcing my promise – and her lie – in front of Edward. What is this sick power-trip she's on?

I catch Edward's eyes in the rear-view mirror, but he has sunglasses on and I can't tell what he's thinking.

The car starts and he drives cautiously up the driveway. I feel like a child. I'm hemmed in and awkward.

Marnie jokes around in the front, dissecting last night's party with Edward, who hardly responds.

What the hell is going on? How has this happened?

75

I thought we were going to the yacht, but Marnie announces that we're going to their beach apartment. I didn't even know they had one, but Edward tells me that this is where Marnie hangs out when he's sailing. I feel hope flare in my chest. Does that mean we'll leave Marnie there and go sailing together? But at the coast there's not a breath of wind.

In fact, by the time we arrive it's boiling hot and the air-conditioning in the small condo isn't working. It's a small white building with a patchy lawn outside. Inside, there are two bedrooms off a central kitchen, each filled with a wooden double bed. It's basic and beachy, but really quite charming.

'Ah, home, sweet home,' Marnie announces. 'What do you think?'

'It's nice,' I tell her, but the walls crowd in on me. It's stifling in here, and I have a headache.

'The boys love it here,' she says. 'Being so close to the beach.'

She opens all the shutters and then the door to the balcony and attempts to breathe in the sea air, but she can't hold onto the metal rail of the balcony: it's too hot. The white beach stretches out to the exhausted ripple of surf. It really is a stunning location, but it feels like we're totally cut off from the rest of the world. Like we could be stranded on a desert island.

Edward pulls me back into the shadow of the corridor.

'I'm sorry,' he whispers to me. I glance around the wall and watch as Marnie starts looking around the kitchen to see what's in the cupboards. 'She insisted on coming.'

He reaches out and squeezes my fingers. His eyes are full of longing and apology. I'm furious with him for letting this happen, but he knows this. He looks disappointed, too.

'Come and see the best bit,' Marnie says to me, turning brightly. My hand leaves Edward's as if it has been burnt, but she doesn't seem to notice.

She leads me through a door off the kitchen and up some white steps. At the top there's a glass door, which leads to a private roof terrace with its own pool.

'Isn't it great,' Marnie says. 'It's a total sun trap up here, and completely private.'

Quite suddenly she strips off her clothes and dives into the pool in her bikini. She splashes water at me from the pool. 'Come on. Get in. It's wonderful,' she calls. 'Just what we need.'

Then Edward arrives with some cold beers and Marnie climbs out of the pool. She hugs him, making him wet, too, but he doesn't seem to mind as much. He announces that he's going to get supplies. I want to go with him, but Marnie has laid out a sun lounger for me and is waiting for me to join her.

'I won't be long,' he says. 'You ladies have fun.'

'Oh, we will,' Marnie says, patting the sun lounger for me to lie down on. My mouth has gone dry.

Alone with Marnie, I feel trapped.

'Isn't this lovely,' she sighs. 'Getting away, for some time to ourselves.'

I can't say anything. I'm terrified that she'll kiss me again, or mention what happened in the studio, and I'm waiting for her to try and snatch another kiss, but she doesn't. She rubs sun-tan lotion on my back and talks about the party and what a success it was.

I barely listen to her. I want her to shut up and be truthful. Does she know about Edward and me? Does she suspect? Is that why she came? Is that why she's being so excruciatingly nice?

I don't get a chance to talk to Edward alone for the whole afternoon, as some elderly neighbours come round and Marnie insists on making iced tea for everyone, like we're suddenly in the 1950s. And, oddly, the setting could be from another century. I excuse myself and take a walk along the beach as they chat. It really is stunningly beautiful here, but the heat-haze on the sand only reinforces how confused I feel, like there's a swarm of bees in my head. I glance back often at the condo, hoping that Edward will make an excuse and come and find me, but he doesn't. I only go so far, before I lose my nerve and head back.

In the evening, at Marnie's insistence, the three of us go to the little town and eat outside by the harbour, sharing a giant platter of seafood. She keeps touching Edward and flirting with him, and I can't help feeling that she's deliberately laying claim to him. Edward takes it all in his stride and, when she excuses herself to go to the bathroom, he grabs my hand.

'I'm sorry,' he whispers. 'Oh God. This must be awful for you.'

Only for me, I wonder? He can't exactly be loving this.

When she comes back, he presses his foot against mine under the table. But, despite his efforts, I watch Marnie and can't help the sinking feeling that something is over. That this must be it. Marnie has cleverly staked her claim on him and I'm here to witness it.

'Won't it be lovely when we come back here with the boys,' Marnie gushes, tipping an oyster into her mouth. 'They love the clam-bake they do here. And Ed can take them sailing, and you and I can have a long girlie lunch and hit the shops,' she says, grinning at me.

'It sounds wonderful,' I tell her and in a way it does, but somehow the future she's talking about seems impossibly far away. Because that will be then, and this is now.

And I can't cope with now.

'Our sweet Miss Henshaw is very quiet tonight,' Marnie says.

'Sorry. It's been an exhausting few days,' I mumble.

'Then let's get you to bed,' Marnie says with a grin. There's a glint in her eye. She looks like she wants to eat me for breakfast.

When we go back to the condo, Edward announces he's shattered and says that now the air con is finally back on, he's turning in too, and Marnie says she'll join him. He doesn't say anything to me. He doesn't even look at me.

'Goodnight, little bird,' Marnie says, blowing me a kiss, as she goes into the room opposite mine. 'Sleep tight.'

I stay up on the roof terrace for a while, mournfully sipping a beer as the moon rises and the stars twinkle, hoping that Edward will come. After a couple of hours I tread carefully back down to my room.

Their door is closed. I hear low voices beyond.

I go into my room, feeling injustice rising up in me. How can she treat me like this, after what happened between us? How can Edward let her?

I'm trapped. Trapped by this insufferable situation, but also by a longing I can't shake.

I can't bear to think of them together next door. Are they talking about me? What if they confide in one another? What then? Is Edward just going to pretend everything is normal? I feel the weight of the pretence we're playing at like it's a physical burden.

I get up and open the window, hoping to let in a cool breeze, but the night is still. I hear a noise and turn to see the door handle of my room turn, and I hold my breath.

76

It's Edward. He's got away. I'm so relieved to see him, I race across the room and throw myself into his arms.

'Hey,' he says as I plant small kisses all over his face.

He laughs gently and takes my face in his hands and stares at me. Then he leans down and kisses me.

'Oh, Sophie,' he breathes.

Even before I open my eyes, I know she's there. I sense her in the doorway, watching us. I pull away quickly from Edward and put my hand on my chest. She's wearing a thin white negligee from her collection and she's naked beneath it. She looks amazing in the warm light from the hallway, all her curves backlit.

'Don't let me stop you,' she says, walking towards us. Her eyes are blazing.

Oh God, this is a nightmare. She's found us. The truth is out, but I suddenly sense something else going on.

It's Edward. He's smiling, watching her. And, in that moment, I realize.

Oh my God. She knows. She knows about Edward and me. Has she known all along?

'You told her?' I ask Edward. 'I thought . . . I thought it was our secret.'

He stares right back, kind of sympathetically, and then takes my hand and I realize the absurdity of the statement. There never was our little secret. He wouldn't keep a secret from Marnie.

'Actually, it was me,' Marnie says, glancing at Edward. 'I told him about us. About what happened in the studio.'

Oh my God. She told him that?

I don't know how to respond. Of course I know why she told him. How she felt our secret was too big to keep. I've been feeling like that, too. But I still feel caught out. I feel completely naked. I can feel my legs shaking.

She reaches Edward, and he puts his arm around her shoulder.

'You OK?' Edward asks her and kisses her hair.

She puts her arms around him and touches his chest. She's staring at me. Her eyes are bright and sparkling, but I see her hand is shaking, too. I've never seen her like this before. She looks like I feel – frightened.

'Now we're at this moment, it's quite scary, isn't it? Quite . . . well . . .' She bites her lip, her eyes glittering at me and then up at Edward.

'Only because it's up to Sophie now,' Edward says, smiling back at her and then at me.

They both stare at me, and my breath catches. Because I suddenly see what they're suggesting. What they've discussed.

Oh my God. What they've *planned*.

Because that's why we're here. I see that now. Everything that has happened has been leading up to this moment. To the three of us . . . being here . . . together.

'If you want this, then it has to be your choice,' Edward says. His voice is serious.

'Ed's right, darling,' Marnie says. 'It's up to you.'

77

The moment stretches, as I stare at them both.

It's Marnie who breaks the silence with a nervous laugh.

'It doesn't have to be awkward, if you don't want it to happen. We have rather sprung it on you. Just say, and we'll go.'

It. Us. All three of us. That's what she means. I look at Edward and see him staring intently at us both. I feel absolutely terrified. I can't believe this is happening. I can't believe that they're suggesting what they are suggesting.

But at the same time, why wouldn't they? If they both know everything? In some ways, it's a relief. It's a relief that I'm not storing up this huge secret any more. It's out in the open. We're out.

But this is completely new territory.

New and thrilling. Despite myself, the idea of a three-some with them starts to take shape in my mind and, even though I can't make sense of it mentally, my body can physically. I glance again at Marnie in her negligee and how hot she looks, and I think of what we did together – only with Ed watching and participating – and my breath catches.

Marnie takes a step towards me. Wordlessly she leans

down and kisses me softly on the lips. 'It's OK. You're in charge here.'

I can't breathe. I stare at them both.

'Am I?' I manage, because I don't believe her for a second.

'Of course you are. We're totally at your mercy,' Marnie says. 'We both want you. That's all there is.'

Marnie is very competitive. Especially with me. Edward's comment rings in my ears and I feel like I'm starting to grasp a much bigger picture, as if I'm about to stumble into the light.

'I don't know what to say,' I manage.

'Then don't say anything,' Marnie says gently.

So I don't. I break away from Marnie and I'm suddenly working on instinct alone. Because this is the only thing that feels right. The only honest thing to do. I go to Edward and reach up and kiss him. I want Marnie to watch us. I want her to see how much he means to me. That, whatever she thinks is between me and Edward, it's more.

We share a deep kiss, and then Edward pulls away.

'Oh God, I love that,' Marnie says. 'I love watching you kiss. It's so beautiful.'

She smiles at me and I can tell that she means it. That she's not laying claim to Edward, but to me. She's not jealous. She wants me.

And as I stare at her in her negligee, knowing it would only take one word for me to crush her, to reject her, instead I feel a surge of affection for her. She's taught me so much, and now I want her here on the next bit of this crazy journey.

'Sophie, darling, are you sure? We don't want to force

you. This has to be your decision,' Edward says. I can see him staring at me and Marnie, trying to fathom out our sexual connection, too.

I try, but fail, to imagine the conversations that have led them both to this moment, to being this cool . . . because they are being cool. They are propositioning me in the most natural, flattering way, and all I have to do is say yes.

But the decision isn't mine – it's my body's, which has already responded. I feel hot and sexual as I stand between them both and they wait.

'I want it,' I breathe, reaching out my hand to Marnie. Because I do. Oh God, I do.

Marnie's hand slides into mine and she smiles stupidly.

'Then, for God's sake, let's do this thing properly,' Marnie says, breaking the tension. 'Let's celebrate with some champagne. We all need a drink. I'm so nervous.'

Ed laughs and I laugh, too. Marnie squeezes my hand.

Nothing has happened, but everything has, as we go to the small condo kitchen. Edward opens a bottle of champagne, whilst Marnie puts on her iPod and plays funky, cool music. Is this her threesome soundtrack, I wonder? I can't believe this is happening.

Edward pours three glasses and we clink them together.

'This is going to be the best night of our lives,' Marnie says.

Edward smiles. 'I'll drink to that.'

And I can't help it. A nervous laugh bubbles up inside me. 'How does it work?'

Marnie takes the champagne from my hand and puts it down. Then she comes behind me and slides the robe from my shoulder and it falls by my feet, so that I'm bared to Edward, as if she's presenting a concubine. I'm trembling all over with excitement. Her hands caress my shoulders and she kisses my neck as Edward watches. I feel him devouring my naked body with his eyes, but it feels wonderful. I turn my head and kiss Marnie on the lips.

Quickly, Edward takes off his T-shirt. He's in his shorts and I can see his erection straining against the fabric. I put my hand out and stroke his chest. He smiles softly at me and strokes my face, like he's cherishing me and drinking me in.

Marnie goes to him and eases the elastic shorts over him until he's free. She looks at me and looks down at Edward. Then she takes my hand and puts it around his stiffness, so that I'm gripping him. He moans gently. Then she smiles and kneels and pulls my hand towards her, so that she can take his tip in her mouth. Her eyes don't leave mine as I watch him disappearing inside her lips.

I kneel too and she offers him to me and smiles at me, and we kiss and lick our tongues over the end of his shaft, and Edward puts his hand over his face and moans.

And I smile at Marnie and kiss her some more.

It's begun.

78

I wake up alone. I'm on the sun lounger next to the pool in the cool morning air and a patchwork quilt is covering me. I squint up at the early morning sunlight and listen to the seagulls and the whoosh of the surf on the beach. I struggle up on the lounger and see a champagne bottle on its side by the pool.

I flop back down and run my hand over my hair, then slowly smile to myself as I remember last night.

Oh my God. Last night.

Snippets of it flash through my head.

That first time we all crashed onto the bed. How we all seemed to coordinate lying together, until we became more confident and started making requests.

How it was Edward's turn first, and I knelt on all fours side-by-side with Marnie, as Edward stood behind us, taking it in turns to find us with his tongue. Then how he slowly dipped into one of us and then the other. How thrilling it felt for us to be consenting to this together, with no boundaries or fear.

And how Marnie and I wrapped together in a delicious sixty-nine as Edward watched, and then I touched Marnie as he slowly fucked her, and I kissed him deeply as he slid into his wife. How it was so intense and beautiful.

And later, I remember our laughter, how we drank and ate and then we sat here on this lounger, candles around the pool, soft jazz playing. How Edward sat behind me, his hands over my breasts, as we watched Marnie dance for us on the side of the pool. How beautiful she looked in the moonlight.

And how we all skinny-dipped and let our limbs tangle together in the water, and how we kissed. How Marnie watched as Edward and I made love on the sun lounger in front of her. How he filled me up, and how I feasted on her at the same time.

Marnie was right in her prediction. It was the best night of our lives. I know that. For them and for me.

Because what we had was beautiful and moving, and almost spiritual in its intensity. Like the three of us have been on a journey all by ourselves. In one way, I want to yell it from the rooftop and let everyone know how I feel, but I know that I can't. That it won't be possible ever to tell anyone what we experienced. But rather than feeling undone by our secret, like I have before, now that the three of us are all equal, I feel completely empowered. As if I've finally become what I wanted to be the first time I met Edward: a real woman.

But what will happen now, I wonder? How is it going to be between us all? What are the rules for this thing, now that the normal rules have been thrown out of the window?

All I know is that I want them both. That the intensity

of our threesome has blasted open a sexual door for me and there will be no going back.

I yawn and stretch, then shiver in the cool morning air.

They must have gone downstairs, because we were all up here together when we finally fell asleep. I wrap the quilt around me and shuffle to the door.

The apartment is silent inside. Edward and Marnie must be asleep. I wonder why they didn't wake me up to come inside with them.

'Edward?' I whisper, but an empty silence greets me. I creep down the corridor and stop. 'Marnie?'

Their bedroom door is open. The bed is made, like it hasn't been slept in. The curtains are open. Sunlight is pouring in. I look the other way. My bedroom door is open, too. The bed in there has been made as well.

And then I see something that makes me gasp. My pink wheelie-case is upright next to the bed. My case from home – from Thousand Acres.

How the hell . . . ?

I'm both hot and shivery as I make it to the bed, where there is a thick white envelope with 'Miss Henshaw' written on the front of it. I open it up, and inside there's what looks like thousands of dollars in cash. I've never seen so much money. I pull it out of the envelope and let the fifty- and hundred-dollar bills cascade to the floor.

I unfold the piece of paper, my eyes welling with tears:

Our dear Sophie, how can we ever thank you enough for what you've done for us both. We never dreamt that it would work out like it did, or that you would have fulfilled our fantasy so completely. By the time you read this, a cab will be outside. The driver will drive you straight to the airport. A first-class ticket back to Manchester is booked for lunchtime today. We hope that will be convenient for you.

I walk over to the window and peek out of the blind. On the street, a little way past the front lawn, is a yellow cab. Slowly I sink to the bed and read the rest of the letter, which shakes in my hand:

I'm sure you understand that we won't be requiring your services any longer and to that extent, so please don't try to contact us or there will be serious repercussions. After last night, we can't have you in our lives, but we wish you every happiness in yours. Edward and Marnie Parker

'No!' My anguished scream sends the seagulls into flight.

79

I'm hyperventilating and shaking as I put my case on the bed and unzip it. All of my clothes have been neatly packed. Marnie's tissue-wrapped underwear is in. As well as the vibrator. Who packed all my stuff? When did they pack it?

Yesterday, after we'd left Thousand Acres, I guess, which means that the Parkers were always going to send me away. They knew they'd booked my flight and they had my bag on its way, even before Edward kissed me.

The knowledge of this – the betrayal of it – feels like a gunshot wound in my chest.

How could they? How could they do this to me? After everything we shared yesterday. It felt like love.

But they only loved each other.

I'm aware of a buzzing and, trying to control my breathing, I go to the door.

For a second I think it might be Edward. That this is all a big ruse to get rid of Marnie, so that we can be on our own, but it's just a fleeting thought. I know they've gone. I know this is final.

I open the door. A guy who looks like a driver stands sheepishly on the doorstep.

'Miss. We have to leave, to get you to your flight.'

What does he know about my flight? I glare at him and he recoils from my look.

'What did they tell you? What did they pay you?' I yell at him. 'Are you working for them? Are you in on this scam?'

Because it does feel like a scam. It feels like I've been played, in some fundamental way, and the impotent fury that I feel is out of control. I feel like I'm a dragon who wants to flame-breathe anyone in my way.

'Hey, lady, I'm just from the cab company. Just following what the controller told me.'

He looks worried, and I know he's telling the truth. He looks nervous. Like he's just a regular guy.

He glances behind me. I see him clocking the notes all over the floor. All that money: 30,000 dollars. That is what they have paid for their ultimate fantasy. That is what I'm worth. It's written on the back of the envelope. A little pencil number. That's how I've been bought. I know it's a fortune, but it feels insultingly little. Because I don't want their *money*.

'I can come back in a while,' he says. 'Wait till you're ready.'

But ready for what?

The fairground ride is over.

80

The tears come as I sit in the back of the cab. I don't even try to hide them, and I sense the cab driver glancing nervously in the rear-view mirror.

'Boyfriend trouble?' he ventures, after one particularly choked sob.

I shake my head. What has happened to me is too cataclysmic to begin to explain. I can't be sure I could even explain the full Technicolor gamut of emotion that I'm experiencing.

The ridiculousness of describing Edward as a boyfriend is not lost on me. He wasn't a boyfriend. He was someone – *is* someone – that I love truly and deeply. And I was so convinced, up until just a few hours ago, that he felt the same.

How could he do this to me? Is total severance what Edward wants, or has Marnie imposed that? How could he endorse such a cruel letter? Doesn't he feel anything at all? It's just the rejection – oh, man, the overwhelming and absolute rejection – that gets me. The fact that I gave them everything of myself, bared myself utterly and completely, and they just . . . vanished. Vanished like thieves in the night. Closed ranks and left.

I'm so underslept and overwrought and shocked that all I can do is sit, helpless, as the great waves of emotion rush over me. I am awash with snot and tears, and in the fifty minutes it takes the driver to get me to the airport, I hardly pause from crying.

I've barely noticed where we're going, so I'm surprised when the cab stops outside a large, glitzy-looking terminal.

'This is Departures,' he says. 'You'll be met just inside the door. I'll get you a trolley.'

I wipe my eyes ineffectually and try and find some shades in my handbag. My nose is red and blotchy. I blow out breath from my mouth, trying to regain some sort of control. I force myself to get out of the cab and watch as the cabbie smiles apologetically and loads up my pink wheelie-case from the trunk. I can tell he is confused. I don't really look like a first-class kind of traveller.

I fumble around and, with no smaller change, offer him fifty dollars. His eyes widen.

'No, Miss, really. I can't. I've been paid in full. Seriously.'

The Parkers have thrown money at him, too, then. Paid for his efficiency and discretion. Paid him to make their embarrassing problem go away.

Where are they now, I wonder? Back in Thousand Acres, advertising for a new nanny for the kids? Lining up their next victim. How will they explain my sudden absence to Gundred and Laura? But, even as I think it, I know that my absence will make absolutely no difference to any of them. That they'll just carry on like before.

The airport is blissfully air-conditioned and the hushed, carpeted comfort of the first-class lounge feels kind of dreamy. I'm offered breakfast and juice, but I can't eat anything. My bag is whisked away, and I'm told by a woman in perfect make-up that the plane has been delayed, due to bad weather in England. She hopes my stay in the first-class lounge will be very comfortable. She guides me, as if I'm an invalid, to the seriously squashy leather armchairs by the window. I get the feeling that she's talking to me as if I've been recently bereaved. In a way, I have. I can sense that it's on the tip of her tongue to ask me who has died.

'Would you like to use one of our complimentary laptops whilst you're waiting?' she asks softly, pushing a MacBook across the table. 'Free Wi-Fi. Help yourself.'

'Thank you,' I mutter.

Bad weather in England.

England.

Oh God, just the thought of home. Of FunPlex, and Dad in the flat, and Ryan and Scott. It feels like it's hurtling towards me, like a tornado in the distance, and I know I'm stuck in its path, ready to get sucked into oblivion.

Manchester flashes onto the Departures board with a 'Delayed' notice next to it. I swallow hard, trying to compose myself. My tears have led to a sort of startled numbness, and I stare out of the window for a long time at the scorching tarmac, the mirage of heat mirroring my thoughts. Then I pull the computer towards me and log into my email. There's a barrage of unopened emails, but they're mostly from online shopping companies, a couple from the bank, and loads from Tiff and Scott.

There's ones from Gundred, too, from before I got to America. What would she do if she knew what I'd done last night with the Parkers? She'd be horrified. I slept with Edward, then with Marnie, and then I slept with them together. It doesn't sound like very responsible nanny-like behaviour. It sounds like the actions of a crazy woman.

Am I crazy? A crazy sex addict?

Is that why they're sending me away?

I turn my attention back to my in-box, scanning for something from Edward, but I know there won't be anything. Marnie has severed him from me forever. She's made that perfectly clear.

I brace myself and open the last email from Scott. It was sent yesterday:

I miss you, Soph. Please come home. I don't know why you've run away like you have, but surely this break has been long enough for you to sort your head out? We have something special, baby. I know I make you happy. Come back to me. I'll wait for you.

I feel a tortured kind of pang. I didn't come away to sort my head out. I came away to have an adventure, but in the process I've totally scrambled myself. Like I've wiped my hard drive.

I stare at Scott's words, feeling overwhelmingly sad. Because the truth is: I wasn't ever unhappy with him. I remember the familiarity and safety of his grubby bedsit and the predictability of our sex life. The times we laughed in the pub. The crap TV we watched together, our ceaseless failure to win the Lotto. Why wasn't that enough? Why wasn't I satisfied with that jokey companionship? That kind of relationship would be more than enough for most people.

Why did I have to go and stick my hand in the fire?

Because I can only blame myself. I chose this. Well, not to feel like this, right now. But I chose adventure. I was looking for thrills. I was looking for life to be different, challenging, exciting. And I found it, in spades.

I walked into the situation at Thousand Acres with my eyes open. I might have been deluded, but I never pushed for answers, like I should have. I never questioned the Parkers. I was happy to be dazzled by them and their extraordinary lives. I got swept up in the fantasy, and now I've been spat out on the other side.

In twenty-four hours I could be back at home, down the pub with my old gang, and back in Scott's bed, as if nothing has happened.

But everything has happened.

And I realize with a sickening jolt that, whatever the future holds, I can never go back. That even if I fly to Manchester, I'll just get straight on a train to London and start again. I doubt I'll even tell anyone I'm home.

I'm just about to pack up the laptop when I see a new email. It's a Facebook friend-request from Harry Poulston.

81

It's a long time since I've logged into Facebook. There are so many notifications. The world has been jabbering on in my absence. Scott has changed his status to single – despite his needy email.

I ignore them all, accept Harry's friend-request, and immediately a direct message pings up.

Hi Sophie. Do you have any time to talk?

I stare at the words, and the blinking cursor waiting for my reply. Why have I let him into my life? I'm about to type that my plane is about to leave and I don't want to talk to him, but realize that I've just accepted his friend-request and, if I tell him I'm leaving, he'll want to know why. Do I have time to talk to him?

Why am I even thinking of speaking to him? Because he's my last possible link to the Parkers? Because I want to know what he knows – the secrets he's hinted at. Harry is the only person who will enlighten me as to just what a huge mug I've been.

But it's too late. I'm leaving. My chance has gone, surely?

And then it hits me.

I don't have to leave on a plane at all.

Since I opened the Parkers' letter this morning, I've just

been going along with their plan, like an automaton. Still on the conveyer belt of their wishes.

But they don't have to be in charge any more. They've given me enough money for me to make different choices.

Sure, I type back.

Sixty SoHo. Say, 7 p.m.?

I confirm it, but I have no idea what or where he's talking about. I google it and realize it's a funky boutique hotel with a rooftop bar in SoHo, in Lower Manhattan. I feel a sharp sensation, like I've been woken up from a sleep with a slap.

I quickly call the hotel and, without even planning it, a lie trips off my tongue. About how I'm Edward Parker's PA and I'm staying in town for a couple of nights to oversee a gallery show. Do they have a suite? Oh, good. Yes, that sounds perfect.

The thrill of making a hotel booking that I'm going to pay for in cash ignites me.

Suddenly, I can't sit still. I can't stay here. I won't stay here.

'Miss! Miss!' the assistant calls, as I stride towards the 'Exit' doors. 'Where are you going?'

'I'm not taking the flight.'

'But your bag . . .'

I wave my hand. I'll deal with it later. Right now, I need to get out of here. And fast.

82

It's the first time in my life I've ever checked into a hotel by myself and, despite being a complete novice, I manage to bluff it out. It helps that the hotel staff are so nice to me. The Parker name clearly carries some weight around here. I half-hope they'll check with Edward that I'm for real – that I am his PA. I entertain a fantasy that he'll show up here. That everything will be OK. But the staff don't check with his office; they just take my word for it.

I'm shown up to my colossal suite, which is just achingly cool. There's a huge king-size bed with the fluffiest of duvets, and I can see a large marble bath in the bathroom. There's funky Latino jazz playing softly. I tip the bell-hop, again with a fifty-dollar note, and when I explain that the airline has lost my suitcase, he organizes for Lauren, a hipster personal shopper, to come to my room.

Lauren – slim, mid-twenties, snakeskin trousers – arrives moments later. She explains that she has a great relationship with a boutique around the corner and, if I don't like anything, it can be returned. I want to tell her that I'm mates with JoJo over in José's boutique in the Meatpacking District, but I don't. Instead I explain that I have a meeting later with a journalist, which is actually true, and that I need make-up and some underwear. I also assure her that money is not a problem.

Ha! Money is not a problem.

Money has *always* been a huge problem in my life, but now I have 30,000 dollars burning a hole in my pocket and it feels like, now I've started, I just need to spend the lot. Fuck the Parkers and their blood-money!

As soon as Lauren has gone, I flop down onto the bed and sink into its luxury softness. Then I strip off and get into an oversized terrycloth robe. I can't bare to be naked for too long. I still feel too exposed.

In minutes, the coffee and croissants I've ordered arrive and are placed on the table on the private balcony, which has an unobstructed view of the Manhattan skyline.

I stare out at the view as I sit alone and pour my coffee. I could be on a plane to rainy Manchester, but instead I'm here. In New York. In the heart of things. It's so unexpected that it feels unreal, like I've shaken off a skin and emerged like a different person. I'm no longer the Sophie Henshaw of old. But I'm not sure who this new me is. I guess I'll just have to make her up as I go along.

I notice, though, that at least I've stopped crying. Lifting my face to the sun, letting my ears fill with the sounds of the traffic and people on the street below, I have at least salvaged something from my earlier despair. I've staked a claim on myself, before it was too late.

I sigh, open my eyes and squint at the view. Somewhere in all those buildings is Marnie's boutique. I wonder what would happen if I were to go there. Even as I think it, I know I won't have the nerve. Her note made it very clear:

there is to be no contact. I wouldn't make it through the door. I know that for certain.

Even so, I can't help wondering where she is. Has she gone into work, after last night, like nothing happened?

Last night. The memory keeps assaulting me. Marnie by the pool. Marnie and me. Marnie and Edward. How could it not have rocked her to her very core? How could she just have walked away? It was so intimate. So real.

It's like I've seen the most amazing film of all time and I have no one to analyse it with, or discuss it with, and now it's too big an experience to process on my own. Marnie must know that. Which is why what she's done feels so cruel.

And how is Edward feeling right now? Has this shaken the way he feels about Marnie? About their marriage? Out of all of us, it was Edward who seemed to be the most awe-struck by what was happening. It was Edward who said it was the best night of his life.

But maybe the Parkers have done this before. The thought strikes me like a thunderbolt. I remember the gagging order I read about, the porn movie playing in the middle of the night. Maybe it *was* Edward and Marnie in it. They'd certainly meant me to see it, I realize, grooming me all along for what happened between us all last night. They played me and played me, and I fell for their tricks at every turn.

The croissant solidifies in my mouth. I can't swallow. I can only stare out, wondering what the hell I do next.

83

Harry Poulston is waiting for me in the rooftop bar. I'm bloody glad that Lauren, the lovely personal shopper, came up trumps with my outfit of skinny jeans, boho loose top, wooden wedges and a loopy necklace and earrings, otherwise I'd feel like a right numpty in this trendy crowd.

She's also supplied a whole bag of complimentary MAC make-up, and I feel like a chameleon. Dressed in clothes I would never have had the nerve to choose for myself, wearing brand-new underwear and make-up, I feel stronger. Like I've put armour over my battle scars.

I'm not intending to have a great time with Harry Poulston. In fact, as I see him standing to greet me at a table in the corner, I have an overwhelming urge to turn on my heel and run away.

But maybe he senses this, because he smiles warmly, his hands out in a gesture of surrender. He looks like he's half-expecting me to go, and his eyes beg me to come forward. He looks less dishevelled than the last couple of times I've seen him. He's clean-shaven, which makes his soft grey eyes more defined, and he's wearing jeans and a cashmere jumper and cool sneakers, rather than his crumpled corduroy reporter look. The change of image makes him look younger.

'Sophie,' he says. 'It's great to see you.' He smiles, like he means it, and takes my hand. Then, to my surprise, he leans in to kiss my cheek. He smells of nice aftershave. Different from Edward – more clean and soapy. 'I know we haven't hit it off before, but I'm hoping we can start over? I'm not going to mention the Parkers. I absolutely promise.'

His eyes search out mine and I nod and smile, despite myself. It's such a relief that the Parkers are off the agenda. I'm not altogether sure I want them to be, but I'm grateful to Harry that he's left it up to me how much I reveal. I still can't process last night. I know that now, right here, I'm not ready to talk.

I'm certainly not going to think about last night, in front of Harry. He's a journalist. Surely he would be able to sniff out the colossal secret I'm keeping, if I gave even the tiniest hint?

I squeeze onto the little stool on the other side of the candlelit table. I have to admit that it's so nice to be mingling amongst ordinary people, to not be trapped with my thoughts. I say ordinary, but the bar is far from my kind of ordinary, back home. Behind us, the Empire State Building is lit up in coloured lights. Funky music plays. The people around us look like actors and musicians and film people. It's how I imagined New York to be. Vibey and fun.

Harry orders cocktails, and mine comes with a wisp of dry ice swirling from its tower of lime and strawberries. It's delicious. I tell him about the clubs I go to back in Manchester, and he surprises me with his knowledge of The Smiths and The Charlatans, who were my favourite bands, growing up. He tells me a funny anecdote about interviewing Shaun

Ryder from the Happy Mondays, and the more we banter and quote song lyrics to each other, the more I realize the colossal level of stress I've been living under for the past few weeks.

As the first hour easily slips into two, it dawns on me how pleasant it is to be having a conversation that's not about Marnie or Edward. It's so great to be able to prove to myself that I can function as an entity independent from them. And the longer Harry doesn't mention them, the more I respect him. It's an elephant on the rooftop, so to speak, but I can live with it.

At some point in the evening we order delicious Thai food and I discover that I'm ravenous. I haven't eaten properly for days, and it's fun to share food with Harry. He tells me about a disastrous trip to Thailand with his ex-girlfriend. He always struck me as quite sneery and hard-nosed, but the more he talks, the more I see that he's just a regular guy trying to make a living as a journalist. As the moon comes up high in the sky and the bar starts thinning out, he tells me about his unfinished novel about a man trying to investigate his own dreams.

'Sounds interesting,' I tell him. 'Would you like to see my suite?'

84

I haven't intended to sleep with Harry, but the second we're in the door, I lean in and kiss him. I'm drunk, wrung out and flying by the seat of my pants, but it feels like I've got nothing to lose. Besides, it's cathartic: to have sexual power over someone else.

He's clearly up for it, although he's surprised I've been so forward. He starts to talk, to discuss what it means, but I silence him, taking off his shirt.

'I wasn't expecting . . .' he mumbles, between kisses. 'I mean, I thought you were with Edward Parker?'

'Well, I'm not. I'm right here with you.'

It's the right thing to say. For him and for me. I've dealt with the Edward Parker issue without making a big deal of it, even though the fact that I'm admitting there's nothing between me and Edward – that it's over, whatever *it* was – stabs me deeply.

Harry kisses me gently, tentatively undressing me. He fumbles with my bra, laughing at himself, until I help him.

'It's been a while, since . . .' he says, apologetically.

'Don't worry. Me, too,' I lie.

And what a lie. The biggest I've ever told. Last night is still physically with me, but doing this with Harry now feels painfully right. Like I'm deliberately trying to erase what happened and, in doing so, inflict some of the pain back onto Edward and Marnie.

Soon Harry is naked. He's more stocky than I thought and more hairy, too. He has a tattoo on his hip, which he admits was a drunken teenage mistake. He hasn't the aesthetic beauty of Edward, but I don't care; I just want to be in his arms. I need to be held. I need to feel physically tethered to someone – anyone – to stop myself drifting off into misery.

He goes down on me straight away, quickly taking off my lovely new black knickers and diving enthusiastically between my legs. I try to get turned on, but as I watch the shadows criss-crossing the ceiling, I can't help remembering Marnie and her beautiful wet softness against me, and a tear leaks out of my eye and drips into my hair. I grab Harry's head and force him away, up towards me.

'You want to stop? I like giving you head,' he grins, like a schoolboy who should be given a medal.

'I need you to fuck me now,' I tell him.

He seems surprised by my seriousness, and so am I. I'm not usually like this. Never so matter-of-fact, but this is a practical matter. I need him.

He sorts out a condom and I realize how little I've thought about contraception, or STDs. I remember Edward in the porn movie, Marnie with the black dancer in the club. God knows how many people they've been with. How many others they've fucked, then fucked over?

I lie on the bed and Harry thrusts inside me, but it's like he can't get to me. Like I'm numb. Because all I can think about is Edward and Marnie. It's not that I can connect with them sexually, which I thought would happen, now that I'm having sex again. Instead, a film of memories plays through my head. Edward's smile when he saw me stepping out of the car in the gallery; Marnie squealing with laughter as I gunned Edward's car down the road; Edward drawing a sketch of me on the yacht; and Marnie teaching me to twirl my nipple-tassels.

And God, how I want to hate them, but my heart is breaking.

85

Afterwards we half fall asleep and I'm shocked when I wake up, spooning next to Harry. His arm is across me, holding me tight, and for one fraction of a moment I think I'm in bed with Scott and the whole thing has been a dream. But then my eyes flick open and I see that we're in a hotel room and it's Harry's hairy arm. I see the watch on his wrist ticking. How is time still marching on, after everything that's happened? What is this new today going to bring?

He stirs and, when I turn, he smiles at me. His hair is rumpled.

'Hey,' he says, softly.

I half-smile at him, but I know immediately that I want him gone. I don't want Harry here in this room. I don't want a post-coital conversation, or for him to suggest that this may be the start of something. I've used him. Used him as much as I needed to, and now I need to face the shame alone.

I swing my legs out of bed and grab the robe, covering myself as quickly as I can.

'I have an early start,' I croak.

Harry sighs and rubs his face. 'Ah,' he says, understanding the code.

He gets up and pulls on his trousers quickly. I don't look at him. I wish suddenly that I smoked. This would be a perfect time to light a cigarette.

'So I guess you're still busy, then,' he says.

'Busy?'

'Being Edward Parker's latest muse,' he says, a leading edge in his voice.

Now I stare at him and he stares back. He's no longer Mr Nice Guy, but a hard-nosed journalist who has me cornered.

Latest muse. What does that mean? Am I just one of many?

'I'm not his muse. Actually, I'm . . .' I pause, jutting out my chin. 'I'm the Parkers' nanny.'

'Their *nanny*?' Harry checks, pulling on his jumper.

'For their boys. Their twins,' I tell him, defensively, bunching up the robe in my fist to cover my chest.

There's a long pause as he pulls on his sneakers. Long enough for the hairs on the back of my neck to stand up. Then he stands and faces me.

'What?' I snap.

'Oh, man,' he says. He brushes his hair back. 'You don't know . . .'

'Know what?'

'Edward and Marnie Parker are childless. Famously so. She couldn't have kids and—'

'What?' I gulp.

'She had several miscarriages. Then they tried to adopt, I think, but it didn't work out.'

'But they have boys. Twin boys,' I say, but my voice is

shaking. 'They employed me from England to look after them and . . .'

Harry laughs. 'And did you ever actually meet these so-called twins?'

'No, but—'

'So they got you. Huh! Go figure,' he says smugly. He doesn't say, 'I told you so', but it's implicit in his tone. 'So, right now I guess you're about ready to tell me what you know. I know a breakfast bar around the corner?'

He knows. He knows that I've been done over by them. I get a horrible sense that he's been waiting for this revelation all along. I swallow hard. I'm desperate for Harry to be wrong, but my mind is whirring back to the interview in London and back further . . . to the advert for the job. *An exclusive domestic position . . .*

There was never a mention of any kids. Ever.

It was one long sexual fantasy right from the beginning. Oh my God.

They invented this whole scenario and I went along with it, until they'd reeled me in and I'd made the choice.

They lied about the kids. They lied time and again. Lie upon lie.

I remember Gundred and how confused she looked when I asked about the kids, and how Laura avoided every question . . .

'Sophie?' Harry says. I glance at him. He has a triumphant glint in his eye.

'Just leave,' I croak.

86

I'm still boiling with rage as I persuade the yellow cab driver on the Manhattan street to take me to Thousand Acres. The cabbie has never heard of it. Upstate New York is about as specific a detail as I have. He has to make a call to his operator, before he finally works out where it is and how far. I promise to pay him extra. When I show him the cash, we begin the long journey.

How amazing cash is, I think, riffling my thumb along the edge of the bank notes. How powerful. I never realized before just how powerful, but how easily it makes life slide along. Everything falling neatly into place in front of you. Every problem solved. I can see how being rich must be addictive. How you must want to make your cash buy you more and more outrageous things. How the thrill of just being able to buy an expensive dress quickly turns into furniture, houses, cars, yachts – each cash 'fix' getting more and more outrageous.

Like buying a young girl from England to fulfil a sexual fantasy, for example.

The cabbie asks me for more details about Thousand Acres, and I feel like a fool for not being able to tell him exactly where the Parkers live. I spent all that time in their home, but I don't know even the most basic facts about it. I didn't once open my eyes.

I stare out of the window, thinking everything through in the cold, hard light of Harry's revelation – Edward and Marnie's letter playing over and over in my mind on a loop.

I have to see them. I have to hear their explanation. I don't care if they don't want to see me – I just need them to know that I know. That I know what they've done. How they've used me.

Finally the cab stops at the gatehouse to Thousand Acres. I get out and am so relieved to see the security guard inside. It's the same one. The balding guy with the moustache, whom Marnie charmed that day after our joyride.

I tell him that I'm here to see Edward and Marnie in the end house, but he stares at me blankly.

'Who?' he snaps.

'Marnie Parker. You know, you talked to her that day. That day we drove up the road,' I say. 'I'm their nanny. You know that. You recognize me, right?'

'Miss, I've never seen you before in my life,' he says, looking me dead in the eye.

For a moment I think he's joking, but his look doesn't change.

'You've got to be kidding me,' I laugh, outraged. 'Marnie and Edward Parker live here. At the bottom of this road. The big house. The house with all the art . . .'

'I don't know to whom you're referring, Miss,' he says.

I can feel the discomfort of the cab driver behind me, who is listening in. He coughs, embarrassed.

This is unbelievable. Impossible! How can he be *lying* like this? Who has *paid* him to lie to my face?

'But you must know. They are in the final house along this road,' I protest one last time, but he shrugs and looks through his computer system.

'I'm afraid you must have made a mistake. That house has been empty for a year. The owners are abroad.'

'They're not. They're here,' I yell at him, exasperated. 'I live there.'

'Hey, lady, I'm just doing my job.'

I know he is, and I know he's lying and he knows I know he's lying, so in the end I resort to bribery. For the princely sum of 300 dollars he tells me that the cab is allowed up for five minutes, and then he's calling the police.

Fucking bastard.

87

I get to the gates of the house, but they're locked and, when I press on the buzzer, nothing happens. I stare at the security camera above the gates. Are they watching me? Are they deliberately not letting me in?

I make the cab driver promise to wait and, ignoring the insects that buzz around the hedge, squeeze through the bushes at the side of the gate and then push through the undergrowth until I'm on the other side.

I run up the grass verge of the drive, desperate to get to the house. But when I get there, it is closed and shut up. They aren't ignoring me. They just aren't here.

No one is here.

I run up the front steps and try the front door, but it's locked.

Desperately I run around to the back, but the house is locked.

Where is everyone? Where are the Parkers? Where are Gundred, Laura, the gardeners?

I race along the back terrace and cup my hand against the window of the sitting room and my heart suddenly thuds.

At first I can't quite believe what I'm seeing.

The room is empty. The white shelves are there, but the

books have gone and the drinks cabinet and record player, the sofas, table and sculptures. Even the rug has gone.

What's happened? Where have they gone?

I'm shaking with frustration and fear. I have to get in there. I have to find out what's going on.

I yank the handle of the French-window doors, but they're locked. I stare through the glass again and see that the key is in the lock. Desperately I heave one of the stone pots of hydrangeas over and thrust it into one of the lower glass panels. The glass shatters and I reach in and turn the key. I snag my T-shirt on the sharp shard of glass and feel my skin puncture beneath, but I don't care.

I run through the sitting room and into the corridor.

'Edward? Edward?' I call, but the house is eerily quiet. I run to the end of the corridor to the stairwell, and the glass door of the gallery doesn't slide back. The walls beyond are empty. All the pictures have gone.

I feel a sob escape me as I race up the stairs, two at a time. My arm is hurting. Blood runs out from under the sleeve of my jacket, and drops run off my fingertips onto the black-and-white tiles.

I get to the first floor. My floor. All the furniture has gone. All the art. Even the bronze nudey man.

I race to my room. The door is open and the round waterbed has gone. The side table, lamp and dresser have gone.

There's only one familiar thing. The pencil drawing that Edward did of me on the yacht is abandoned on the window-seat cushion.

88

When I get back to the cab I can see a police car arriving slowly over the brow of the hill.

'Just get out of here,' I yell at the cab driver, thumping myself into the back seat. I'm trembling violently. 'Just take me into Manhattan.'

I'm going to find Marnie and demand an explanation.

'Hey, you're bleeding,' he says. 'Don't bleed over my seat.'

The police car is getting closer. The driver can see we're about to move off. I hear the siren sound briefly.

'Oh, man,' the cab driver says, 'I knew you were trouble.'

The policeman doesn't know that I've broken into the house, but he wants to know why my arm is bleeding. I make up a lie about knocking off a scab from an old wound, but the officer doesn't believe me. He's looking at me like I'm crazy. I'm bleeding badly, but I don't care. I can't feel it. I'm too shocked.

'Can you call the owners of this house?' I beg the policeman. 'It's very important that I speak to them. Please, Officer.'

He finally strolls to the police car and I see him picking up the radio. He seems bored and annoyed as he talks into it. We wait for an age, as I explain that I live at the house, but the owners have forgotten to give me a key. He clearly thinks I'm nuts.

The radio inside the car comes to life and the policeman walks to get the message. I see him nodding and then he comes back.

'The owner of this house lives in Singapore. It's managed by an agency.'

'An agency? No, that's not right. It's owned by the Parkers. Edward and Marnie Parker.'

The policeman refuses to do any more research for me, and he's keen for us to move on. Nobody has heard of the Parkers. The policeman checks with the guard at the gatehouse. The house has been empty for a year.

Am I going insane?

89

I stare out of the window, hardly seeing the blur, just seeing my own reflection as the cabbie takes me back to Manhattan, occasionally tutting to make sure I've registered his displeasure.

I look different. Even to me. I look serious and jaded, tainted by an overwhelming experience that I simply can't get my head round.

They planned it all. *You fulfilled our fantasy.* I fully get it now. Their note makes complete sense. Without all the emotion of yesterday, I can finally understand. Our spontaneous threesome really was meticulously planned all along, and I was too naive even to suspect it. The Parkers are extraordinary people, all right. Extraordinarily rich people, who will do anything they can to get what they want. Even if it means faking having kids, or faking a whole life together, to ensnare someone they can both have fun seducing. Did they compare notes about me? Did they know everything all along, when they were telling me to keep secrets?

Of course they did.

Is *anything* they told me about themselves true? Was any of it real?

I will do anything to keep him happy, Marnie's voice bangs around my head. *Anything at all.*

The audaciousness of her plan is breathtaking. They picked me and played me, knowing all along that it would end the way it did. They made it seem so plausible. They made it seem like it was my choice all along, but I was just doing exactly what they wanted.

They had already begun the process of moving out of Thousand Acres when I was with them at the condo. Maybe they hadn't really moved into it at all. That's why there were red rooms. Empty red rooms. Rooms they hadn't moved into – which they never had any intention of moving into.

And now the Parkers don't want me to find them, but I'm not going to let them do that to me.

I resolve to find out the whole truth. I'll go to Marnie's studio and challenge her. I'll tell her that she mustn't be scared. That I'll never say anything, so long as she lets me stay.

I can't leave now. I can't. I have to see them one more time.

And then I remember.

Marnie's studio.

I picture me in it with her, and suddenly my throat goes dry. Because I remember the photoshoot, and the toys and the handcuffs and all the pictures she has of me.

What if I try and track her down and those pictures are the 'serious repercussions' she mentioned in her letter? She has all the incriminating evidence that she needs to make sure I'd never be employed again.

90

I go back to the hotel, but I can't stay in my room. I'm too jangled. Instead, I wander around SoHo, staring in shop windows and not seeing anything.

Eventually my feet get sore, and I find a table under an awning in a cupcake cafe on the sidewalk. The smell is delicious, but I'm too churned up to eat anything. Instead, I watch the queue of kids being swallowed inside, to gawp and gaze at the glass counters full of pastel frosting. I would have brought the Parker twins here, I think – if they'd ever existed.

I shake my head. I still can't believe it.

I'm vaguely aware of a phone ringing, but it takes a grandma on the next table to point out that it's coming from my bag.

I thank her and, embarrassed, take out my phone. I'm sure it'll be Harry. At some point in the evening last night I gave him my phone number, I remember. He'll be wanting that kiss-and-tell and, for the first time, I'm tempted to give it to him. Blow up the Parkers' world. Tell the truth about the kind of people they are.

When the phone rings again, though, I bottle it. I don't want to speak to Harry. I'm too confused. Too stunned. I'm not brave enough to confess what happened. I'm not ready to soil it, stamp on it and make it public. I know instinctively that it would crush whatever I have left of myself.

Besides, I'm frightened. Frightened of what Marnie might do with those photos. If she and Edward were prepared to go to the lengths they did for their own pleasure, then what might they be capable of if I incurred their wrath?

'Are you gonna answer that?' the waitress asks, pointedly.

I glower at her and pick up the phone and press the Answer button, steeling myself.

'Miss Henshaw?'

It's a woman's voice. Not Harry. She sounds vaguely familiar.

'This is Laura.'

I sit upright. 'Laura?' It doesn't sound like mousy Laura, with her chainmail braces. How has she got my number? From the Parkers?

'Could we meet?' she asks.

91

I wait for her outside the Guggenheim Museum on the edge of Central Park. I'm exhausted and weepy as I sit in the sunshine. I stare around, waiting to see Laura and her terrible haircut emerge through the crowds of Japanese students.

I wonder why she called me, and why she wanted to meet me. I'm nervous about what she wants to tell me and, more specifically, what she knows. What small nugget of truth she's picked up, whilst she's been vacuuming around the Parkers' locked doors. I think of how she refused to tell me anything about the house or the kids. Why has she changed her mind now?

Does she know about what happened between me and the Parkers? Does she know what the Parkers really employ their staff for? Oh my God – has she been duped by them, too? Has she had a threesome with them?

I doubt it, but I'm really hoping that, if she's asked to meet me, she'll be able to shed some light on why Thousand Acres is suddenly empty. And where Edward and Marnie Parker have gone.

'Sophie,' someone says in my ear, making me jump.

I look up and see a woman standing next to me, and I stare at her in shock. Laura is no longer Laura, as I knew her at

Thousand Acres. Her hair is blonde and her figure has miraculously changed, but it's still her. She's wearing a green wrapover dress with sexy high heels. And she's carrying a bag. A toffee-coloured designer handbag . . .

A distant memory chimes. I stare at her again. And then I realize who she is. She's the woman who spilt coffee over me at FunPlex. The woman who gave me the copy of *The Lady* . . .

She cocks her head and smiles sympathetically, acknowledging my shock.

'It's a long story,' she says. 'Shall we?'

I stumble to my feet and walk with her. I see the limo on the pavement a little way up. The Parkers' limo. Oh my God. Has she brought Edward?

Because, in spite of everything – everything he's done – a part of me still yearns to see him. A part of me still wants not to have been discarded by him, but still to have him as mine. Hopes that, even if this all might have begun as a game to him, he really did fall for me. And when he held me like he did, looked at me like he did, that it was as real for him as it was for me.

Laura nods to Trewin, who stands next to the passenger door, like she's in charge.

And then I realize . . . she *is* in charge.

He smiles at me for the first time.

'Laura, I don't understand,' I gasp, as we're sealed into the back, on the familiar fawn seat.

'I know that the Parkers think you have left already, but I'm glad you haven't,' she tells me. She has an English accent. I stare at her, dumbfounded. She knows? She knows what happened?

'You're English?' I blurt. My mind is going crazy.

'I'm mainly based in London, yes. My agency is.'

'Your nanny agency?'

Because the Parkers don't have kids, I want to blurt, but I don't, because she shakes her head. She knows that already.

'No. It's a different kind of agency. You could call it bespoke.'

'But I don't understand?'

'You sent your CV and a photo to a nanny agency in London, and we pay them a very healthy retainer to look through their books for the right sort of girl for us. And we found you,' she says with a smile. 'Then it was a question of tracking you down.'

'But the advert in *The Lady*?'

'It was step one of a long strategy we had planned. I was only really there, that day in FunPlex, to see you. But when I left you the magazine, and you fell for it straight away, it made our lives very easy.'

So the Parkers paid her to find me. To find someone innocent they could corrupt, and to play out their ultimate fantasy. I stare at her, dumbfounded. They didn't just meet me and seduce me. There was a plan in place long before I ever set foot on a plane.

'You have to know that the Parkers chose you very carefully. There were fifty or more candidates, Sophie, but there was no doubt in their mind that it had to be you. Only you. They absolutely guaranteed that they wouldn't hurt you, and I hope that's the case?'

I nod slowly, but I can't speak. I stare out of the window

at the queue of tourists near the museum, trying to absorb all of this. So they chose *me*, together. I'm kind of stunned and flattered at the same time.

I thought they loved me, a little bit, but it wasn't that. It was something else. They *chose* me for their fantasy.

I sit back and try and take it all in. I almost want to laugh at the audaciousness of it all.

'Why . . . I mean, the Parkers . . . I don't understand?'

Laura smiles at me and I can see she does, if I don't. 'I know you're confused, but Edward and Marnie are very special people. I vetted them myself, and spent a long time discovering what they wanted to happen. I know that they love each other very much.'

I think back to them in the kitchen, the first time I saw them together. The way they touched each other unconsciously. The way they loved each other. And I know Laura is telling the truth. They do love each other. And that's what hurt. Because I thought they loved me, too.

'They have highly sophisticated tastes – as you have discovered. Personally, I think that perhaps a childless marriage allows a couple to be that way.'

Again Laura smiles at me, her eyebrow rising.

I can't believe I'm in this car, having this conversation with her, but suddenly something slots into place and I feel calmer. A lot calmer.

She's right. They do love each other. I see that so clearly now. That bit wasn't a lie at all. And if planning an elaborate fantasy is what they have to do, to keep each other happy, then who am I to judge? If that's what it takes to mend the heartache of a childless marriage, then so be it. But why did it have to be me?

'I see,' I nod.

There's a small pause, and I let it sink in. They chose me. I start to see it all in a different light. It's premeditated, calculated . . . yes. But bad? No, not bad, I decide. Flattering, actually.

I suddenly see Marnie so clearly, stroking my face. And how she held my hand in this very limo when we came back from the photoshoot and that incredible evening together. She was taking care of me.

And Edward, too, when he came to me after we'd been sailing, like he was lost and couldn't help himself. That wasn't faked. That was real. He was just as desperate for me as I was for him.

'I hope you've had a good time, Sophie,' Laura says, interrupting my thoughts. 'It looked to me like you were enjoying yourself. They wanted it to be just as much of a fantasy for you, too. They planned it so carefully.'

I blush, looking away. She's right. I did enjoy it. Every minute of it. Right from the start. And it was a fantasy for me. The plane, the limo, their home, their friendship – the wonderful, incredible times we shared. And although it's all over, I know deep down that I wouldn't have missed it for anything. That, if I had the choice, I'd do it all over again in a heartbeat.

In the moment that follows, a steady realization comes over me: that in the light of everything Laura has said, I can't hate them, or continue being angry with them. They didn't set out to hurt anyone. Certainly not me. So maybe the fault was mine. For falling too deep. For them both. In what was just meant to be a game.

But they saved me, too. Because I remember how crushed I felt at home back in Manchester, that day Laura came all the way to 'check me out' in FunPlex. How stifled I was by my dead-end future. How bored I was, and scared. Scared that nothing brilliant or extraordinary would ever happen to me. And then this happened. The Parkers happened. And I got to have an adventure. An amazing, thrilling, life-changing adventure. I can't hate them for that. Because it was everything I wished for, and more.

They trusted me. They still trust me. And they've spoilt me, too. They've opened my eyes and, yes, let me be complicit in an amazing sexual experience. One that I know now really will stay ours. Just ours. Have I really come out of it so wronged?

'Sophie, are you OK?' Laura asks.

'Yes,' I tell her, turning back to her. 'Yes, I'm fine.'

She checks my eyes to see if I'm telling the truth, then turns to face me more. 'The thing is, I wouldn't have normally blown our cover like this, but we feel—'

'We?'

'Oh, right, yes. I think you thought she was Mrs Gundred, but she's Sarah, my partner at the agency.'

I stare at her. Mrs Gundred was in on this, too? She had an acting role all along as well?

I close my eyes and shake my head a little. Laura lets out a comforting kind of laugh and puts her hand over mine.

'Yes, I do appreciate it's a lot to take on board,' she says.

'It's OK,' I tell her. 'Go on.'

'Well, we both feel that you've been an exceptional candidate. One of the best we've ever had. And I think you've enjoyed your experience. Am I right?'

I nod slowly. She looks relieved.

'We just wondered, before you go home for good, whether you'd consider another assignment?'

'Another assignment?'

'Yes. Not immediately. You deserve a break, obviously. In fact, I wondered if you might want to come to Venice with me for a while.'

'Venice?'

'Yes, I have some business there, and I could explain the next . . . adventure.'

I stare at her, trying to wrap my head around what she's saying. The choice she's offering me.

The choice not to go home. Not to go back. But forward. Forward into a bright, unknown future. A future that could be as amazing as the recent past has been.

Because I see now, sitting here, that my episode with the Parkers is over. Our perfect fantasy has run its course. All my angst and fury at them have been totally misguided. They have treated me in the only way they could. They had to cut me off. I see that now. They had to let it be the perfect night, to make it special. For both of them – and for me, too.

I am so grateful now that I didn't tell Harry anything. That our shared experience is still intact. That it will always be safe. A sacred memory for all of us. I know that now.

'What sort of adventure?' I ask Laura.

'Well, it would involve travel again. And a hefty fee.' She

smiles at me and cocks her head. 'And, of course, it would involve a certain amount of discretion. But then you're more than capable of handling that.'

Edward's voice chimes in my memory, along with Marnie's. *It's just ours. Our little secret.*

'So, Sophie?' Laura says, smiling at me. 'What do you say?'